Alison Cooper started writing fiction at the age of 62, after a long career in academic research administration. Her final position before retirement was at the Leverhulme Trust where she worked for thirteen years. Her first novel, The Rapallo Legacy, was published in November 2009.

Adrian's Journey is a story based loosely on the family circumstances of a friend, adapted and altered for the actions in the novel.

Alison has a degree in Chinese and French, a working knowledge of Italian, and enough German and Spanish to read essential notices. In 1977-78 she spent nine months as a student in Beijing. Now living in London and Italy, she enjoys classical music and jazz, (in the past she played the timpani, the viola, and the piano, and even conducted a little), collecting Chinese stamps, ballroom and Latin dancing, and gardening, about which she knows very little.

D1428827

For my nieces Emily and Vivien, my nephew Mark, and in memory of their father, Tony.

And for Roddy Gruzelier, whose family circumstances inspired this story.

Alison Cooper

ADRIAN'S JOURNEY

AUSTIN MACAULEY
PUBLISHERS LTD.

A CIP catalogue record for this title is available from the British Library.

ISBN 9781786295712 (Paperback)
ISBN 9781786295729 (Hardback)
ISBN 9781786295736 (E-Book)

www.austinmacauley.com

First Published (2017)
Austin Macauley Publishers Ltd.
25 Canada Square
Canary Wharf
London
E14 5LQ

Acknowledgments

My sincere thanks go to my friend Doreen Shafran who, having pointed me in the right direction for my first novel, The Rapallo Legacy, continued to help me with advice on the content, characterisation, and shape of this story.

Helen Fearnley and Professor John Davies read my manuscript with a keen eye for spelling, punctuation, and other inaccuracies, and also commented on the plot and construction of the book. I am very grateful for their help.

I am also particularly indebted to Craig Larkin who provided information on Lebanon and the Middle East, making many useful suggestions as to pertinent and reliable sources of background information.

Many thanks also to Austin Macauley for taking me on, and to all the staff involved in the production of the book. Thanks also to Gordon Bottoms for my photograph.

Time does not change us. It just unfolds us.
[Die Zeit verwandelt uns nicht, sie entfaltet uns nur.]

Max Frisch (1911 – 1991)

One

October 2000

Sunshine filtered through the flimsy curtains, whilst a bright ray from underneath them emblazoned a stripe of tartan duvet. Adrian was lying on his back, gradually coming to. He brought out a warm hand from under the duvet, rubbed a little itch on his nose, and shifted the pillows. Turning on to his left side, through his scarcely open eyes he could just see the outline of a figure in the doorway; it was Gemma of course. Perhaps a sense of her presence had jogged him into consciousness.

"Are you awake?" she asked in her soft high-pitched voice.

"Uh. Mmm. Sort of, or if I wasn't, your voice woke me up," he answered, lifting his eyelids a little higher to look at the tall gangly figure of his teenage sister. She was wearing cargo trousers and a T-shirt, her mousy brown hair held back in two plaits showing up her little oval face which briefly betrayed a slightly hurt expression.

"Would you like a cuppa?"

How like her, he thought guiltily, always doing something for him while he did nothing for her.

"What time is it?"

Gemma looked at her bright pink watch. "It's exactly ten thirty-two."

"Oh dear."

"Well, would you?" she asked again after a few seconds.

"Yes, I would. Please."

What a little sweetie she is, he thought.

She disappeared, jumping down the stairs two at a time. He could hear her chatting and clattering in the kitchen with Fen, their mother, and then Gemma's footsteps coming back up, slowly, carefully. Adrian could imagine her round blue eyes flitting between the mug and the stair treads, her hand gripping the handle steadily so as not to spill the tea. She came in, put the mug down on the bedside table, and looked at him expectantly. Adrian readjusted the pillows for upright sitting and stretched for the mug. She watched him as he gulped down a first mouthful loudly then rested the mug on his chest.

"Sit down, Gems, and tell me what you've been doing since I went to London," he said. Her face lit up with pleasure as she plumped herself on the end of the bed.

"School's cool. I'm best in my year at lots of things."

"I bet you are."

"History, especially history, I love history, I'm going to be an ancient historian, like, well, before I'm ancient, if you know what I mean." She giggled.

"I do, Gemma." Adrian lifted his mug lazily from his chest and took another slurp, "What else do you like?"

"Science; you see, it's very important for ancient history, archaeology."

Adrian nodded. "I got tired of science."

"Yes, I know. I heard Mum and Dad talking about it."

Adrian's expression changed. "What did they say?"

"They were saying, well…" She hesitated.

14

"Come on Gems, you can tell me. I won't go grassing on you."

Gemma took a deep breath. Her loyalty to Adrian was and always had been unwavering.

"They said they were surprised you didn't decide to do science at uni."

"Anything else?"

Gemma looked away, then back at him. "They said it was a pity, and that they didn't know what you were going to do with your Chinese."

"Hrumph. Nor do I." He looked up and smiled at her. "But then you can't predict everything, can you?"

"I know, but I plan lots of things," said Gemma, eagerly bouncing a little. "I know exactly what I'm going to do."

"Yes, ancient history and archaeology."

After a pause, she added: "And I know why you chose Chinese."

"Why did I then?"

"Because it looks different, all those squiggly things."

Adrian laughed. "So what are you going to do today?"

"First Nell's coming to fetch me and Mum's taking us to the pool for the swimming club, and then we'll have our sandwiches there and then Mum'll come back to fetch us and take us to art. And then Nell's Mum'll fetch us to go to her house for tea. Susie and Sausage'll be there too. And then I'll come home." She took a swift gasped breath in between blurting out each activity on her list, as though to emphasise their separateness and importance.

"Who on earth is Sausage?"

"Susie's dog, silly!"

"Of course, silly me indeed." He paused. "It sounds like a busy day to me. Where do you do art now?"

"Where do you think? At the new Arts Centre."

"Oh, yes, the pride and glory."

"They have special interactive groups on Saturday afternoons. You work with other people on a subject, like, at the moment we're doing dancing. So we do drawings and paintings and photos of people dancing, and we learn about the different dances and we look at pictures and sculptures etc. of dancers, like Degas, and then we dance. Me and Susie dance together. But the teacher says I've got two left feet."

"Swing your legs up on here, Gemma, so's I can look at them," said Adrian invitingly, with a wicked look.

She screwed up her face. "You're teasing me…"

"No honestly! Show them to me."

Liking the idea of Adrian examining her legs which everybody said were long and slender, she leaned on her arm and swung them both up so that he could see them.

He grinned. "Well, I'm sorry to tell you Gems, but they are both the same, lefties. God must have had an off-day when he invented you."

She took a swipe at him and he ducked.

"Hey, mind the tea."

Gemma looked thoughtfully at her feet, and Adrian at the last drain of tea in his mug. After a moment she said:

"Adrian, it feels funny without you at home."

He looked up. "No funnier than this past year though, surely."

"But it *does* feel funnier. Last year you came and went, you were really away some of the time, far away, but you were living here while you worked, and your things were

16

here. This feels different, 'cos you're not far but you're just … not near either. It's not the same."

"You'll have to get used to it, Gems."

"Yeah."

They were both silent.

"I s'pose I'd better get up," said Adrian.

"Yes, 'bout time too, lazybones," squeaked Gemma jumping off the bed and taking Adrian's duvet with her which she dumped unceremoniously in a heap on the floor. Adrian was naked. Gemma's hands went up to cover her flaming cheeks as she turned her head away.

"Gosh, I'm ssss…sorry, I didn't know…"

"It's all right Gemma" replied Adrian soothingly. "I'm only a bloke, with the usual things blokes have. Anyway, you can turn back now, I'm wearing a pillow to cover them."

Gemma turned her head back and then made a gap between her fingers through which she peered as a smile turned up the edges of her mouth. She looked at him for a moment then said abruptly "I'd better go. Nell'll be here any minute now. See you later."

Adrian got up slowly and shuffled off to the bathroom for a shower before pulling on jeans and a t-shirt with upside-down Chinese characters on the front. Down in the kitchen, he took two crumpets out of the freezer to defrost and toast. He ate them with gusto, butter and marmalade dripping down his fingers. It was quiet; Gemma had evidently gone, and nobody else seemed to be around. Sitting by the window, Adrian could see across the garden to where, beside the gate into the field on the far right side of the terrace, the weeping copper beech glowed in the sun, protecting under its fronds private places where ten-year old Sebastian often acted out bits of his imaginary life, peopled by football heroes. Wearing the latest trainers and sports gear, Sebastian won computer games against them, and went sailing with them on his father's boats. To the left of the tree was the wooden summer house (a grand name for a shelter), its weathered walls warm and welcoming. Under its rickety roof stood a rusting metal table bearing a chunky blue and white striped mug. Adrian let his eyes roam right round, taking in the whole garden. It was a curious shape, probably staked out from a large estate by members of a family in fulfilment of a succession clause in a will. It was overgrown in places; their father John and mother Fen tamed its unruliness with sporadic enthusiasm; bedding plants made occasional appearances only to wilt in the wind and die of neglect. The many shrubs tufting randomly in clumps or alone were more resistant; their subtle greens, greys and purples, changing constantly with the seasons, provided an irregular patchwork of colours. Everybody in the family loved the messy garden and enjoyed watching the frolics of the rabbits which found sanctuary there from the neighbours' dislike. The rabbits' voracious appetites made short work of the salads that Fen planted hopelessly each year.

Finishing his crumpets, Adrian went back upstairs and into the study, a room lined on three sides with warped shelves deep enough to hold two layers of books. The floor space was cluttered with family belongings – a cricket bat, an ironing board, a bean-bag pouffe, a large cardboard box with a huge bird-kite poking out of it, a cello in a case. He sat down at the family computer, booted up and clicked on the Met Office website to look at the weather patterns for places he had been to during his gap year.

John and Fen had been relieved when Adrian had returned from his wanderings; they saw his move to university as the beginning of his adult life, and an especially significant time since Adrian had abandoned science for Chinese studies. Adrian himself had no such recognition of a new epoch in his life. He had moved seamlessly from school to work and work to travel. His time in the pea-processing plant and in Elsie Pittock's shop were just some of the next things to be done, with the object of earning money for vagabonding in Europe and the Far East, for seeing new places, and for socialising. University was but the next stage and beginners' Chinese seemed to him much like being back at school: a classroom of people struggling with a new language.

By the time he had finished sixth form, Adrian had realised that his appetite for chemistry and physics had been satisfied and that he wanted to channel his analytical bent into something different. John and Fen had not objected. John was a shy retiring person who disliked interfering in other people's decisions and eschewed confrontations, while Fen, a large motherly person with a placid personality, steered John into making responsible family decisions when necessary but felt she had little to contribute in questions of education. The fact that Adrian was neither Fen's nor John's blood relation had made no difference to them or to Gemma and Sebastian.

John appeared in the doorway of the study almost timidly, a slight smile creasing his cheeks, his chin tucked in, and his huge floppy hands dangling on the end of his elongated arms. Adrian looked up.

"Hi Dad," he said.

"Hullo old thing."

John's father had always called his son 'old thing'; it had been instinctive for John to continue the tradition.

"Computer going ok?"

"Yes, it is. I couldn't be bothered to bring my laptop with me. You haven't got all the software I've got, but it's quite fast. Where is everybody?"

"Gemma's off for the day with her friends and Fen's taken Sebastian into Ipswich to get something. I forget what...oh yes, sports socks."

Adrian grunted.

John went to look over Adrian's shoulder at the screen where every possible statistic about Beijing was displayed. Adrian looked up sideways at John and smiled.

"I'm checking up on things, living backwards vicariously."

"No harm in that. You'll need to stay in touch with things in China for your year abroad."

"Yes, I will."

Conversation lapsed. Adrian knew John had something to say – interrupting wasn't one of John's habits.

"Adrian," said John quietly, "now that you're back and settled in at university, there's something…" he tailed off.

"Yes Dad?"

"There are some things you ought to know. Fen and I both think it's time to tell you."

John's left eye twitched slightly – it always did at times of stress.

"What about, Dad?" Must be really serious, he thought. John sat down on the other seat – a rickety office chair which clicked and tilted as he shifted anxiously. He moved the sole of his right squashy shoe to cover the top of his left, as though one could gain comfort from the other. Adrian swivelled round to face him.

"It's about your… your family. Not us, your, er, biological family, as I think it's called nowadays."

Adrian didn't answer. He had no recollection of either of his real parents nor had he ever been interested. As far as he was concerned, Fen and John were his mum and dad, Gemma and Sebastian his siblings. John again searched for words.

"Do you remember anything about them?"

"No."

"Well, you do know that your mother went off, cleared out, just before you were two?"

"I know, Mum told me, but I don't remember her or anything about it." Adrian's voice betrayed a slight annoyance.

"No, I suppose not. You were too small." John paused. "The reason she left was because Leslie, your father, wasn't good to her... sort of...er, violent."

Adrian sat bolt upright. "What do you mean, sort of?" he asked angrily.

"He beat Patti up and she left. And then he met Fen and they got married very soon afterwards, in fact as soon as your parents' divorce came through. Leslie was very charming. Fen said it was love at first sight. That's rather an old fashioned thing to say, I know."

Adrian relented.

"It still happens, only we don't call it that. These days it's called falling for someone big time."

John afterwards couldn't remember what the new expression was; for the moment he was intent upon continuing with what he had to say.

21

"Oh. Then Leslie carried on with Fen where he had left off with Patti. Huge mood swings, drunken rages, unprovoked attacks. Poor Fen, it was terrible for her."

John was looking at his hands, spreading and un-spreading his fingers.

"How terrible! I can't imagine that happening to Mum – she's so strong, physically and psychologically."

"Leslie was very big, threatening and domineering. Fen couldn't stand up to him, so that's why she, too, started to get ready to scarper. She said you never saw what was going on because you were with your grandmother most of the time."

Something stirred in Adrian's memory; an image of someone flashed before his eyes and promptly vanished.

"I have a vague memory of someone tall and thin. Presumably she was Leslie's mother?"

"That's right. She always looked elegant. Anyway, Fen wanted you home with her and Leslie. But he was scared that you'd see… well, what he was like, what was going on. He often went for Fen just before you were due to go to them. He pretended to everybody that you didn't visit often because Fen, not being your mother, didn't want to have much to do with you. But it wasn't like that at all."

Adrian was shocked, silent, not wanting to hear more. John continued haltingly.

"Just as Fen was preparing to walk out, Leslie died in a car crash – it was only a few months after he and Fen were married. I suppose you know about that?"

"Yes, someone must have told me some time how he died."

"Leslie was well over the limit, had just had a set-to with Fen, and had banged out of the house saying he was going to the pub. He swerved to avoid an oncoming car and smashed into the wall of a house. He died in the ambulance on the way to hospital. Fen suffered awfully after his death – she somehow blamed herself, as though his behaviour were partly her fault. When she and I first met, she was very nervous about getting close to anybody ever again." John swallowed the excess of saliva produced by his uncommonly long speech. "It was ages before she came to trust me; our engagement lasted over a year, and it was a further year before we got married. I knew something terrible had happened and eventually, once we were husband and wife, she started to tell me about it. I think she told me most of it over some weeks. I'll spare you the details." John swallowed again, hoping that Adrian might fill in the silence with a few words, but Adrian only grunted, his eyes fixed on his shoes. John took a deep breath to help him into the next bit of the explanation he had set himself to give.

"She told me not only what Leslie had done to her, but also everything he'd said. It was awfully painful for both of us." There was another long silence. Adrian stared out of the window at the brambles. The fruit must be over by now he thought, then looked back at John who was again struggling to find his voice.

"Go on," said Adrian finally.

"Fen told me what she knew from Leslie about Patti, about your mother. We thought you should know now." John took a deep breath and exhaled it in a hurry.

"I don't want to know, really I don't. I'm not interested. It doesn't have anything to do with me, with us," answered Adrian quietly.

"I know old thing, I didn't think you'd want to hear it. But you're a man now" – Adrian squirmed – "with a life of your own, and Fen and I wouldn't like the information to slip away, erm, sort of, into oblivion. You're moving ahead, university, holiday jobs, travel, new friends. You won't be coming home so much."

"Like I said, I really don't want to know." There was a hard, crackling edge to Adrian's voice, betraying a nagging fear of the truth which might split open a section of his past until now buried deep within the recesses of his brain.

Taken aback by Adrian's tone, John stood up and took a couple of steps towards the doorway.

"I can't force you to listen," he said with his back turned to Adrian. He hesitated. "Perhaps you'd rather hear the rest another time, later?"

"Whenever, it doesn't make any difference."

"Then I'd rather get it over and done with now," replied John, turning back decisively and going to lean up against the bookshelves, a little further out of Adrian's range than the chair he had been sitting on previously. Adrian's mouth was, unusually for him, set in a firm line, his chin protruding and his eyes negative. John took the final plunge.

"What we know is that Patti took a job teaching English in Beirut. We think that before marrying Leslie, she had done a TEFL course – you know, the qualification you need to teach English to foreigners. She met someone from the Middle East in London who had waxed lyrical about that part of the world. When she left Leslie, she wanted to get out of reach, so to speak. She had kept in touch with her friend – wherever he came from. Leslie told Fen a sob story about Patti being unfaithful to him with an Arab but that was probably a fabrication. After Leslie died, Fen came across an address for Patti amongst Leslie's papers. I don't think Leslie and Patti had been in touch after she left, but he had evidently made it his business to find out where she was. He was a bit of a control freak and he might have thought to use the address later, for something unpleasant. Fen wrote to Patti's address in Beirut to tell her about the accident and Leslie's death. The reaction was a very brief note saying, basically, good riddance, and that she, Patti, was doing fine, teaching. She didn't ask about you nor suggest she wanted you back. That was when we decided to begin adoption proceedings. Patti agreed to our plan." John came to a halt.

"My mother didn't want me. Is that it?" asked Adrian aggressively.

"Yes. Soon after that Fen burned everything – a big bonfire she said. But she copied Patti's address on to a slip of paper that is with the adoption papers about you. It was the right thing to do."

John was motionless, looking at Adrian, who was sitting very still avoiding John's eyes. After a moment, Adrian looked up, knowing he should say something. John's mouth was opening and shutting as he tried to find words which might comfort Adrian. Adrian cleared his throat.

"Is that all?" he asked after a moment, a little ashamed of his truculence and softened by John's anxiety. After all, John was doing what he thought right. "I suppose you want to show me the address?"

"Only if you want to see it. I hope all this isn't too much of a shock to you. You know that you've always been our son, Fen's and mine - our first son. There's never been any…"

Adrian interrupted him.

"Dad, I know that. You're cool parents. I suppose it's partly because you're so cool that I don't want to think about 'family' in any other way. You and Mum and Gemma and Sebastian are my family. It'll always be like that. I'll ask you for the address if I'm ever curious about it."

"OK old thing, enough said. I'll leave you to get on with following the Chinese weather patterns." He smiled before going downstairs. Adrian heard him putting on his garden boots and soon glanced through the window to see him in his shirtsleeves fighting with overgrown shrubs.

Presently Adrian heard the car return, doors slam, and family talk downstairs – not all intelligible; first John's quiet voice interrupted by the others, then Fen's clear mellow tone.

"I don't know, Seb. He's probably on the computer."

A mini-stampede up the stairs followed and Sebastian, stocky and muscular, burst in, punched Adrian on the arm, and said:

"Dad's taking me to the boatyard this afternoon to help! Are you coming too?"

"I don't think so. I've got things to do."

"What things? Computer games?"

"I don't play computer games any more," replied Adrian. "I'm trying to get to grips with Chinese and it's more interesting. And I have some other stuff to do."

"All this serious university stuff! I hope I don't ever have to do it."

"It's much too early for you to think about it. What's Mum doing now?"

"What she calls grooming the terrace and Dad calls whirling the dust."

"Oh." Adrian wanted to relax privately with Fen a bit. Not necessarily to talk about Patti, but at least to settle himself back into his relationship with the person he felt to be his real mother.

"And then we're having lunch. And then me and Dad are going to the boatyard."

"Buzz off now, Seb. Call me when lunch is ready."

Sebastian bounded noisily back down the stairs.

In the end, Adrian's desired peace was rather short-lived. After John and Sebastian had left for the boatyard, Fen tidied up the lunch things whilst Adrian sat drinking a mug of coffee at the kitchen table. She broached the subject.

"So Dad's told you about Patti and Leslie?"

"Yeah. What a mess. How horrible."

"You didn't know what your father was like?"

"No. I'd never thought about him. I suppose that might have been because I *had* seen something disagreeable which I buried away in my subconscious. Since I don't remember anything about him, he's not a real person for me." Adrian was running his hands through his light brown hair.

He was quiet for a moment. "But…"

Fen turned to look at him.

"But what?"

"But when Dad told me I'd spent most of the time with my grandmother, I did remember somebody tall and thin who looked after me. I imagine that was her."

"Yes, she was thin but not particularly tall. She probably looked tall to you because all adults do when you're small. Before marrying she'd been an actress. Rather a stagey person but very sincere and concerned for you and she was nice to me. She was desperately proud, and mortified when Leslie turned out the way he did. He was her only son."

"Did… does Leslie have any sisters?"

"A younger sister, called Margo. She married an American and disappeared off to America. After your gran died, she would have nothing more to do with Leslie. And your grandpa was long since gone."

They fell silent. Fen had finished putting things away and sat down at the kitchen table across from Adrian.

"Mum, it must've been awful for you."

"Yes – it was, I can't describe it. John was marvellous, so kind, the opposite of Leslie. Meeting him helped me through a lot, in getting on with things. Either you survive in your head or you don't. I did. Enough said. And, Adrian" – she reached across the table to grasp his arm – "it was lovely having a ready-made son – it made the three of us into a comfy family straight away. You know you're not a bit like Leslie, except in looks."

"Oh, really? Dad said he was very attractive."

"Yes, more immediately attractive than you. He was bigger than you, dominating and persuasive, with a wicked streak, which turned out to be vicious."

"I suppose you never saw his first wife?" Adrian couldn't bring himself to describe her as his mother or say her name.

"No, she kept well away. She went off to the Middle East, anyway. She'd found somebody else."

"I wonder where she is now."

"Mm."

"Leslie and Patti Sandling. It sounds odd. He's dead and she's somebody else, Patti-somebody with an Arabic name perhaps."

Fen looked at her watch. "Gosh, look at the time. I must go and get Gemma. You know we've got an address for Patti. You can have it if you like."

Pressing her hands on the table, she levered her bulky body up from the chair, and lifting her apron over her head, used it to wipe the beads of perspiration off her face before hanging it on the peg on the back of the door.

Adrian watched her affectionately, calling to mind how her soothing voice and robust arms had, fifteen years ago and longer, protected a small boy from Dangers. He remained at the kitchen table. Fen, now wearing a voluminous jacket called from the hall.

"I'm off now. See you later."

"OK. I don't want the address now," he called after her. "I've got to digest all the other stuff first."

Two

"*Nimen xue shenma?*" asked Sun Qianghan.

"*Women xue hanyu*" replied the class in ragged chorus. Sun was his surname, Qianghan his given name, meaning doughty, intrepid. He doesn't look intrepid, thought Adrian, turning back from the contemplation of London University roofs to scrutinise Sun, who seemed discouragingly distant, humourless, retiring.

"*Ni xing shenma?*"

The lecturer's long thin finger was pointing at him. Quick, what does "*xing*" mean? Ah yes, surname.

"*Wo xing Goodfield*," he replied after a couple of seconds.

"*Zhen de ma?*" The questions and answers continued, the lecturer's finger selecting different students to reply.

"I think we've got the gist of that," the person sitting beside Adrian said in a low voice. Adrian turned to smile at him – he had dark curly hair, pronounced cheek bones and deep-set dark eyes. It was unlikely, thought Adrian, that Sun would have heard or understood enough to take offence. Sun's long-winded description of himself, including his expected contribution to the first year course, his background, and much more besides, had given no hint of familiarity with colloquial English; when the students spoke to him he simply looked bemused by the language, or the content, or even by the circumstances in which he found himself, unsurprisingly since he had arrived from China only a few days before the beginning of term. Obtaining a British visa, for a Chinese, was a notoriously slow process.

"All standard stuff, not very inspiring," said Adrian, at the end of the hour.

"No" replied his neighbour.

"Coming for coffee?" asked Adrian.

"Great, yes. I'm Max, by the way."

"I'm Adrian."

"I've not had a look around yet – where's the refuelling pump?"

"I think I know. Follow me in case I do."

Adrian led Max out along the corridor, through swing-doors, down two staircases, and through double fire doors into a very large room with blue plastic tables and grey chairs arranged in rows. The odour of aeons of frying was aggravated by the combined heat of the sun shining through the grimy floor-to-ceiling windows and by the central heating, doubtless switched on habitually at the beginning of every academic year regardless of the weather.

A very large girl from their Chinese group approached them as they grimaced over a milky brown liquid in plastic cups.

"Mind if I join you?" she asked.

Max pulled a chair back from the table for her and gestured to her to sit down.

"Hi, I'm Sadie," she said, in unmistakably transatlantic tones.

"This is Adrian and I'm Max."

"Hi there."

"Where do you come from?" asked Adrian.

"Toronto Canada," said as though the words were hyphenated. "Say, where did you get that coffee?"

"If it *is* coffee, doesn't look or taste like it to me. It's from that machine over there," answered Max.

Sadie dropped on the table a motley pile of things – denim jacket, scarf, bum bag, sheaves of papers, mobile phone, and a book. She extracted a purse from the bum bag and sauntered over to the machine where she fiddled with coins for a few moments, glancing back at Adrian and Max for possible help. Just as Adrian stood up to go to her rescue, the machine groaned into action, spitting hot water in and around the plastic cup. On the adjacent counter she helped herself to a blueberry muffin, leaving some coins in a bowl. She didn't know if it was the right amount, but it didn't seem to matter anyway – there was nobody behind the counter to ask.

"How long've you been here, Sadie?" asked Max as she sat down and took a large bite into the muffin.

"Let me see, three weeks, yeah, just a bit more. But I've been here before, often. My dad comes on business, and my mom comes with him sometimes, if she feels like it. We've got relatives in Scotland who we've visited with several times, and we always stop in London to go to a show. We just love Scotland and London too. My folks were glad when I said I wanted to come here to study and when I got the grades I needed, wow, no stopping me! You Briddish are cool." She spoke artlessly.

Max was examining her attentively, but turned his face away at her last remark to put his smirk out of ken. She seemed even larger sitting than standing, the top of her head higher than Max's, and he was over six foot two. She had large thick hands with brightly painted nails, short-cropped carroty hair which emphasized the thickness of her neck, and a receding dimpled chin. Her eyes were magnificent, hazel, oval, set wide apart, and her complexion a smooth, clear, light olive colour.

"Sadie, where are you living?" asked Adrian, managing to avoid catching Max's eye.

"I'm staying temporarily with a friend, someone studying political science, in his uncle's flat – his dad's a friend of my dad's. But I can't stay there permanently – I have to find somewhere else soon. I've always stayed in a hotel before."

"Try the accommodation office. They were quite helpful to me" suggested Adrian, "although it may be a bit late for somewhere good."

"What do you mean?"

"Students' rooms in London are rather grotty, none of your north American luxury."

"Really, you mean dirty?"

"Most of them," said Max. "Greasy kitchens and peeling wallpaper and smelly loos." He smiled cynically.

"Oh dear. Oh well, all part of the experience," she said with an unconvincing note of optimism in her voice and a girl-guide-ready-for-anything look.

"You won't say that after a few months," replied Max darkly. "Anyway, by all means go to the accommodation office."

"Yeah, I will." Sadie drank her coffee in one go and then, in the ensuing uneasy silence, looked at her watch. "Say, you guys coming to linguistics?"

"Linguistics? When and where and why?" asked Max.

"In a few minutes. My tutor said it was a good idea, get embedded, he said, get a feel for where Chinese is in

33

relation to other languages. And I'll get to meet some more people."

"I don't know about that sort of pay-off," replied Max. "What do you think, Adrian? Sounds a bit like hard work to me."

"Nobody suggested I should do linguistics," replied Adrian.

"Mmm, nor me," said Max.

"Well, I'm going to see if I can find the room," said Sadie. "See you later." She scooped up her untidy heap of possessions from the table and ambled off, leaving her emptied cup, ringed by light brown liquid, on the table.

"So it all begins," said Max wearily. "Did you count how many there were of us in our group?"

"No. But it looked like about fifteen to me."

Max observed Adrian for a moment, then said,

"You seem to know a bit of Chinese."

"I went to China in the summer, part of my gap year."

"Ah. I intended to, but it seemed a bit keen and needed an awful lot of organising, so instead I did some work for my father and went to France to laze around." He paused. "How long were you in China?"

"Just a couple of months. I spent the rest of the time earning money and helping in a shop and inter-railing in Europe."

"Where are you living?"

"In a hall of residence down near Aldgate tube station. It's okay, not your actual five-star hotel, but there's an oven to heat up a pizza. I don't know if I'll stay there all year. How about you?"

"I've got a room in a flat, friends of friends of my sister, Tazie, that sort of thing."

"Whereabouts?"

"Close to The Globe – about five minutes' walk from London Bridge. Quite convenient, and it's relatively easy to get home to Sussex from there."

"I'm not planning on going home often, there seems to be so much to get into here. Anyway, my parents are near Ipswich which is a bit of a trek."

"I suppose they're there for work."

"Yeah. My dad's a boat-builder. It's a fun job. I mess around in boats with him sometimes. My little brother loves it."

The conversation lapsed. Then Max continued:

"Look, I've got to meet someone now, but I'll be free later. We could go for a Chinese together if you like? It must be the right thing to do at the beginning of term."

"Yes, it must. Where shall we go?"

"Are there places near your hall?"

"Yes, round two corners. Call me when you're ready."

Max took a large sheet of lined paper from his neat canvas bag, folded it exactly in half and tore it in two, giving one piece to Adrian. They exchanged numbers; Adrian added his address. Max stood up purposefully and walked off, turning to nod to Adrian from the door.

Adrian sat on for a moment wondering what to do next, feeling a little aimless. Perhaps he should have followed Sadie into linguistics. Too late now anyway. A walk back to his hall of residence seemed a good idea.

Armed with his new A to Z, no crumpled pages yet, he set out diagonally across Russell Square where idlers were sitting or lying on the grass, singles, pairs, groups. Many looked like students, closed pads and books beside them. The scruffiest man Adrian had ever seen lolled on a bench,

35

empty lager cans beside him and on the ground underneath. Adrian thought it was a man because of his hirsute face, although he was wearing a long skirt which covered his legs, leaving visible only his feet, clothed in holed odd socks. Under his bench, pigeons and sparrows competed for the remains of a snack and its paper bag. On another bench, a very skinny young woman was combing a tiny fluffy pooch which had a small pert face resembling its owner's.

Halfway across the square, Adrian stopped to look at the towering red brick edifice of the Russell Hotel, a monument from a past way of life. His feet led him without thought across the street and to the front of the building where he climbed the steps and pushed the doors round slowly. Inside, all was brown marble and chandeliers, imbued with the grandeur of England leading the world, an atmosphere curiously at odds with the people in the reception area who were casually dressed in jeans and anoraks. Deep in contemplation of Britain's global position, Adrian wandered unchallenged down corridors and into public rooms.

Finding himself once again outside in the oblique sunshine, he turned into Queen Square where he found, to his surprise, a pleasing pedestrian area with a village atmosphere, far removed from the splendour of the hotel. Outside a corner café, a petite oriental girl was neatly folded up in a small aluminium chair, constricted by its arms, her bare feet on the edge of the seat and her flip flops on the ground below her. Her mouth was talking quietly without facial expression to a small western man with glasses. From time to time, she stretched out a thin arm only just long enough to reach its goal – a tall glass half-filled with puce liquid which she sucked up delicately through a green-striped straw. The man nodded every so often. Adrian smiled to himself as he tried to imagine Gemma fitting into such a chair.

Great Ormond Street was adjacent; so this was its position in the London scheme. The hallowed hospital couldn't be missed – it almost brazenly declared its prominence, drawing attention to its existence, self-congratulating. Across the road, just a few paces further on, a door opened invitingly into a second-hand bookshop, faded maps in the window. Outside the adjacent newsagent, the evening paper hoarding announced 'Killer Wasps Alert'. After a moment's hesitation, Adrian went into the bookshop. Nobody seemed to be about, but some rickety folding steps were leaning up against a big pile of ancient volumes with torn yellowed pages falling out of them; the steps were tall enough to enable Adrian to reach the China shelves at the top of a section marked *Far East*. He moved the steps over and climbed up them warily, head back to peer at the book titles. He wasn't looking for anything in particular and soon realised that the China section was limited to a number of language text books printed in the 1960s by the Chinese Foreign Languages Press. Still nobody came. Feeling suddenly like an intruder, Adrian stumbled down the ladder to bid a hasty retreat.

Adrian walked down Lambs Conduit Street, looking for information about Lamb, but discovered nothing. At the bottom he continued on into Holborn, noisy and steaming with traffic. He felt suddenly tired and wished he had taken a bus; indeed, he still could, but he had decided to walk, and walk he would.

He scarcely noticed St Paul's – his family had visited it recently on a day trip to London. Beyond the new and old architectural monuments of the City of London, the streets became intimate, lined with ordinary shops where people hurried in and out, dangling plastic bags, intent upon catching something or someone. A tower of text books in a small stationer's window looked as though it could topple over with the slightest tremor from the tube running audibly below. A large handwritten notice invited 'Get things here for Back to School'. The notice was faded, no wonder, since school term had started a few weeks earlier. Inside, Adrian found a notebook with large squares intended for primary school maths. It would do nicely for practising writing Chinese characters.

Buildings, buildings, Adrian said to himself as he turned the corner past a small general store with a Post Office counter. Fifty yards on, he stopped in front of Fletcher's Hall to consider it for the first time, something he hadn't bothered to do until then. It was an austere grey brick building with sash windows and a heavy stained door, open now, inside which a further door with a coded number entry system led into an unprepossessing hall. Adrian thought it must have been an orphanage. Not a warm attractive place but dignified, self-respecting. He let himself in and walked slowly up the stairs, wondering whether he would become accustomed to being there, or whether it would remain as it was now, somewhere to dump his things, sleep and study. To personalise his room a little, he had put up a couple of posters of China on the wall opposite his bed as well as a photo of a very elegant boat his father had built for a local electrician. In the musty cupboard behind the door, two pairs of jeans were hanging alongside the shelves bearing his underwear, t-shirts and socks. He pulled off his trainers and pushed them under his bed, beside the suede lace-ups, his 'better' shoes, just about smart enough for … what? A special invitation? A meeting with his tutor? A date? Perhaps he would never wear them. Or would a holiday job at Sainsburys' impressive headquarters put them to good use? Suppose he were to teach at St Paul's Cathedral School? Doubtless the historic baggage there would require incumbents to wear respectable shoes. Adrian slung his bag on to his bed, filled his kettle and plugged it into the multiple adaptor strip connected to one of the two sockets in his room. While it was boiling up, he spooned instant coffee into a mug, added powdered milk and opened a packet of chocolate biscuits. He realised with a start that he had no idea when Max intended to turn up, not that it mattered much; restaurants were open very late.

Wo, ni, ta: Adrian practised writing the characters, counting the strokes carefully. He had what his mother called an 'artistic hand': shapes came to life, lines curved gracefully, static objects moved and flowed effortlessly. His Chinese characters looked naturally stylish already.

An hour later, his coffee long finished and the chocolate biscuit packet a couple of inches shorter, Adrian flopped on to his bed with an English translation of 'The Water Margin'. Just three pages into the second chapter he dozed off, the open window leaving a gap through which warm air wafted in to lull him. He felt anyway in limbo. Term had started but hadn't really. There were as yet no serious challenges, no essays to write, only characters and sentence patterns to learn and books to read.

A loud knock at the door roused him. He pulled on his jeans and went to open it to a small untidy person wearing glasses held together at the left hinge by a lump of sticking plaster. An ample dark blue t-shirt with "STRANGER THAN" on its front dangled loosely down over his threadbare jeans which, instead of being trendily tight around his hips, were as loose as his t-shirt; the belt which must have been preventing them from falling down was hidden. Slung over his shoulder was a brown anorak daubed with some incongruous pink blobs, more likely, thought Adrian, to be the result of decorating than of fashionable design. He wore brown boots with the remnants of laces keeping them from being stepped out of.

"Hi," said the person. "You're Adrian, I know because you've got your name on your door."

"Yeah. The doors are all the same so I put it there to make sure I didn't try to barge in on anyone else."

"Oh. Well, I'm Benny and I haven't got my name on my door. But it's two along, that way." He raised his right arm and waved it up and down. A book fell from his pocket. They both bent down to pick it up, banging heads.

"Sorry!"

"No, I'm sorry" countered Adrian. "Come on in then."

Benny hesitated. "I was wondering if you'd got any tea or coffee? I haven't got round to buying any yet."

"Yes, I have. And I've even got a spare mug." Adrian refilled the kettle, set it off and prepared both mugs of coffee. "Milk?"

"Yup, and sugar if you've got any?"

"No, I don't take sugar."

"Never mind. I'll fix things up in my room one of these days."

"Sit," said Adrian. Benny took a step towards the only chair, hesitated, then seeing Adrian return to sit on the bed, sat on the chair.

"What are you studying?" asked Adrian.

"Linguistics. Terrifically interesting. I did some on my own last year. And you?"

"I'm doing Chinese. I was supposed to be a scientist but thought better of it. My A levels were science. What did you do?"

"Greek, and Latin. And Russian and maths."

"That sounds like lots."

"Mm. I liked it all though. I did some software development too." His smile was charming, almost childlike, spreading from ear to ear on his small irregularly shaped spotty face.

"How are you liking London? You don't come from round here, I can tell." Adrian spoke gently.

"No, you couldn't mistake me for a southerner, could you." Benny took a gulp of coffee then added self-deprecatingly, "it's me vowels, isn't it. To answer you, I've not been here long, so I don't know what I think about it. It's not like Newcastle. No mates around."

"You'll meet people here. It won't take long. Have you seen Sadie, the monumental Canadian? She's doing Chinese with us, but I think she went to linguistics today."

"Yeah, how could I have missed her, she's as physically odd as me. She doesn't look like a clown though, not like me. When you've got a mush like mine, you become a clown in spite of yourself. Besides, me Dad's a clown."

"You mean he's funny, tells jokes, that sort of thing?"

"No. He's a real clown. Professional. In a circus."

Adrian was startled. "That's cool. I like that." They observed each other with interest for a moment.

"So that explains all about me, or almost," said Benny.

41

"What about your Mum then?"

"Guess. What do you think? Of course she's in the circus too. She used to be a trick cyclist but now she looks after costumes."

Adrian said: "My Dad's not very conventional either. He's got a boatyard. We all help, me less than the others now though."

"Who's we?"

Adrian wasn't sure about all this home chat. It felt as though he was being asked to walk backwards rather than forwards. On the other hand, Benny seemed lonely, needing to link up his life so far with the place where he now found himself, by talking about his circumstances, assuming or hoping that Adrian would accept the invitation to respond.

"My little sister and brother – she's not so little now and he's quite chunky and strong," he replied. "And my mum, she comes along with the tea. And to chivvy us to come home when supper's up. Dad's got no concept of time."

Benny smiled. "You're not quite as peculiar as me." His face fell a little as he took stock of what he'd just said. "I don't know if I'm going to fit in here." Adrian remained silent to encourage Benny to continue; not in vain.

"It's great to have got here but… It's the first time I've been away from home, although my mum and dad are often away."

"No gap year?" Adrian already knew the answer.

"No. People like us can't do that. I've always worked. I got a job when A levels were over, and then came straight here. I'm the oldest of five." He laughed. "My Mum's Catholic."

"I see."

Benny tipped up his empty mug, pretending to pour the last drops of coffee down his gullet – a time-to-go gesture.

"Thanks anyway for the coffee. I'll leave you in peace now. See you around."

"Yes, come any time. Bring your own sugar though. I'll remember which room is yours."

Benny grinned and shuffled off, leaving the door open. Adrian shut it and returned to lie on his back on the bed.

By a quarter past eight Adrian was hungry. Presumably Max wasn't coming which was a nuisance; it meant Adrian would have to go out and get something. Baked beans from the newsagent would do, and some bread to toast. Or he could finish the packet of chocolate biscuits. He picked up his keys, felt in his back pocket where he found a fiver, and bounded out. Back in his room, he searched amongst his things for the tin opener. His mobile rang. It was Max.

"Sorry I'm so late. I got tied up. I've found your place and I'm on the pavement outside. I hope it's not too late." He sounded neither contrite nor insecure. "Are you ready to go and eat?"

"I've just been out to get baked beans. I thought you weren't coming, it was so late." He knew he sounded peeved as he said it. Altering his tone, he said: "But we can still go out. I'll be down in a few minutes, unless you want to come up?"

"No thanks. I think I'll forego the pleasure of seeing your cosy little nest this time. It'll only delay our meal while I run my fingers across all the surfaces to check the dust…"

Adrian joined Max on the pavement. They walked along the dimly lit road to the right, and then turned into a quiet street with a betting shop and several restaurants:

Indian, Mexican, Lebanese and Chinese of course. It was a glorified takeaway with a counter to the left and several tables in the back. Max hesitated outside as Adrian stepped firmly towards the door.

"Are you sure you want to go in here?" asked Max.

Adrian turned to look at him.

"Why not?"

"Well, it doesn't look very, er, appealing."

"I don't think there's anywhere else close by. Besides, I'm rather hungry. Aren't you?"

Max relented. "Yes. OK, let's go for it. You can make my apologies tomorrow if I get food poisoning."

A friendly man behind the counter called to them. "You want takeaway? You want table?"

"Table please" replied Adrian, and they followed the man through to the back. Large shiny pictures of the Great Wall confronted each other across the room, while a Chinese girl beamed down at them from a poster advertising toothpaste. She and the tube were the same height.

"Sit here," said the man gesturing briefly to a table against the right wall, and walked back to the counter. It wasn't clear whether this was a command or a question, it sounded like the former.

"Oh, all right then and God Bless the Middle Kingdom," said Max to the man's retreating back.

Two unmarked phials containing brown liquid stood on the edge of the table against the wall. Adrian removed the screw tops to smell the contents.

"Nothing sinister," he said, "Just soy sauce and vinegar."

"Fine," said Max.

The owner produced two greasy plastic menus – Chinese characters on the left and English on the right. Adrian pored over it, trying in vain to recognise some of the characters to match up with the English words. Max glanced at the menu briefly. "What do you think? There's nothing on here that particularly grabs me."

"I can't work out what any of the Chinese dishes are from the characters, and as for their English equivalents …" The spelling was indeed peculiar. "I suggest we just ask him what's good. If he comes up with tasty stuff, we can come back another time."

Max looked doubtful. "We always choose rather carefully when we go to Chinese restaurants, but they're rather more … um… well, a bit smarter than this."

"OK then, you can choose between egg rice and steam rice if you like. Same between bake duk and wet duk. Heaven knows."

"You're right. We'll just let him drop us in the soup so to speak. You talk to him. In Chinese."

"Too soon," said Adrian with a smile. "Next month, I promise, although he probably speaks Cantonese, or something else."

The owner was surprisingly forthcoming, although neither Adrian nor Max understood what he said he would serve them. They did grasp however that he would give them what his invisible family, now talking loudly in the adjacent kitchen, had eaten that evening and that it wasn't on the menu.

The beer came first, and by the time the owner had fried up the leftovers for them, Max and Adrian had relaxed. They consumed various mixtures of pork, bean sprouts, cabbage, peanuts, chicken and rice, sprinkled liberally with vinegar and soy sauce. A clear soup with bits floating in it also appeared which, the owner explained, was the house speciality, served only to special guests. A woman in an apron came out of the kitchen to sit down at a corner table, her head angled backwards so that she could watch the television fixed high up on the wall. Two children darted back and forth between her and the kitchen, settling down finally on chairs beside her. Adrian called for maotai – lethally potent, but never mind, he thought. It came in a medium-sized carafe.

The conversation moved on to families. Adrian learned that Max's father was one of two founding partners in Britain of a large multi-national with offices in Paris, Moscow and New York, and that he often worked in London and Paris. The plan was, Max explained, for the small operation in China, where he would soon be doing vacation stints, to expand and for him to become, after graduation, the 'key player' there. Max described his future proudly and, Adrian thought, pompously. He had to agree that there was plenty of potential, but he couldn't imagine himself in Max's position.

His own plans were non-existent, as he revealed. He had decided to change tack from science to try something new, although his parents had hoped he would get a good position as a research chemist in a pharmaceutical firm. Meanwhile, in four years some sort of career would suggest itself to him. So there he was for the time being, drawing squiggles.

"They say the more languages you know, the easier the next one becomes," said Max.

"Yes, and since I haven't done A-level languages…"

"Well, never mind, I'm sure you've got the talent for it." Max was animated, reassuring. "Tell me about your inter-railing," he continued warmly.

Adrian sketched, fleetingly, the places he had visited; some were familiar to Max, who understood well the swing of things: moving on to the next place, meeting new people every day, and thinking about nothing that had any connection with home, school or family. Adrian described some of the unhealthy places where he had stayed, the dodgy food he had eaten, and the substances he had smoked. There had been a few girls too, one of whom, an Aussie, he had liked particularly, but there had seemed to be no point in trying to establish a relationship, since their journeys were pointing in different directions. His memory of her had dimmed; she had become a name in his past.

Max had a steady girlfriend who lived close to his family home in Sussex. He had spent some lazy months with her and in the South of France, on the beach and in a borrowed boat. She was now in her first year at St. Andrews University; they planned to meet once a month.

"My mother thinks I'm going to be a great entrepreneur. All the opportunities are there, but I'm lazy, when I know I can be."

Adrian rather admired Max's boasting self-assurance. He poured out more maotai and then said: "Ah well. My parents know I'm not going to follow in my father's footsteps and be a boat-builder, and to boot they're disappointed I gave up science. They don't see a career for me with a Chinese degree; nor do I, to be honest. I'm not focussed like my sister. She's only thirteen and very firm about what she wants. She'll change her mind, but she'll get there."

"My sister's an accountant."

The maotai was flowing. The owner came in with another carafe and put it down on the table with a toothy grin. Adrian, who was taking two gulps to Max's one, felt slightly dizzy.

"What's your name?" he asked the owner, expecting an answer in Chinese which he wouldn't understand.

"I'm Jack," he replied. Adrian was taken aback.

"Oh. What about your Chinese name?" Adrian's words were slurred.

"Too difficoot. Juzt Jack. You?"

"Adrian, and this is Max."

"Adrian, Max, I hope you come here often. Please, drink." And with that he disappeared into the kitchen shouting something to his wife as he went.

Half an hour later, Max and Adrian called for the ridiculously cheap bill, paid, and wove an unsteady path out into the street. Max, by dint of serious concentration, kept his feet more or less in order, while Adrian lurched from one side of the pavement to the other.

"Our greasy chopstick," said Max.

"What?"

"You know, not spoon but chopstick."

"Oh." Adrian hadn't quite got it.

"Hey, I'd better come with you to your place," said Max. He put his arm through Adrian's and steered him round the corner to his door. "Are you ok to get upstairs?"

"Yeah. Funny stuff this maotai. It doesn't taste strong." His words tailed off. "Thanks for the company Max. See you tomorrow."

Max helped him with his key, and then held the door open to watch Adrian fumble for a moment before finding the right number combination to get in through the inner door. Round two corners back towards the tube station, Max hailed a passing taxi. As it rumbled along, he thought of the pleasant evening he had spent. Adrian fell fast asleep without even removing his trainers, to wake at five with a terrible head. It took him until lunchtime to stir into action. Max, perky as ever, attended the morning classes.

Three

Thursday, 7.46 p.m. His chin cupped in his hand with his elbow supporting it on his desk, Toby was looking with mild dismay at his computer screen and a reproachful pile of files. He felt harassed and weary. Every morning he planned his work day, and towards the end of every afternoon he admitted defeat and flipped through the neglected papers, hoping he had at least got the priorities right. If only… if only he could lock his door, ignore his emails, phone calls and colleagues, and avoid being called into meetings at three seconds' notice, he would be able to achieve what he planned. At the end of each day he vowed not to be over ambitious for the next, but by morning his optimism took over and he would once again overload his mental list of urgent matters.

He took off his glasses to rub his eyes. Through the glass panels of his cube-office, Toby could see the abandoned grey work stations arranged carefully to improve the feel-good factor of the staff. He got up, stretched his arms above his head and went out to sniff at the emptiness, to rejoice in the tranquillity spoiled only by the hum of equipment. Poking out from under the desk to the right of his door was a pair of dark socks crumpled up beside a pair of well-worn black leather shoes. He looked more closely. The socks were decorated with bright green frogs. He walked past to the next desk. There the shoes were neatly on the chair, as if to remind their owner to put them on in the morning. A stroll round the room revealed office shoes under many of the work stations; they were nearly all black, some shiny, some scruffy, some with laces, some with high heels. It was the first time Toby had noticed them. He sauntered around bending and craning to look at them, considering how much one could infer about people by the shoes they wore. The shoes under the desks had evidently been changed out of, and were likely to belong to walking or biking people; a desk with no shoes underneath could therefore belong to an incumbent who took less exercise on the way to work. To test the theory, he walked over to Cedric's desk – he was the fattest member of his staff by far – and looked under it. As he had expected, no shoes. What about the skinniest, who was that? Maybe Mimi, who sat in the corner to the other side of a bank of filing cabinets. And lo, there were the shoes, long thin pointed ones, probably plastic, they were so shiny.

Suddenly he felt eyes on his back and turned to see them gazing at him, dark strong eyes belonging to Tazie Bobrikov who stood immobile, black coat and bag over her arm. He felt embarrassed.

"Hullo Tazie," he said. "Just going?"

"Yes. I've done enough for today."

"I wish I had."

Toby looked at her shoes: white trainers with green and black stripes. Better come clean.

"You're a walker then, or a biker? Got your trainers on I see."

"Yes – I've got quite a walk at the other end. But what an odd thing to say…"

"I hadn't noticed all the shoes under the desks until just now, so I came out to test some theories about who left shoes in the office and why." Tazie's face broke into a smile; she nodded.

He continued. "You're slender and you walk. Others…" he tailed off. Tazie laughed.

"You shouldn't make personal remarks to or about your staff, but I'll ignore them. I saw you looking under Cedric's desk. No surprises there I think."

"No not one."

They looked at each other silently. Tazie made a move.

"Well, m'off. See you tomorrow."

"Have a nice evening."

"Thanks, you too. By the way, do you fit your model? Where are your trainers?"

"Come and search if you like – no trainers at all."

"Then you don't fit the model."

She disappeared into the lift. Toby returned to his desk and once more surveyed the pending work on it. Tomorrow he would have only a couple of hours before going to the airport. It was inconvenient having to take leave at this time with the structures report in preparation. Besides, Toby didn't want to go to Israel. His self-confident leadership in the office belied a shyness which seemed to twist his intestines into knots at large social gatherings. He could manage at official work functions; they were bearable because he had common concerns and interests with the other people there. But big family gatherings were a different matter. To be surrounded by relations he scarcely knew was a severe trial. Nevertheless, he had agreed to go to the wedding to please his parents, flying out with them from Birmingham and returning a week later. His mother, a nervous flyer, was calmer with her adored son seated beside her. But he rather dreaded the questions about girlfriends that awaited him in Israel, and the introductions to suitable young women, with encouraging words from the aunts and whispered innuendo from the uncles. His father and mother refrained from any direct mention of Toby's bachelorhood at home, but once in Tel-Aviv they would somehow be swept along by the tide of family fervour and join in the exhortations. What, thirty-six now, and still not married?

Toby reorganised his piles and updated his electronic diary. That at least would help him in the morning.

He could hear his phone ringing from outside the door of his flat as he arrived but it had stopped by the time he put down his briefcase. He went into the kitchen to pour a cold ginger beer from the fridge, took a ready provençale chicken meal from the freezer, and set it to cook in the microwave. The phone rang again.

"Toby, my boy, where've you been?" asked his mother shrilly. He knew that she knew perfectly well. "Not at work all this time? It's late."

Toby sighed. "Yes Mum, at work. That's what I do."

"You're a workaholic. You never seem to do anything but work. Good thing you're coming with us tomorrow, give you a change, a rest. You need a holiday."

Some holiday, he thought. Whisked around in a coach with a hundred and one relations to whom he would be obliged to make polite conversation. Admire the bride, congratulate the groom. It wasn't that Toby was against marriage; on the contrary, he felt it to be the bedrock of society, necessary and right for many people but not for him.

Mrs Sterne continued. "What time do you arrive in Birmingham? You won't miss the flight will you? Your Dad and I couldn't get on the plane without you – we'd be so worried."

"Worried about what?"

"Well, worried about what would happen at the other end, all the family waiting. And how would you get from the airport to your Uncle David's house?"

"They have taxis in Israel. Don't worry, Mum. I'll be there. My train to Birmingham allows me plenty of time for getting to the airport. And I'll only have carry-on luggage."

"What? Only carry-on luggage?" clucked Mrs Sterne disapprovingly. "What are you going to wear then? You can't wear a suit all the time."

"Don't fuss. I've got it all sorted."

Mrs Sterne subsided: her marvellous and successful only child, of course he would be wonderfully organised.

"Well then, if we get to the desk first, we'll check in and say that we want to sit together with you. Do you think they can do that, if we don't all check in at the same time?"

"I can check us in online probably. I'll let you know."

"Good. I'm so looking forward to it. Did you know that Becky was pregnant? Again! That'll make four. She's really hoping for a girl this time, after her three lovely boys."

"Mum, you can tell me all that tomorrow. It's after nine, I'm hungry and my meal's in the oven and almost ready. So I'll see you at the departure gate tomorrow. I'll probably be there well before you."

She wasn't to be shrugged off.

"Our hand baggage will be rather heavy, with the presents and things…"

Toby groaned inwardly. Presents, yes, plenty of them doubtless. But his relations did seem to appreciate them.

"I'll be able to help with that. Must dash now, the oven's just pinged and the food's ready. See you tomorrow. Lots of love!"

"And to you darling. I suppose we'd better get on the plane even if you aren't there."

His mother hung up. Toby's meal wasn't quite ready, but tomorrow would be a better time to hear the latest family news. There were, he reflected, some compensations to going away: at least he wouldn't have to plan meals. And he knew one or two of his cousins rather well – he would enjoy seeing them again.

It was well past midnight by the time he went to bed.

Four

The garden looked as though a pack of wolves had rampaged across it; foxes probably had, Fen thought. The leaves carefully stacked by Gemma three days previously were scattered, a squelchy mass now clogging all available furrows and corners. Tufts of weeds sprouted healthily in the grass, if the green blades of various hues and types could be called grass. The bean poles down near the summer house were lying flat on the ground, uprooted from the thick clods of sodden earth to point in all directions. On the terrace a pair of grey wellies stood miraculously upright, toes against the wall, held in place no doubt by the quantity of water in them and prevented from falling because the wind came from behind the wall. Fen thought they were John's.

And the fence, what a sorry sight. Fortunately most of the confines of the garden were marked out by laurel hedges; but on one side there was only a straight wooden boundary fence on crumbling concrete posts, all in sad need of attention. Its panels leaned in perverse ways, battered over the years by gales whipping across the flat countryside, and weakened by downpours. Fen and John had talked about renewing it, but it had never come to anything. John was in favour of pulling out that last fence and planting hedges which would eventually reach a height to which the others could be trimmed. "Baby hedges reaching upwards," Fen had said, "and we won't see them from the graveyard." So the discussion was never concluded.

Fen felt a bit guilty about the garden. Neighbours had beautifully tended plots, be they small or large, tidy beds brimming with bright flowers in summer and lumpy with carefully turned soil in winter. Her guilt wasn't caused by envy of neighbours' horticultural prowess, or by worry about what they might think of her own garden. No, it was because she felt that she, John and the children, weren't doing justice to what they possessed. Gemma nagged about it every few months; Sebastian laughed, and Adrian was simply uninterested.

What different people, pondered Fen, as she watched the rain sheeting down the windows, blown there in torrents. She was fortunate to have three healthy children, all adorable in their own ways. Gemma's teens would become more difficult; such a determined and pig-headed person was bound to throw herself into heated confrontations with others who cared less than she did about the environment, the truth, poverty in the third world, and all the other important causes she was impulsively espousing. Her teachers said that as long as she stuck to her studious path, she could go to a top university, and thereafter reach whatever goals she set herself, including satisfying her declared intention of being an historian. She was securely one of the stars in her year. Seb was different. Not particularly able intellectually, he was just short of being uncontrollable about everything physical, sliding down the banisters, playing football, fighting with his classmates, running to school, bounding up and down the stairs three at a time. As a baby, he had soon discovered how to wriggle free of restraining belts. He regularly fell out of his first bed, never cried and never minded bruises. Fen wondered what would happen at puberty. She hoped he wouldn't change from a cheerful bouncing ball into a silent and moody teenager. She couldn't imagine it. John often remarked how like her he was. His body was solid and muscular, his voice very low for his age, and his nature open and direct. Unlike Fen, though, he was competitive and confrontational, but perhaps those traits in Sebastian belonged in the world of boys, in the atmosphere of the classroom, in the home where he was the youngest child. Anyway, most important of all was that he should remain healthy and honest.

Neither Gemma nor Sebastian took after their father physically, but Gemma's academic bent came certainly from John's side of the family. John was knowledgeable about everything, albeit modestly, never stating his opinion unless there were an opening in the conversation, always ready to give way. He had never been ambitious and wanted nothing better than to run his boatyard. They had been through good times and bad with it. Some years John had been overwhelmed with orders for new boats; in others, he had been reduced to mending small craft, varnishing them in winter, and sprucing them up inside. Not that it mattered as long as he was happy. There was family money to tide them over.

And Adrian, what of him? Fen wished she had had him from birth. He had adapted so quickly to being her son, touchingly responsive to affection and care, showing no signs of trauma or complexes from his babyhood. What mysterious genes had made him charming and amiable? He had been a delightful toddler, grown into an obedient and attractive child, slipped easily into untroubled teens and was now almost out at the other end with no tumultuous upheavals, no worries as he would say. Sebastian, with whom Adrian capered tolerantly when required, heeded and looked up to him. And Gemma simply adored him. Fen wondered, with some concern, how he would develop. He took everything almost too easily. His first weekend home from university had taken both John and her by surprise. They had expected that he would be unnerved by the revelations about his parents, but having talked about it with both of them, he had filed the facts away in his mind and got on with being normal, too normal. He was settled, almost passive. They asked him how his first weeks in London had gone. Yes, the course was good and he was doing fine. Yes, he had already made some good friends (never a problem for Adrian – everybody always wanted to be his friend). Yes, London was interesting. But where was the brimming enthusiasm that might be expected of a first year university student? In less than three years' time, he would need to be considering a career; up to now, he had shown no inclination to think about it, and Chinese did not seem to Fen and John to lead anywhere in particular. She realised that she had put her finger on Adrian's weakness: he had no direction, no sense of purpose.

It was almost unbelievable that he was Leslie's son, thank goodness. How magnetic and compelling Leslie had been, how presumptuous, precipitous and predatory. He had swept Fen off her feet at the outset. leading her into mind-blowingly wonderful sexual pleasures, far more intense than any she had experienced since. But Fen remembered with crystal clarity the day, date and time when it had tipped over into violence, curdling everything that had gone before: it was five days after they were married. She had never told anybody the details of the subsequent attacks and disgusting sexual activities he had forced her to undergo. She shuddered, disturbed by these memories, suddenly insecure. So many years had passed since Leslie's death; but when, albeit only occasionally, her brain locked itself on to him, the bile rose to her throat. She had learned slowly and painfully to quell this symptom of her past suffering and expunge the line of thought from her head.

John was her bedrock. Their attachment was like superglue. Fen turned brusquely from the window, shaking her head to settle its grains back in place as though it were a salt cellar. She called him at the boatyard; as usual, it rang and rang before he replied. Fen could see him in her mind's eye, extricating himself from under a boat and wiping his hands on a dirty rag to pick up his mobile. Briefly, she told him she would be on her way with tea and that she wanted to talk to him about something important; he replied as he always did that he hadn't noticed what time it was. Fen warmed the thermos, made tea in a pot and decanted it. Milk, sugar, a spoon, plastic mugs, and biscuits in a basket along with the thermos, and Fen was ready to brave the dash to the car. She drove slowly down to the boatyard along the bumpy road pitted with huge puddles. John looked, as always, foolishly pleased to see her. She reminded him that they had promised the family a dog for Christmas and that if they wanted a pedigree, they needed to start the search straight away.

Five

In retrospect, it had been an odd evening, Adrian thought. His attempt, with Max, to get a good group together for an enjoyable hour or two in a pub hadn't really turned out as he had expected. It had started well, in the refuelling station, with the arrival of Max's sister, Anastasia Ludmilla Bobrikov, otherwise known as Tazie. Adrian liked her looks: her wide face framed by thick brown hair similar to Max's, her voluptuous lips and deep brown eyes.

"I'd forgotten you were Russian," said Adrian. "So what's *your* full name, Max?"

"I'm Igor Maximilian Pyotr Bobrikov. Our parents were Russian but are now British like us – except that we were born here."

"That's a lot of names," remarked Adrian.

"I don't know what I did to deserve one more than Tazie, but that's how it is."

"It's because Ma and Pa were in Russia not long before you were born," said Tazie, sitting down on a chair that Adrian had wiped for her with a paper napkin from the holder on the table. "And there was pressure from some relation or other for you to get Pyotr as well as the names the parents wanted for you."

"How come you know that and I don't? It is me we're talking about, after all." Max prodded her on the shoulder.

"I can't remember who told me, but I've always known. People told me things about that trip because I was there, although not old enough to know anything about it at the time."

"Are there any more of you? Siblings with lots of interesting names?" asked Adrian.

"No" answered Max hurriedly. "We had a sister but she died."

"Oh, I'm sorry," said Adrian. Tazie was looking at the floor. "Anyway, it's nice to meet you Tazie."

She raised her head to look straight at him then, her face neutral. He looked very young to her, with a relaxed freshness as though he had just come in from a long ramble. He had a pleasant open face with docile eyes, and his light brown wavy hair looked as though it would enjoy being ruffled by a gentle hand. He wasn't obviously handsome but warm and alluring in an indefinable way. Nice.

Adrian, not for the first time, sensed Max's impatience; he was tapping two fingers on the table and glancing at his watch. Next, he stood up and flexed his arms backwards, then demanded to know where 'everybody' was. Soon Benny appeared, his arrival heralded by a brown boot which kicked open the swing doors to admit a bundle with a person inside. It was impossible to discern his shape under the floppy clothes he was wearing as well as the things he was carrying: a sweater, an anorak, and a huge bulging backpack. A bunch of keys dangled from his belt. He dropped on to a chair, his keys clanging against it. On being introduced to Tazie, he remarked how nice it was for Max to have a sister in London. Adrian filled in a gap in the conversation by telling Tazie that Benny came from Newcastle and was doing linguistics.

The conversation turned to the choice of venue for the evening. Max had a favourite bar in South Kensington and tried to impose his will on the others. Benny had never before been for a drink in London. Tazie suggested a place up at the Angel where she said there was an eclectic mix of people and drinks – something for everybody. Max wondered if it was the pub belonging to an acquaintance. Adrian didn't mind, but wanted to shield Benny from the embarrassment of expensive drinks.

Hardy, a friend of Sadie's whom nobody knew, was the next to arrive. He looked round the room, searching for a group of people to fit Sadie's description. She had called him briefly urging him to join the others without her as she would be late.

Hardy felt uncomfortable about all aspects of his connection with Sadie and had every expectation of feeling ill at ease with her friends. Because of a connection between their parents she had, on arrival in London, temporarily moved into Hardy's uncle's large comfortable flat, on the understanding that she would find university accommodation as soon as possible. Early on, Hardy identified a wayward streak in her which, coupled with her guileless innocence, got under his skin. Sadie, on the other hand, revered Hardy and was a little afraid of him, while his perfect manners and upright bearing impressed her, making her feel part of a sane and secure world where her erratic impulses might be concealed.

A couple of weeks after the beginning of term, Hardy's uncle, stopping unexpectedly in London overnight on his way to New York, had seen the state of the flat and correctly attributed its disarray to Sadie. A quiet word settled the matter. Hardy broke the news to her as diplomatically as he could. With bad grace, she had to take such accommodation as was available at that late stage in the term: a room in a large flat with several others – the numbers varying according to love, homelessness, sex, hunger, thirst and public transport.

Having found the whole episode embarrassing, Hardy had been glad to see the back of her. Since her departure, a maid did the laundry once a week and cleaned. Hardy stocked the freezer with the best ready meals he could find and buried himself in his study of politics. A postgraduate place at an Ivy League university had been set up for his return to the U.S. which would prepare him for whatever opening he fancied afterwards. It was all clearly charted. He had every hope that once Sadie moved out she would be too tied up with new flatmates to see him; but on the contrary, she had kept in touch with him, calling him regularly to propose outings.

On this occasion, he had persuaded himself that it would do him good to go out with a group. His eyes came to rest on Max whom Sadie had described as a smart dresser. He walked over quietly, unwilling to interrupt the raised voices which petered out as he approached. He introduced himself, apologised for being late, and explained why he had come alone. Max immediately stood up to shake hands and pull up a chair beside him. Benny grinned and Adrian smiled. Hardy towered over Max – himself over six feet – by a couple of inches. This might, along with the fresh shirt and tie he was wearing, have given him a certain authority, but Max was impervious to such influences.

The group settled on Tazie's suggested place at the Angel, to which Adrian summoned the remaining friends. The bar there was a cavernous room with a large oval serving counter at the centre within which a dozen people dressed identically in purple trousers and black tops whizzed around getting drinks. The lights were so angled as to cast peculiar reflections from mirrored walls, making the space seem misshapen and eerily larger than it was. Max began a low-toned conversation with Hardy which was to last much of the evening. Tazie watched her brother with amusement; he never failed to collar well-dressed acquaintances, assuming them to be the sort of people he could associate with, and adopting a confidential pose, subtly flattering.

Max's conquesting was interrupted by the arrival of Sadie who, eyes shining and clothes skimpy, wove unsteadily towards them, put her hands on Hardy's shoulders and awkwardly kissed the bit of him nearest to her – the back of his neck. Adrian noticed how, looking acutely uncomfortable, he jerked his head sideways. There being no available seat beside Hardy, she sat down grumpily next to Benny, not even feigning interest in his analysis of that day's linguistics lecture.

The last to turn up were Sujit and Lian Hua, fellow residents from Fletcher's Hall; their presence altered the dynamics of the group. Sujit was, in Adrian's eyes, small and perfectly formed; his round smiling eyes and graceful movements exuded gentleness and tranquillity. Lian Hua was brash, dynamic and self-assured. She stood watching and listening before fetching a chair and squeezing it in beside Hardy's, much to Sadie's dismay.

As the evening progressed, Adrian looked round at them all. Sujit and Benny were carrying on a conversation about university funding which they had evidently started a few evenings before. Lian Hua was getting her teeth into Hardy, at least that was how it seemed to Adrian and apparently to Sadie too, who downed several drinks with ostentatious abandon, watching her adversary. Tazie commented quietly to Adrian that Sadie might need some support later on. Soon enough there was indeed a rumpus when Max, observing the way she was conducting herself, asked if she were ready to go home. Sadie was angry at first at the implication that she had had too much to drink. She then tried to inveigle Hardy into seeing her home, but he replied that he would soon be leaving to meet his uncle who was due to arrive from Heathrow. Sadie had some bitter words to say about the uncle. Max and Adrian eventually succeeded in steering her outside and sending her on her way.

Adrian felt hungry as he sat down again beside Tazie.

"She's in a taxi" he announced.

"Say, thank you very much," said Hardy. "You guys got me out of a spot. I'm real grateful."

"Don't mention it" replied Adrian.

"Thank goodness," said Tazie to Adrian quietly. "The poor girl looks really smitten with Hardy."

"Mm. I shouldn't think she's got much hope there. He seems very formal and straight-laced – I don't suppose he'd want to get enmeshed with someone who has a potential drink problem."

"It's sad for her, though. I'm sure she minds towering over blokes, and Hardy's the right height for her. It's difficult for women her size to find anybody."

"I suppose it is. But she's fleshy and floppy too," said Adrian.

"That's not very kind," replied Tazie.

Adrian turned to look at her. "I can see why Hardy's not interested. She wouldn't turn me on."

"What sort of woman would then?" asked Tazie with the ghost of a provocative smile, interpreted by Adrian as encouragement.

"That's a leading question. Pass – for today, anyway."

Comfortable, neither spoke. Tazie glanced up to see Max raising his eyebrows at them. She looked away. Max was used to the magnetism his sister exercised on the opposite sex, unwittingly bewitching boys when in her teens and now perhaps more knowingly. He knew also that she was circumspect in the matter of relationships. He wondered for a moment about Adrian; perhaps there was someone in Suffolk. He sighed. It was none of his business anyway, Tazie could pull the strings competently.

Adrian's last memory of the bar was potentially embarrassing. Somebody was shaking him and calling his name. He roused himself to discover that his head was on Tazie's shoulder. He sat upright with a jerk and apologised, to be informed by Max that he had been asleep for nearly ten minutes. Tazie accepted his apology, brushing off her shoulder as though Adrian had left dandruff on it.

For a couple of days, Adrian thought intermittently of Tazie with regret, for surely his slumber had not impressed her and her earlier encouragement must have evaporated. On the third day, he decided to find out – no harm in asking.

"Max," he said at the end of a two hour long language slog which left them all wilting, "will you give me Tazie's number? I want to apologise to her for the other night."

"Ho hum," grinned Max. "If it's just apologies, then I could pass them on without giving you the number?"

"But," smiled Adrian, "apologies don't fare well second hand. Anyway, whether or not it's just apologies will depend on her, not me. So come on, give me the number."

It was easier than he had expected. Again she accepted his apologies and she even agreed to call him the following week to arrange to meet.

Six

This was the third time Adrian and Max had played squash together. Max had years of practice behind him; with many hours of supervised training, he had learned that an eye for the ball and good anticipation could compensate for sluggish footwork. On the other hand, Adrian didn't like indoor sports – he particularly disliked the gym and everything to do with it – but squash had turned out to be more fun than he had anticipated, and in his games against Max, his speed and flexibility made up for his lack of experience. They were well matched, although Max had the edge and was very pleased about that. Adrian was glad for him too and minded not in the least losing each time they played. Afterwards, they ate fried noodles in a Chinese café they had found near the sports centre, or in the one near Adrian's hall where they had first eaten together – their 'greasy chopstick'.

On the bus home, Adrian thought about Max and Tazie. There were tangible likenesses: similar colouring and facial bone structure, similar speech lilt, similar self-confident demeanour. But in temperament, thought Adrian, they were different. Tazie was considered, almost slow, whilst Max was brisk and impatient. Tazie seemed tolerant whilst Max was perhaps not. Adrian pulled up short in his comparison, surprised by his implicit criticism of Max whom he liked. As a plus, this friendship with Max had led to an attractive girl, or rather woman. Tazie was older than both of them. Adrian knew Max was twenty; Tazie could be as old as twenty-five. She had the bearing of a woman, unlike the girls Adrian had met on his travels.

Their date the previous week had left Adrian feeling buoyant. The Italian restaurant close to her gleaming glass office building was not smart but neither was it scruffy. They had enjoyed bruschetta and olives, pasta and salad, and while Tazie indulged in a cappuccino, Adrian tucked into tiramisu. Not especially refined fare, but at least tasty and nourishing.

Adrian was relaxed, at ease (as he was with everybody), self-confident and cheerful; awkwardness was alien to his body and his mind. After the date, he gave scant thought to the impression he might have made on Tazie – either she liked him or she didn't, either she found him sexy or not; he hoped for positives in due course. But for now, Adrian and Tazie remained decorous, parting at the tube station, agreeing to go out again some time in the next couple of weeks.

But something that Tazie had said dropped a seed in the buried areas of his mind, eventually growing up to the surface - something that had disturbed him; it was when they were talking about their families. Tazie had asked whether he was curious about his birth mother, where she was and what she was like. He hadn't been. Moreover, the Middle East was a closed book to him apart from what he learned from news bulletins. Chinese language, culture and institutions filled his days while shapely Chinese characters insinuated themselves into his sleep. But... was he like his mother? Fen had said that in temperament, he was unlike his father; was he therefore like her, Mrs somebody? Did his mother ever think about him? Had she remarried and did she have other children? Perhaps Adrian had half-brothers and sisters. If they existed, they could be in their teens now. What might they be like? Were they Arabs? Did they speak English or Arabic or both? Would he, in his mother's shoes, have abandoned a baby because of marital violence? Impossible even to guess. Adrian had no experience of marriage, babies or violence other than boys' tussles at school.

His bus stop. Quickly, he roused himself from his brown study and jumped off. A full moon in a cold limpid sky created strange hues and shapes on the pavement and reflections in the window panes. In his room, Adrian turned on his blow heater (the central heating system was less than adequate), filled the kettle and got a mug ready with coffee and milk in it. Time to practise writing characters. He ruled three columns on a sheet of lined paper, wrote a random series of English words in the left column, then without looking them up, he added characters in the middle and the transliterated pronunciation in the right column. After half an hour, he checked what he had done. A few mistakes in the characters, so he spent some time writing and rewriting them. My mind's wandering, he said to himself. He was imagining the Middle East, countries he had never seen, unfamiliar people, food, clothes. Idly, he went on to the internet and typed in *Patti Sandling,* knowing it would be in vain. Many solutions and sites for Patti offered themselves: a basketball player in Kansas, a horse trainer in Australia, a sauna in Sweden, a golf instructor in Bermuda, as well as the inevitable salacious offerings. For *Sandling* there were but few entries: a state university in Canada, a lifting equipment manufacturer in Norway and other such irrelevances. There were no results for Patti and Sandling together. He typed in *find people* and up came plenty of UK sites. Perhaps she was back in the UK.

An impatient fist banging on the door interrupted him. Lian Hua was there. Somehow she always managed to erupt when Adrian was concentrating on something. As usual she had a list of requirements. The first was to ask if Adrian knew where Sujit was, as he hadn't turned up to meet her after a late lecture. Adrian had no idea, but suggested that an extended question and answer session might have detained him. Lian Hua looked astonished, as though she expected everybody to conform to her timetable, and as though seeing her was more important than doing anything else. The next was a peremptory demand that Adrian should go with her to see the latest Kung Fu film. Adrian agreed – it was no hardship as he liked Kung Fu films.

The final matter was more delicate – the upshot of an evening earlier in the week. Sadie had once again asked Hardy to go for a drink. He had skirted round the request, avoiding refusing her outright by asking who else was going to be there. Sadie, fearing with reason that Hardy would not go out alone with her, had included some of the others in the plan, and thus it was that Adrian, Max and Sujit had gone too. And Sujit had brought along Lian Hua who had wasted no time in homing in on her opportunity. Hardy, thought Lian Hua, was the ideal date, distinguished, serious and pleasant looking. She had sat beside him, smiled at him and agreed with everything he said. He was flattered and intrigued by this small person with a heart-shaped face and thick black shiny hair who spoke wisely of the need to get a good degree and to avoid wasting time.

Lian Hua's plans were concrete: she was determined to dangle her fish hook, and she needed Adrian's intervention. First, she told him, she would adopt an English name; she had decided on Lily although, as Adrian pointed out, a lily wasn't the same as a lotus blossom – the meaning of her Chinese name. But she was adamant. Her Chinese friends had all adopted English names and it was time for her to do likewise; none of them was called Lily and they had all agreed it was a good name. Adrian doubted privately that this could bring down the odds on her chances with Hardy but heard out her planned bait: a meeting between Hardy, Adrian and her, from which Adrian would be called away. Adrian prevaricated. Lian Hua was pushy, Sadie was easily thrown off balance, and Adrian had not perceived any interest in Lian Hua on Hardy's part. Furthermore, he was unwilling to do anything that might tip Sadie and her alcopops into another muddy pit from which they would be obliged to extricate her.

Lian Hua was a go-getter. Her family was originally from the countryside near Shanghai. They had made money quickly in the 1980s' boom and her father had moved on to invest in shares in state owned industries to which he, as a communist party member, had special access. He was now rich, but speaking no English had decided that his only child should have the opportunities that had eluded the family until then. So it was that she found herself, aged sixteen, in a sixth form college in Britain where she became a star pupil, particularly in maths, all the while not quite managing to get her mouth round English consonants and vowels. A student's visa for undergraduate economics followed, the subject chosen by her father as being the most useful for her business career in the Far East. Lian Hua was as ambitious as her father was for her. Her progress and achievements were remarkable, exceeding their hopes.

Adrian agreed to think about her suggestion and to try to remember to call her Lily. She departed with alacrity; he returned to his computer. By the time he went to bed, he had registered doggedly on several people search sites, without any conviction that he might find Patti Sandling.

Although at first unsurprised at his lack of success, by the following week he had grown grumpy as nothing he entered led anywhere useful: Max, noticing that he seemed out of sorts, tried to pry subtly but to no avail. In the end, he took the direct approach, believing probably with justification that he was the only immediately available person who could prise something out of Adrian.

"You got a sore toe or something?" he asked the next time he and Adrian were alone over coffee. "There's a cure for it you know."

"What do you mean?" replied Adrian, offended.

"You're not your usual cheerful self. You slink off and don't react to anything people say to you. Bit dull for me, you know."

Adrian turned to look at the damp, opaque window then back at Max.

"Leave off Max. I've got something on my mind."

"So I see. What else is new?"

Adrian turned his cup round and round on the table without replying.

"Your business, anyway," said Max offhandedly.

"Yes it is." Adrian slid his bottom from side to side on the sticky chair. After a moment he relented, just a little.

"Did Tazie say anything to you… about me?"

"She said she liked you."

74

Adrian smiled then returned to the essence.

"Not that sort of thing, about me personally, my family." He was struggling with the words.

So that was it, thought Max. "You mean about your parents?"

"Yes…"

"Mm. She did say that your father was dead and you were adopted without knowing your mother."

There was a silence. Adrian licked his finger, dabbed it in some stray sugar crystals on the table and put it in his mouth.

"I've got this thing about who and where she is."

"Well that's quite normal."

Adrian warmed to the subject, and to Max. "Mum and Dad said she went to Lebanon, and they have an old address for her there. I've asked them for it and will write to her, although I don't know what to say. Anyway, I don't hold out much hope that she's still there. I've been looking in vain on the people-search websites. But I don't know her name now. She's probably remarried – an Arab."

"Oh," said Max in surprise. "Do you think that she could be here, in London, or somewhere else in the UK?"

"She might be, but the last Mum and Dad knew was that she was in Beirut, teaching English."

"Ah. So why don't you start searching Beirut? Do the people-search sites reach Beirut?"

"No, I don't think so."

"Then there's no reason for you to be dis-chuffed yet. You're looking in the wrong direction. A bit of lateral thinking, my boy," he said, somewhat patronisingly, unnoticed by Adrian.

"You're right, but I am dis-chuffed all the same. I'm not expecting anything special, but I'd just like to know about my mother."

"Why not try schools or colleges in Beirut? What do you know about them?"

Adrian was taken aback. It hadn't occurred to him.

"Nothing."

"Then time to start, Adrian. There must be stuff on the net about them."

"You're right" answered Adrian slowly. "Yes," he replied more briskly "I'll do that."

Seven

3.00 p.m. Back at his desk, eating a tuna-mayo sandwich on the day after returning from Israel, Toby was thinking about matrimony. Despite his reservations, he had to admit that the wedding in Tel-Aviv had been spectacularly successful: his relations had been more than welcoming and the bridal couple looked ecstatically happy. And on a more private level, he thought with satisfaction that he had forgotten, some of the time, about feeling different, having matured enough for his shyness to dissolve in the momentum of the event. He had danced with the best, talked to strangers about all and nothing, and eaten with relish. People had asked him with genuine interest about his work and he had replied with warmth and animation. But he still didn't identify with the country nor did he recognise in himself any profound Jewishness, whatever it was.

The parade of young women had been duly marched before him by his uncles and aunts, almost as though he were expected to choose there and then, to waltz off into happy-ever-after land, fulfilling their wishes and presumably those of the chosen spouse. Even in this unwelcome inspection of troops, Toby had been cordial and attentive. One young woman had appealed to him more than the others. She was a distant relation by marriage; Toby had forgotten the exact connection, but it was deemed by his sundry relations to be useful. "People you know, people you can count on," said Uncle David. After the wedding celebrations were over, he invited her out for coffee the day before his flight back to London. A final year medical student ("even better" said Mrs Sterne to her husband a few days later), she had apparently had neither the time nor the inclination to become romantically attached. Selena Bonstein was no beauty: rather thin, of medium height and soberly dressed. Nevertheless, her face became pleasing as she talked with an endearingly pronounced lisp of the things that were important to her – her work, life in Israel and the orphanage founded by her aunt of which she was to become a trustee. With enthusiasm she outlined to Toby her future as she saw it: in Tel-Aviv, married with children, pursuing her career. Was she sounding him out, he wondered, probing to see if he would consider moving to Israel so that if not, she could write him off? It seemed obvious to him, sitting at his desk back in London, that moving to the UK was not something she would want to consider.

It was all irrelevant anyway, he thought impatiently, taking a large bite out of a spongy apple. He could never marry. It would be near criminal to inflict his illness on a wife, although doctors had assured him that he could "lead a normal life", whatever that was. Toby could never forget the accident in Istanbul, seven years previously. A business trip intended to last two days had had to be prolonged, bridging a weekend. Toby's hospitable Turkish hosts had arranged a day's sightseeing including a scramble over some recently discovered Roman ruins on a stony hill. The view over the city was magnificent, although the ruins were little more than a pile of rocks, some just recognisable as fragments of columns. On the way down, Toby's leather-soled office shoes had slithered sideways, projecting him forwards on to a sharp flint which had made a deep gash through his trouser leg into his left shin. Profuse bleeding had landed him in hospital where in due course he had been given a blood transfusion. Hepatitis B was the result; it provoked some red faces amongst his colleagues, since Turkish blood supplies were believed to be free from the virus. Toby had never felt so ill. Six months later he had still tested positive and was therefore considered to be a carrier. Although he had forgiven himself for falling and did not indulge in self-pity, his stoicism in accepting the consequences became the foundation stone of a wall which he started to construct as soon as he became interested in a woman. Stifling his yearning for love became second nature.

Mr and Mrs Sterne's attitude was that most people had something wrong with them and that Toby's condition should not hinder him in anything. For many months after his symptoms were gone, they were gushingly attentive; when he was with them, they asked him several times a day how he was feeling, and when he was away they rang him twice weekly, reminding him boringly to go for a check-up if he suffered the slightest malaise. Toby bore it all philosophically, swallowing down his irritation. Eventually, they simmered down, although there was always a note of anxiety in Mrs Sterne's voice when she asked him over the phone how he was. They naturally continued to encourage him to set himself up with a wife; Toby continued in his resolve not to marry and, wanting to avoid needless and endless debate, had never revealed his decision to them. So his eyes and theirs never focussed on the same horizon.

All this wound its way through Toby's mind as he finished eating and went to fetch a cup of coffee. He was a workaholic, he recognised, and pleased to be one, his nose in his papers until late every evening, isolating him from the difficulties he had in socialising. He had exchanged email addresses with Selena; he would send her a polite but cool message saying he was busy and had much enjoyed meeting her. Under the circumstances, it wouldn't be right to say more.

A shadow appeared in the doorway: Martin, Chief Executive.

"Had a good trip?" he asked. "Wedding good, family pleased to see you?"

"Yes" replied Toby with more than usual enthusiasm, surprising Martin. "The whole thing went off very well. It's good to see life somewhere else, blows away the cobwebs."

"Yes. Well. I wish we could do it more often. It's so difficult to get away. Annual leave entitlement's all very well, but juggling things and people...." he tailed off. Martin halted to clear his throat and look around himself vaguely for a moment. Toby waited.

"Anyway, we've got a new problem," continued Martin, "in the Tyneside office. It seems that one of the supervisors has been doing less than he should, and that his two sidekicks have been auditing accounts cursorily without supervision, leading to a series of penetrating questions from a small business client when HM Tax Inspectors prised open the can of worms. The sort of thing that I hate and which gives us a bad reputation."

"Bother, to put it mildly" replied Toby, shaking his head.

"Yes, shit."

"Should I go and sort it?"

"Someone must, but I don't think you need go yourself. Send one of your whizz kids – Jeremy for instance – and tell him to take Tazie with him, it will be good for her to see it."

"OK. Jeremy's good, and Tazie's ready for something new."

"Fine," and with that, Martin disappeared.

Tazie, thought Toby. Now there was a special person; quiet intelligence along with, seemingly, a beautiful personality and a sexy body. He wondered for an instant if she had a partner. He didn't recall her bringing anybody to an office function, but she'd not been in his section long.

He went out to Jeremy, explained to him what needed doing, and told him to take Tazie with him. Ten minutes later, Tazie was outside Toby's office wearing a large smile. She thanked Toby warmly for the opportunity and was pleased that she would get her first taste of trouble. Toby, gratified, remarked that a couple of days should be enough to clear up the mess, and suggested Tazie might enjoy looking round Newcastle which had become an interesting place. He hoped that on her return, she would tell him personally how she had fared.

Eight

In the end, Adrian gave in to Lily's badgering but organised the meeting with Hardy in his own way. A threesome suddenly interrupted by an emergency phone call for him seemed just too contrived, so instead Sujit, Benny and Tazie were included (without an explanation) in the event, and while he, Adrian, would be pleased to go off with Tazie, Lily would have to countenance the possibility that Sujit and Benny wouldn't take the hint and disappear together, although a good friendship had developed between them. Sujit's gentle personality put Benny at ease, while intellectually they were a match for each other. Benny was the more academically focussed of the two, but since they were on different courses – Sujit was studying development economics - there were never clashes. Benny had described to Adrian the taunting he had been subjected to at school because he was, according to his teachers, 'university material', and how he had become expert at suddenly not being there when the more violent bullies were on the march. No wonder Benny had come to London full of apprehension; it had taken time for him to understand that being a misfit at school didn't kit you out for being one at university. Friendship with Sujit was rewarding for both of them. Sujit too had been on the receiving end of unwanted attention and threatening behaviour at school because of his dark coloured skin and beautiful body.

Of his three candidates for inclusion in what Adrian came to call the "Hardy exploit", he first approached Benny who agreed innocently to come along and suggested bringing Sujit. This, Adrian felt, was a good start, and it dispelled some doubts about the whole undertaking. Although the others were sympathetic with Hardy, understanding his reluctance to be anywhere near Sadie, actually guiding him towards someone else was a somewhat different matter.

It was the first week of November. They met in a pub in Pimlico close to Hardy's flat. Punctual as usual, Hardy was sitting alone at a round table in a corner when Tazie, umbrella under her arm and wearing a smart aubergine raincoat open at the front, arrived to join him. She kissed him, remarked that she was apparently the first on the scene, and let him get her a rum and coke, noticing that it took only four strides of his long legs to reach the counter. He returned with some nibbles too.

They filled in the time by conversing about Hardy's initial impressions of his economics degree course which, he confessed, he found disappointing. There was little supervision; students were expected to attend lectures (which didn't always start on time) and plan their work alone, and competition for the limited copies of recommended books in the library was irritating, especially since some were out of print and unavailable to buy. Tazie was sympathetic, contrasting Hardy's experience with hers. The highly structured nature of her course in accounting and finance had allowed students to build up knowledge and techniques systematically within a specific timeframe.

This way of working had suited Tazie, and she couldn't imagine any other.

Lily appeared. She had slipped into the pub behind a very tall couple and was standing before them, looking cross: although she was early, Tazie had beaten her to it. Hardy jumped up with alacrity and put out his hand to greet her; she took it and shook it enthusiastically. He gestured towards the empty seat beside him where she immediately sat down. He fetched her a drink.

"Hullo, Lian Hua," said Tazie.

"I've changed my name" announced Lily firmly. "I've taken an English name, it's Lily. Lian Hua is too difficult for people to remember. Please call me Lily."

"Right, I will," replied Tazie, realising that her peremptory tone reflected her usual tone in Chinese rather than any wish on Lian Hua's part to be disagreeable. When Hardy returned with Lily's drink, Tazie said at once "Hardy, Lian Hua's got an English name now. It's Lily."

"Is that so Lily?" said Hardy, sitting down between them. "Well, that's a gorgeous name, such a lovely flower. It suits you." He looked at her with beatitude. Suitably gratified, Lily flashed him a winning smile.

Benny and Sujit turned up next and Adrian last, on purpose. He had wanted the hellos and awkwardness to have been done with before he got there. He wasn't disappointed. Hardy and Lily were by then deep in conversation whilst the other three were discussing football. After the greetings, Adrian sat unnoticed, observing them all, wondering how long to allow before escaping with Tazie.

Then after less than half an hour, Hardy surprised them all.

"Lily, to celebrate your new name, I'd like to take you to dinner. How about it? This evening?"

Lily's face flushed with unbridled triumph.

"Oh yes Hardy," she breathed.

"Do you like Mexican food? We eat it quite often back home."

"I've never had it. I'd like to try it."

"Splendid. There's a restaurant which my uncle and I like very much. Shall we go? Are you ready now?"

"Yes," replied Lily, standing up swiftly to thread her arms neatly into the sleeves of her coat. It was clear from Hardy's demeanour that the thought of asking anybody else to go with them had not occurred to him.

"Let me see now. I think we can get a taxi outside." And with that they were gone. Four mouths were left hanging metaphorically open in surprise. Tazie looked penetratingly at Adrian. Benny and Sujit looked at each other.

"Well, that was a bit quick," said Benny. "She looked as though she was getting what she wanted."

"Mm," agreed Sujit. "I hadn't thought of Hardy as being a fast worker."

Tazie and Adrian said nothing.

"I'm going to get a beer," said Benny. "Anybody else? Another of those Sujit?"

"Yes – it's pineapple juice."

"Not for me, thanks," said Adrian. "How about you, Tazie, another drink?"

"No thanks. I must be going soon."

After a few more minutes of desultory conversation, Tazie stood up to leave, followed by Adrian. When they got outside, she confronted him accusingly.

"You set that up, didn't you?"

"Sort of."

"What do you mean, sort of?"

"Lian Hua, I mean Lily, asked me to. She kept pestering me. In the end I gave in, but tweaked the whole thing a bit."

"Asking us to come too, you mean?"

"Precisely that."

"And what about poor Sadie?"

"Sadie's got nothing to do with it. The way I see it is that Hardy's not interested in her, and she may anyway not get to hear about it for a while, by which time water will have passed under the bridge. Perhaps Hardy and Lily won't hit it off or Sadie will find somebody else."

"Pigs might fly, but I hope she does. I feel sorry for her."

"I know you do, and I do too, a bit. But it's a tough world."

Tazie rejected Adrian's suggestion of a bite together, pleading work to do at home. Adrian went off feeling somewhat disconsolate. Once in his room, he forced himself first to write a composition in Chinese, and then eagerly went to his computer to continue searching for Patti Sandling. He was using several different websites and methods to find the names of teachers in Beirut.

He had just finished eating a salad when a long-faced Sujit knocked on the door. While Sujit commented on the gathering earlier in the evening, Adrian got coffee and biscuits. He was intrigued by Sujit, whom he'd never seen long-faced before.

"Adrian, I'd like to ask you something," he began.

"Go ahead," said Adrian.

"I've met someone, and I'd like to know what you think." His limpid brown eyes betrayed anxiety.

"Good for you, but you know I'm no expert in matters of the heart."

"But it's different for me – I need help from someone who's worldly. You see, I'm gay."

Of course, thought Adrian, that fits. I should have realised. "Go on," he said.

Sujit explained that he had always known, but came from a traditional Hindu family. His parents lived in an imaginary world where homosexuality didn't exist. So Sujit had bottled it up and had never had any sexual contact with anyone, nor told anybody about himself. Thinking that coming from Southampton to live in London would open things up for him, he had started going to a few clubs and pubs but had shied away from going off with anyone he met. On Saturday he had been to a quiet gays' pub in Clerkenwell where he got talking to a dark, chunky bloke who seemed nice. They had exchanged mobile numbers; the man had texted Sujit suggesting going for a pizza together. Sujit was scared and wanted Adrian's advice about what to do.

After discussion, it was arranged that Sujit would tell Adrian the name of the restaurant, where Adrian and Benny would go in advance and remain anonymous, to give the man the once over.

"Then, you and I could go for a pee at the same time and exchange a quick word. Not that I know anything about gay body language. Of course we couldn't follow you anywhere. You'd best not go home with him after the first meeting anyway" said Adrian.

"Adrian, that's awfully kind. Yes, please."

"Presumably Benny already knows that you're gay?"

"Yes. But I thought you'd be a better person to help me decide what to do."

"Let me know where and what time, and we'll be there."

Sujit left looking cheerful.

Adrian was as good as his word, meeting Benny as arranged and sitting at a table next but one to where Sujit and Mike were deep in conversation. The pizza was mediocre – but Sujit and Mike appeared to be connecting nicely. Adrian gave Sujit a cautious yes in the loo before going back to Fletcher's with Benny.

***

It was the following week that Tazie and Adrian became lovers, unplanned by both of them, with no momentous build up but just a growing awareness that this was how it was going to be, naturally and when the appropriate time presented itself. Their mutual attraction had never been in doubt; making love was the logical consequence. Tazie had been able to leave work relatively early and wanted to go home to change before going out. As Adrian had never, as far as he could remember, been to Battersea where Tazie lived, she suggested meeting there in an Indian restaurant. Adrian, unusually for him, arrived early and had almost finished his first beer when Tazie appeared, looking wonderful in casual clothes. The sight of a different version of her stirred Adrian; they had previously met only on weekdays immediately after she had left the office, and she went almost invariably to her parents' home on Fridays. He stood up for the customary kiss, feeling that it was somehow a different sort this time, a step further on.

Tazie listened with genuine interest and sympathy to details of Adrian's trawling on the internet through names in search of someone with at least his mother's first name. She understood well why it had become so important to him at this juncture, and that it was the first of several complicated crossroads which he could not foresee. She discovered that her earlier questions about his attitude had been a catalyst, awakening his curiosity. A desire to know about his mother would anyway have been awakened some time, by someone else, under some other circumstances.

When the conversation came to a natural close, Tazie looked straight across the table at Adrian.

"Well, is it tonight?" she asked.

Adrian understood immediately.

"Yes, please" he answered calmly.

The flat she shared was quiet and dark; there was neither sight nor sound of flatmates. Tazie's room was along a corridor, next to the bathroom. By the time he had washed, she had drawn the curtains and was pulling the duvet back. The bed was cold and had a fresh washing-powder smell. Afterwards, Tazie lay awake, happy and tranquil, whilst Adrian slept deeply, his head in the crook of her arm. There was no question of Adrian going back to Fletcher's.

The next day, Benny accosted him in the canteen.

"I looked for you last night," he said. "Even very late, you weren't back."

"No, I wasn't" answered Adrian in a non-committal fashion.

"Anything special?" grinned Benny bluntly.

Adrian decided quickly that there was no reason to be secretive.

"Yes, quite special," he replied, smiling.

"Great for you," said Benny. "Nice lady if it's who I think it is... happiness, warmth. Lovely."

It was more than a week before Max knew – there seemed to be neither reason nor opportunity to tell him. A chance remark of Benny's – not even an indiscretion since there was no question of secrecy – imparted the information. Wanting always to be in control and considering himself to be Adrian's earliest and thus closest friend in London, Max was proprietorially piqued not to have been the first to know. Later that day, he hunted out Adrian who was deep in a journal in the corner of the canteen. He strode across purposefully to stand almost threateningly over him, one hand on the back of his chair.

"So, you've been hitting it off with my sister without so much as a by-your-leave? How come everybody else knows except me? Were you afraid I'd withhold my brotherly permission?"

"No, no, Max," said Adrian looking up wearily. "Sit down, don't lean over me like that. It wasn't a big planned event and it didn't occur to me, nor to Tazie I think, to announce it."

"No, well I've not spoken to her for a few days." He sat down expectantly, hoping for more information.

"So who told you?"

"That's classified information. You tell me first who you told and we'll see if it matches."

"I told Benny only because he was looking for me the night I was at Tazie's. I didn't go out of my way to tell him, it just fell out."

"All right, all right. You're forgiven. Should I ring and congratulate Tazie?"

"Please yourself. Up to you." Adrian returned his eyes to his journal. Max softened.

"Want a mug of glop?"

"Yes please, a milky one."

By the time Max returned from the coffee machine with two plastic cups of brown liquid, Adrian was his usual affable self again.

"Adrian, I haven't asked you for a while how you're getting on with your parent search: any news?"

"I took your advice and I've been surfing all sorts of websites looking for names of teachers in Beirut. It's a bit difficult when the only sure information I have is her first name. And come to think of it, even that may have changed. She might be calling herself Blossom by now for all I know."

"Blossom? What on earth are you talking about? Where did you dream up that name from?"

Adrian grinned. "Lian Hua wants to be called Lily; all her Chinese friends have English names now, and she thinks Hardy will like her the better for it. So why not Blossom for my mother?"

"Hum. Lily and Hardy eh. Not surprising, he innocent and gentlemanly, she determined and predatory. I can see it. And two fingers to Sadie."

He glanced at the journal in front of Adrian and snatched it away.

"Hey, what are you doing reading Middle East stuff? You're supposed to be doing Chinese."

Adrian looked slightly guilty. "It's just recreation. Ringing the changes."

The heading on the page was 'Security aspects of Palestinian refugees in Lebanon'.

"Looks heavy stuff to me," said Max thoughtfully and glanced at the article. "Just a minute," he said slowly. "You're not thinking of … you're not thinking of going there, are you?"

Adrian didn't reply.

"Adrian, I asked you something" he reiterated insistently. "Are you thinking of going there?"

"Well, it did occur to me that I might get more information on the spot."

"You must be mad! It's dangerous. You haven't a clue where to go or what to do or anything. You don't speak Arabic; you don't know where to stay or how to get around or anything useful." Max's voice was becoming louder and angrier.

"I am thinking of learning a bit of Arabic," said Adrian, hoping to mollify Max.

Max exploded. "Even madder! For fuck's sake, as if one difficult language weren't enough, you're launching yourself into another." An expression of dawning suspicion spread across his face.

"Don't say that was Arabic you sloped off to in a hurry on Monday after linguistics? An Arabic class?"

Adrian faced him. "Not exactly. It was an Arabic Society get-together. I didn't stay long – I felt a bit out of place."

Max subsided. They eyed each other in the silence that followed.

"Adrian," continued Max quietly and slowly, as though addressing a child, "I know I sometimes sound a bit detached and dilettante about doing Chinese, but I do actually take it very seriously, and I'm going to do well. I've got a goal to achieve and a career waiting for me, all being well. Now you haven't, but at least you've got a real gift for Chinese which is bound to lead to something good. We both know how much effort it takes just to begin to get a handle, in a very elementary way, on the language, and a feel for China. You can't start buggering around just now. For goodness' sake, stick to Chinese."

Adrian looked at the table and said nothing.

"I'm your mate, Adrian. I'm not saying this for me."

"I know, I know. But this mother thing is preoccupying me. I know my parents thought it the right time to tell me about it, but it seems to be getting to me a bit."

"Look at it this way. You've been fine up to now without knowing your mother, and you've got years ahead in which to find her. Give yourself a chance here first."

"You're right, of course" nodded Adrian.

"And you get on fine with your parents, don't you? I've never heard you speak ill of any of your family."

Adrian smiled.

"They're cool, Max. They've never been less than completely supportive."

"Well, there you are. Go and spend a weekend at home. Do you good."

The idea gave Adrian momentary relief from what had become an obsession.

"Max, come with me, if you like?" he said impulsively. "It's a different world there. Have you ever been?"

"The Broads? No."

"Then come?"

"When? I can't do this weekend."

"All right, next weekend?"

"Yeah, that'll be all right. My parents are going to a wedding in Bolivia."

Adrian wondered whether Max would pull out the following week, but he didn't.

Nine

Max, looking smart-casual with a waxed fabric grip in his right hand and a leather briefcase in his left, was ready to leave for Ipswich with Adrian as soon as the Friday afternoon lecture was over. But Adrian hadn't got his bag with him and had to return to Fletcher's to collect it and change his shoes, accompanied by Max. It was late by the time they set off for Liverpool Street Station. Max's patience was sorely tried. He was used to being punctual and well prepared; he had scant sympathy with people who, as he put it, farty-arsed around. He had all but reduced Adrian to sullen silence by the time they reached the station, where they discovered that all the trains were running late because of excessive water somewhere on the track. Autumn rain, what a surprise, said Max. He began to think perhaps it had been a mistake to agree to this jaunt to Adrian's home. However, after some laden silences, comradeship in railway adversity prevailed.

John and Gemma were waiting outside the station in the gloom, she under a dripping umbrella with station lights reflecting in the scattered raindrops on it, and he with saturated hair and a very damp collar. Gemma sat with Adrian in the back of the car, her arm through his, regaling him with colourful accounts of her recent activities, whilst John and Max in the front began tentatively to make acquaintance. Fen opened the door to them with a broad smile and led them all straight into the kitchen where she dished up a thick soup of pearl barley and chicken with hunks of heavy white bread for Max and Adrian. Max had never eaten pearl barley before and didn't take to it, but was too polite to say so. Fen was, on first impression, one of the warmest women he had ever met, her size and volubility offsetting John's almost deferential timidity. Gemma sat at the table too, scrutinising Max openly and coolly, watching his every movement; he, unused to a young teenager's focussed gaze, surprised himself by being slightly unnerved. It crossed his mind that, however far off the mark, Gemma might be regarding him as a potential competitor for Adrian's friendship and affection.

Awake and alert in the morning (with Adrian still dead to the world as was his wont), Max thought about the development of Adrian's comfortable personality in these surroundings. Presumably the nature/nurture balance varied from person to person; what was the percentage for Adrian? It was a futile train of thought, he knew, and an unanswerable question. What mattered was that Adrian was a charming person, and his family loved him.

Max pushed the duvet off, swung his legs down to the floor and went out in his pyjamas. He could hear loud voices through the open door of an adjacent room: Fen was evidently trying with limited success to persuade Sebastian to excavate his 'bomb-site', i.e. his room. Max poked his nose round the door to say hullo. Sebastian pranced over to greet him with a painful twisted handshake and a laugh; Fen reproached Seb and reassured Max that the bathroom was empty. They had been planning for many months, she said, to build another in the large roof space, but hadn't got round to it yet.

96

Ten minutes later, freshly dressed, Max ventured downstairs to the kitchen where Gemma was sitting alone at the orange formica table. She stood up as he came in and went to the kettle, asking him if he'd prefer tea or coffee. Then she took a bowl out of a cupboard, a spoon from a drawer, and pushed the cereal packets towards him. There was milk and sugar already on the table. Max decided that until he had established some kind of rapport with her, kid gloves would be the right approach. By nature a manipulator, he knew instinctively how to go about it; a few years on, Gemma would have recognised his strategy but for the time being, she was innocent of it. He started by asking her about school and her hobbies, listening seriously to her hopes for the near future and plans for the more distant. Forgetting her self-imposed reserve and carried away by her ideas, Gemma explained, in a surprisingly mature way, her passion for ancient history and archaeology; there was a fire about her interest which Max had never experienced, nor did he believe, had Adrian.

Soon Gemma looked at the clock and announced with a little smile that it was time to see about Adrian's tea. Max noticed how cleanly and precisely she prepared it, just as she had prepared his coffee; not a drip slopped out of the kettle or over the rim of the mug. Max tried teasing her for spoiling Adrian but soon discovered that he had overstepped the familiarity mark, for Gemma replied perfunctorily that Adrian was special.

So special that Gemma, with Fen's agreement, had planned a 'proper dinner' for that evening since, she said, not only was Adrian home but they had a 'proper' weekend guest. What was it, wondered Max that fitted him for propriety; did he really qualify? The meal should be in the dining-room, with candles and tidy clothes, and naturally not before 7.30 pm although both Gemma and Sebastian were ravenous at least an hour before. By six, wearing a mauve t-shirt with a frilly border and a long lime-green denim skirt, she had already started laying the table; with laborious care she tried out different arrangements of cutlery and side plates, positioned and re-positioned the old brass candlesticks, and considered where everyone should sit. John was on hand to advise. He reminded her that the principal guest should sit to the right of the main host of the opposite sex. Gemma postulated that Max was of her generation and that he should therefore sit on her right, but John pointed out tactfully that for the time being, Fen was the hostess, as she was in charge of all household matters. Gemma conceded. Sebastian bulldozed in from time to time, ran round the oblong table and tweaked the knives and forks out of position causing Gemma to screech at him. Max, ensconced at the kitchen table with Adrian where they were watching Fen trying, as she said, to live up to Gemma's high entertainment standards, listened with amusement to the dining room frolics. Gemma had even chosen the menu: Cromer crab with lemon mayonnaise and pitta bread to start, followed by pasta, salad, and then the gungiest, stickiest, toffee-chocolate thingie to finish. With double cream. A few minutes before they sat down, Gemma demanded a hurried lesson in table manners from John. This, she thought, gave her the moral high ground from which to berate Seb if he misbehaved his way through the meal. He was not remotely interested in anything other than eating voraciously as fast as possible. Candles and table manners weren't on his menu. He was at no pains to conceal this, but didn't go so far as to flout Gemma's instructions deliberately, perhaps precisely because there was a stranger at the table.

Seb was at an age when family visitors were nothing to do with him. So Max had been, to start with, completely irrelevant, someone with whom he simply had no common ground and therefore no contact until on Saturday morning at the boatyard, when the rain had let up. Max had offered to sit in the front passenger seat of the battered station wagon with Seb at the wheel, and to suffer the hacking and spluttering of Seb's efforts to engage first gear. Eventually they managed several excursions up the lane but Max drew the line at letting Seb try his hand at reversing back down, preferring to take the wheel himself. Seb listened attentively and respectfully to Max's driving tips as well as to some colourful accounts of Max's previous exploits in the driving seat. From that moment on, Max had a firmly enthusiastic new friend. Not that he wanted one.

Sunday morning at breakfast, Max found himself, to his displeasure, embroiled in a discussion about the Sunday family walk. He had woken, as usual, at around six. Pushing aside the old cotton curtain, he saw that mist lay over the garden between the dark sky and the earth. A fox was just visible on the grass, ears pricked up, attentive. Any sound outside was muffled; indoors the floorboards creaked and somewhere water was gurgling in the pipes. Max got back into bed and lay on his back. After some minutes, he stretched an arm to recover *The Economist* from the floor. Soon, a gentle tap at the door announced Gemma's arrival. She was bearing a mug of coffee which she handed him with a nod but not a word, to retreat leaving the door slightly ajar. In a few minutes, voices could be heard downstairs. In due course, showered and dressed, Max joined the others in the kitchen. Adrian was evidently still asleep.

The habit of the walk had been slipping and Gemma was trying to revive it. Her instinct was to round up the herd, introduce Max into it, and thus strengthen the bond between them all. The presence of their visitor was a good reason why they should all walk together, she thought: he should be entertained by the whole family, and she would countenance no suggestion that any of them might stay at home. Max, when challenged, averred that he was not a good walker and had only one pair of shoes with him which would not be improved by getting wet. This proved to be a mistaken excuse. A multitude of garden shoes and boots lay on the floor in the hall in disarray and Gemma lost no time in telling Max, who had noticed them with dismay, that he could borrow a pair, or two separate boots if his feet didn't match each other, since there were all kinds and sizes. Max, smiling at the implied affront to his anatomy, suggested that Adrian might not want to walk and if not, he Max wouldn't go either. Gemma countered this with the information that Adrian was the keenest, after herself, and would certainly walk. She enumerated the reasons why the walk was a good idea, including the flippant suggestion that it would allow her mucky little brother to cover his boots, legs, face and hair with mud. A predictable spat ensued.

Seb, swinging his feet back and forth on the floor under his chair, insisted that his hair had never got dirty on a walk and chucked half a bagel at Gemma, prompting Fen to order him not to speak again until he had finished his breakfast. He lapsed into resentful silence and continued munching. Gemma appealed to Fen, whose evasive response was to say, all in one breath, that she had the roast to do and it looked like rain. Her private view was that it was inappropriate to push a visitor into an activity that he didn't like. Gemma asked Max pointedly what he would do if he and Fen were the only people not to go for a walk, to which he replied that he would talk to the plants, help Fen with the lunch, or play the bagpipes. Seb guffawed, spitting grains of cereal on to the table to be severely reprimanded by John, who supported Gemma. He loved the family walk.

A few minutes into the argument, Adrian, face puffed up with sleep and eyelids drooping, appeared at the door in his pyjamas to complain that the raised voices had woken him up.

"Good thing too," said Gemma. "It's about our walk. Mum says it's going to rain, Dad wants to go, Seb just laughs and Max is trying to get out of it. But it'd be nice to go, wouldn't it Adrian? We always do when we're all here, and besides Max hasn't seen the ponies and the ducks and swans." She sounded plaintive.

"I'll come, Gemma," said Adrian. "But you mustn't insist on Max doing anything he doesn't want to."

In the end, Max capitulated with good grace and they all went except Fen. Gemma found some wellies only one size too large for Max which he first sniffed, then pulled on reluctantly. She and Sebastian ran ahead, back, and around, speculating about the possible gift of a dog for Christmas and trying to winkle information out of John, who remained non-committal. Gemma pointed out many animals and insects to Max, whose kindly feigned interest was convincing enough to fool her. Seb slid around purposely in mud patches but didn't fall. John and Adrian walked steadily through watery meadows on knobbly paths they had evidently trodden hundreds of times. Occasionally, the damp torpor of the air was interrupted by a wood pigeon which, disturbed by their passage, rose suddenly from the hedgerow, flapping its wings noisily, and escaped. The area was unrelentingly flat, the sky like a wide grey blanket composed of seemingly immobile clouds. Max had never before seen so much sky.

On the train back to Liverpool Street, in the companionable semi-silence of Adrian's gentle snores, Max sifted through his impressions. Habitually aloof, he had been charmed by Adrian's family, although he would not admit it: his own family, where individual success was everything, was a world away. His perfectionist and critical father, his tough mother, and the flaming rows between them, had not made for a tranquil childhood. True, he, Tazie and Natalya had responded to the challenges set by their parents, but Natalya... Max remembered once again the afternoon when he had returned home from school to be told by his father that Natalya had committed suicide. Tazie and their mother were locked in each other's arms sobbing violently while their father paced up and down, up and down, his shoulders shaking, until late in the night. Max wondered for the hundredth time whether Natalya had eventually crumpled under the burden of parental expectation.

In contrast, Adrian's parents accepted their children's characteristics without fuss, showing no excessive ambition for them, nor trying to make them fit into a preformed mould. Decency, respect and kindness were required of everybody; Sebastian would be calmed by example. Max had watched carefully for any word or gesture that might suggest that Adrian was considered or treated differently because of his parentage, but to his relief there was no such indication.

His thoughts turned to Gemma. After a sandwich lunch on Saturday, Max, Adrian and Sebastian had gone to watch her in a swimming competition. She was evidently proud to present her brother and his friend to some of the other competitors, and looked tall and slender in her swimming costume. Afterwards, having done creditably in the competition, she revelled in Adrian's praise. Her attachment to him was overt and appropriate for her age, but there was an anticipation about it, as though her feelings were ready to swell into something more than sisterly love for him, her non-brother. Could mean trouble, Max thought. He was under no illusion that while he himself was the excuse for the special dinner, Adrian was the reason. Adrian had not, Max thought, sensed this; he would doubtless continue, for the foreseeable future, to treat Gemma as he always had done.

Thinking over the weekend, Max recognised that Saturdays and Sundays with his own family bore no resemblance to what he had seen at Adrian's. His own parents were frenetically busy people, whose free time was always crammed full of useful, cultural and social appointments. By contrast, this weekend had been relaxing and surprisingly entertaining, although Max was not inspired to include country walks and messing about in boats on his list of desirable activities for the future. Nevertheless, a small rowing boat in the shed had caught his eye; John told him he had built it some twenty years earlier for an American couple who had gone bankrupt. John had decided never to sell it because he had constructed the boat, at the request of the Americans, using

103

greenheart timber, the best wood for boats: strong, heavy and more resistant to water than almost any other timber.

Adrian stirred.

"I hope you enjoyed yourself, Max," he said.

"How could I not. Your folks are great people, and we had fun."

"Come again some time?"

"Indeed, I will."

Ten

For a few days after Adrian's return to London from the weekend at home, he felt at ease. The affection of his family, the comfort of familiar surroundings, as well as Max's evident pleasure in the visit, had brought repose. But it was ephemeral, soon suffocated by his increasingly persistent urge to find his mother, and thereby a thread of his identity. He asked John to give him his mother's address intending to write to her, but each time he started a draft, he quickly scrapped it. He continued searching the internet but found no reference to anybody called Patti Sandling in educational establishments in Lebanon. He had to concede that she was probably no longer working, and since schools' sites naturally provided no information on previous employees, he had drawn a blank. It was anyway possible she had married the 'someone from the Middle East' referred to by his dad, someone who was doubtless seriously wealthy and whose position and circumstances made it unnecessary for Mrs S (Sandling or Somebody) to continue working. Despite his lack of progress, Adrian felt frustrated rather than thwarted, and became convinced as time went on that the Middle East was the place to find a clue, since there was no lead to or from anywhere else.

Adrian began to plan. First, he should prepare himself for the Arab world. Every day, he scoured the internet for news and articles about the area and in particular about

Lebanon. Then there was the language; he had already bought a book outlining the rudiments of the Arabic language. Just glancing at it showed him how impossibly difficult it would be to learn without tuition. He needed help, a pipeline, somebody who could lead him into the maze. Timetables of lectures were posted up; Adrian had no difficulty in finding first year Arabic. All that remained was for him to insert himself into the class, although of course he had missed the all important introductory lessons. After a day's hesitation, he bit the bullet and gate-crashed a class which fortunately did not clash with anything on his timetable. He waylaid the lecturer on the way in, explaining that he was a student of Chinese and was doing some comparative work on *ab initio* language learning. The young lecturer, who was beginning only his second year in London and was preoccupied by many more important matters, merely gave a brief nod of assent without bothering to ask Adrian what his name was. Adrian sat quite near the front at an extended table along from a dark-skinned young man who, seeing that Adrian had no textbook, moved his own between them. After the hour was over, Adrian had to admit to himself that he had gleaned almost nothing from what he had heard. His desk mate waited for him outside the door and suggested tea, which Adrian felt was just the window of opportunity he needed.

Hassan was British, the son of Jordanian parents originally from Palestine. His parents had changed domicile several times before settling in Britain when Hassan was in his teens. He possessed only spoken Arabic which gave him comfortable contact with relations everywhere – many were in America and Australia – but no core to his knowledge and no feel for what it was to be Jordanian. A degree in Arabic would, he had thought, be a step towards remedying this lacuna. He and Adrian exchanged information about courses and swopped first term experiences. When Hassan asked Adrian why he had chosen to look in on Arabic, Adrian was ready with the story he had told the lecturer. There would be time enough later, he thought, to mention a possible relation in the Middle East should Hassan prove to be really useful. Hassan was anyway receptive, and immensely informative. In half an hour, Adrian had received in his eager ears a thicker wad of information than he was able to absorb. Hassan's spoken English delivery was unfortunately monotonal which, along with a lack of emphasis and some doubtful grammar, created a woolly fuzz in his listener's head. Nevertheless, thought Adrian, a useful contact and amiable at that. Voluble was good in this case.

The next Arabic language session was on Thursday and that day it did clash, with Chinese politics. Too bad, thought Adrian. He could catch up at any time by reading, whereas he was seriously at sea in Arabic. Max, though, had expected to see Adrian at the politics lecture. It was their habit to refuel together afterwards, sometimes with Benny, and often with Sadie, who was becoming increasingly neurotic. She had the habit of flouncing in, throwing her pile of belongings on to the table, and going without a word to get coffee from the machine. On her return, she would listen briefly to what Adrian and Max were saying, only to interrupt and contradict. Her concentration would then lapse, leaving her frowning absent-mindedly at her plastic cup, waiting and hoping that they would ask her what the matter was. Adrian usually did, whilst Max would sit back and listen, hardly bothering to hide his contempt. Her stories were long and complex, always with a mention of Hardy's lack of interest in her, and leading often to the confession of a scrape in a pub with people she hadn't met before, sometimes ending in her room – no details offered. Adrian would give her no advice but did express genuine sympathy; Max would wade in to chastise Sadie for her behaviour which often led to harsh words between them, occasionally with Sadie in tears.

This time, in Adrian's absence, Max sidled straight off, leaving an unhappy Sadie waiting in vain in the canteen. The following day, after Chinese language class, Max and Adrian went together for coffee, Sadie having announced that she was going home "to sleep off her fatigue". She said this with a look which invited questions, but these remained unasked. Max and Adrian suspected it had more to do with Smirnov than Chinese four-character phrases. They were both relieved that she didn't join them.

Max, never one to mince his words, laid in to Adrian immediately.

"So where were you yesterday, at politics?"

"Miss me, did you?" asked Adrian with a slight smile, twirling an elastic band around his forefingers.

"No, not at all" replied Max in an offhand way. There was a silence. "Come on," he continued, "you don't usually skip things. Sadie's the one to do that. And it's going to get worse."

"Yes, poor Sadie. One day she's going to come in seriously, definitively the worse for wear. Then we'll have to mop her up."

"She's foolish. Wants a kick up the backside. Wasting her opportunities. And somebody else I know may be doing that too," Max added darkly, watching Adrian's expression intently.

"What do you mean?"

"Well, you were obviously somewhere else yesterday, since you weren't at the lecture, and you don't look ill and have no horror stories of being run over by a bus, so I can only assume you thought something else was more important."

"Mm."

"And that something else probably had to do with the Middle East, didn't it?" he challenged.

Adrian gave in.

"Yes. As a matter of fact, I went to Arabic."

Max shook his head despairingly.

"You're stark staring bonkers Adrian, for Christ's sake… What sort of lecture?"

"Language, of course" replied Adrian irritably.

"And what did the lecturer say about your being there?"

"Not a lot. He's young and new and innocent and fortunately doesn't mind if extra people, or an extra person, arrives. At least he doesn't seem to. He probably doesn't understand about fees and registration and that sort of thing." Max was silent.

"And," added Adrian, "people working on the Middle East are in a permanent state of dislocated apprehension about what's going to happen next. So his mind's not on who's there and who isn't."

Max looked at Adrian wordlessly, leaving him space in which to continue should he so wish.

"I know you don't understand, Max. But it's this mother thing. Mum and Dad gave me an address for her in Beirut and I've tried to draft a letter, but I don't know how to do it. I'm sure I can find my mother somewhere in the Middle East, and I shall need to be able to understand something when I get there - both language and culture. Assuming she's there, she'll have become very integrated, won't she? She may have married an Arab and perhaps I have siblings, real blood siblings." He lapsed.

"I heard you. 'When I get there', rather than 'if I get there.' Adrian, you're not an idiot, but you're behaving like one. You've got plenty of time in which to find her, but you haven't got several shots at beginners' Chinese. Why not write the letter, and then put off the hunt until summer when you could dabble in a little Arabic? I'm sure there are plenty of people around here who'd be willing to earn some extra money."

Adrian shook his head.

"I just don't feel I've got any time to lose. It feels as though with each day that passes, she slips further away from me."

"When is this journey to take place?"

"I thought maybe just after Christmas. I've not yet tackled Mum and Dad, and I'll need some financial help for tickets and things, but I think they'll understand."

"Yes, I expect they will." They eyed each other cautiously. Max continued after a moment.

"So you've not found any trace of her yet?"

"No. It's very frustrating. That's why I need to go."

"I suppose you've tried the British Council? They run English language courses abroad."

"Oh," said Adrian in surprise. "That hadn't occurred to me."

"She wasn't necessarily employed in a school. She might have worked freelance, or even lectured at a university."

"I doubt the latter. From what mum and dad have said, she wasn't very academic. But you could have a point about the British Council. I'll have a go."

"And you could always try the Foreign Office, though I imagine they're a bit stuffy there. And what about putting a notice in *The Daily Telegraph*? I assume she was a *Telegraph* reader?"

"I suppose so. Good ideas, both. I'll try."

They parted awkwardly, Max exasperated and more concerned than ever, Adrian determined, disturbed, and dogged. He hoped Max wouldn't discuss their conversation with Tazie; he would tell her himself, all in good time.

***

Tuesday, 4.00 pm. Back and forth Adrian strode in his room – three steps this way, three that. He had finally written a brief note to Mrs P Sandling at the address in Beirut, enquiring if she might be his mother. He had looked up the British Council on the internet and found a 'General Enquiries' number, but he wasn't sure that his question could really be classified as general. However, the only other number was for callers who had a name or extension number to ask for – clearly inappropriate. He sat down in front of the window at his desk looking out distractedly at the windswept street where an eddy of rubbish was whirling around on the opposite pavement. The British Council wouldn't ask him anything he couldn't answer. He reached for a sheet of paper and a pen, and pompously wrote 'Mrs S – Action Log' at the top, then the date on the left hand side, and 'British Council' with the phone number in a hypothetical middle column, leaving plenty of space on the right for information. He tentatively called the number. A bright female voice answered immediately. Adrian haltingly explained that he was searching for Patti Sandling, last heard of in Lebanon and thought to have been teaching English there. Could anybody help trace her? The telephonist replied that his enquiry was rather unusual but that perhaps the External Relations Department could help and she would put him through. After several clicks, a voice said, "External Relations, Monty Simons speaking." Adrian repeated his query. Monty was neither encouraging nor the reverse. He was a bit busy this week, but if Adrian would like to call again this Friday he would see if he could put aside a few minutes to see him some time next week. Adrian thanked him and wrote appropriately on his piece of paper.

Next, the Foreign Office. More difficult, Adrian was sure – busy people who could be dismissive. There was a number for a 'Consular Assistance Team' under which the heading 'Missing persons' appeared. Mrs S wasn't missing in the usual sense, but she was missing for Adrian; besides, there was no other more appropriate department or team. By now more confident about his explanation, Adrian called. A throaty man's voice answered 'Consular Assistance Team' so Adrian duly asked to speak to the person responsible for missing persons.

From the outset, Francis Hacker couldn't have been more helpful. He explained, as Adrian had expected, that missing person enquiries were usually about people who had disappeared abroad within the past couple of weeks and whose relations were surprised not to have heard from them. Very often it was a case of a stolen or lost mobile phone; many times it was a misunderstanding about different time zones and flight times, or names of cities or hotels. Nevertheless, Francis always sent appropriate messages to the consular offices in the relevant country whose replies were mostly preceded by a call from 'Mrs Worried of Hatfield' to say that the missing person had been in touch and thank you, no further action was called for.

However, 'intriguing' was how Francis described the idea of searching for someone who had definitely been in the Lebanon, although several years had elapsed since she had gone there. He had, he explained, spent two years in the Consular Section at the Beirut Embassy, having first completed an FCO intensive Arabic language course. The conflict and danger in the area had given him a buzz, and being at the geographical centre of the action had been stimulating and revealing, as had mixing with many experienced Middle East experts. Contact with the local intelligentsia of all political shades had filled in many gaps in his knowledge.

To be of help in this case however, he needed more information. In a light and airy way, he asked if Adrian would like to meet for a drink after work later in the week, so that he could learn more about him and the circumstances surrounding the disappearance of Patti Sandling. Adrian agreed readily and the appointment was fixed for Thursday at 6.00 pm in a quiet bar round the corner from St James's Park tube station. They would both carry *The Financial Times*.

It was an occasion, Adrian felt, for wearing his tidiest clothes. He managed to unearth a good striped shirt, found trousers with a crease and dug out his lace-ups from under the bed. A navy blazer and thick scarf completed the outfit. He took the tube, arriving early at the appointed place. On a tall stool at the bar, a lanky man was bent forward reading a pink newspaper folded down the middle. Walking over, Adrian noticed a smart, dark blue pinstriped suit and well-polished shoes which were resting on the bars of the stool. A pale face supporting rimless glasses looked up as Adrian approached; the man slid off the stool and removed his glasses. With a smile, Francis led Adrian to a corner table for two with rattan armchairs. They studied the extensive cocktail menu under the patient scrutiny of a waiter who didn't hide his disappointment when they both ordered house wine.

Francis introduced himself rather fully, describing fluently in a smooth voice the steps in his Foreign Office career as though he were setting out his credentials. From what he said, Adrian gathered that he was in his mid-thirties and had joined the Foreign Office some eight years previously. Looking for missing persons was only one part of his brief, but Francis did not touch on any other activities and Adrian thought it would be indiscreet to ask. Francis evidently enjoyed work and indeed the rest of his life too, as he enthusiastically described outings to theatres and cinemas. Adrian warmed to him. When Francis came to the end of his verbal cv, he paused to take a sip of wine and looked expectantly at Adrian. Adrian didn't know how to start, so Francis filled in the silence with a question.

"Tell me about Patti Sandling?" he said, "who she is and how you know her."

It wasn't as difficult as Adrian had imagined, Francis filling gaps in Adrian's halting story with questions. Adrian had realised, while Francis was talking, that it would be impossible not to reveal that Patti Sandling was his mother, even though he felt oddly as though he were betraying her. He was able to omit that his father's violence had caused her to desert him, and related the other facts that John had passed on to him which were by then etched on his brain. Francis listened attentively, prompting Adrian to supply extra information, including details of his efforts to trace Mrs S on the internet. He asked finally about Adrian's current circumstances and then signalled to the waiter to bring two more glasses of wine. The effort of recalling the information made Adrian suddenly feel like crying so he swallowed thickly, turning his head to look at the window. Francis let him be, then said gently, "sorry if I've been pressing you."

"No, no, it's all right, it really is. Thank you for helping me tell you. It's just that this is the first time I've spoken to anybody officially about it." He smiled.

"Well I'm not sure how official this is going to be. A search of this sort may not really be within the remit. I've not been asked before to find anybody who went off so long ago. But I'm not going to abandon such an interesting challenge. I'll try to help you via my contacts in Beirut, Amman and so forth. I suppose you've been in touch with the British Council as your mother was a teacher?"

"Yes, I've spoken with Monty Simons on the phone, and I'm hoping he'll have time to see me next week."

"Ah yes, Monty. He's a good chap. They're frightfully busy over there you know. Everybody's doing two people's jobs following the drastic redundancies."

"He sounded a bit frazzled."

"He always does." He paused. "So now, have I your permission to pass on everything you've told me to my diplomatic colleagues in the Middle East?"

"Yes, certainly. How will it go, by email?"

"No, it'll go as a letter in the diplomatic bag within the next few days, when I've had a chance to draft it up. Email's not protected from enquiring eyes, and although your case couldn't be described as sensitive, I'm sure you'd prefer it not to be peered at."

"You're right, and thank you, it's reassuring."

Francis pulled out a diary from his inside pocket, noted down Adrian's mobile number, then stood up and went to pay for the drinks at the bar.

"Must go," he said on rejoining Adrian. "It's been a great pleasure meeting you, but uxorious matters await me. Here's my card. Get in touch if you find out anything. I'll call you next week, just to reassure you that I've not forgotten – it'll probably be a bit soon for any news though. Bye Adrian."

"Bye Francis, and thank you again." Watching him stride purposefully away, Adrian somehow felt that they had clicked and that Francis's friendly noises were genuine. On the way home he thought over their conversation, ready to record the salient points on his log sheet.

The next day he called Monty as arranged; Adrian was summoned to the British Council on Monday at 4.00 pm. Again he wore the tidy clothes.

Having described the whole case once, to Francis, he was well rehearsed for this second meeting, in a small stuffy room off a large open plan office. Monty was older and stiffer than Francis, balding, jacket-less with clearly visible underarm stains on his rumpled shirt. As Adrian spoke, Monty made notes on a thick pad. When Adrian had finished, Monty explained simply that he would send an exploratory email to his colleague at the British Council in Beirut, but that it was a small office and it was unlikely that anybody could look into it straight away. If records of past employees, whether part-time or full-time, temporary or permanent did exist, somebody would have to find the time to look through them page by page, as data of some seventeen years ago had not been entered on the computer databases. The interview was over in fifteen brisk minutes, whereupon Monty advised Adrian to call him in a couple of weeks to find out if there were any news.

Eleven

On the first Saturday in November, John and Fen took Gemma to London for a long promised visit to the British Museum, postponed from August. Sebastian and museums didn't mix; eventually they had all agreed with him that a trip to London on a precious summers' day would not be 'fair' on him, nor would it be the best use of the time. Autumn would do instead for the outing. Sebastian could visit a friend and the absence of the 'china shop bull' on Gemma's much heralded museum day would be a relief to all of them. Gemma had been to the museum once before, "in my pre-teens, when I didn't know anything," as she said. This time her aim, she declared pompously, was to sort out in her mind where her real interests lay. Fen privately thought that the prospect of lunch with Adrian and a visit to his hall of residence was more than an added attraction, but wisely said nothing.

The day started well. Sebastian was dropped off, promising not to do anything dangerous and to think before jumping into mischief. John parked at Ipswich station and they made a dash in the rain for the ticket office. John gave Gemma the money to buy the tickets – something she loved doing as it was part of the magic of travelling. She led the way on to the platform and when the train came in, she plumped herself beside the window so as to watch stations, towns, and fields flashing by, imagining herself a few years hence with a season ticket, belonging to the adult world. First it would be university and then she would earn her living; she would step off the train in London and hurry to be *there* where she was expected and respected.

Inside the entrance hall to the Museum, there were several groups standing around: about 20 Japanese, huddled together, the women wearing neat little round rain hats, the men with caps, all soon herded off by an English woman with a raw voice waving high a closed orange umbrella; a dozen jostling teenage boys, wearing grey blazers with badges on the pockets, and five small girls practising ballet steps in a line. Gemma, watching them whilst John fetched the Museum map and guide, thought they looked rather silly.

Since this was Gemma's treat, it fell to her to choose the exhibits to see. She had done her homework online and had decided they should start in the Centre for Young Visitors on the lower level of the Great Court. John handed her the map, giving her the responsibility of finding, at each stage of their tour, the way to the relevant rooms. In the Centre, Gemma found a large quantity of leaflets and educational material which she handed to John to carry. He teased her for treating him as a packhorse. Then they moved up to the Greek and Roman sculpture on the ground floor where Gemma was astonished at the size of the some of the pieces. After looking at half a dozen, she got John to put his hand over the identifier labels as they moved ahead, so that she could try to guess whether they were Greek or Roman. She had little success. They skipped through the Asia section and moved up a floor to where Gemma became absorbed in Greek and Roman Life. Next they went into the Medieval Europe gallery. It was here that Gemma's love of Byzantine artefacts was born. Fen and John, although tired, rejoiced in her pleasure.

Their lunch arrangement was to meet Adrian at the long tables in the Court café at 12.30. While they were waiting for him, Gemma walked up the winding staircase to the higher level Restaurant admiring, at each step, the different vistas. Fen had to wave her down when Adrian arrived. To their surprise, he was accompanied by Max and a young woman. Gemma paused on the stairs to scrutinise them, wondering who she was. On the phone, Adrian had not mentioned bringing anybody with him. After greeting Fen and John, Max introduced his sister and kissed Gemma affectionately. He explained that he and Adrian had spent the morning in the library comparing notes from a Chinese politics lecture, and Tazie had dropped by with some keys Max needed, so he'd brought her along too to say hullo. In truth, Max had been talking Adrian through the Thursday lecture which Adrian had missed because it clashed with Arabic language. Max was angry, but acknowledged that it was a good exercise for him to synthesize the salient points of the lecture.

They all sat down to have a drink together, John and Fen asking many questions about the course and life in London, whilst Gemma sat beside John, a little apart, observing Tazie in silence, a knocking in her head. Max's attempts to include Gemma in the conversation met with little response. Wounded puppy love, Max said to himself – a bad move to bring Tazie; or had some demon prompted him to do it? Gemma would probably have had to meet Tazie some time. Discovering she was Adrian's girlfriend would be the next step. Better not tarry, he decided. In a gap in the conversation, he looked at his watch.

"Goodness, you're going to be late for your whatever it was, Tazie," he said. "And Hardy's expecting me. Excuse us. We've got to go." Fen and John said how nice it was of Max to have brought Tazie while Gemma remained distinctly cool. As Max and Tazie walked away, they talked and looked back at the family. Evidently they are discussing us, Gemma thought.

She remained quiet throughout lunch, although her appetite was not affected. Was it her imagination or did a special look pass between Adrian and Tazie when the family discussed visiting Adrian's hall of residence? Suddenly the idea of seeing his room wasn't so attractive, but Gemma knew she had to go through with it. While they ate, Adrian plied her with questions about what she had seen; after some minutes she thawed enough to launch into a description of her favourite piece of Byzantine jewellery.

They took the bus to Fletcher's Hall. John immediately remarked what a depressing building it looked, grey and austere. Inside, the long anonymous corridors did nothing to soften the impression. Adrian's door was like all the others except that it had his name on it, stuck there, as he explained, on day one for his own guidance and left there to ensure that Benny didn't get lost.

"Who's Benny?" asked Gemma.

"He's my mate from a few doors along. He's very very bright, from an unusual background."

"What's 'unusual' Adrian?" asked John.

"His dad's a clown in a circus, his mum works there too. They live in Newcastle, he's the oldest of five children and he'd never been to London before coming here. He got all A*s in his A levels and loves studying. He's small with

121

a funny little face, rather unprepossessing. You'd love him, Gemma."

"Is he here now? Can we meet him?"

She liked the idea of him living just along the passage.

"No, he's at a one-day seminar on something or other. But I'll arrange it for next time you come up."

"You mean I can come again?"

"'Course you can, Gems."

In the pleasure of anticipation, she forgot Max's sister for a moment, but her face fell a moment later when she remembered.

Inside his room, Adrian had spruced things up. His clothes were all out of sight, and the duvet was smoothed out. Four mugs stood on the table alongside a box of teabags and a packet of chocolate biscuits. There were many books and papers on the table too, although Adrian had taken the precaution of moving everything connected with Arabic and the Middle East into the cupboard. He opened the window to bring in a carton of milk and switched on the table lamp to make the room look cosier, leaving the ceiling light on too. At least the room was well heated, Fen remarked. John gestured to her to sit on the chair while he and Gemma perched on the bed. Adrian filled the kettle and put it on to boil, then made tea and handed out biscuits. There was even sugar for Gemma; Adrian explained he had got it for Benny.

Gemma was keeping a grip on essentials.

"Next time I come, I suppose I'll be seeing Max and his sister again?" she asked artlessly, looking straight at Adrian. Fen glanced at John who was turning the pages of a book he had picked up off the table and appeared not to have heard Gemma's question. Adrian busied himself making tea, his back turned towards Gemma.

"Maybe – it depends what they're doing," he answered in a non-committal fashion.

Gemma fell silent, whilst Fen filled Adrian in on the news from home of which there was little of any importance except that Seb had been chosen for the junior hockey team. Half an hour later it was time for them to head home. Fen asked where the toilets were, allowing her to inspect the showers, which she declared to be rather dilapidated.

"Apart from that, you look rather well set up here, Adrian," said John standing up, "quite adequate anyway. And you've made friends."

"Yeah, it's ok. The room's not too bad, and it's very convenient. And we've got all sorts of cheap restaurants nearby. Max and I often go to a Chinese round the corner. Of course, maybe next year I'll get something better, perhaps share a flat with some people. But for now this is fine."

Fen kissed Adrian, John patted him on the shoulder, and Gemma threw herself at him for the biggest hug she could get.

"I still miss you at home" she said. Adrian stroked her head then detached himself. There were a few tears on her cheeks which he wiped away gently with his thumbs.

"It'll soon be Christmas and I'll be home."

"Come on now," said John. Adrian showed them out.

Gemma was uncommunicative on the bus to Liverpool Street, but in the train she asked Fen earnestly whether she thought Tazie was Adrian's girlfriend. Fen replied truthfully that she had no idea, nor did she remember either

Adrian or Max mentioning her existence. Gemma lapsed into silence for the rest of the journey, glancing distractedly at the Museum guide. At Ipswich, as they walked to the car, Fen held her hand out to Gemma who, at this moment, was not too old or too proud to take it; besides, it was dark. When they got home, having fetched Sebastian, Gemma went up to her room and only came down, her nose red and damp, when Fen called her for supper. Seb lost no time in saying:

"Tee, hee, did the Museum make you cry of boredom?"

Fen told him he was a tactless little monster and that he would get no supper if he uttered one word more. After swallowing down half a bowl of soup, Gemma excused herself and went upstairs to run a bath. Half an hour later, Fen heard her bedroom door shut. She looked across the table at John who was drinking coffee.

"I think I'd better go up to her now, don't you?" she asked.

"Yes, I think so. Definitely a woman's job. Nothing to do with me." He smiled. Fen blew him a kiss, took a glass of water and went upstairs. She had foreseen this crisis without knowing when it would occur, or how to forestall it.

"Gemma!" she called, tapping gently on the door, "may I come in?"

Fen interpreted the muffled grunt from inside as an affirmative.

Gemma was sitting on her bed with a packet of tissues in her hand, her legs drawn up, and her arms around her knees. Her favourite teddy was beside her. Fen put the glass of water on the bed frame then sat down beside Gemma and put her arms round her.

"Is it what I think it is, Gemma?"

"What do you think it is?" replied Gemma, with a note of aggression.

"Is it Adrian?"

"Yup."

Gemma dissolved into sobs. Fen thought carefully before deciding how to tackle the subject.

"Didn't you enjoy seeing him today? We had a nice time, didn't we?"

"'Course I did, we did, but…"

"But what, sweetheart?"

"Why did that woman have to come?"

"You mean Tazie?"

"Yes, Tazie. What sort of a name is that anyway? It's a stupid name." She spat out the words.

"It's probably short for something. It's no stupider than any other name."

"Anyway, it was supposed to be our day, and then *she* came along."

"She was hardly with us for ten minutes!"

"That was long enough to spoil it," said Gemma petulantly.

"No it wasn't." Fen paused, then continued, "you know, Gemma, that Adrian doesn't belong to you."

"I know. He belongs to all of us, but I thought I was special."

"Of course you're special. You're the only sister he's got."

"But I'm not his sister, and I thought I was special in a different way. You know…"

"Know what?"

"Because we're not blood relations."

"Ah, so that's it," said Fen, glad that Gemma had opened up; now perhaps she could help. There would have to be some home truths.

"Gemma, Adrian *is* your brother. John and I adopted him. He thinks of himself fairly and squarely as being our son and your and Seb's brother. He was always going to meet a girl and fall in love, and get tied up somehow. And quite right too."

"I'm sure she's his girlfriend. I'm sure this *Tazie* is his girl and he sleeps with her. Why would she have come to meet us otherwise?"

"I don't know, Gemma. But after all she is Max's sister, and he seems to be Adrian's closest friend in London. However, it's possible that she is indeed Adrian's girlfriend, and there's nothing you can do about that."

"I thought that perhaps, since he loves me – he's said so you know – he would wait for me and we could…." she stopped short of saying get married.

"Darling girl, Adrian doesn't think of you like that. He's known you since before you were born. There are many different kinds of love. John and I love you, and Sebastian does too, and Adrian's no different."

"How do you know he doesn't think of me like that? Has he ever said so?"

"Yes, as a matter of fact he has. He said he was looking forward to discovering what sort of bloke you would go for in due course and that it would have to be somebody very intelligent and very tolerant."

"Oh!" Gemma was shocked. "I had just been hoping… I love him awfully but now *she's* come along to spoil things."

"She's not going to spoil anything to do with your relationship with Adrian. In due course, Gemma, you'll have a boyfriend, and this will all seem rather different."

"I'll never love anybody as much as I love him" she said defiantly.

"Yes you will. Think about it. Meanwhile try not to make yourself unhappy with unrealistic wishes. Leave Adrian to get on with his life and you get on with yours."

"It's so hard." She was crying again.

"I know darling. But you'll see I'm right. Adrian will have a partner in due course, who might or might not be Tazie, but anyway it won't be you."

"You can't be sure."

"I'm 99% sure."

Fen was quiet for a few more minutes until Gemma's sobs subsided.

"Are you all right now my pet? Do you think you can go to sleep?"

"I don't think so, but I'll try. I'll just read a bit first. Are you going to tell Dad?"

"Do you want me to?" She was going to, anyway.

Gemma nodded. "But don't tell Sebastian, Mum."

"All right then."

John was still in the kitchen when Fen went down.

"All ok then?" he asked.

"Yes, she's a wise little person, although very smitten with Adrian – who wouldn't be? I wonder how long it'll be before reality sinks in. A stubborn little puss like her may yet stick to her fantasies and throw a few wobblies. She'll be sensible in the end though. By the way, she asked me to tell you about it. I think she'd like it if you went up to say goodnight. She's going to try to sleep soon."

John did as Fen suggested.

"Did Mum tell you?" asked Gemma, as John bent to kiss her. She was by then lying in her bed with a book in her hand.

"Yes."

"Thanks for coming to say goodnight, Dad. And by the way, I'm going to do Byzantium."

"Good for you, my dear. Night night."

"Night."

When Fen looked in on her half an hour later, she was asleep with her teddy in the crook of her arm. Subject closed, thought Fen, at least for tonight.

***

"Adrian," said Max on Monday, "you've got to be careful about Gemma."

"In what way?" asked Adrian, surprised.

"She's got a huge crush on you, and knowing that you're not a blood relation, she's building up hopes of your becoming an item."

"Oh gosh, really?"

"Sometimes I think you're really dim, you twit. Fancy not noticing the way she hangs on your every word and fawns …"

"But she's always been affectionate and sweet and helpful..."

"But she's not always been a teenager. Things change at puberty. Even you must know that."

"I just think of her as my sister."

"Well, make sure you carry on thinking like that and, most importantly, that she knows it. You don't want to hurt her, do you?"

"No I most certainly don't. Thanks for the advice Max."

Twelve

In the days following the visit to London, Gemma was distracted by a nagging curiosity as to the nature of Tazie's and Adrian's relationship. Were they lovers, or just good mates? Did he find her enormously attractive? Gemma had to admit that Tazie wasn't ugly. Did they go out for cosy little meals together in the restaurants around Fletcher's? How could she find out? Max knew, surely, but she couldn't ask him, nor could she bring herself to ask Adrian, in case the answer was yes. She wanted to know, but she didn't. At night in bed, she tried to imagine herself as Adrian's girlfriend, kissing him on the lips, but the picture was blurred because her thoughts kept harking back to the scene at the British Museum café where the bombshell of Tazie's existence had dropped. At school, her fits of abstraction didn't go unnoticed. Her history teacher, for whom Gemma was the prize pupil, had to rebuke her.

There was only one thing for it: she had to go to London on her own to see Adrian with Tazie and observe them together. He had said she could come again and that she might see Max and Tazie. Perhaps after all she would ask Adrian about Tazie, or if she were alone with Max, she could ask him. But that would mean Adrian and Tazie would be alone together – a disturbing thought, although Gemma knew nothing prevented them from meeting when they wanted. Thus her thoughts rambled on until she called

Adrian to ask if she could see him again in London on Saturday. It would be two weeks since the museum trip.

"Yes, you can come if you like. What do you want to do?" said Adrian.

"Christmas shopping in Oxford Street" she answered promptly, "and meet Benny and see Max and Tazie again."

Adrian, recalling Max's advice, smelled a rat but didn't have the heart to discourage her. "You mean this Saturday?"

"Yes, after all it's nearly Christmas."

"Well I've got one or two things to do, but ok. I can't promise for Benny etc. I'll ask anyway. Oxford Street in the morning, coffee, a sandwich, and if you like, come back to my place for tea? Will that do?"

"Wicked! This Saturday, perfect! Then I'll ask Mum and Dad," squeaked Gemma.

Fen and John also smelled the rat but agreed privately that Gemma shouldn't be protected from anything she might find out. It would anyway be her first visit to London on her own: she was sensible enough to manage the train journey and Adrian would meet her at Liverpool Street.

***

Sadie reached out a lazy arm to turn off the nasty bleeping of her alarm clock. She rolled over to see if it really was eight in the morning, hoping that the clock had gone wrong and she could stay on in bed nursing her muzzy head. The prospect of getting up now was awful, but it was indeed eight. Perhaps with a pick-me-up she could manage to move. She could see her plastic bottle, a quarter full of colourless liquid, just out of reach at the back of her bedside table. She sat up, reached for it, and swallowed down a mouthful. That's better, she said to herself. It was very quiet this morning – none of her flatmates had stirred.

Soon she got up, waved her toothbrush at her teeth and dressed – underwear, fleece trousers and top, thick anorak, scarf – grabbed her keys and backpack and stumbled down to the door. Shit, the plastic bottle. Back upstairs, she topped it up from the bottle on the floor of her bedroom and put it in the backpack. Outside it was raw and misty but Sadie, undeterred, pulled her hood up and struggled off to the tube. At Bayswater, she got out and walked automatically until she was outside the building where she had lived when she had first arrived in London. She was for an instant tempted to ring Hardy's bell, but as reason triumphed, she crossed the street and walked along a little, keeping the imposing porch and door in her sight line. A convenient letterbox afforded some cover but Sadie towered over it, feeling exposed despite the anonymity afforded by winter layers. It was bitterly cold; she warmed herself up with a sip from her bottle.

The riddle she planned to solve was whether Lily and Hardy were sleeping together. If they came out together, that would prove they were. A Saturday seemed a likely morning for them to spend time with each other – a day on which people didn't get up early to go out. Sadie fed her hungry jealousy regularly, vividly imagining the couple in bed. Confirmation of their closeness would be further good food for it. Why didn't Hardy want her? She would do anything for him. She could have been in his bed now, warm and caring for him. She deluded herself into believing that if he were not stepping out with Lily, she herself would be his girlfriend. She needed to find some way of impressing him properly so that he would desert Lily. A big success of some sort, or an especially kind gesture towards him or towards somebody he knew. She mulled it over as she watched.

A small woman walking briskly along on the other side of the street caught Sadie's eye. Funny, she thought, the woman's got the same coat as Lily's, dark red, calf length and padded. Just as the woman was about to go up the steps to the front door, she turned round to look up and down the street and seemed to have caught sight of Sadie who instantly leaned over the letterbox pretending to post a letter. Lily – indeed it was she – made as though to cross the road towards Sadie, but in an instant turned back and went up to the door. She pressed a bell, the door clicked open, and she went in slamming the door behind her. Sadie's heart was palpitating as she grasped the letter box to steady herself. In an instant she bent over to vomit in the gutter and then burst into tears. A few moments later her head cleared enough for her to fumble in her backpack for a tissue. Not an overnight stay then, but a 9 a.m. get together. She wondered what Lily and Hardy would be doing. How would they spend the day? Recovering a little, she staggered along the pavement, away from her sight line of the doorway, and slumped against a high-sided parked van. A moment later, there were footsteps behind her and a gruff male voice said, "Oi! What you doin' loitering by my van? There ain't nuffin' in it for you. Shove off!" Sadie obeyed. She walked back unsteadily in the direction whence she had come, looking for more camouflage. There was none. The only thing to do was to continue walking up and down; she could just manage it in her present state, glancing regularly behind her at the hallowed doorway. Some five minutes later, her patience was rewarded. Hardy and Lily emerged into the winter chill, he wearing a smartly tailored overcoat. Sadie swayed as she ducked down behind a car. They walked off arm in arm in the direction of the tube, chatting cheerfully.

Sadie didn't have it in her to follow them. She had in all likelihood been spied by Lily, her height making her particularly conspicuous, and she was now shivering and miserable. It was time for a bit of comfort.

***

Gemma gulped down a bowl of cereal with a glass of orange juice and called to John that she was ready. The previous evening, in high excitement, she had carefully stowed everything she needed in a large shoulder bag of Fen's: purse, ticket, mobile, umbrella, water bottle, and some peppermints in case of emergency, as well as a folded waterproof carrier bag for Christmas presents. John dropped her at Ipswich station, reminded her that she should at all times wear the shoulder bag across her front, and waved her off on the train, not fearing for her safety but keeping his fingers crossed that she would have a happy day. On the train Gemma felt very grown up, as though this were the beginning of a new phase in her life, a taste of independence. She looked at the other passengers and was glad of her secret from them, that this was her first journey to London on her own. Across from her, round a table, were two children with their parents. The boy looked about her age but, she said to herself triumphantly, he wasn't on his own.

"How was the journey, Gems?" asked Adrian as they hugged.

"Fantastic! I felt great, doing my own thing."

"Splendid! And there's good news," said Adrian. "We're having coffee with Max and Tazie at eleven, and Benny will be back after a linguistics lunch to join us for tea in my room."

"Cool, lucky me!" said Gemma. "And in between there's my shopping list!"

"Indeed, there is. But you won't be able to get anything for me because I'll be watching you like a hawk."

"Watch me all you like. You won't see anything 'cos I'm getting yours in Ipswich with Mum," replied Gemma in a self-conscious and superior tone. "I know what it's going to be."

"Tell me, tell me!"

"No Adrian, it's got to be a surprise."

"I'll ask Mum."

"Don't you dare! Or I'll ask her what you're getting me."

Adrian felt momentarily guilty. He hadn't thought about Christmas presents, but he knew it would be easy enough to find something for Gemma and Seb with Fen's advice.

"We're going to Selfridges first," he said. "That's where we're meeting Max and Tazie."

"Good. I want to get something for Mum and Dad there."

"What do you think they might like?"

"Perhaps a new blanket; Mum said the other day that the one they'd had since they were first married was wearing thin."

They got the tube to Oxford Circus and pushed their way through the throng to Selfridges, Adrian guiding Gemma by the arm. The first port of call was the sports department where Gemma, on Adrian's advice, bought Sebastian a red training shirt with a lime green and navy shoulder motif. Then she led Adrian to what he called 'the Girlie Department' to look for gifts for her school friends. A bored Adrian wandered off telling Gemma he would see her in ten minutes at the cash tills, hoping she would manage to finish by then. She didn't, but by dint of choosing indiscriminately for her from the articles she was considering, he managed to winch her away after ten more minutes. By then it was time to meet Max and Tazie.

To Adrian's dismay, there was a huge crowd milling round the lower ground floor coffee shop. Out of nowhere Max appeared to explain that he and Tazie had got there a few minutes earlier, seen the queue and opted instead for a small coffee shop round the corner from Selfridges where Tazie was waiting for them. They found her ensconced at a round table in the back, with her coat, scarf and bag on three stools.

"Here we are!" said Max cheerfully. Tazie stood up to kiss Adrian on the cheek then stretched out both hands towards Gemma, who stepped towards her.

"May I kiss you too, Gemma?" asked Tazie.

"Yes," she replied, gratified by the suggestion, forgetting momentarily her animosity. It was a warm, neat kiss. Left with Tazie at the table whilst Adrian and Max went to get the drinks, Gemma felt suddenly shy; the purpose of this encounter seemed engulfed by the occasion itself as Tazie asked about Gemma's shopping. Max and Adrian returned with one hot chocolate and three coffees to find a sports shirt and an array of small cuddly things on the table, whilst Gemma named the friend for each gift before scooping them up to make room for the cups. Next, Max asked her about her visit to the British Museum whereupon, eyes shining, prompted from time to time by questions from Tazie, she described to them some of the beautiful Byzantine gold and silver artefacts she had seen. It was not only kindness that drew Tazie in; she sensed and even admired Gemma's genuine enthusiasm, which she recognised as being more than teenage fancy. In passing, Gemma turned to Adrian and said:

"You know, after the museum visit, I know what I want to do – it's Byzantium of course. I saw a marvellous section on Byzantine churches – they're everywhere. It's such an exciting idea, travelling to loads of places to see them."

"That's great Gemma," said Adrian moodily. "I wish I could feel as good about Chinese as you do about your subject."

"Maybe if you were to concentrate on what you're supposed to be studying, you might find a fire within yourself," said Max with a wry smile.

Adrian gave Max a withering look. Gemma, engrossed in her thoughts and her hot chocolate, neither noticed the remark nor the look, which was just as well, thought Adrian. Max broke the silence that followed by asking Gemma how her parents were, and whether Seb was still driving the station wagon around the boatyard. Gemma replied that he was, and moreover was hoping Max would come again soon to give him some more driving tips. She described the boatyard in detail for Tazie's benefit, asking Adrian for corroboration of details from time to time.

"We could invite Tazie to come and visit us with Max some time," suggested Adrian. Max gave Adrian a warning glance as Gemma's face changed whilst she searched for words. Meeting her enemy in London was one thing, but welcoming her at home was another.

"If she's free some time…" started Gemma but then ran out of suitable words.

Tazie, noticing the glance, rescued her.

"It's a nice thought, but I'm awfully busy now till Christmas, and then when new year comes I always have a lot of work to finish before the end of the financial year. My weekends just get lost."

Gemma managed a smile as she said, in a conciliatory tone, "Perhaps some time later in the new year, Tazie." Maybe Tazie wasn't interested in Adrian after all. Max kicked Adrian under the table. Adrian smiled at him.

Tazie revived the conversation by asking what they were all planning for the holiday season. Gemma explained that there was a mysterious treat in store for them, or at least for Seb and her; she was suspicious that Adrian was in the know. Adrian was indeed and lost no time in floating fanciful ideas about what it could be. Perhaps a Father Christmas outfit for Seb? Or money for a weekly gardener? Or a barbecue for the terrace? Or a Greek statue? Or tickets for a holiday in Rome? Gemma pooh-poohed them all, knowing that Adrian wouldn't include the secret present in a list of silly ideas. Max said he was spending Christmas with his girlfriend, Arabella Winton, and her parents. Tazie said she would be with her parents and other family members, but had to come back to work on 27th December and would perhaps be working during the New Year holidays. At that point she looked at Adrian; Gemma thought she saw him shake his head, a second intimation that something special might be going on. She sighed loudly.

"OK Gems?" asked Adrian. "Are you ready for a sandwich yet? We could have one here. Go and see what they've got."

While Gemma was at the counter, Tazie said quietly to Adrian:

"She doesn't know about us, does she?"

"No," he replied. "Nor does anybody else at home."

"That's fine. So long as I know what's what."

"I'd like crispy bacon and avocado please," said Gemma when she returned.

"Time for us to push off, I think," said Max. "Leave you to your eatings." More kisses and then they were gone. Adrian and Gemma tucked in silently.

"She's nice, Tazie," said Gemma in due course, with a tinge of doubt in her voice.

"But what Gems?"

"Nothing, really…" It was the moment to ask, but she couldn't do it.

They spent the next hour searching for Gemma's presents for her parents. In the end she couldn't decide on anything, so they headed out of the overheated shops for a walk in Hyde Park. The mist had lifted leaving a wintry sun casting long shadows of chunky trunks and spindly branches. Gemma put her arm through Adrian's.

A tube and a bus got them back to Fletcher's where they found a note from Benny on Adrian's door saying: "m'in and reddy 4 t". Adrian sent Gemma to collect him.

There was an instant rapport between them. He, witty and guileless, charmed Gemma with his funny stories, his

139

simplicity and his wide knowledge. He was used to looking after his three sisters and slipped easily into that mode with Gemma, who was happy to accept his protection. He liked her perkiness, her individuality and her giggle. There was plenty of that in the hour that followed, Adrian observed, contentedly.

A call on his mobile interrupted the chatter. He listened a moment, then said loudly:

"Oh goodness! Sadie! Sadie! Hullo! Hullo!" He shook the phone and listened again. "Nothing! She's gone."

Then, "Oh, hullo." His screwed his face up as he listened.

"What am I supposed to do?" he asked next. "Right. I'll be there." He switched off his phone and chucked it angrily on to his bed.

"It's Sadie!" he said. "She's been arrested and she's at Paddington Green Police Station. Stupid bitch. She tried to phone but couldn't manage, so the policeman took over. I suppose I've got to go."

"I'm coming too," said Benny immediately and stood up. "Poor Sadie, I wonder what's happened."

"Me too, I'm coming," piped up Gemma. "Who's Sadie?"

"Gems, dearest, I don't think that's a good idea…"

Gemma interrupted him:

"Don't be so stuffy, Adrian. I'm coming and that's that. But tell me who she is."

"She's doing Chinese too. She's Canadian and very big and not very good at managing her life."

Benny went to his room to get his jacket. As Adrian picked up his and Gemma's, he said reluctantly: "Oh well, I suppose it is simpler if we all go."

140

It was heaving at the Police Station. They had to wait fifteen minutes to be seen until a well-dressed family was through with shouting shrill insults at one of the police officers and surged out. On either side of Gemma, Benny and Adrian clung to her arms to prevent her getting swept away by the departing family. Along the counter an elderly man with a bent back was complaining plaintively that his pot plants had disappeared again. More people came in.

"I'm here because somebody called me on Sadie's behalf," said Adrian when they reached a space in front of a big, burly officer with a moustache.

"Sadie, Sadie, unusual name but we've got two of those so far this evening. Funny that. We don't often get more than one name at a time. Which Sadie is it?" he asked, smiling. Adrian turned to Benny.

"What's her surname, Benny?"

"Erm…" Benny was concentrating.

"She calls you to help and you don't even know her name?" teased the officer.

"We're fellow students… We're all in a group together," said Adrian lamely.

Benny's face suddenly relaxed. "I remember, it's Klein."

"OK, I'll go and see what's happening and what I can tell you. Who are you?"

"We're Adrian Goodfield, and Benny Hooper, and Gemma Goodfield. We're her friends."

He disappeared.

"Blimey," whispered Benny, looking round at the other people, "this lot isn't your actual silk sock brigade, is it?"

"How soon will the policeman come back?" whispered Gemma.

"Gems, I know as little about it as you. I've never been in an English police station before."

"Meaning you have been in a foreign one?"

"Not there either, smarty pants."

Ten tense minutes later and the officer returned.

"I expect you want to know why we're holding her?"

"Yes, we do" answered Adrian.

"At 1.47 pm she was arrested on suspicion of having committed ABH – that's assault occasioning actual bodily harm."

There was a short silence while they all looked at each other.

"Can you tell us any more? What does that mean?" asked Adrian.

The officer scrutinised the three young people; they didn't look aggressive and had waited their turn quite patiently, so he decided he could tell them more, although the little lass looked rather young.

The story was that at 1.14, the Police had received a call from the landlord of a pub called "The Six Steeds" in Notting Hill. It was known as being a rather quiet place, well-kept and respectable, where officers themselves quite liked to drink occasionally after work. The landlord reported that a woman – Sadie – had attacked a man with a bottle.

"She had been in the pub for quite some time, putting away vodkas. She was angry because the landlord suggested she had probably had enough."

"Oh dear," said Adrian.

"He said she was eyeing up the men," said the officer, "not that there had been more than one or two punters, it being early, you know. One of the regulars came in, got a

142

drink, and sat on his usual stool which happened to be beside Sadie's. She started talking to him, chatting him up like, but when he saw she'd had a few too many, he moved off to a table. She picked up a glass bottle of Buxton water on the bar, walked over to him and hit his hand with it. He was holding his glass, which smashed. Nasty cuts with bits of glass and blood all over the place."

The landlord, with the help of the only other customer in there, had immobilised the woman, "no mean feat, she's a big 'un, although she wasn't very steady on her pins," while the landlord's wife had called the police as well as an ambulance. The man was taken to St Mary's Paddington. The police arrived as the ambulance was leaving, just in time to take details of the injured man so that they could get a statement from him later.

"That's all we know so far," said the officer. "She's in the Custody Suite, but she hasn't been charged yet."

"Are we supposed to see her?" asked Adrian slowly.

"You don't sound very keen, young man. Don't blame you. Chums, eh! You won't be able to see her until after she's charged. After that, she might be bailed tonight, or if not, she'll be going to court from here on Monday and will be released after the hearing, assuming she gets bail then. Sadie passed out and she's in a rather, well erm, unhygienic state. She's quite safe and we're keeping an eye on her. If you like you can wait a while to see her, and if she's released on bail, then you can take her away."

"Oh," said Adrian.

Two policemen arrived with a foul-mouthed man handcuffed between them. Adrian made a decision.

"I ought to wait, make sure she's ok."

"Right you are," said the policeman. "By the way, I'm Constable Geoff Henshaw. I'll get her out here to see you as soon as I can."

"Thank you," said Adrian. He turned to Benny and Gemma. "I think you should go home now, Gemma. It's past six." She opened her mouth to protest but Adrian forestalled her. "No, don't argue. Benny, can you take her and put her on a train? Then call me to tell me which train it is so that I can let my parents know?"

"'Course," said Benny, "but which station is it? I've not been to all the London stations yet."

His remark triggered a sudden giggle in Gemma, who had kept very cool throughout the proceedings, eyes wide open, watching and listening. The tension was broken. Benny joined in, as did Officer Henshaw, and finally Adrian. Their laughter caused everybody else in the room to stop talking and stare at them. Mirth was not common there. Adrian described Liverpool Street and how to get there. Gemma asked whether she should tell the parents about Sadie and Paddington Green. Adrian hesitated whereupon Gemma decided for him: she would tell them – after all, nothing bad had happened to her, and they might hear about it later anyway because of a chance remark. Adrian agreed.

"Bye sweetie. We'll talk tomorrow. Thanks, Benny. See you later."

"I'll be in my room. Come and see me when you get back" replied Benny. Adrian watched him lead Gemma out by the hand. At Liverpool Street, they vowed to meet again as soon as possible.

On the train, Gemma had much to reflect on, not only the unsettling scenes she had just witnessed, but her new friendship with Benny. Funny, she felt very safe with him. The atmosphere and conversations at coffee with Max and Tazie were beginning to sink in. Hostility towards Tazie hadn't seemed appropriate at the time because she had been charming, but inside Gemma the seed of jealousy was sprouting. I've not found out what I wanted, Gemma said to herself and, I'm still in love with Adrian, however nice Tazie is.

For a couple of hours, Adrian sat on a hard chair, waiting to see Sadie, with nothing to do except read a *Daily Mirror* he had picked up off the floor, and play games on his iPod, whilst an endless stream of people in various stages of intoxication were led in. Benny duly called to give him the train times and he relayed the information to his parents. He got a coffee from a machine, but it was even more disgusting than the university stuff. All the officers were fully occupied, coming and going. Once, when the crowd thinned, Adrian went forward to ask Constable Henshaw how Sadie was getting on, only to be told that she couldn't be seen yet. There wasn't any point in protesting that he had been waiting a long time. Finally, Henshaw beckoned him to the counter to tell him that Sadie had been charged with ABH and was to stay in the police cell until Monday morning when she would go to the Magistrate's Court. Since Sadie was in a distressed state, Henshaw offered to bring her out briefly (this was somewhat irregular) to have a word. Adrian, although dismayed, felt obliged to acquiesce.

She limped in hanging on to the arm of a female officer. She was dirty and dishevelled; an attempt had been made to wash the vomit off the front of her clothes, and Adrian couldn't help but notice wet patches around her crotch and down the inside of her trouser legs. Her face was puffed up with tears and alcohol, and when she spoke, her voice was husky, her speech muddled. On seeing him, she stepped towards him, calling out his name loudly. She smelled disgusting. In the next breath, she begged him to help her get away. Adrian tried to explain that he was powerless to do so, but she wasn't listening. When Adrian repeated it, she muttered that she didn't believe him; he was lying. Adrian questioned her as to what had happened. Gradually the words tumbled out, snippets of information which Adrian was eventually able to construct into Sadie's version of the story. She had been to see Hardy, but hadn't seen him. Then she'd gone for lunch in a pub where a nasty man had insulted her, so she'd had a go at him in self-defence. She remembered little thereafter; however, snuffling and sobbing, she launched into a vindictive diatribe against Lily without connecting her to the day's events.

Adrian was both sorry for her and exasperated. To be desperately, shamelessly in love with someone who didn't reciprocate her feelings must be miserable. Evidently Lily was somehow involved in what had happened. That someone as intelligent as Sadie should let herself go to such an extent was pitiful, although intelligence wasn't a factor. She was one of nature's innocents, wearing her heart on her sleeve, ready to be a victim. Adrian realised with dismay that Sadie needed his help in the short term and that he owed it to her, having been partly instrumental in bringing Lily and Hardy together. In the longer term, Sadie probably needed professional guidance, as well as understanding from her flatmates and all of the rest of them. But for now there was nothing more to say.

"I think she'd better go back in," said Constable Henshaw, seeing Adrian grab her to stop her from swaying over. "I'll be back in a moment."

He returned with the female officer who took Sadie firmly by the arm. "Time to go back now, Sadie," she said.

"Don't go Adrian!" croaked Sadie, squirming in vain to free herself.

"I'll be back tomorrow" he answered.

"When you come," said Constable Henshaw, "be so good as to bring some clean clothes with you for the Court appearance."

"Right you are," said Adrian.

On his return to Fletcher's, Adrian went to see Benny. He described Sadie's condition in detail, and retold her story. They agreed that it would be useful to talk to Lily. Next morning, Benny found Sadie's address and he and Adrian trekked round to her flat in Tooting. Luckily one of her flatmates, a tall thin girl with prematurely grey hair, was in. Not wishing to reveal Sadie's predicament, they told her that Sadie had had a cooking spill and needed clean clothes for the day's outing.

Constable Henshaw wasn't on duty at the Police Station that day, but after checking their identity, another officer informed them that Sadie had slept off her hangover and now, following a meeting with the Duty Solicitor, realised that she was in quite serious trouble. He would give her the clothes.

***

It proved difficult to approach Lily informally. Her life was strictly time-tabled, leaving little opportunity for casual conversation which might lead to the subject of Sadie. Lily was reputedly always where she should be, punctual for lectures and tutorials, and well prepared for them thanks to steady hours working in the library or in her room. She was physically fit from regular sessions in the gym and the swimming pool, and her free time was carefully apportioned for leisure activities, including spending time with Hardy. Saturday was their usual day together, as well as occasional evenings during the week. Sundays were for family matters or for anything else that needed doing; Lily had a cousin who ran a business in Bristol, and Hardy's uncle was sometimes around at the weekend. Adrian gleaned this information from an innocent conversation with Hardy (full of admiration for Lily), about the different ways in which people went about organising study time. Lily's schedule seemed to Adrian and Benny to be extremely restrictive and lacking spontaneity, but evidently Hardy was content with it – and her.

On the other hand, reasoned Adrian, perhaps Lily wouldn't bridle at a direct question. She had after all demanded imperiously that Adrian help her to get fixed up with Hardy. Adrian asked Benny what he thought, without of course divulging the part he had played in getting Hardy and Lily together. Benny's view was that a direct question would be acceptable to Lily. They both knew, however, that they might have to explain Sadie's predicaments – all of them – to Lily.

Accordingly, Adrian knocked on Lily's door one evening later in the week.

A face peered cautiously round the door.

"We need to talk to you, Lily," said Adrian. "Come and have a cup of coffee?"

"Who's, we?" she asked.

"Benny and me. We want to ask you something."

"What about? I'm writing essay."

"It won't take long. Just a few minutes."

"OK, but no coffee." Her monosyllables in a clipped Chinese accent were definitely off-putting. Decidedly, thought Adrian, the charm was reserved for Hardy.

Benny was already sitting on Adrian's bed. Lily sat in the chair while Adrian made coffee for himself and Benny.

"You sure about no coffee, Lily?"

"Sure."

Adrian cleared his throat.

"It's about Sadie."

"What about her? She what you call lush, no?"

"Why do you think that?" asked Benny.

"I saw her Saturday morning, holding on to letterbox near Hardy's house, to stop from falling, pretending she posting a letter. I almost went crossed to speak to her but Hardy expects me – we going shopping for Chinese food – and I couldn't be bothered, too busy. Don't like her."

"Did you tell Hardy you'd seen her?"

"No, he gets cross with mention of her. She's been a nuisance, writing notes, phoning, hanging round after lectures, trying to talk to him. I didn't want Hardy to bothered on our day."

"Have you any idea what happened next?" asked Adrian.

"No, and not interested. She got gone by the time we got back."

Adrian and Benny looked at each other.

"Erm, she got into a spot of bother, but it'll be coming out ok," said Adrian.

"Is that all?" asked Lily. "Can I go now?"

"Yes," said Adrian. "Thanks for helping us."

"She won't get life like that," was Lily's parting remark as her back disappeared down the corridor.

"Blimey," said Benny as Adrian shut the door. "Watch your jugular when she's around. Single-minded isn't in it. She's aiming big in every way. And nothing will stop her, especially not the Sadies of this world."

"Made it easy for us, anyway. Not having to tell her anything. And she's not even interested enough to gossip."

"Remember to ask her when you want help with Chinese! She'll fall over herself with agreeableness."

"I tried asking her something once," said Adrian, "but she didn't want to understand my question and gave me a very strange answer before stomping off."

"I wonder why Sadie went to Hardy's place? Just routine spying or something more complicated?"

"We'll probably never know. It's good that Hardy didn't know she was there."

"Mm."

Thirteen

By the beginning of December, the idea of a trip to the Middle East was preying on Adrian's mind. He had mentioned it again to Max, who was predictably dismissive as a matter of principle, not in the belief that Mrs S couldn't be found there, but that Adrian would be surfing a rolling wave into a dangerously deep ocean. Where were the solid foundations for this trip? What leads did Adrian have? Who would guide him? Adrian tried in vain to win Max over by filling him in on his contacts and plans. The information forthcoming from Monty Simons at the British Council had been the name of his Beirut colleague, who had located the archives from the period when Mrs S first arrived to teach in Beirut, but had not yet started opening them up. Meanwhile, Adrian felt bolstered by contacts with Francis Hacker at the Foreign Office who, some days after their meeting, had called Adrian to confirm that he had written the letter to Beirut and that it was on its way in the diplomatic bag. And only yesterday, Francis had called to propose meeting again for a drink. Adrian felt that at this stage of his search, it would be useful just to have a first glimpse of the Middle East, meet the relevant people if possible, and perhaps look in on some schools. Furthermore, Hassan had a cousin living in Beirut who would be pleased to meet him and show him round Beirut. All these contacts, Adrian said, were encouraging. Max, having asked and discovered who the hell Hassan was, remained unconvinced, cautioning Adrian about trusting someone he had only just met and about whom he knew practically nothing.

A couple of days later, Adrian set out, prepared for disappointment as that seemed the sensible way to be, to the bar where he and Francis had met last time. A smiling Francis was again there in advance, this time already seated at a table with a bottle of wine and two glasses. He stood up, waved Adrian into a chair saying "Good news. My colleague Glyn Morgan in Beirut is curious, but busy."

Adrian nodded. "I understand."

"I want to tell you a bit about him. He's on his second posting there, in the Consular Section, and has many contacts, some dating from his first posting. One of them is a kind of long term 'eminence grise' of the British education scene in Lebanon. He's called Vic Appleton – a retired mathematician whose father had owned a spice business in the Middle East. The family lived there until the 1970s when the civil war propelled them back to England, where Pa re-established the business successfully, having taken all the proper precautions for protecting his capital and funds." Francis took a sip of wine before continuing.

"Vic, however, found nothing to attract him to living here, so returned to Beirut for good – teaching, dodging bombs and terrorists, gathering information, and keeping copious written records of everything and everybody. He has a phenomenal memory for events, dates and faces. He also has a reputation for being in touch with both high level officials and dubious fraternities, although nobody has ever challenged him on that score nor found any proof." Francis smiled. "I've met him on a few occasions and found him to be affable, although somewhat eccentric and evasive. Subtle probings about his connections are met with a blank face and a joke. His discretion, when needed, is legendary. Glyn meets him to exchange Middle East news and play backgammon, sometimes in Vic's large bachelor flat."

"He sounds like a good contact," said Adrian, "as long as his discretion doesn't prevent him from pointing me in the right direction."

"If he won't or can't help, he'll say so. He's rather straightforward in that sense, but you'll never discover the reason why he does or doesn't help."

"Well, it sounds like a possible thread leading somewhere, some sort of progress at last. I might be on the way to finding my *bio-bod*."

"That's an apposite appellation, if I may say so."

"And that's a pompous pronouncement, if I may say so."

Francis twinkled. "We get used to pompous pronouncements at work. I'm spearheading a campaign for straight talk and straight prose. No euphemisms, no nebulous sentences, clauses, or phrases. They all hate me for it, because I'm always picking holes in what they write. Anyway, Adrian, don't build up your hopes too quickly. After all, Mrs S might have moved on and now be living in Archangel or Mandalay, assuming that she isn't neatly concealed somewhere in the UK."

"I'm almost sure she isn't. I've searched everything possible on the internet."

"Mm," said Francis in a non-committal fashion. "You *think* you've turned over all the stones, but in my experience there's always one more. She's probably got an

English lawyer somewhere. Perhaps you could put a notice in a legal paper?"

"You're right," said Adrian, smiling, "I've not done that. Worth a try."

While Francis refilled their glasses, Adrian decided quickly to show his hand.

"I'm thinking of going out there after Christmas before term starts again."

Francis raised his eyebrows. "That may be a bit premature," he said slowly. "Glyn's got to look at a few records and find time to talk to Vic. And what about Monty? I don't suppose the Council's come up with anything yet?"

"Monty's given me the name of his colleague who's going to look through the relevant archives."

"And hasn't started yet…"

"No, I don't think she has."

"And you need to get into the right frame of mind for going there – read up, get a grasp of the geography, not to mention the difficulties of Arabic."

"Ah, well…," said Adrian, then stopped abruptly.

"What were you going to say?"

"That I've already started. I've been looking at journals, and begun on the language," he hesitated then continued. "I've been going to some lectures at SOAS…"

"*Two* difficult languages at the same time? Not a good idea, I would have thought. How do you manage your time? And how does Arabic fit in with Chinese?"

"Not too well actually. There have been some timetable clashes."

Francis burst out laughing. "A neat way of putting it. You're doing a degree in Chinese but goof off and slide into Arabic!" He looked straight at Adrian who returned his gaze. "I don't need to tell you, do I?"

"No, you don't. I know what I'm doing, and that I shouldn't be."

"Adrian, you've got to do well, get a first or an upper second, otherwise you won't be able to get into the Foreign Office, for example."

"The Foreign Office? Me?"

"Why not you? A first degree in a difficult global language plus a politics and economics Ph.D, or vice versa, is always useful. Come to think of it, there are now plenty of British graduates in Chinese but fewer in Arabic." He laughed. "I shouldn't have told you that. It might have a detrimental influence on your conduct."

Adrian was stunned into silence. He had never thought of a career as a civil servant, in fact had not thought much about the future at all.

"So supposing I were interested," he said slowly, "I might do better with Arabic than Chinese. Is that what you're saying?"

"Circumstances change and the position may be different by the time you graduate – assuming you get sorted out and do graduate – but at the moment, yes, that is so."

"Interesting. My parents do worry that I don't have an ultimate goal in mind, but allaying their fears on that score hasn't been at the top of my list. For the time being, I've got to talk them round about my trip to Beirut."

Francis was looking at his watch. "Time's up. Drink up. Last round gents. Wife calls." They swallowed down the last of the wine and walked out together. On the pavement, Francis, looking serious, said: "Adrian, I do think it's too early for your trip, but if you do decide to go, get in touch so I can talk you through a few things and alert Glyn."

"I certainly will, and thank you again," said Adrian.

**

He had saved up a little over a thousand pounds, but guessed that this would not be enough, which meant asking his parents for funds. His casual references to his mother in conversations with them had alerted them to his awakening interest in her, tinged naturally by his feeling of alienation. In due course, he had told them that he knew their decision to put him in the picture had been the right one, and that he appreciated it. During a later phone conversation, he mentioned that he felt compelled to search for her; they were not surprised and John offered both moral support and financial help.

Now, it was time to put his cards on the table and plan the journey, to take place immediately after Christmas. There was no doubt it would be a difficult project. As Max took every opportunity to remind him, Lebanon had only that year despatched home the Israeli occupiers of South Lebanon, and the Middle East could erupt at any time. However, Max seemed to have decided that the best course at present was to try to prevent Adrian from missing any more Chinese lectures. Despite the dangers attached to such a trip, of which Max reminded Adrian at every opportunity, Max was by now expressing cautious optimism about Adrian's intention, hoping it might get the whole matter out of his system. He wasn't surprised when Adrian informed him that he was going home to talk to his parents, but he tactfully declined Adrian's invitation to accompany him, feeling that his presence would be a distraction rather than an asset.

It was Saturday morning. Gemma was again at the station, this time with Sebastian who was wearing a red and blue sports outfit with shiny badges. Pushing through the ticket barrier, Adrian was almost knocked over by a bouncing bullet of a person.

"Hi Adrian. Look at my new gear! Great, isn't it?"

Adrian pushed Sebastian away, holding his arm in a firm grip.

"Don't rush at me. I can't see your gear if you do that."

"It's for the hockey team. We've got hockey now, it's not compulsory though. I like it lots and I'm in the junior team."

"Very smart gear, Seb, and well done for getting into the team," said Adrian in an older-brotherly voice.

"Will you come and watch me in the match this afternoon?"

"Why not! Yep, I will."

"Cool!" said Sebastian, wrenching himself away from Adrian's grasp and punching him in the chest.

Gemma stepped forward, pushed Sebastian away and stretched up to kiss Adrian. "Dad's waiting in the car," she said. He held her around the shoulders, feeling how quickly she was growing. They linked arms to walk over to the car where John had the engine running already. Sebastian ran on ahead.

The first thing Gemma asked over lunch was how the 'Sadie situation' had developed.

"She's in trouble," said Adrian. "She's well over six foot tall, has an amiable face with an olive complexion and lovely eyes, but she's clumsily built, and doesn't have much self-esteem. So she goes about relationships with men in the wrong way. She's fallen frantically in love with Hardy, who's from South Carolina, taller than her, smart, courteous and correct. But she's absolutely and utterly not his type. What's worse is that he's seeing Lily, a Chinese student whom Sadie knows too, very compact, very neat, very complete, who is just his type. So Sadie's jealous, and a bit of her wants to be. She keeps trying to get Hardy's attention. She's drinking too much, probably not an alcoholic yet, but putting away quite a bit every day and more at the weekends ending up, we think, in the arms of pub punters."

"How sad," said Fen. "Dangerous too, I would think. Who knows what nasty diseases pub punters have!"

"Quite," replied Adrian. "Anyhow, on the Saturday Gemma came up, Sadie went to spy on Hardy's house, saw Lily going in, and went off upset to comfort herself in a pub. There she tried it on with a punter who turned his back on her, so she smashed his glass and his hand with a bottle. He went to hospital where he had stitches and the landlord called the police who took her to Paddington Green Police Station. She was in a bad way, passed out, and was still barely able to stand when I saw her much later at about 8.00pm. She had been charged with ABH – assault occasioning actual body harm – and had to stay in the police cell until an appearance before the magistrate on the Monday morning. The Duty Solicitor acted for her. She pleaded guilty, got bail under all sorts of conditions, like reporting regularly to the police, not going near the pub where she had attacked the man, etc. I even mentioned Alcoholics Anonymous to her when Benny and I collected her. Anyway, the next thing is the Crown Court, where she'll again plead guilty. The solicitor thinks she'll get a fine and a suspended sentence. Trouble is, being the person she decided to call for help, I've sort of got caught up in it, about the last thing I want – best friends with Sadie isn't a role I aspire to. But she knew she'd have got short shrift from Max, and Benny's not London-wise enough yet to sort that kind of thing out. And as for Hardy, forget it. He puts miles between himself and Sadie. Benny and I have been trying to give her a bit of advice. One of her flatmate's quite friendly with her too, so we hope she's watching over Sadie a bit."

"I wouldn't mind getting advice from Benny," squeaked Gemma. "He's cool. Wait till you meet him, Mum!"

"I hope I will, dear." She turned to Adrian. "Gemma told us all about their chats and him looking after her and seeing her on to the train. In fact we heard almost more about that than anything else you did!"

"Ah well, there you go."

Adrian didn't mention his proposed trip to Beirut until after they got back from Sebastian's hockey match, when he told John and Fen he wanted to speak to them privately. Gemma, who had returned from spending the afternoon with a friend, was banished upstairs protesting hotly, and only went when Adrian promised to tell her his news later himself. Seb was sent for a shower and to clear up his sports gear. Over a cup of tea in the sitting room, with the door shut, Adrian outlined his plans. He proposed to fly to Beirut where he would be met by a cousin of a Jordanian student he knew in London, and would be taken to a hostel – bed booked in advance. He had two solid leads to follow up: someone at the British Council via Monty at the London office, and a contact through Francis whose Foreign Office brief included the Missing Persons Section.

John was taken aback by Adrian's announcement; he seemed to have moved further ahead than John would have expected, bearing in mind his initial hostility to the idea of his mother's existence. Fen's immediate concerns, on the other hand, were for Adrian's safety in that volatile part of the world. Both she and John had thought that Adrian would spend some time searching on the internet and through other channels first without heading off anywhere. In an effort to soften the impact of his resolution, Adrian related everything he knew about Hassan and his cousin who would, he believed, be available to help him if necessary. And if it got hairy, Adrian would hop on a plane and come straight home; it would only be a short visit anyway. Fen grew increasingly vehement as she sketched various disaster scenarios: bombs dropped on the airport and on the port, Hassan's cousin wounded or killed, no taxis available to take Adrian to Israel or any other adjacent country, and the borders closed anyway. In an effort to calm her down, John got out an atlas which they all studied together. Eventually, when John said gently that he understood Adrian's reason for going and that he couldn't stop him, Fen went quickly into the kitchen to fetch a tissue out of the box on the sideboard. She was distressed as well as angry with John for, as she put it, giving in to Adrian. John voiced all the arguments he could find to support Adrian, but Fen was adamant: she could not approve of Adrian's intentions, and she wanted him to know it and remember it when he was on the plane going over there. Her opinion had nothing to do with Patti, but everything to do with safety. She realised now that Adrian would go, but it was to be without her blessing.

Then came the discussion about money. Here, Fen agreed with John: Adrian should have plenty of funds so that he could look after himself in case of emergency. John decided to make £2000 available to Adrian in Beirut by whichever method the bank suggested. And the amount could be topped up if necessary.

Adrian's conversation with Gemma was not a comfortable one, either. He found her at the computer in the study. She looked up nervously as he came in and asked immediately if he were going away; she started to cry as soon as Adrian began to unfold his plans. When he had explained everything as fully as he could, including their parents' role, she calmed down enough to echo Fen's worries about his safety. More importantly, she gave voice to her personal anguish: the idea, which had often been at the back of her mind, that Adrian would prefer his real mother to Fen and decide to abandon them all. Adrian tried his best to persuade her of the impossibility of such an outcome, and although mollified by his insistence upon the strength of their family ties, his loyalty to them all, and the enormous affection in which he held them (feelings which he had never before put into words), she was still afraid that they might be losing their Adrian.

The news was broken to Sebastian over supper. His reaction was one of surprise, for the idea that Adrian might want to find his mother had never occurred to him. Nor were the dangers of the Middle East anything that he had ever considered. He accepted Adrian's decision with equanimity, moving swiftly on to the details of the hockey match which he expounded at great length to Gemma.

On Monday, Adrian told Max that he would be flying to Beirut before the end of the year, and that he had decided to tell Hassan the reason for his trip: Max insisted on meeting Hassan, despite Adrian's objections. It was not a congenial occasion: Max's impatience was palpable as Hassan struggled to make his English intelligible. Alone with Adrian afterwards, Max admitted that Hassan seemed helpful and that reading Middle Eastern body language was not amongst his strengths.

Fourteen

Sadie's Crown Court appearance had been scheduled for February, but a call from a Court official changed all that: a major fraud hearing on the list for the week before Christmas had had to be postponed, leaving a gap to be filled by some small cases, of which Sadie's was one. It was a relief to everybody, but in the days leading up to the hearing, Sadie's self-confidence reached a new low; as well as dreading whatever would take place in court, and the possibility of having to face her victim, she had realised that strait-laced Hardy would never go out with her, however hard she might try to attract him, especially since the story of her misdemeanour was likely to reach his ears. Indeed, he and Lily were now 'dating'. Max had heard from Hardy that Lily and he had done 'family things' together: dining in London with Hardy's uncle, and spending a Sunday in Bristol with a cousin of Lily's, who owned three grocery stores. This, Max declared to Adrian, was getting to be serious stuff since, he supposed, Hardy wasn't looking to run a grocery in Bristol.

Sadie's three flatmates were all drinkers and she had always joined in; however, one of them, Holly, who was fond of Sadie, had noticed several empty bottles in her room and had tried to stop her from drinking on her own. It was fun to binge together a couple of times a week, she said, but they all had lectures to attend and assignments to complete, and Sadie needed to buckle down. Holly was short, fat and jolly, and her wide feet were planted firmly on the ground as far as studying was concerned. She had a deep, buttery voice (she sang tenor in a well-known choir) which she used regularly to warn Sadie of the dangers of the booze shelves in the supermarkets (they sometimes shopped together), the off-licence round the corner, the newsagent who winked at her, and casual encounters with men in pubs, especially when they led to sex.

For two days following her Magistrates Court appearance, Sadie had been too traumatised by her experiences to leave the flat; she finished her bottle of vodka in rationed amounts, knowing that the next bottle would entail an expedition outside, which would be torture. On the second evening, Holly, guessing that Sadie hadn't been out and ignorant of her saga, bounded into her room and challenged her. What was going on? Had Sadie stayed in? Had she skipped lectures? What was the matter, was she ill? Sadie burst into tears; coaxed along by Holly, she recounted a self-pitying version of the story. Holly, suspecting that she wasn't getting the whole truth, reacted sympathetically but firmly. First, she went out to buy sandwiches, then, while they ate them together, she extracted a promise from Sadie that she would return to college the next day and try to forget what had happened until her Crown Court hearing. Sadie did indeed return to SOAS but her mind strayed obstinately back to the incident in the pub, the police cell and the Magistrates' Court; she was also suffering withdrawal symptoms but did not recognise them as such. For the rest of the week, Holly checked up on Sadie each evening, glancing around for bottles and glasses, but finding none.

By Saturday, Sadie's craving for alcohol got the better of her. A trip to the supermarket soon set her up for a weekend alone with the television – her flatmates were all away. She remembered to have a sandwich and a chocolate bar every so often to accompany the vodka and coke. By Sunday afternoon she was comfortable enough within to forgive herself in advance for not going to college on Monday.

Holly, returning on Monday evening, found her sitting in a chair with a rug round her, a glass in her hand and a bottle on the floor. This time Holly lost her cool; searching the room, she shouted at Sadie that she wasn't even trying to help herself. She removed all the bottles – full and empty – and prised a half-full glass from Sadie's hand. As she left, she slammed the door. Her heavy footsteps thumped into the kitchen where she emptied the bottles, then resounded on down the staircase and outside where she put the empties in the recycling bin, returning to her room without speaking to Sadie.

Sadie felt abandoned. Alone, she sobbed for a few minutes, then levered herself to her feet and shuffled over to stand in front of her cupboard mirror. She found her image distasteful: she was too big, too clumsy-looking, too floppy. Her eyes were bloodshot, her cheeks seemed to sag, and her hair was dirty. She returned to her chair, trying to trace back how she had become the person she had just seen in the mirror who, she had to admit, deserved Holly's reprimands. Was she indeed an alcoholic, as suggested by Adrian's allusions to AA? Surely not. In Canada, she had never drunk more than a couple of beers; her first vodka had been with her parents on a visit to London. Perhaps London was the wrong place for her? But she had been happy at first, starting an interesting degree course, meeting new people, staying in a comfortable room in Hardy's uncle's flat, seeing Hardy every day, trying to please him. How and why had that gone wrong? Of course, she wasn't the tidiest person alive – her mother had always said that – but Hardy wasn't perfect either: he left empty glasses on the draining board. At SOAS, she had made encouraging progress in Chinese; Sun Qianghan had complimented her on her pronunciation and her initial grasp of word order, even though her written characters were untidy. Looking back, Sadie concluded that her unhappiness had started when she moved out of the flat, and when that awful stuck-up prig Lily dug her talons into Hardy. She went to bed to cry herself to sleep.

The next morning, Holly woke her at 7.00 with a cup of sweet black coffee, pushed her into the shower and got her clothes ready. When Sadie was dressed, Holly marched her down the stairs and out into the cold, grabbing her by the arm to steer her to the tube. Sadie thought she would remember that morning for ever, the terrible chill of her shaking body, her thudding head, and her disobedient legs which did their best to wobble her off the damp pavement. Luckily she arrived at SOAS at the same time as Adrian who asked solicitously whether she was all right, making her feel a little less wretched. Smelling a combination of toothpaste and alcohol on her breath, he took her for coffee and a muffin which she surprised herself by eating with relish. She survived the day's obligations, and when she got home, Holly was preparing a meal for both of them, accompanied by a glass of water and a catalogue of stiff advice.

As the days passed, Adrian and Benny did their best to help Sadie to stay away from pubs and bars, but it was impossible and undesirable to monitor her all the time. Sadie attended her classes and lectures and said pointedly at the end of each day that she was going straight home. Max noticed how sad and withdrawn she had become. He mentioned it to Adrian who decided on the spur of the moment to tell him why, since Max might be useful while Adrian was away. Max was predictably contemptuous; he had always known she was a disaster waiting to happen, a personification of trouble. But if his help were needed at any stage, he might be able to spare a little time.

Holly was the home gatekeeper. She listened out for Sadie's comings and goings, found pretexts for going to her room to see if Sadie were drinking, and took Sadie out to the cinema with her. Benny persuaded Sadie she should go home to Canada for Christmas and supervised her booking a ticket online. Eventually Sadie plucked up the courage to ask Adrian and Benny if they would accompany her to Court. Benny agreed immediately; Adrian, preoccupied by his Lebanese trip, stalled, hoping to get out of it, a position justified, he thought, by the fact that Holly and Benny would be there. Benny however pointed out gently to Adrian that as he had been Sadie's first port of call when she was arrested, he should continue to support her. Adrian gave in.

Two days before the hearing, Holly called Adrian.

"Sadie gave me your number and asked me to ring you. She's started calling you, Benny, and me her 'Salvation Team' and wants us to meet her for a drink tomorrow to prepare, as she calls it, for Court. Not that there's anything to prepare, but she's feeling rather low at the moment and was too embarrassed to call you herself. It would obviously do her good. Can you and Benny do it?" Her deep steady voice bore conviction.

"Oh dear," said Adrian. "Not cool, not cool at all."

"Do you think Benny will be ok with it? Can you ask him for me?"

"Benny's much nicer than I am, and I'm sure he will if he's free."

"I don't know you at all, Adrian, but Sadie speaks warmly of you. It will make a difference to her if you're both there."

"Flattery and wheedling will get you nowhere. But I suppose I must. Are you training to be a barrister by any chance?"

Holly laughed. "Yes I am, as a matter of fact. But barristers don't flatter and wheedle – whatever gave you such an idea? Or at least, this one won't, or not all the time."

"Ha!" replied Adrian. "So what time's this thingie tomorrow supposed to take place and where?"

"At 6.00pm. Meet at SOAS in the entrance."

It was, as Adrian had anticipated, an awkward encounter. They repaired to the pub at the Union. Sadie gushed out gratitude and apologies, hopes and promises, all muddled up together. Benny spoke the kind words she needed, Adrian tried to avoid catching her eye, and Holly told them all firmly where to be in the morning and when. She also mentioned that, as far as she knew, Sadie had not touched a drop since returning to SOAS, and was to be congratulated for her abstinence. Sadie almost smiled; Benny and Adrian murmured appropriately. And indeed, Sadie was on orange juice while they were drinking beer.

Once the arrangements were settled, Holly, Adrian and Benny chatted for some minutes while Sadie sat staring into the distance, frowning. Soon Holly drank down the last of her beer and got up decisively to lead Sadie off; Sadie, though, insisted on first kissing Adrian and Benny.

"Ugh," said Adrian when they had gone, "there's something about her, physically, which I find a bit repulsive. I hope she doesn't make a habit of kissing us."

"It's part of the event," said Benny.

***

They assembled outside the Court at 9.30. Holly and Sadie arrived early, Holly serene and in control, Sadie shaking all over, convinced that Adrian and Benny wouldn't turn up and threatening to be sick. However, Benny and Adrian were soon there. Inside, the Duty Solicitor was waiting to tell Sadie the welcome news that her victim was not planning to attend. While Sadie went to report in, Holly led the Salvation Team over to meet the legal team; she wanted to get talking to the barrister, a blonde man with a sunny face who looked about fifteen. Indeed, this was his first case. The previous evening, Holly had explained the court procedure to Sadie, but the young barrister went through it again when Sadie reappeared, because she was so nervous. Holly led Adrian and Benny confidently into the front row of the visitors' seats where they listened with great interest to two cases before Sadie was finally called. The charge was read, and the barrister declared that the offender was pleading guilty, whereupon the Judge released the members of the jury.

Were there circumstances he should take into account in pronouncing sentence, he then asked? The fresh faced barrister said he would like to make a plea in mitigation; the Judge agreed he might do so. The barrister explained, haltingly at first but soon with confidence, that Sadie had no previous convictions nor had she ever before been in any kind of trouble with the police. She had been upset by a personal disappointment in the days leading up to the incident at the pub which was where she had imbibed too much alcohol, causing her to attack a member of the public who had spoken offensively to her. She was a regular and model student at London University where she was successfully pursuing a difficult course in Chinese studies, and where she had good friends who were helping her to remain sober, as was her flatmate. She was in touch with Alcoholics Anonymous. And most importantly, she had recognised her culpability and pleaded guilty to the charge, thereby sparing public resources. The judge withdrew to consider his verdict, returning after ten minutes to announce that as this was Ms Klein's first offence, he was granting her bail on four strict conditions. First, she should report to her local police station every week for the next six months, unless she were in Canada with her family; second, she should never return to the Six Steeds public house in Notting Hill Gate; third, she should attend Alcoholics Anonymous regularly; and fourth she should pay a fine of £500. Through the barrister, Sadie agreed to the conditions.

Outside, Sadie produced a wan smile, the first for many days, and kissed the Salvation Team. She even turned towards the legal team as though to do the same, but the Duty Solicitor and barrister were apparently well up to avoiding it. Holly led Sadie, Benny and Adrian to a café frequented by lawyers for lunch, after which she went her separate way and the others returned to SOAS. Later, in private, Adrian told Max the outcome. He snorted.

Fifteen

Tazie was shocked. Eating steak with Adrian in a tidy little bistro round the corner from her flat, she listened to him explaining his planned journey to Beirut. She remained silent when he stopped talking.

"You're not saying anything" he said, after a moment.

"What should I say Adrian?"

"Tell me what you think."

Tazie sighed. "You probably won't want to hear it."

"Yes I do."

"All right, here goes. It sounds premature to me. After all, you've only known about your mother for a few weeks – you've not really had time to get used to the idea of her existence, and now you're charging off into the unknown to look for her."

"I know it seems that way to you, but I feel an awful urgency about it. I feel as though she's been escaping from me all these years since she first scarpered, and that I'll never catch up with her unless I start out now."

"I see," said Tazie doubtfully. "But you've nothing really to go on. You've no idea if she's still in Beirut, and you don't know of anybody who's seen her there in the past."

"My mother," said Adrian. "Somebody must know her or of her. I've got these useful contacts from Francis at the Foreign Office and from someone at the British Council.

And there are several schools where she might have taught."

"But how are you going to get around? You can't expect everybody to speak English."

"Ah well, Hassan's being very helpful. I met him at SOAS. His cousin lives in Beirut and will meet me at the airport etc. And Lebanon used to be a French Protectorate so I expect there are still loads of people who know French, which I speak quite well. Besides, I've been reading up a bit, doing a bit of Arabic."

"Oh, in your spare time?" she asked sarcastically, with raised eyebrows.

Adrian met her gaze. "Yes, I've been going to one or two lectures on politics and society and stuff, and to tell you the truth, I've also attended some language classes. That's where I met Hassan." He paused. "Max didn't tell you?"

"No."

"The soul of discretion. Great, Max! Well, confession time: I've missed a few Chinese classes which have clashed with Arabic things. Max is cross with me."

"As well he might be," said Tazie, heatedly. "You must be mad, Adrian. I can understand your feelings about your mother, but I can't understand your throwing away the opportunities you've got at the moment. This could all go belly-up. Missing Chinese lessons and lectures! If you don't stick with it, you'll be letting yourself and everybody else down." She shook her head and said, almost to herself: "What a fool!"

"It's all right, Tazie. I can cope. I can catch up when I need to. I'm doing quite well really."

"Says you."

Adrian shrugged.

"So when are you leaving, and how long will you be gone?" she continued.

"I'm going on 29th December, coming back on about 9th January, when term starts."

"'About'. What does that mean? Have you got an open return?"

"No, it's booked for 9th."

"Then why did you say 'about'?"

"Tazie, it's just a way of talking. I wasn't thinking."

"Or you were being devious. It sounds as though you don't want me to know."

"Of course I want you to know. I wouldn't be telling you now if I didn't. It's only that I'm very preoccupied with this whole scenario. It was just words that slipped out."

"I'm disappointed Adrian," was Tazie's bitter pronouncement, which closed the subject.

After a short stony silence, they resumed talking, edgily exchanging snatches of news. Their lovemaking later in Tazie's flat was tinged with doubt, lacking flavour and fervour. Adrian didn't stay the night.

*****

It was now time to enlist help. First, Hassan. Adrian had prepared the ground earlier by telling him that he wanted to visit Lebanon; at that time Hassan volunteered his Beirut cousin's assistance. Adrian's description now of his family circumstances and his search for his mother touched a nerve in Hassan, who spoke with first-hand knowledge and sincere feeling of detached families and lost relations. He would contact Khalil, his cousin, immediately. Khalil would arrange for Adrian to stay in a clean, cheap place and would meet Adrian at Beirut airport. He worked freelance on computer software, so would have time to accompany Adrian wherever he wanted. That all sounded good. Hassan then launched into convoluted descriptions of the charms and pleasures of Beirut where he often visited family members. Adrian listened patiently, grunting occasionally, and mentally losing his way in peregrinations around the town.

Next, Adrian called Francis, who promised to email Glyn Morgan. Francis asked if Adrian had had suitable inoculations, and advised him to buy a local mobile phone on arrival. Monty at the British Council was elusive at first; when Adrian finally got through to him, he dismissed Adrian's journey as hare-brained. He nevertheless gave Adrian the contact details of his Beirut colleague, Jean Stavropoulos.

Finally, before the end of term, Adrian took Benny out to dinner, during which he explained where he was going, why and what his feelings were. Benny had never heard Adrian speak so long and intimately of himself, and was touchingly concerned that the venture should go well.

***

The Christmas party season had arrived in the City of London. Toby knew that in addition to celebrations with clients there were two office functions he couldn't skip. The first was a sit-down dinner by invitation of the CEO which was part ordeal and part pleasure. The second was his Department's knees-up. He dreaded the latter. Each year he floated the suggestion of a sit-down meal in a pub restaurant, but each year his staff insisted that they preferred the informality of the staff dining room where, they said, they felt comfortable. Indeed, Toby knew that the atmosphere there was less constrained; in particular, it was more convenient for the sorts of activities which were common at office parties and which made Toby cringe.

The party began at four. Just before six, Toby sidled in, his heart sinking at the prospect of empty words to be spoken with people in a particularly empty mood. From the door he could see Tazie sitting at a table with a group of colleagues playing some kind of game which seemed to entail swilling down a drink, calling out something, and then touching different parts of the head with the hand. She looked as though she were enjoying herself. Toby picked up a glass of elderflower cordial and looked around the rest of the room. Some older long-serving members of staff were sitting in armchairs talking. Toby went over thinking to join them, but the subject was fishing, about which he neither knew anything nor wanted to. Music blared from a couple of floor speakers and someone was screeching down a mic.

Drawn to Tazie as Toby always was, he wandered over to stand behind her, thinking to find out the rules of the game.

"Hey, Toby, come and play this!" called a voice from the other side of the table.

"I don't think I could manage it" he answered. Tazie turned to look at him.

"Merry Christmas, Toby!" she said quietly.

"And to you," he replied, touching her lightly on the shoulder.

"Would you like to play this silly game with us?"

"Not really," answered Toby. "That is, unless you tell me it's fascinating, demanding, and rewarding."

"None of those," she replied, standing up. "I'm ready for another glass of wine."

They walked together over to the drinks table while the game continued without her. She was drinking red wine. Toby took a glass of white for himself.

"What are you doing for Christmas, Tazie?"

"The usual things; I'm going to my parents in Sussex on 23rd in the evening. There'll be various relations joining us on Christmas day. My brother, Max, will be with his girlfriend some of the time – she lives close to us. And then I'll be back here working before New Year." It was true; he knew all about her workload during the run-up to the end of the financial year. He understood too that she wasn't trying to impress him but was just stating a fact.

"How about you? Is your family in London?"

"No, my parents are in Birmingham. I'll be going there. But we don't do much for Christmas. You've probably guessed – we're Jewish."

"Yes, I thought so. And you probably know I'm Russian."

"A hundred percent?"

"Yes, I'm second generation."

"You know, I've never bothered to find out what that means. Are immigrants first generation, or does it mean the first generation to be born here?"

"Max is a bit obsessive about accurate meanings. He says that first generation means the children of immigrants, and I believe him. So according to his definition, the fact that I'm second generation means that my grandparents were immigrants."

With a comic expression on his face, Toby started counting on his fingers. "Fourth, third, second, first…"

"Which are you, then?" asked Tazie, smiling.

"I'm second too," he laughed.

"Well counted! I'm glad you can manage ordinals backwards."

"Mm. My grandfather came with nothing from a desolate village in Poland." Toby realised, suddenly, that he was opening up to a sympathetic woman, something which was not a habit. Suddenly, he said: "Look, I've got to hang around here for about another hour, but should we go later and get something to eat together? Or are you an inveterate party girl?"

"Definitely not that," said Tazie. She hesitated.

"But perhaps you've got something else on later?"

"No, I haven't," she answered decisively. "Yes, let's go and eat together."

They went home their separate ways after an adequate meal at an Indian restaurant nearby where Tazie had been before. On the tube, Tazie recalled her impressions of Toby. Although she wouldn't describe him as good-looking, he had a pleasant demeanour. He was tall and slender – nearly six foot she guessed, with thick black hair, funny prominent ears, and wide lips. His eyes were black and deep-set. He spoke quietly with a slight Birmingham accent and was unassuming, shy almost, with a subtle sense of humour which soon revealed itself. He was a good listener – a person with whom she felt at ease. She learned that any spare time he had was spent running and playing the horn – not concurrently; he had excelled at both at school and joined an orchestra when he first arrived in London, but couldn't make it to rehearsals, which prompted the conductor to ask him to step down to give more regular musicians the opportunity to play.

Meanwhile Toby's musings on Tazie were of the sort that he could never discuss with anybody.

Sixteen

The chocolate Labrador puppy didn't come in time for Christmas, but Gemma and Sebastian heard the news of her existence and imminent arrival with great excitement. They each received two framed photos, one of the litter and a recent one of the puppy herself. Amongst other presents were a kennel for outdoors in the summer, a basket, two bowls and some toys. They chose her name: Cadby, in honour of Sebastian's favourite chocolate. When Gemma asked Adrian if he considered himself too grown-up to be given a picture of Cadby, he swiftly countered that he intended to take his own pictures of her with his new camera, bought for his visit to Lebanon. Gemma was touched that Max had thought to send presents for both Sebastian and her via Adrian. Sebastian got an illustrated boys' guide to car maintenance; Gemma's present was a book about Byzantine churches. Benny sent her a calendar showing photos of London museums.

There were eight people at Christmas lunch. Aunt Melanie and husband Derek always came and this year a recently widowed neighbour, Brenda Smallbone, joined them. Everybody enjoyed themselves. They ate turkey and played games: ping pong, darts, monopoly, cards. Sebastian, Adrian, Derek and John kicked a football around in the boatyard. Only Gemma wasn't quite her usual perky self, with Adrian's forthcoming trip weighing heavily on her mind.

Adrian refused John's offer to take him to Heathrow by car from home. He opted instead for going to London by train the previous day and taking public transport to the airport – more reliable if the roads were congested. As he explained to Fen and John, this would also give him an opportunity to spend the evening with Tazie who was working between Christmas and the New Year.

On 28th December before Adrian left for London, John gave him some cash for the trip and explained how the bank deposit in Beirut would work. Fen reiterated her disapproval of the whole undertaking. Gemma went to her room while that conversation was taking place. It was there, privately with Adrian, that she afterwards sobbed her heart out and clung to him, voicing her worry that he might go to live with his biological mother. Eventually, reassured a little by his protestations, she wished him a safe journey while he stroked her face; he knew that she would soon be taking his absence in her stride. Sebastian's farewell was a new feeble joke, a punch in the chest and an arm twist.

***

Tazie invited Adrian to dinner at her flat. It was a still and frosty evening. London was clear of revellers, now no doubt curtained indoors gearing themselves up for potential New Year's Eve excesses. Adrian bought nine pink roses in a fancy flower shop, and a bottle of Chateauneuf-du-Pape. Tazie thought how attractive he looked, standing smiling on the threshold. She wanted to make amends for her harsh words last time they had met. They were alone in the flat;

Tazie's flatmate Claudia was still away, and a third bedroom was vacant. Tazie had chosen to cook some Russian Christmas dishes: mushroom soup, goose baked with apples, and vzvar – dried fruit poached in honey, to which she had added a thimbleful of vodka. Adrian, especially impressed by the prospect of goose, uncorked the wine while Tazie put the roses into a vase. The kitchen table looked immaculate with a tablecloth and shiny glasses.

Their conversation ranged from impressions of China, which Tazie had visited, to images of Russia, which Adrian had not, as well as places they would like to see. Tazie talked about her job, and Adrian talked about university life.

"That was delicious, Tazie," said Adrian, swallowing his last mouthful of fruit. "I didn't know your qualities included cooking."

"I don't cook properly often," she answered, "Only on special occasions."

"So this evening's special is it?"

"Yes, there's a leisurely feeling – it's the first evening we've spent together during a holiday period."

Over coffee, sitting comfortably away from the table, with their arms around each other, Tazie ventured down a potentially hazardous path.

"Adrian," she said, "I wonder where you think we're heading? You and I together, I mean."

Adrian was taken unawares.

"Enjoying each other. It's good, us, isn't it?"

"Yes, it is. But do you think there could be more?"

Adrian was now on his guard.

"I don't know, really. I'm not saying there couldn't be, but is now the right time to think about it?" He pulled away from her. "I've got a lot of things on my mind at the moment you know."

"Oh yes, I realise that," said Tazie, taking his hand. "I just thought that now we've known each other for about three months, we could perhaps sort of see if our hopes coincide."

"Who's counting the months? What's the hurry? Tazie, frankly this is bad timing for me. Searching for my mother is my number one priority. There are all sorts of questions charging around in my head. You don't know what it's like."

"Adrian, you've become a bit fixated," replied Tazie slowly. "Yours isn't the only mixed-up family in the world. There are lots of unanswered questions in my family too, things to do with my great grandparents. For instance, my mum's grandpa was an officer in the Imperial army. Did he kill anybody? Where did his loyalties lie? Why did my grandparents come to Britain? Was there some kind of scandal they were fleeing from? Nobody ever speaks about them, and when I've tried to ask, I've been warned off."

"But at least you know your real mother and father and they're still together. My father was a villain, and my mother was irresponsible, leaving me behind when she ran away. I need to find out *now* why she did that and what she's like."

"I do realise that's different from my circumstances."

"You can say that again. The question mark over her makes me feel, well, rather insecure. Who am I? Where do my genes come from? What traits have I inherited? Will I be violent like my father or a bolter like my mother? Can I avoid being like them?" He lapsed into silence.

"Adrian you're one of the most nonviolent people I know. You don't have to be like them. You can choose."

"I hope so."

"Maybe a sort of commitment between us would help you to feel more settled, particularly while you're away in the Middle East."

"You don't get it, Tazie, do you?" said Adrian stridently, standing up and knocking over the coffee table. "I don't want anything that will complicate my life. And any kind of an understanding for the future between us would be just that sort of complication. If you're after a commitment, you'd better look for it elsewhere."

Tazie pulled the table back up, went round to pick up the coffee cups and saucers which fortunately hadn't broken, and into the kitchen for a floor cloth. As she wiped up the spilt coffee, Adrian hovered over her helplessly.

"Sorry, that was clumsy of me," he said contritely.

"It's all right," she replied quietly without looking at him, and took the cloth back into the kitchen. She returned wiping her hands on a tea-towel. They looked at each other for a moment. It was Adrian who broke the silence.

"Look," he said, "I think I'd better be off. I've not done my packing yet."

"I see," said Tazie. "Aren't you going to stay…" then stopped short.

"No I'm not," he replied quietly, turning to go to the door, "I've got to go."

"But Adrian…," said Tazie to his retreating back.

"Sorry, sorry."

She caught up with him in the doorway, where he planted a perfunctory kiss on her forehead.

"Bye, Tazie. See you when I get back."

"Bye. Have a good journey and take great care of yourself."

Adrian ran out into the street and breathed deeply. Escape.

Like his mother, said Tazie to herself acrimoniously, can't face up to things. Tazie's heart was thumping; she hated scenes (there had always been many at home), and she was bitterly disappointed by Adrian's rejection of her tentative push ahead. She recognised that he had spelled out his position. Clearly she had misjudged and mistimed her approach, but she realised that his reaction would have been the same however she had expressed herself. He was simply not ready for a solid relationship. He and she were at different stages in their lives, and this was the first time that gap had been a factor in a disagreement between them. Nevertheless, Tazie had to admit to herself that she had occasionally thought of him as juvenile.

So how did Adrian regard her? Was she just an affair, someone to be sexy with for as long as it lasted, until he moved on? How strong was his feeling for her? They had never spoken the word 'love', but Tazie felt that, as well as great sexual compatibility, there was a robust bond of affection there; Adrian had never, until now, shown any sign of feeling otherwise. And indeed, thinking about it, even now that wasn't a factor. He had looked genuinely sorry as he left, but hugely impatient too.

Tazie examined her own feelings. Yes, she thought she loved Adrian, whatever that meant, although his abrupt departure hadn't made her weep. Previous relationships had lasted only months, apart from an unhappy affair with a married man which had nearly ended in disaster. She knew she was anyway seeking stability; was she perhaps letting this desire colour her feeling for Adrian? She tried to imagine herself living with him, married or not, and found it hard, not because she could foresee disagreements, but because of his easy-going attitude to, well, almost everything, and his apparent lack of ambition. She herself was aiming for a successful career, a loving partner, a good marriage, and a family of children. And prosperity too, she realised. Adrian seemed to care nothing about any of these.

She cleared up the kitchen and went to bed where she slept fitfully. Back at the office the next morning, the previous evening's scenes interfered with her concentration. At lunch time, Adrian called her briefly from Heathrow. They spoke in polite but guarded tones.

Seventeen

31st December

Dearest Mum, Dad, Gems and Seb,

All going well here so far. As I said in my text, the journey was fine. I sat next to an attractive stylishly dressed woman who, shortly before we landed, tucked her hair under a hijab and pinned it in place. Evidently her escape was over. The views of the Med and the islands on the way were absolutely stunning as were the snow-capped mountains in the east of Lebanon. The first thing I noticed after landing was that the airport smelled different, not neutral or plastic like European airports, but exotic, scented with cigarette smoke, spices and perfumes. Of course it's warm – about 15°, which was nice after London. The airport is full of security people and well organised; my bag appeared quickly, and Hassan's cousin Khalil was holding up an A3 sheet of paper with my name on it – spelled with an 'E' on the end! He's quite a bit older than Hassan – I'd say in his late thirties or even early forties, but it's difficult to tell when you're in an unfamiliar country with physical types you've not come across much previously. He's got lots of grey hairs anyway, but who wouldn't, living in that part of the world.

We went off in a battered taxi – not to the YMCA which doesn't have sleeping accommodation here – but to a block of independent rooms which are let on a short (minimum one week) or longer term basis, mostly to students. It's called *Residence de l'Aube*. Each room has a kitchenette (just a couple of hot plates, a tiny fridge and a sink), and a bathroom. It feels quite safe as there's an inside bolt as well as a lock to the room, and an entry swipe for the main entrance. The room is tiny with a small window: apart from the bed, there's a table, a chair, and some shelves. The bathroom is old-fashioned but clean – a cracked basin pedestal, a wobbly shower and a spotless loo. The building's near the American University, in an area called Ras Beirut (don't know yet what that means) – very central so of course it's noisy but convenient for the many local schools. Perfect, and cheap. Just beside the building there's a dingy grocers selling a wonderful variety of delicious dates. The owner, who speaks some French, seems to be suggesting that I might like to marry his daughter. If she's the one behind the counter (stunted with a squint), I won't be taking him up on it!

I left my bag and then Khalil took me out to eat in a cafe close by. The choice of food there was similar to what I've had with Hassan in London. Khalil and I talked a lot over the meal. He isn't a bit like Hassan, who speaks fast and rambles on, making it difficult to follow what he's saying; Khalil's English isn't very good but he searches carefully for words and corrects his sentences as he goes along. It's easier listening to him than to Hassan. He asked me about my search for my mother and made some suggestions about schools to see and people to contact. Folks eat late in Beirut – we didn't finish until about one, so I flopped thankfully into bed and slept well.

First thing yesterday, Khalil (who's a self-employed software designer) took me on an orientation tour of Beirut on public transport – a bit confusing, but I grasped as much as I could. It helps that most street signs are in French or English as well as Arabic so I hope I'll be able to follow the map I bought in a bookshop. There are loads of books in French and English available. I'll explore that later. Beirut seems to be a very lively place, people milling around everywhere, going to work, selling things. Visually, it's modern and a bit chaotic, and of course there are plenty of bullet-pocked buildings, as you can imagine.

In the evening I started to plan out what to do first. There are several historic English language secondary schools as well as many French ones – as Lebanon used to be under French mandate – where my mother could have taught. I'll be going along to all those to see if anyone can tell me anything. By the way, the school children here all wear immaculate uniforms, the little girls with starched pinnies all round.

Today I'll phone the contact woman at the British Council and the man at the Consulate, as well as another contact mentioned by Francis Hacker at the FCO.

I keep pinching myself to make sure I'm really me, here. The place excites me. And I feel well placed to set things in motion to find Her.

I hope term starts well, Gemma and Sebastian. I'll be home soon to find out for myself.

I'm writing this on a grimy old computer in the reception area of the Residence. I've bought a token which should give me ten half-hour internet sessions. I hope it works! Please can you mail me back to confirm?

Bye and best of love to all of you

Adrian

Adrian clicked and his text disappeared. Next, he emailed Max and Benny briefly and then logged off. Back in his room, he reorganised the things on his shelves before grabbing his jacket and backpack, impatient with himself for procrastinating. Heart in his mouth, he went out for his first day without Khalil. He had insisted that he could manage.

The traffic was ferocious. Adrian consulted his map and, dodging dangerously between cars, buses, trucks and carts, headed for Hamra, where the previous day he had noticed a shiny shop selling mobiles, laptops and other electronic goods. It was next to Dolce Gabbana. He hesitated on the pavement; should he buy the mobile here or look for a cheaper place in a back street somewhere? Was he ready to start bargaining? Khalil had told him that he could bargain in most shops except the really posh ones. How did this one rate? Undecided, he turned away to walk along Hamra for a few minutes, looking into all the cafes, shops, and even venturing up the steps of one of the most opulent hotels. When stopped by a helpful doorman, he asked boldly for the coffee shop where he was shown to a deep armchair beside a low round table. Most people in there were very smartly dressed, making Adrian feel shabby. Slightly self-consciously, he ordered a Lebanese coffee and drank it slowly, as he told himself, with all the time in the world. It cost an arm and a leg; he paid in dollars left over from his gap year cash.

Outside, he retraced his steps to the phone shop. He didn't feel up to bargaining yet, nor did he think it worth trying to save money on such an important item, so he

191

would buy a reliable mobile here at whatever price was quoted. He would have liked the latest smart phone but, never a profligate spender, he knew this would be a foolish expense. The salesman, who spoke good English with a strong American accent, laid out on the counter seven medium-priced models, some made by companies unknown to Adrian. Then, naturally hoping to tempt Adrian into buying something expensive, he added a row of five prestigious brand mobiles. Adrian kept his head. When pressed, the salesman recommended a locally made mobile which offered, he said, the same high quality as the internationally known brands, at a substantially lower price. Adrian bought it, as well as a sim card with a hundred US dollars' worth of calls. Next, he looked at prices of laptops, since he had decided not to bring his from England for fear of theft; there was too much of importance on it. With foresight, he had also created a new email address specifically for this trip and any future trips to Lebanon. After a few minutes, the salesman excused himself to take care of another customer, leaving Adrian looking at the laptops. He left, deciding he needed Khalil's advice.

Returning to his room, he pulled out his list of phone numbers. Anticipating a negative or at least neutral reception from the British Council, he began by calling Jean Stavropoulos there. At first, she didn't recognise his name, which wasn't surprising, so he explained. As he did so, she interspersed his words with little recognition noises, "Oh yes", "Ah", "Indeed", "Monty told me", and when he had finished, she bubbled over with sympathy and apologies for not remembering his circumstances. She told him that she had enlisted the help of a diplomat's son called Mark, who was on a gap year and had nothing much to do.

He had gone through about half the data on computer, but had not so far come across a reference to anybody called Patti. There was a record of a British woman called Mrs P Hajjar which Mark had researched, since it was possible that Adrian's mother had married a Lebanese, but Mrs Hajjar's first name had turned out to be Prudence. Jean suggested that they could get together with Mark, preferably after work, to talk things through and see what was what. They made a tentative appointment for the following week, to be confirmed later. As Adrian was thanking her, ready for the call to end, suddenly Jean interrupted him to say:

"Look, its New Year's Eve, and I bet you've got nowhere to go! There's a party on at Glyn Morgan's tonight. Would you like to come?"

"Being here, I'd forgotten that the day existed. And I..."

Jean bubbled in again. "You needn't worry about not knowing Glyn or anybody else. They're very hospitable, are Trisha and Glyn, and there are always hangers-on at these parties, businessmen on their way somewhere, Foreign Office people, students. And Mark will be there, and I expect you were planning to call on Glyn anyway. Do come! It'll be fun."

"You make it sound very attractive. I..."

"Where are you staying, Adrian? May I call you Adrian, and you can call me Jean?"

"With pleasure. And I'm staying at the Residence de l'Aube."

"That's settled then. I'll square it right away with Glyn and come to fetch you at 9.00pm. I've got an orange Beetle. Be outside, but don't be outside early. It wouldn't be good for you to hang around on your own. And by the way, it's a masked party, so I'll get one for you. Any preferences?"

"Gosh, it's very kind of you. Perhaps an animal face would be nice?"

"I'll see what I can do. Perhaps a wolf?" Jean giggled. "Bye, see you later."

"Bye."

Excited but tired, Adrian moved over to the bed, where he immediately dropped off to sleep. He woke with a start some twenty minutes later, rubbed his eyes then looked round at the walls wondering where he was. Piecing himself together, he realised he was hungry; he had forgotten to buy anything to eat and now it was 2.15pm. Better brave the grocer and his daughter again. On the counter was a metal dish containing a pile of aromatic falafels. The grocer explained that his wife had just made them, so Adrian bought four, a jar of instant coffee, a tub of powdered milk, two mangoes, and a packet of sweet biscuits. Fortunately the daughter was nowhere in sight. Back in the Residence, he took out a bottle of mineral water from the slot dispenser in the lobby. The falafels were delicious and the mangoes ripe, although he ate only one, and a couple of biscuits.

Next was a call to Glyn Morgan at the Consular Section; he was in a meeting and therefore unavailable. It was easier that way: Adrian didn't need to explain that he would be at Glyn's home that evening; instead he left a message and his mobile number. He also called Khalil who was pleased that Adrian was now reachable, and suggested eating together later in a trendy American-type diner in Hamra. Adrian explained what had happened, hoping that Khalil was glad to be let off the hook. They agreed the

American diner would be for another night. Khalil didn't sound put out.

Jean was as good as her word. Promptly at nine a Beetle drove up on to the kerb. A small chubby young woman, with masses of blonde curly hair framing a round face, got out of the driver's seat. She looked shorter than 5ft to Adrian.

"Welcome to Beirut," she said, pulling his head down to deposit three neat kisses on his cheeks. "We kiss three times here, like in France. But don't do it to people you don't know."

"But you don't know me," exclaimed Adrian laughing, the imprint of soft round lips still on his cheeks as they held arms.

"Well I will soon! Come on get in, Beanpole's in the back."

Adrian and Mark shook hands.

"You can't see at the moment," said Jean, "but Mark is well over six feet tall, and very thin, hence the name I've given him." As she drove along, weaving a path deftly through a cluster of would-be formula one drivers, swearing at them as she went, Mark produced three masks: Adrian's was a lion's head, Jean's a flying helmet with goggles, and his own a head bandage.

"We'll put on the masks in the lobby. The general idea is to be unrecognisable."

"But you'll introduce me to Glyn and Trisha, won't you?"

"Oh yes. As they're the hosts they will know everybody – security, you see. The caretaker of the block will have a list too. There are all sorts of safety checks in place here. You'll get used to it. Glyn's mask is the same

195

each year, recognisable. It's Venetian – a white plague doctor's mask."

The flat was on the second floor of a medium-sized block at the top of an incline, where a rough access track ended on the edge of a building site – or bomb site – Adrian wondered which. Jean managed to find a space in which to squeeze her car, beside a pile of rubble over which Adrian had to scramble to reach the track. Lower down, a few corrugated roofs were visible in the faint moonlight and further on, the sea. Lights from dark blobs of ships winked into the ripples of the water where they flashed momentarily and disappeared. Adrian stood on the track staring for a minute, contemplating the scene, the enormity of the Middle East problem, and the size of his own quest by comparison. Jean and Mark came to stand beside him, wordlessly. After a while, Jean tapped his arm.

"Adrian," she said gently. "Don't worry, if she's here, we'll find her."

The sympathy brought tears to Adrian's eyes. They turned to walk back across the track, and into a square marble hall. At the caretaker's desk, they were signed in. They then donned their masks, and went up in the lift discussing how to pour drinks into their mouths. There were already some one hundred people in the vast open plan living area of the flat - at least that was how it looked to Adrian. Jean led him by the hand to meet Glyn, a big man with a booming Welsh voice and extremely long arms.

"Ah, the mum-seeking lion!" he said jovially, after welcoming Jean with three noisy kisses, and shaking Adrian's hand. "Welcome to my madhouse. A drink first, and then you must meet my wife Trisha, she's somewhere around. Are you settled into a room somewhere? Good,

good. Ah, there she is. Trisha! Trisha!" He beckoned expansively to a small thin woman wearing a white cat mask with escaping strands of jet black hair, who was talking to four unmasked Arab men in well-tailored suits, one of whom turned to stare at Adrian. A waiter appeared with a tray of drinks.

"Champagne all right for you? Good." Without waiting for Adrian's reply, Glyn handed him a glass just as Trisha joined them. Jean moved away.

"Darling, come and meet this lion, alias Adrian Goodfield! He's here on a search mission, looking for a lioness."

"How interesting!" she said. "What kind of a lioness?"

"Actually, my mother. And I don't know if she's a lioness or not because I've never seen her. She left when I was a baby."

Trisha was unfazed by Adrian's abrupt words. With persistent questioning, she prised the short version of his position out of a reluctant Adrian who wasn't in the mood for confidences. When he was done, Trisha plied him with sketches of all the relation seekers she had ever known, none of whose circumstances resembled his in the very least. Jean came to rescue him; there were some students studying languages who would like to meet him.

"She's ok really," said Jean as they sidled away. "Not very tactful but a good sort. She's does get up people's noses though sometimes."

"Jean," said Adrian quietly, "see that unmasked Arab man over there? Do you know him? He was talking to Trisha earlier, now he keeps looking and smiling at me. Why I wonder?" Jean glanced across in the direction of Adrian's nod.

"Oh that's Hameed el Saad, a close relation of the Minister of Transport of Sharjah. He likes boys and springs into action on occasions such as this. He's a devout Muslim, so his wives can't come to parties, nor can the wives of the other chaps with him. The others don't like boys though, they just home in on the girls. I keep out of their way. They like my shape while I don't! That's life."

"But he can't see what I'm like."

"That doesn't matter to him – a new body is a new body."

"So he got married all the same?"

"Yes, I think he's got three wives. Arab men have to get married. I suppose he's bisexual, but I don't want to know. Steer clear, that's my advice."

"I certainly will."

The two students were third year European linguistics people from York who were staying with a Lebanese fellow student for ten days. As they were talking, Adrian suddenly thought of Max and Benny, and wished they were there too. And Tazie. Since the evening he had spent with her, Adrian had tried to avoid thinking of his knee-jerk reaction. He had behaved badly, he knew, but his negative response to her approach was a true one: he wasn't ready for a serious relationship. Their phone conversation the next day had done nothing to improve things. He must email her next time he went on the computer.

Soon he withdrew politely from the language group. Attracted by a large expanse of deep indigo sky visible through sliding doors, he edged his way through the crowd until he was looking out on to a wide terrace. He shuddered, suddenly aware, for the first time, of the potential danger of living there, and wondered what aspects of Beirut would compensate for that. A waiter tapped him on the shoulder, took his empty glass from his hand and substituted a full one for it. Adrian turned back to contemplate the great expanse of sea. After a moment, he felt a presence behind him and turned to find the Arab pederast there, smiling. A hand was proffered, which Adrian felt obliged to shake. The soft fingers caressed his.

"I am Hameed el Saad. I am from Sharjah. I assume you are a British lion?"

Adrian nodded. Hameed continued.

"I had the privilege of graduating from your very prestigious military academy, Sandhurst. Now I work in defence business. What is your name, please?"

"I'm Adrian Goodfield," said Adrian lamely. He was cornered.

"It's a very great pleasure to meet you. Do you stay here in Lebanon? I would like to show you around."

"I'm only here for a few days. I'll be going back to England just as soon as I've accomplished what I set out to do," replied Adrian primly.

"And that is…?"

Adrian kicked himself.

"I have a small family matter to sort out."

"Perhaps I can help you?"

Decidedly, this man is persistent, thought Adrian.

"Thank you, but I don't think you can."

"Where are you staying?"

Avoid this one.

"With a friend, in a flat."

"And where is that?"

Must get him to push off.

"To tell you the truth, I don't know. I've only just arrived. We came almost straight from the airport."

Hameed stretched up haughtily.

"I think you don't want my hospitality, then."

"It's very kind of you. But everything's been organised for my short stay."

Hameed took a visiting card out of an inside pocket of his suit.

"This is my card, in case you change your mind. I could show you plenty of exciting places in Beirut."

I'm sure you could, thought Adrian as he watched the man stroll away, his back displaying huff.

As Adrian made his way around the room looking for Jean, a crisp voice suddenly said in his ear:

"What were you doing talking to that creepy customer?"

Adrian swung round to find himself face to face with Gene Kelly. White socks, loafers, short-sleeved shirt, and a very accurate mask.

"He cornered me."

"Well you're all right as long as it isn't a private corner in a quiet room with a bed in it."

"So I gather."

"So you're Adrian."

"Yes, how did you know?"

"I guessed."

"You mean Jean or Mark told you. Or Glyn or Trisha; these are the only people I know, so it must have been one of them."

"Well, as a matter of fact, it wasn't. Anyway, come and see me in three days' time."

"I might like to do that if I knew who you were and where to go."

"You'll find out all in good time."

And with that he was gone, slipping away through a group of women talking about holidays in the Caribbean. What was all that about, Adrian wondered fuzzily, emptying his glass. He was rather thirsty.

Just before midnight, Glyn banged a large gong hanging on a chain beside the door to the flat, and demanded silence. He bade everybody welcome and invited his guests to remove their masks and disguises on the final stroke of midnight. Then he switched on a local radio station for the chimes. At the stroke of midnight, the sky lit up over the sea revealing clear outlines of ships, whilst the air exploded and windows rattled. There was much clapping, shouting and kissing as masks were removed. Adrian, startled by the noise and hoping that war hadn't broken out, found himself in the comforting clutches of an elderly sari-clad woman. A second bang on the gong demanded silence again, this time, said Glyn, for the loyal toast, to be followed by Auld Lang Syne. Lubricated voices sang out lustily while a few non-British guests looked on, puzzled by the linked arms going up and down. Adrian noticed the Arab pederast standing aloof outside the circles. There was more hugging and kissing when the singing stopped.

Mark appeared. "You got nobbled by that man," he said.

"Which one?"

"The gay Arab."

"Yes, nasty piece of work. Jean told me."

"I should've rescued you, but I didn't want him to recognise me – he tried his charm out on me a few weeks ago and I was quite rude to him."

"'He wanted to know where I was staying."

"I bet he did. You didn't tell him, did you?"

"No way."

"Good. Now come and meet my Pa and Ma. They've just arrived from dinner with the Ambassador."

Dr. and Mrs Arnott were on the far side of the room, a small dapper man with a moustache and a taller, broader woman. Mark introduced his father as the 'political guru' at the Embassy. Mark was more like his mother in stature, but his long thin nose, narrow mouth, and bright deep set eyes were his father's. Dr. Arnott issued Adrian an open invitation to join them for a meal, echoed by Mrs Arnott, who sought to reassure Adrian by remarking that she did ordinary English home cooking.

The rest of Adrian's evening was a blur. He remembered trying to find Gene Kelly's feet, and that someone asked if he always looked at people's shoes at parties. His incoherent description of the problem to Mark, Jean and the York students provoked plenty of hilarity when he said, stubbornly, that he was looking for Gene.

Sometime between midnight and 6.00am – Adrian could not say when – Jean and Mark woke him from a deep sleep in a comfortable armchair. It was a good thing, Mark said, that slimy Hameed el Whatsit had left, otherwise who knows what might have happened to Adrian.

"Funny thing," said Adrian, as his new chums helped him into Jean's car, "my legs don't seem to be working." At the Residence, Jean found his entry swipe and key in his jacket and despatched Mark with him up to his room, gazing anxiously around herself whilst waiting in her car on the kerb.

"He's fun, isn't he?" said Jean as Mark shut the car door.

"Yes," said Mark, "He's all right. I hope we can help him."

Eighteen

Every year, Toby divided half of his bonus into equal portions to give to the staff reporting directly to him. He paid out the sums by personal cheque in the run up to New Year's Eve. His habit was to see each member of staff separately, in order to offer personal thanks. Toby never announced in advance his intention to share his bonus. However, when a member of staff was called in and the door closed, a ripple of hope would run through the office until the person emerged; he or she was expected to give a thumbs up if the cheque had been offered.

This time, Toby wanted to get sessions with two members of his team out of the way first; their work had not been up to scratch, and he knew he should say so now, giving them a chance to improve in time for the formal assessment at the end of the financial year. He hated such confrontations, but had never excluded anybody from the handout except once, when the person was leaving under a cloud. So he dealt with the two difficult interviews first and then called the others in one by one, leaving Tazie until the last on New Year's Eve so as to be able to end his conversations on a cheerful note. As this was her first year reporting to Toby, she was unaware of his generous annual gesture, but couldn't help noticing the thumbs up and a feeling of complicity among her colleagues.

At last her turn came. Toby explained that she and her colleagues were receiving a share of his bonus, and that he was satisfied with her adaptation to the work in his section. Handing the envelope over, he complimented her on being perspicacious, hard-working and accurate, i.e. someone with a good future ahead. Blushing, Tazie thanked him for his confidence in her and assured him that she was enjoying the job.

"Well, despite that, I absolutely forbid you to come in tomorrow," said Toby. "Such devotion shouldn't stretch to New Year's Day. Besides, don't forget you'd have to go to the trouble of getting special access to the building; you know I'm sure, about the alarm which prevents even key-holders from entering between midnight and six a.m. every day, and all day on public holidays. The caretaker goes round to make sure that all the offices and wash rooms are empty before he sets it."

"I accept your prohibition with relief. I wasn't thinking of coming in anyway, although I can feel the end of the financial year creeping steadily towards me. So you're not coming in either."

"No, my parents keep telling me to take time off, and although I could ask to be let in, I've got lots of neglected things piling up at home: on my desk, on my draining board, in my linen bag, not to mention the relations' names on the list beside the phone."

"Yes, that's another thing – phoning all and sundry to wish them a happy New Year. That takes time. Sometimes I think it would be nice just to forget about all of them and go out for the day, to the races in Cheltenham, or greyhound racing, or orienteering, or a fabulous tea at Fortnum and Mason, or a New Year concert, but I usually end up just trailing round the flat picking things up and putting them down again, accomplishing nothing."

"Well I know which activity I would choose from your list."

"I've got it Toby, the dogs!"

"Funny you should say that. My dad used to go to Perry Barr Stadium every Saturday night – it drove my mum crazy. She said betting on dogs was a waste of money, which of course it was. When I was about fifteen, he started taking me along with him – to make a man of me, he said; I hated it on my mum's behalf, and I've loathed the idea ever since." He paused, thoughtfully. "Which activity would you like best?"

"Something sedate and civilised. Tea, I think."

Toby got up and started pacing round the room.

"Well there's a thought – tea out, with tiny scrumptious sandwiches and scones! What a good idea! My parents took me for tea at the Ritz when I got into university. I was overawed by the whole occasion, as they were too. All that delicately prepared food. I say, Tazie…" he tailed off.

"What?"

"Why don't we meet for tea tomorrow? I hereby invite you to the Ritz. It will be an incentive to get all the jobs done in time to go out."

Tazie was surprised that Toby had taken her literally. She didn't answer immediately. Toby stood alongside her with his hand on the back of her chair, looking down at her, then said:

"What about it? Don't you like the idea?"

"I like it very much, and I must confess that when I mentioned Fortnum's just now, I had the same thought as you."

"Good. Hang on a minute while I try to book it."

The website told him that tea was fully booked for tomorrow. Feeling it was worth trying by phone, he called. An odd conversation ensued.

"It sounds as though they're allocating us a table that was cancelled just a moment ago; easier to give it to us than to pull out their waiting list. Perhaps we're in luck. If not, it may have to be McDonalds. 3.30pm in the Palm Court."

Tazie went home smiling to herself. After eating a meal composed of what she could find in the fridge and freezer – fish fingers, fried eggs and warmed up broccoli – she switched on her computer to see if there were a message from Adrian, but there was nothing. She wasn't surprised, for he had made his position clear, but she was sad, wondering whether he intended her to interpret his hasty departure that evening as his final exit.

The next morning she set about home jobs, which bored her enormously, especially since she was fussy about every little detail: no dust in the corners, no creases in the ironed shirts. Everything had to be done properly. After she had finished and made some of the required phone calls, she sat down with a cup of coffee to think about the new year. She made no resolutions, but wanted, rather, to sketch out her expectations of herself, and to guess at the possible impact her potential achievements might have. Adrian was immediately back in her mind. She now knew what she couldn't hope for from him: a commitment. So did he expect their relationship to continue, when he returned from the Middle East, in just the same way? If he had found his mother, would that influence the way he regarded the people close to him, his step-parents, Gemma, Sebastian, Max, and herself? If he didn't find his mother, how would he be feeling? It was impossible to predict, and pointless to think about it. Better to plan improving her knowledge of the tools of her trade, and to contemplate her possible advancement. She intended to push forward, learning new techniques, and staying on an even keel with her colleagues, despite the usual office peccadillos.

It was time to get ready to go out; she should look classy for the Ritz. She chose a deep red cashmere dress with a dark coat, black hat, boots and bag. She left home in good time, but an accident south of the river caused a build-up of traffic in the whole area. Tazie contained her frustration, knowing she would be late and hoping Toby wouldn't give up on her. Worse, she didn't have his mobile number. She ran up the steps and into the lobby of the Ritz at twenty to four; Toby was waiting for her by the revolving doors. Before she could apologise he said, with a naughty smile, "Take your gloves off. I'm sure kissing your hand is *de rigueur* here."

Tazie obeyed, and Toby performed. He brushed aside her abject apologies, saying that foolishly, they hadn't exchanged mobile numbers, and that they should do so as soon as they sat down. Their coats were taken from them and they were led up three steps and through an archway to their table near the centre of the Palm Court. Gleaming silver cutlery and fine china plates proudly displaying the Ritz crest shone up at them, fit for film stars. Toby caught Tazie's eye and they both laughed.

"Great to see you, Greta!" said Toby, as Tazie's chair was pulled back and pushed in under her.

"Kind of you to invite me, Clark!" she replied as he sat down.

They both chuckled. The crisp, starched waiter standing by had evidently heard it all before, and didn't react. While Toby ordered Darjeeling with the Traditional Afternoon Tea, Tazie looked around herself. The drapes (surely these were not curtains), the napery (not a tablecloth in sight), and the napkins (definitely not serviettes) radiated opulence, while the light, glittering brightly down on them from crystal chandeliers and reflected back on mirrored wall panels, enhanced the splendour of the scene.

At the table next to them, there was a party of noisy Russians – three adults and five children; the adults talked amongst themselves while two small boys, dressed in identical midnight blue velvet waistcoats, tucked in hungrily to everything they could reach. Meanwhile two little girls showed off their frilly party frocks and knickers by doing pirouettes all round the table, watched by an elderly couple at an adjacent table, frowning and muttering. The fifth child, a baby girl on a highchair, wailed fruitlessly from time to time in an effort to attract somebody's attention.

Many of the patrons were over sixty, Tazie thought.

Toby leaned across the table to remark, in a low voice,

"The clientele here spells wealth."

"Yes, almost everybody is of an age and well-heeled," she replied, equally quietly. "This is one of the most expensive hotels in London. I thought that when I came once before," Tazie paused as she noticed Toby's raised eyebrows, "but it was only to collect my Pa from a business meeting. I was eighteen and had just passed my driving test. I had to wait over half an hour for him in the entrance and when he appeared he was in a hurry so didn't offer me a drink, or tea, or anything."

"Poor Tazie!" Toby sat back.

"I can't remember where I parked" she continued, "but I do remember going to fetch the car after he had appeared, and getting lost in the one-way systems."

"I don't like driving," remarked Toby. "I passed a driving test, but I haven't got a car. You can't tell how long it's going to take from A to B, so you have to leave awfully early not to be late."

"Thank you!" said Tazie archly with a small smile.

"I didn't mean to take a dig at you," said Toby, laughing. "Besides, you were on a bus, and you're not the late type."

"Oh and how can you tell?"

"If you were the late type, you'd be one of the last to arrive at work in the morning, but in fact you're one of the first."

Tazie was silenced.

"Talking of which…" continued Toby. He took his mobile out of his pocket. "Before we forget, mobile numbers." As they keyed in the numbers, Tazie wondered fleetingly how Toby's wish for future outings might fit in with her plans. She was distracted as strains of *A Nightingale Sang in Berkeley Square* wafted up from the piano a few steps below the Palm Court. The choice of music was in perfect harmony with the decor, redolent of a past era, sentimental yet tasteful. A waiter with a trolley arrived to unload on to their table a pot of tea, a milk jug, a sugar basin, and a silver cake stand bearing tiny sandwiches. The waiter explained that scones and cakes would come when they were ready. Toby decided he would pour the tea rather than let the waiter or Tazie do it.

They were hungry, both confessing to having saved up their appetites for tea. Toby was a considerate host, ensuring that Tazie had everything she wanted at each stage of their meal. He asked her about herself, never indiscreetly, having apparently no wish to know about her emotional life or past relationships. He turned out also to have a quirky sense of humour, recounting stories of language misuse, misshapen events, and celebrations which went harmlessly wrong. Toby felt at ease with Tazie, not inhibited by her or anxious about his usual chronic shyness. Nor did he need to worry about whether his humour was to her taste; he soon discovered that she was alongside him, responding quickly to even his most obscure jokes and appreciating the import of his stories. Just as a second cake stand with several types of scones, butter, cream and jam arrived, they discovered a common interest in the cinema; Toby was knowledgeable about early films and the first 'talkies'. Tazie's father was a Russian film enthusiast, and she had made this interest her own.

An enjoyable hour into their tea, the conversation moved on from Tazie's father to a conversation about families, starting with amusing circumstances and peculiar remarks that parents and siblings were apt to make. Toby laughed about his mother's nagging, directed sometimes at his father, and sometimes at himself. They always fell in with her wishes, if possible, to stem the flow of advice.

"What does she nag you about?" asked Tazie.

"Oh, mostly about looking after my health and not overworking."

"Were you a sickly child?"

"No, not that." Toby was silent for a moment, looking at the tablecloth.

Tazie observed his sudden sombre expression. Intuition prompted her next remark.

"Toby," she said gently, "you can tell me if you like, but don't if you don't want to."

He looked up at her and made a snap decision.

"I'll give you the short version. I'm not a hundred percent healthy and probably never will be. My mum's right, I have to watch it. And I'm an only child which makes it worse for my parents."

"Poor you. I can't imagine what that would be like. A sort of shadow following you, I suppose." She paused, in case Toby wanted to add something, but he just nodded. "I won't ask you any more," she continued. "If ever you need any help, I'm there."

"Thank you for that. I hope I never will need you."

His face relaxed and he smiled at her, the most benign smile Tazie had ever seen.

"You look pretty healthy to me," he said after a moment.

"Yes, I am. But like you, I have a few family problems."

"Want to tell me?"

"There's nothing much to tell except constant squabbling, mostly between my father and my brother Max and sometimes between my mother and me. It's often about money and I hate that, especially since we're not short of it. My insides curl up in embarrassment when these arguments happen."

"I sympathise. Are there just the two of you?"

"Yes. We had a sister but she died." Tazie stopped talking and swallowed. Toby watched her. After a moment, she was able to speak again.

"Max is younger than me; he's a first-year university student. But he wants to marry his girlfriend soon, because he'll get a substantial legacy from a great-uncle when he does so, and will be able to buy his own home. My parents don't want him to; they say it's too early altogether and that he should get settled into work before tying himself down. His fiancé is also a student – a girl from a posh family. She's ok but I don't have anything in common with her; we're not on the same wavelength."

"Well, there's nothing unusual about our circumstances, yours or mine."

Their conversation turned to Christmas, the relations they had seen and even the presents they had received, allowing plenty of scope for mirth. Eventually when they had gone through the cake stage and eaten as much as they wanted, Toby looked at his watch.

"Goodness, it's seven already. No wonder they're laying up the tables again. It's time to go home, isn't it?"

"Yes, it is."

Toby jumped up to deal with the bill. In the entrance hall, when they had donned their outdoor wear, Toby put his hand under Tazie's arm and turned her to face him.

"I've enjoyed myself enormously. I hope you have too," he said seriously. "And there are plenty more stories to tell. Can we do this again? A film perhaps? Lunch, or even dinner?"

"I don't see why not," answered Tazie thoughtfully.

It had started to snow. Toby offered to see her home; when Tazie refused, he took hold of her arm firmly to prevent her from slipping on the icy pavement as they made their way to her bus stop. There, despite her insistence that he should go straight down into the tube, he waited until she was safely sitting on the bus. On the way home, he wondered if he should have kissed her goodbye.

Nineteen

Adrian was woken by the trilling of his mobile. He reached to the floor beside the bed where he usually left it at night, but it wasn't there. Cranking himself up into sitting position, he looked around the room, bewildered. Where was he? Ah yes, Beirut. Phone may be in jacket pocket. The trilling stopped. "Shit," he said, aloud. Never mind, the person will call back. He pushed his legs sideways from under the covers and gingerly tried out his feet on the floor. Swaying, he accomplished the two steps to his jacket, fumbled for the mobile and, hand clasped firmly round it, returned to bed to nurse his sore head. The mobile trilled again.

"Hullo," croaked Adrian.

"Adrian, I'm Khalil. Did I wake you?"

"Yes, you did. What time is it?"

"Twelve and thirty."

"Crikey. I'd better get up."

"You had a good time last night and you were late home?"

"Yes, to both your questions. I'll tell you about it when we meet."

"How about the Burger Hall tonight?"

"Good idea."

"I pick you up at the Residence at eight?"

"Great. See you. And the meal's on me."

Adrian made himself a coffee. Some minutes later, remembering it was 1st January, he got dressed and went down to the computer to write some New Year's greetings. Max, Benny and the family were easy: he wrote about the helpful British Council people, Khalil and Mukhtar, the party at Glyn Morgan's flat, and his search for schools where his mother might have worked. Tazie was more difficult. Adrian would have liked to apologise for rushing out on her, but this would raise the inevitable question as to whether he regretted having done so, and the answer was that he did not. He was sorry for hurting her, but the thought of going down an extending path towards a closer connection had the effect of rooting his feet to the ground. After several botched tries, he wrote that he had arrived safely, had met some kind and relevant people, and was searching out schools where his mother might have taught. He wished her a very happy and successful New Year and was looking forward to seeing her again soon. Despite his behaviour, this was true.

Khalil was late collecting him. Waiting apprehensively on the pavement outside the Residence in the dark, Adrian wondered what he should do if Khalil didn't turn up. Keep calm, he said to himself, as Beirut tension attacked his nerves. Cars cruised past, jumbled into traffic jams, pulled up on to the kerb to collect or let out passengers, horns blared, people shouted, and a couple of men in uniform strolled past Adrian, turning their heads to stare at him, then continued on their way, talking. It all made him feel dizzy. Finally at ten past eight, a rambling old Renault pulled up and Khalil jumped out. He opened the back door and pushed Adrian in, then got in quickly beside the driver.

"You must not wait outside, if I'm late." He sounded angry.

"Sorry," said Adrian.

"The traffic is awful because New Year holiday, and Saturday." After a hurried conversation in Arabic with the driver, Khalil turned to Adrian.

"This is my cousin. His name is Mukhtar. He works some time as taxi driver. He says I give you his cell phone number so you can call him when you need him."

"That's very kind. But does he understand English?"

"No, you just say, Adrian Residence, and he will come." Another quick burst of Arabic and Adrian was invited to say the two words several times. Mukhtar himself had a try too, and they all laughed.

"Khalil," said Adrian. "What if I'm not at the Residence?"

"Then you say slowly Adrian, Adrian and the name of the place where you are. You have to try to pronounce it in Arabic."

"OK then."

They had some tries at that too.

A few bursts of speed interspersed with screeching brakes brought them to the Burger Hall. They had to wait several minutes for a table in the vast brightly lit space, which was divided into sections with brass rails. Once they were sitting down and had ordered burgers, chips, and beer, Khalil explained to Adrian that it could be dangerous to stand alone on the street at night. Hostage-takers could appear from nowhere, and while Beirut residents had special ears for listening and watching, newly arrived people were unaware and could be targeted.

"You stay inside to wait. If I don't come in fifteen minutes you try to call me. If no reply, you go back to your room to wait for my call."

"I understand," said Adrian.

"It's different for us Lebanese people. We have I think you call, is it 'sick smell'?"

"You mean sixth sense," said Adrian, trying not to laugh.

"Why, six scents?"

Adrian explained, and spelled out the words which Khalil penned promptly in a notebook he took from his hip pocket.

"Adrian, 'the meal's on me', what does it mean?" was Khalil's next question.

"It means that I'm paying, it's my invitation."

"Ah," said Khalil. "Then thank you for this evening."

"It's a pleasure, it's to wish you a happy New Year and to thank you for helping me."

Khalil held out his hand to shake Adrian's across the table then entered that expression in the vocab book.

"While I remember," said Adrian as they sat down, "there's another useful expression for you to learn. It's 'Going Dutch' which means that each person pays for him or herself."

That got entered too.

"It's good for me to be with you. I improve my English."

"I'll think up some more useful expressions for you to learn."

Two Almaza lagers arrived quickly, followed soon by sizzling hot chips and steaming burgers, with various sauces in small bowls. Having had nothing but an apple to eat since the previous evening, Adrian was ravenous. As they munched, at Khalil's request Adrian described the party, the people, the food, the drinks, the toasts, and Auld Lang Syne. Khalil said that he had never attended such a New Year's celebration in the private residence of a foreigner; his family was a traditional one, gathering together often with relations and friends, many of whom lived close by. They would eat, drink, dance, share a narghile (a water-cooled pipe), and exchange gossip.

"We are not so many now – many have left for safer places – grandparents, uncles and aunties, young people too. Some dead in the war, two murdered for political reasons, and others just missing." His speech became staccato.

Adrian was shocked. Although by now alive to the potential for trouble, he had not considered the impact of the Lebanese conflict on folks he knew. It had all seemed distant, words in a newspaper column, pictures on television, sorrow in general, but removed from people you could speak to and touch. He confessed that he had never asked Hassan about his family and regretted not having done so. Khalil simply nodded. They were silent for some moments.

"Adrian," Khalil asked eventually, "why you don't know where your mother is? Why you look for her here?"

Adrian didn't answer immediately, contemplating how to make the story short and comprehensible.

"Sorry," continued Khalil, "maybe it is private, maybe you don't want to tell?"

Adrian reassured Khalil, and recounted a short version of his circumstances.

"So I live with my father's second wife," he concluded, "we call her a 'step-mother' in English, and her husband, and their two children who are not blood relations to me. I call them my parents and my sister and brother."

"And you're not happy with your not real family?"

"On the contrary, I'm extremely happy with them. They treat me just the way they would if we were blood relations. They are lovely people and my little sister and brother are great too."

"OK, so why you look for your mother now?"

Adrian continued the next bit of his story, explaining about his parents' decision that it was the right time to tell him what they knew about his biological mother.

"At first I wasn't at all interested – I was happy with my situation. But I did listen to what they told me, and I began to get curious about her, where she was, what she was like, whether she was interested in me, and why she had abandoned me. All my parents knew was that she had gone to Lebanon to teach, and there was an address here. I started to look for her, and put a notice up on the internet and in the newspapers, but all in vain. That's why I had to come here. I wrote a letter to the address my parents had given me, but had no reply. She's anyway probably not Mrs Sandling any longer; she'll be Mrs somebody else by now."

"Show me the address."

Adrian took his diary from his inside jacket pocket and passed it to Khalil, open at the relevant page. He read out the English transliteration of the address then switched it into Arabic before saying:

"This place is in West Beirut, in the part where Saudis live. I will go to see it for you and ask if there is any Western woman there."

"Who will you ask?"

"The man at the entrance of the building, working."

"Ah. He's called the caretaker in English." Khalil scribbled again.

"Good good. But so long ago, your mother could be anywhere in the Middle East?"

"Yes, but I have to begin my search in the place where she started. I feel quite positive. People have been very kind – especially Hassan who was very encouraging."

"My cousin is a good person and a good student."

"Khalil, if Mukhtar is your cousin, then is he Hassan's cousin too?"

"Possible, but he not. A different sort of cousin." He lowered his voice. "I can tell you. It's like your parents and you. Mukhtar isn't the same blood. He is the son of neighbours who disappeared, long time ago, probably murdered. Most of his family were in America so he had nobody. My parents took him in quite young. So we call him our cousin, but it is difficult."

"Why?"

"Because Shiite (includes Hezbollah) don't like Sunnis – Mukhtar is Sunni."

"And you are Shiite?"

"Yes, we are," answered Khalil with a trace of pride, not lost on Adrian, "not so dangerous now, but could become dangerous."

"Khalil, my danger here," Adrian asked quietly, "the danger to me, is it from Hezbollah?"

Khalil answered quickly. "Probably not. There are many aggressive groups with different targets because of maybe religion, or history, or politics, or family connections. For instance, in our parliament, there are 64

221

Christian seats and 64 Muslims seats. Christian includes Maronite, (our President is always a Maronite), Greek Orthodox and Catholic, Armenian, and Protestant, as well as some others. The main Muslim groups are Sunni and Shia (the Prime Minister is always Sunni, and the Speaker of Parliament, Shiite), and there are Alawites and Druze. Seats are given by religion to each region. So there is many basis for conflict, especially as Lebanon is now occupied by at least 20,000 Syrian troops. Foreigners often think that trouble is caused by Hezbollah, but that is not often the case. Trouble can be Syrian."

"I read a bit about the Syrian occupation," said Adrian, "and about the South Lebanon Army. It's all very complicated and difficult, isn't it?"

"Yes," was all that Khalil could answer.

After a moment, Adrian stood up.

"Empty glass, another beer?"

"Yes. You have one also?"

"Yes. It's bribery for a favour I want to ask of you."

When he returned, he explained that he intended to buy a laptop so that he could be on the internet as and when he wanted, instead of using the one in the Residence. He needed Khalil's help to be sure he wasn't swindled. Khalil agreed readily; he knew where to find a good reconditioned laptop. He was busy but could manage it in a couple of days.

When their beers were finished, Adrian paid the bill and Khalil walked him back to the Residence to teach him the route and to show him how to be vigilant.

***

Adrian's optimistic nature failed him in the succeeding days. The Residence computer was a serious challenge: not only was it slow, but the screen frequently went blank, coming alive again a few moments later, sometimes opening at the page he had been using, at others times at a completely unrelated page. He had checked, without much hope, all the connections, but nothing was loose. For his first task, searching schools and listing the likely ones with their addresses and phone numbers, a reliable computer was essential.

Adrian struggled on throughout Sunday morning, trying to save his notes on to a memory stick, but to no avail. Eventually he went out with his map. Sticking to the main streets where he felt safe, he walked briskly towards the sea, where a stiff breeze was whisking up froth, bobbing the small fishing boats around. His map told him that this was the Corniche. In the bright sunshine, people of all ages were jogging, while young boys climbed over the railings to perch on the slippery rocks above the sea. Youths leaned nonchalantly on their parked cars, ogling the women and smoking. Sellers pushed carts laden with cooked sweetcorn on sticks, or fresh vegetables, or soft drinks. A copious snack was being enjoyed by a family group; they were seated in a circle on small brightly coloured plastic stools. The place could have been idyllic.

But it wasn't. There were security check points along the seafront manned by Syrians, as Khalil later revealed. The trunks of the lofty palm trees were spattered with bullet holes. At the Golfe de Saint-Georges, the pink shell of the iconic hotel stood out like a sore thumb against the turquoise of the sea. Along one stretch of about 50 metres, smashed remains of concrete benches scarred the

223

pavement. Further away, wide holes full of rubble were all that remained of them. Adrian returned despondently to the Residence.

The next morning, he called Jean who said it was all right for him to come to the British Council. Through Security, she led him to the reading room where she installed him at a table with a pile of files, explaining as she laid them out, how personnel records were classified at the time and where he might find staff lists. Mark arrived soon to help, and at lunch time Jean joined them, bringing sandwiches. Looking through the records was tedious and unrewarding. Adrian grew downcast, feeling that his days were slipping away as time hurtled towards Sunday 9th January and his plane home. Worse, Khalil called to say that the caretaker of the building where his mother had lived knew of no English woman occupying any of the apartments during the six years that he had held his post there. No, thought Adrian, of course, mother must have moved on before then. Khalil had also questioned the owners of adjacent businesses but none had any information to offer.

That evening, Adrian called Vic Appleton, whose voice sounded somehow familiar. Vic was brief and to the point. Adrian was invited for a drink on Wednesday at about 6.00 pm, and should bring with him all the information he had about his mother. It was precious little: one sheet of paper listing some dates and places in England where she was known to have been, but nothing about her residence in Beirut except the address he had shown to Khalil.

On Tuesday, Khalil turned up with Mukhtar in the car to take Adrian to buy a computer. Contrary to his expectations, Khalil's computer friend didn't own a retail outlet, but ran a workshop in a churned-up suburb of Beirut where, as well as doing repairs, he took in unwanted or used computers, cleaned them up, both the shell and the electronics, installed a new main drive, and sold them on. Adrian chose a solid Dell and a small, light printer. Khalil's friend also sold him a dongle for the internet connection. Adrian had no idea how the prices might compare with new laptops, but he knew he had to trust Khalil. At least he could now sort out his list and make a start on the thankless job of calling schools to ask for permission to read their files. Back in Adrian's room, Khalil connected the computer to the light socket with an adapter, installed the internet device, and loaded a list of all the schools in Beirut. They then went through the list together for Khalil to point out those that he thought might be well organised and willing to show Adrian their staff records. Jean came in the evening to look at the list too; she knew a few of the schools by repute because some expats sent their children there rather than to boarding school in England. They also checked out a list of universities and language colleges.

Contact with the schools was a slow process. Getting through to the right person and department was difficult enough; but once in touch, the responses Adrian received were often negative in tone, some downright rude. He complained to Khalil that he was getting nowhere. Khalil's comment, a fair one as Adrian afterwards admitted to himself, was that so many tragic events had happened in Lebanon, claiming lives and razing buildings to the ground, that the fate of one English woman, who had been in Beirut many years previously, was completely insignificant. Perhaps that was what Khalil felt too, Adrian wondered.

225

His first calls to schools produced two invitations to visit – one run by a German Catholic foundation, the other a French international school. He also reached a sympathetic ear at the AUB – The American University of Beirut, thanks to an introduction from Jean. The Head of English there invited him for coffee, and upon hearing why Adrian was looking for Patti Sandling, asked the University's Head of Administration to pop in and consider giving Adrian permission to go into the archived files. The HoA agreed; Adrian was to return in the morning to collect a permission letter and an identity disk. His spirits lifted. The items were duly issued to Adrian the next day, the HoA explained how the documents were filed, and left him to it. Adrian installed himself at a corner table in the archives room and ploughed through the papers. He read fast, flicking through documents to cast his eyes down personnel lists for any mention of Patti Sandling. But half a day's work didn't take him far down the pile.

At the German school, he was granted access to the files, but it turned out that unfortunately the relevant ones had been destroyed by a fire during the war. The staff at the French school were willing but disorganised: at his first visit he was well treated by the Personnel Manager and invited to return. But the staff couldn't lay their hands on the right records.

Glyn Morgan, who invited Adrian to coffee at the Embassy on Wednesday, turned out to be as genial and expansive in private as he had appeared at his party, but considerably less loud. He first asked Adrian to tell him the details of his family circumstances and his search for his mother, of which he knew only the bare bones, second hand from Francis. Adrian, by then accustomed to divulging his

226

thoughts and exposing some of his feelings, stressed at the end of his account that he was enormously grateful to his parents, and that nobody, not even his 'mother' could replace them in his life and his affections. Glyn listened attentively as Adrian spoke, smiling occasionally in encouragement.

"Sounds as though you've been lucky," he remarked when Adrian had finished, "fallen on your feet with nice people." He paused, looking at him closely. "You're evidently a survivor."

"Perhaps, except that being just a baby, I didn't know what was going on at the time."

"But Adrian, some children would be traumatised by the insecurity of it all, even without understanding the comings and goings."

"Yes, I suppose so. I can only go on my own experience." Adrian took a gulp of coffee from a delicate gilded cup.

"I hope we can help you," continued Glyn. "It's all a question of asking the right people. You know Beirut is a melting pot. People here are escaping from all kinds of tribulations – hiding is a speciality and Beirut the ideal place. That means that there's plenty of money in staying schtum or, conversely, in selling information. The prices get quite high." He illustrated his words with an arm flying up towards the ceiling. "Sometimes it seems as though everybody is just passing through on the way to somewhere else, like slippery eels," he continued, thrusting his arm forward and wriggling his hand appropriately, "places where perhaps comfort, security and happiness await them. As a consequence, people are cagey about passing on information, even when the questions seem innocuous, or there's money in it." He was silent for a moment. "How long are you staying, Adrian?"

"I've got a ticket back to England for the 9th."

"That's Sunday, isn't it? Very little time. I must say I think it's unlikely that you'll get very far in these few days. I gather you've got a local helper."

"Yes, Khalil. He's the cousin of a fellow student of mine at SOAS."

"Francis told me that you're reading Chinese?"

"Yes."

"Not Arabic?"

"No. I liked the beautiful Chinese characters."

Glyn guffawed. "As good a reason for doing Chinese as any, I suppose." He got up and started pacing up and down.

"Of course it's not the only reason," added Adrian. "I got interested in how China ticked, and how the radical changes came about in the twentieth century. And in how it has become what it is now."

"And here you are in rather different surroundings. You didn't even consider Arabic?"

"No, but perhaps I should have. Being here has opened my eyes to the enormous diversity of the Arab world, and to how complicated the politics are. I've also started studying Arabic a bit on my own."

"Good man!" said Glyn, stopping to slap Adrian on the back. "The Embassy uses an excellent teacher who would, I'm sure, be happy to take you on next time you come. For there will be a next time, I'm sure. Anyway, you're welcome to look at some of our archives. I say 'some' because you must know that a lot of what is done in the Embassy is classified. But I can rustle up some payroll papers for the relevant years for you."

"Thank you."

Glyn sat down and moved the discussion on to describe, for Adrian's education, how the diplomatic service was organised.

"And now I must, with regret, throw you out," he said, standing up and making shovelling gestures with both arms. "Come on Friday to have a look at some papers. Una, my PA, will look after you. And come to dinner on Saturday evening, before you leave; I'll persuade Trisha to rustle up a nice meal for us, who knows, perhaps even a roast," Glyn rolled his eyes upwards in anticipated pleasure, "and I'll invite Jean and Mark. By the way, you're going to see Vic Appleton, I hope?"

"Yes, this evening."

"Vic knows everybody – or almost. He'll winkle out the clues if there are any."

On his way out, Adrian's first thoughts were of gratitude for Glyn's amiability. Soon, however, he began to feel panicky: he was only nibbling at the edge of a big plateful of possible sources of information. Why had he thought that he could accomplish anything in ten days? Had he been foolish to come? What if there were no clues to winkle out, as suggested obliquely by Glyn? His fixation had blinded him. He now had to reassure himself that his journey to Beirut was the right action at the right time; after all he had needed to start somewhere, sometime, and these early contacts would have been the same whenever his first visit had taken place. He was anyway doing all he could. It was just that since his arrival, and earlier, he had been so utterly immersed in his search that he had not stood back to take stock of what he was doing.

The help he was receiving, as well as the many useful avenues to explore, fed his optimism, while the lack of any leads dragged him down. Glyn's parting words cast doubts on whether he would eventually find his mother. It irked him also to admit that he was out of his depth. Although he was able, using his map and phrase book, to find his way around, yet he felt he had no connection with Lebanon, nor could he interpret his impressions; facts were supplied by the people around him but he couldn't enmesh them with his observations. It was frustrating, having no understanding. Furthermore, he had long exhausted the possibilities of the few Arabic words he was able to say, and could understand practically nothing of what he heard.

That evening, his mood fluctuating, he bravely flagged down a taxi which took him to the block of flats in a prosperous area of downtown Beirut where Vic Appleton lived. He instinctively wanted to disassociate himself from Mukhtar for this visit. In the lobby, a smartly uniformed caretaker came out from behind a high desk to greet Adrian, who wondered if he were armed. The caretaker asked him whom he was visiting, and showed him to the lift. Vic Appleton's flat was four floors up. Vic opened the door quickly when Adrian pushed the bell, and shook hands with him.

"So, we meet again," he said, ushering Adrian in.

Adrian had worked it out. "Mr Gene Kelly, delighted to meet you," he said solemnly.

"Come in, come in. I won't offer to dance for you now. What'll you have to drink?" he asked, opening a cupboard to reveal numerous bottles and glasses. "There's a bit of everything in here."

"G and T if you've got it."

"Good, I'll join you." He went out and returned with an ice bucket.

As Vic poured the drinks, Adrian noted his physique. He was quite tall, slender with fine, deft hands. His blonde hair was speckled with grey, and straight. He was wearing a soft-looking dark green V-necked sweater over a cream-coloured shirt, and dark well-tailored trousers, greeny-black. His shoes were black suede loafers. Adrian guessed he was in his mid-sixties – a man, he felt, who exuded strength and control.

As Adrian hovered, Vic pulled a small table between two armchairs facing the windows. A bowl of pistachio nuts and the two glasses went on the table. Vic gestured to one of the chairs.

"I hope you won't mind if I ask you some questions about yourself and your family?" he asked, as they sat down.

"No, not at all. And here's all I know about my biobod." Adrian handed him the single sheet of paper.

Vic frowned as he read.

"It's not much, is it?" he said.

"No, but it really is everything I know, or rather, we know – my parents told me all they could."

Vic looked up at Adrian.

"So now, tell me everything that's happened so far."

Adrian launched into the full version; from time to time Vic interrupted him to ask for clarification or additional details. When Adrian had finished, they were silent for a moment until Vic said:

"I'd like to lead you back into the past to try and jog your memory in case you can recall something about your biological parents. I'm interested in how their personalities

231

and actions, together and separately, might have contributed to your being where you are now. There may be no link, but it's worth considering."

Penetrating and astute questions followed, delving into the past, sliding through the present, and prodding into the future, awakening Adrian's expectations and hopes for when he found, or definitively did not find, his mother. Shadows of memories flitted through Adrian's mind, appearing and disappearing; some stopped and became real memories, while others slipped away. Ideas and desires surged and fell, Vic always pushing for more, leading Adrian along deep recesses of his cerebral almanac. Finally, the inquisition stopped.

"I've battered you a bit, haven't I?" said Vic, after a few moments, looking at Adrian with an engaging smile, his brilliant blue eyes alert.

"Yes, I feel as though I've been at a job interview on a psychiatrist's couch." They both laughed, releasing the tension.

"Fear not, I'm only trying to build a context around your pursuit of your mother. Amongst all the morsels you've given me, some will be edible. Anyway, now it's your turn. Is there anything you want to ask me? About me, or about what I do or have done in the past? What did Francis tell you?"

"Only that you're the 'eminence grise' of the education scene in Beirut, and that you have plenty of contacts and an extraordinary memory for people and events. Oh, and that you're a mathematician."

"Hm. A fair assessment."

"At the moment I can't think of anything to ask you, but plenty of questions will occur to me once I get back to my room."

They fell silent. Vic rattled the ice in his empty glass.

"Refill, Adrian? Your throat must be dry after all that talking."

"Yes, as long as you're having one?"

"Yes, I can do with a bit more gin." He refilled the glasses and returned to his seat. "I'll tell you now what I propose to do. First, I'll make a few notes in a very secure file on my computer. OK with you?"

"Yes."

"There are various ways of finding people. My information files could be helpful. I can also think of several sources where there could be stuff about your biobod – your name for her."

"I can't think of her as my mother, nor refer to her as 'Patti Sandling'."

"That's understandable. I'll poke around a bit, discreetly of course. People jabber here. It will all take time. By the way, I gather you're not staying for long."

"No, I'm going home on Sunday. I've got to get back for the beginning of term."

Vic got up and went to the window.

"Come here Adrian. See down there." Adrian joined him. "There are a million people down there of whom several must know of your mother." He put his hand on Adrian's shoulder. "You know, I think we may find her, but not immediately. Don't lose heart."

He released his hold. Adrian, with a dangerous sob in his throat, provoked by the sudden softness in Vic's tone of voice, turned away and covered his face momentarily with his hands. He felt Vic moving away. When Adrian returned to his chair, Vic, already sitting down, was watching him intently.

"I've dug you up," said Vic, "made you face things. Maybe that's good."

Adrian swallowed. "I believe it is," he said slowly. "I'd scarcely given a thought to how I might feel about the outcome, such has been my obsession with the search."

"I understand," replied Vic. "Be kind to yourself now. If you remember anything else or want to ask me something about Beirut, or people, or any subject, just give me a call."

"Thank you, I will." Adrian looked at his watch. "Crikey, I've been here nearly three hours."

"That's not long for the grilling you've had."

They smiled. Adrian stood up to go. Vic assured him that he would be in touch by email as soon as he had anything useful to relate. He accompanied Adrian down to the entrance to see him into a taxi. Back at the Residence, Adrian flopped straight into bed after devouring some biscuits, and fell sound asleep. Vic started on his notes immediately, thinking deeply about the courageous, intelligent and attractive youth, with his engrossing mission.

Twenty

Jean called Adrian at 9.30 the next morning. Excitedly, she told him that a retired QM was going to be in Beirut for a few days, and that he might have known Adrian's mother. Adrian had never heard of QMs; Jean explained that they were Queen's Messengers, i.e. couriers who travelled around carrying the diplomatic bag. This needed a further explanation. Adrian thought back to Glyn's description of the Embassy work and fitted the new information into the picture.

During his hunt for school leads that day, two subjects occupied Adrian's thoughts, both of which mitigated his feeling of despair at his fruitless pursuit. The first was his visit to Vic. He realised that he had learned practically nothing about the man, except that he was razor-sharp and kind. What made him tick? Adrian wondered. If it was true that he knew 'everybody' in Beirut, how come? What was his link to the Embassy? How did he spend his time? Perhaps he was a retired dancing champion? Adrian smiled to himself at the possibility. Vic certainly played his cards close to his chest. Maybe that was it! A professional bridge player or gambler...? Dismissing his fanciful ideas, Adrian realised that the encounter had been a one-way transmission of facts and feelings, but that there was an underlying confidence of success in Vic's attitude towards Adrian's search.

As to the arrival of the QM, Adrian tried hard not to think about it, to avoid inflating the chance of the QM having known his mother. Even if the dates did coincide, the QM must have known many people and presumably didn't spend long in any of the places he visited. But it was important to meet him. How should he go about organising it? Jean hadn't suggested anything, nor did she know the QM's name, or where he could find him.

In the event, he didn't need to decide. On Friday morning, whilst he was plodding round between two schools (both willing to see him but neither, Adrian thought, likely to yield anything useful), Glyn phoned to tell him formally about the QM, whose name was Brigadier Clifford Turner. His arrival was scheduled for the following week; at the moment Glyn knew no details, but Clifford was likely to be in Beirut for several days. Vic would know more as the Brigadier usually stayed with him. It could be to Adrian's advantage, suggested Glyn, to see him, but he should think carefully about extending his stay in Beirut, with the challenges of the new term awaiting him in London. As to arrangements, Vic would doubtless be in touch with him.

Adrian was torn. His conscience demanded that he return to London on Sunday as planned; his instinct told him to stay and meet the QM. After all, he reasoned, it would only mean a few extra days. All he would have to do would be to prolong the room booking, find out about his air ticket, and email home. Even if Brigadier Turner hadn't met his mother, he might know somebody who had. Adrian's spirits rose.

Then, in the afternoon, at the American University, the name Mrs P Sandling suddenly shouted up at him from a

1994 list of teachers paid hourly in various capacities. Her job description column specified 'Untenured hourly rate English teaching, remedial, Arabic students.' Adrian stood up and punched the air. "Got her!" he shouted, to the surprise of two auditors three tables away. He felt like going over to explain and hug them, but remembering where he was, he sat down again, trembling. As his mother had disappeared from England in 1983, he turned hurriedly back in case he had missed something, but no, her name wasn't to be found on earlier lists. He continued to 1985 where she appeared again, and in 1986. Then the trail went cold. Adrian ran through two subsequent years, but found nothing.

He didn't know what to do next, nor could he think straight. There must be a trail leading forward, he thought. He should certainly keep at the archives, in case Mrs P Sandling should return in later years to the same job. But that was enough for today – it was time to celebrate. He closed the folders, returned them to their boxes and checked out of the building. Quick phone calls to Jean and Mark ascertained that they would be happy to join him at the Burger Hall at 8.00 for a celebration evening. They were delighted for Adrian. He, in turn, accepted their congratulations with modesty, praising instead the patience of the people he had met. Soon the conversation moved on to where the discovery might lead and how Adrian should proceed.

"Listen, Adrian," said Mark suddenly. "If, as you suspect, your mother remarried, then it would probably be her married name that would appear in the AUB lists for 1987 onwards."

"Brilliant Mark!" cried Jean. "She might still have the same initial, Mrs P somebody else."

"How clever of you!" said Adrian. "I'd always imagined she might have remarried but hadn't thought about it in this context. I'll carry on with the same files. Also, it's unlikely that the AUB would employ a non English mother tongue person to do remedial work. So I know what I'm looking for: a woman with an Arabic surname and a possible P."

They clinked glasses boisterously. When the second bottle of wine was empty, they wisely decided not to have a third. Jean drove a happy, pickled Adrian back to the Residence.

By the following day, feeling enervated after a night of waging war with the bed clothes, he had decided that he should stay on for the extra days to meet the QM. Vic, sounding sober, phoned him in the morning.

"Adrian, it's about Clifford Turner. Glyn's mentioned him to you, I believe?"

"Yes, he has..."

"Clifford will be staying with me. He's an easy-going chap and would, I'm sure, be willing to meet you, which could be helpful in your quest, since he was working as a QM at the time when your mother was known to be here in Beirut." He paused to lend weight to what he was about to say. Adrian held his breath. "You may wish to consider staying on to see him."

"Yes, I definitely want to do that," blurted Adrian. "Yesterday I found my mother's name in a list of teachers at the AUB. I can't tell you how excited I am. It seems like a good omen for meeting Brigadier Turner."

"Hang on, Adrian! Pipe down! You must think seriously about this. There are different ways of looking at it."

"I know there are," interrupted Adrian. "But you can't imagine the fillip this has given me."

"I assure you I can. And I'm delighted for you. But you shouldn't lose sight of reality."

"I know, I know. But…" he tailed off.

"Adrian, all this is very encouraging for you," said Vic decisively. "I understand. But listen to me a bit. Think about the great opportunity of being at a specialist university, at being able to learn a difficult language. Attending regularly is essential for a good grounding. Then there's your family to take into consideration. Your parents have been very generous to you. They may be worried about you being here."

"They are, a bit, but I'm a good student and I try to be a responsible son," replied Adrian defensively.

"I don't doubt that. But hanging around here to meet an amiable elderly man who may or may not have seen your mother, and if he has seen her, may or may not remember her, isn't necessarily the best use of these days. Consider the *pros* and *cons* properly before jumping in feet first."

"I've been doing that all night, tossing and turning."

"But the night's over now and, as you well know Adrian, things look different in the sober light of day. Besides the academic considerations, there's also the expense of changing your flight." He was silent for a moment. "And I could ask Clifford all the questions on your behalf."

"No, that wouldn't be the same," cried Adrian. "She's my mother, not yours."

239

"You're right. And in the end, it's your decision. Think hard. If you do decide to stay on, I suggest you come to lunch with us on Thursday – I'm sure Clifford will have arrived by then. After lunch, I'll leave you two alone to talk. Call me back in an hour or two to tell me what you've decided. But promise me to give it due thought."

"I promise. And thank you, Vic."

"Bye." Vic ended the call quickly.

Adrian got busy. First he sought out the Residence caretaker who told him that he would have to check with the boss to see if he could make an exception (to what? wondered Adrian) and let him stay on, as he was such a nice trouble free guy. Then he called the airline. The jumbled information he gleaned from a staff member at the reservations office prompted him to grab his e-ticket and go to the airport to sort it out. He took the bus, which was full of large suitcases and their owners. He was pressed against a tiny sinewy man with a big black moustache who smelled of fried garlic. Released into the cool wind blowing down from the mountains, the snow-covered crests and slopes glinting bright white against the cerulean blue sky, Adrian breathed in big gulps of air and blew his nose to expel the smell from his nostrils. At the airline's ticket desk, he was issued with a voucher for about half the cost of the cancelled journey. Then he confirmed to Vic, who sounded neutral, that he had made arrangements to stay on.

Not having spoken to Khalil for a few days, Adrian wanted to tell him the news too. He explained how happy he was that two positive things had happened, but that meeting Brigadier Turner would mean staying on a few extra days and missing some lectures at university. Khalil was glad for Adrian that he was making progress.

Assuming Adrian would still be in Beirut the weekend following his meeting with the QM, Khalil proposed a trip in the car. There were two special places to be seen – places unconnected with his mother. He refused to satisfy Adrian's curiosity as to where and what they were, but would say only that they would be seeing different sides of the country, places that were significant for understanding more about Lebanon. Adrian agreed readily; the trip was arranged for 7.30 on the Saturday. Meanwhile Khalil would cancel Mukhtar for the airport trip.

Adrian now had to face emailing his parents, who would doubtless disapprove and worry. He imagined, with a sinking heart, John's disappointed expression and Fen's tears. Hurting one lovely mother to look for another, unknown? It sounded ludicrous as he thought it over. He considered a couple of coward's options: emailing Max, which he would do anyway, and asking him to pass the message on, or telling them that he was ill? He debated, too, whether emailing them, rather than calling, was cowardly.

Ultimately, he wrote it as he felt it. First, he described the AUB lists where Mrs P Sandling's name had appeared, and the possibility that she might appear in lists for subsequent years if she had remarried. Next, he explained about the QM, and the suggestion made by both Glyn Morgan and Vic Appleton that there was a chance he might have known his mother; they would not otherwise, he reasoned, have mentioned the QM, even though they doubted it was right for Adrian to prolong his stay. He described his new friends, Khalil, Jean and Mark, who were all helping him in different ways, as well as Glyn whose hospitality he had enjoyed, and Vic. He ended with apologies and promises that he would catch up on the missed work as soon as he got back to London. Click. It was gone. Adrian sat thinking about it for a few moments and then opened it up to re-read it, imagining other sentences, other words, other explanations and details that could have made the message more acceptable and clearer. Too late. He would have to face the music anyway.

His message to Max was easy. Although he could imagine the curled lip and the sarcastic comments, Adrian felt no pain. It was nothing like writing to his parents. Max would undoubtedly do as Adrian asked and make apologies on his behalf to the Head of Department, Vernon Buckley. For good measure he also emailed Benny, but not Tazie. One difficult message was enough for the day.

Dinner that evening at Glyn's home was an uproarious occasion. Mark was at his wittiest and Jean was chirpier than ever. A female version of Glyn was there too, a daughter called Marilyn, stopping over on her way back to London after a business trip to Sri Lanka. Adrian, relieved that having made his important decision, he could plot the forthcoming week, beamed at everybody. Glyn boomed forth on the excellent qualities of the Château Musar they were drinking, (the best Lebanese red wine), colouring his words with demonstrative gestures, one of which knocked over a very large pepper mill. Trisha produced a succulent roast leg of lamb with more than the usual trimmings (mint sauce, redcurrant jelly and onion sauce), as well as an array of vegetables; she piled the food up on their plates, especially Mark's, happy to see them all tucking in. Adrian was grateful that Glyn chose not to sour the atmosphere with a discussion of the rights and wrongs of his decision to stay on. Concealed behind a front of universal *bonhomie* was a sophisticated diplomat.

On Sunday when, as Adrian reminded himself, he should have been in the air flying home, he was out with Jean and Mark. "It's only about 40 kms to Byblos," she had said. "I've been there a few times with friends but never driven myself. How about it?" Adrian had agreed readily. Mark knew Byblos well, and thought it would be fun to show it to Adrian. Mark's father recommended a simple harbour side restaurant for lunch, and generously provided the necessary funds.

They left Beirut early in bright sunshine to beat the traffic. It was a straightforward run along the Tripoli highway, through a mainly Christian area. The route was flanked with large commercial billboards showing the name 'Solidere'; Mark explained that the company had been founded in the 1990s by the Prime Minister Rafic Hariri, to undertake and oversee the rebuilding of Central Beirut following the destruction of the war.

On arrival at Byblos, Mark, who was well versed in local history, guided them first to the earliest archaeological site, believed to date back to about 8000 B.C. He went on to describe subsequent settlements, leading them to remains of the first town buildings, then on chronologically to evidence of subsequent settlers in Ancient and Medieval Byblos. Jean and Adrian were astounded by Mark's detailed knowledge of the sites and stimulated by his sharp and humorous explanations of political situations. The history lesson over, they ate lunch and then relaxed outside in the sun. Adrian said the day was unforgettable, both for the trip and the company.

Both he and Mark responded with enjoyment to the attentions of Jean who was, Adrian thought, in her early thirties, and whose instinct was to mother them. Adrian was sure she must have a partner somewhere back in England or posted abroad, but it was too early in their friendship for him to ask. It was impossible that such an attractive and vivacious person had nobody special in her life.

The beginning of the new week proved trying for Adrian, impatient to hear of the Brigadier's arrival, and to receive emails from England. Max was the first to reply. He wrote that he had spoken to Vernon, who had been understanding about Adrian's extended stay and the reason for it. That sentence was followed by two rows of expletives in as many languages as Max could muster up, as well as an offer to do catch-up with Adrian on his return. He signed it: 'Cheerio, bloody idiot! I hope you find her soon so that you can get on a plane and come back to real life.'

A phone call from Vic on Tuesday confirmed that Clifford Turner would be arriving the next day and that Adrian should join them on Thursday at 12.30. If there was a change of plan, Vic would ring again.

Adrian's family took until Wednesday to reply. It was Gemma who wrote the email; neither John nor Fen had made time to learn much about computers. Gemma started by telling Adrian how sad everybody was that he hadn't come home as expected and that Fen, particularly, was extremely worried for his safety. She had cried on and off all day Saturday. Although there had been no news of incidents in Lebanon, there had been a border skirmish in the Golan Heights. The family had got out the atlas to count the miles distant from Beirut. Gemma herself was coping in his absence and loved him lots. Even Seb had become a little bit quiet and thoughtful. But it was good that there were two leads to follow up, and they all hoped that he would find his mother very quickly, partly for his sake but also for theirs so that he would be home soon.

Meanwhile, her history teacher had lent her a glossary of archaeological terms. Cadby had arrived – he was sweet and growing fast; he loved licking people's faces. Benny had called to wish her a happy New Year – they would be meeting again soon. Adrian sighed as he read these snippets of news. He wasn't exactly homesick, but he felt guilty, almost treacherous. He should try to finish this whole episode of his life quickly; once he had found his mother, he could arrange to meet her again in the near future.

On Tuesday he broke off from the 'school-traipse', as he, Jean and Mark called it, to continue reading the files at the AUB. To his joy, a new Arabic name did appear for 1987: a Mrs P Al-Zaini. The description of her work wasn't exactly the same: this entry showed that the person was teaching elementary English to children of Arabic staff members. Adrian called Jean immediately to ask her what she thought; Jean's response was that it seemed encouraging. The trail ended abruptly in 1989, the last year her name appeared. Adrian thought it safe to assume that she had left the AUB rather than changed her name a second time. What he needed now was an address; he returned to the DoA to ask if there were files showing addresses of former employees. There certainly must have been, he was told, but it would take some time to locate them. Somebody would call Adrian the following week if the department secretary managed to find anything useful.

Vic confirmed on Wednesday that Brigadier Turner had arrived and was, as expected, willing to talk to Adrian who should come for lunch as planned. This news, coupled with the family's email, sent Adrian's head spinning. He was excited and apprehensive at the same time. He spent some of the afternoon looking aimlessly at the list of Al-Zainis in the phone book and then went out to walk and shop. His sense of direction had improved and the surroundings of the Residence were now familiar. Unusually for him, he bought *The Guardian* – the previous day's edition.

The next day, in a poorly disguised state of agitation, Adrian arrived at Vic's block of flats seven minutes early. His legs, as keyed up as the rest of his body, walked him fast along the street to the next block and back to kill time. Now with only three minutes to go, Adrian marched in, ascertained with the caretaker that he was expected, and took the lift up. A small brawny man with bandy legs, some bushy clumps of hair, and shrubs growing out of his ears, opened the door.

"Good to meet you, Adrian," he said gruffly, looking at him through thick black-framed glasses. "Come on in." They shook hands; his grasp was strong and his skin rough.

"Thank you for agreeing to see me, Brigadier," said Adrian, stepping over the threshold.

"Call me Clifford. Vic's in the kitchen." He waved in the direction of an open door off the living area and then shut the flat door. Vic appeared in the kitchen doorway.

"Welcome," he said. "Clifford's got something important to tell you while I finish off in here. By the way, come and meet Josette." A small black-haired woman was energetically stirring the contents of a pan.

"Bonjour Madame," said Adrian, hoping he'd got the right language. She turned her head briefly to reply "Bonjour, Monsieur."

"G & T, Adrian?" asked Vic.

"Yes, please."

"Go and sit down with Clifford and I'll bring it."

"So," said Clifford, as Vic handed them their glasses, "I did know your mother, and she was a very attractive woman."

Adrian was dumbfounded. He tried to speak but only gravelly noises in his throat spluttered out. The ice in the glass he was holding rattled noisily as his whole body trembled. Vic took the glass from him, put it on the table beside him, and dropped his hand on his shoulder.

"Are you all right?"

Adrian grunted.

"Take your time, breathe deeply." Adrian obeyed. In a few moments he found his voice again.

"I'm sorry. I er… got a funny er … buzzing in my head. It's such a surprise, talking to somebody who really did know her. I can't believe it."

"Ready for a drink now?" asked Vic, offering him back his glass, which Adrian accepted gratefully. "Sip carefully, you've had a shock."

"Thank you." Adrian remembered, years later, how he savoured the taste of that celebratory gin and tonic. He was tongue-tied until Josette brought in the lunch and set it up on a square table.

"Clifford," said Adrian as they sat down, "what did my mother look like when you first met her?"

Clifford was uncomfortable. He was not in the habit of describing women; Adrian had to prompt him with questions, gradually squeezing out of him a vision of a medium to tall shapely person, with thick shoulder-length hair, or sometimes short hair – a person who wore nice clothes and had expressive eyes.

"Lovely legs," he added after a moment's pause.

"What colour are her eyes? What's her skin like? What's her nose like, and her mouth?"

"I think you're asking a bit much of Clifford," said Vic. "Just think of how you'd describe your girlfriend or sister or aunt. Could you fill in all the details you've just asked Clifford for?"

Adrian had to admit that he couldn't.

"Do you remember your mother at all?" asked Clifford.

"Since I've been looking for her, my imagination and memory have been conniving against reality. I think the answer must be 'no'."

"What progress have you made in your search?" asked Clifford.

Adrian told him about the AUB staff lists which showed his mother to have been working there between 1984 and 1989, and about the possibility that an address for her at that time might be found in the accounting records. Clifford thought that he had first met her towards the end of 1985 at some sort of Embassy do, or with Embassy people in the bar of the St. George's Hotel. He remembered her telling him how pleased she was to have been taken on as a teacher by the AUB, which was more interesting than doing accounts. She didn't mention her marital status but Clifford assumed she was divorced, since she talked about her baby son without mentioning a husband. His assumption was reinforced by the fact that she was openly happy to accept dinner invitations.

"I'm surprised you never met her, Vic" said Clifford.

"Her presence here probably coincided with one of my longer periods in England, when I was trying to please my father by taking an interest in his spice business."

Clifford nodded. "Ah yes, that would be it," he said.

"So she did have another child," said Adrian slowly, "but just a minute, she was divorced from my father before she left Britain, probably in 1983, but she never took me to Beirut – she abandoned me in England. Was this baby with her here when you first met her?"

"Oh yes. Evenings with Patti always had a time limit because of the nanny's hours."

Adrian's eyes widened. "Then I've got a brother, who had a nanny," he said slowly, running his hand through his hair. "I started wondering about it when my parents opened up the whole story with me last autumn. How odd. How peculiar. A person I'm more closely related to than my family - my mother's son."

They were all silent for a minute.

"I'm thinking," continued Adrian, "that this boy must have been born soon after my mother arrived here. In fact, she may even have been pregnant by the time she left England. So it means either that she was indeed, as suggested by my father, having an affair with someone from the Middle East, or that she was pregnant by my father when she left. If you met her towards the end of 1985 …" his voice tailed off. He sat staring at his plate then his shoulders began to heave with sobs. "Sorry, it's all a bit much" he stuttered, "my little brother. Someone she wanted, but she didn't want me - either a brother or a half-brother."

Vic fetched a box of tissues which he put on the table beside Adrian, and ran his hand slowly up and down Adrian's back.

"This is very hard for you. Take your time. And by the way, don't forget to eat."

Adrian cleared his throat and looked up. Vic sat down again, watching Adrian who ate a mouthful absent-mindedly, before continuing his questions.

"She was called Sandling wasn't she, when you met her?" he asked Clifford.

"Yes, she was."

"And Sandling was my name, before I was adopted. She disappeared from the AUB records under the name 'Sandling' in 1986, but a Mrs P Al-Zaini doing similar teaching appeared in 1987. Presumably she had got married. Then that person disappeared after 1989."

"I never knew her by any name other than Patti Sandling. And as I never called her at work, I didn't need to know any other name. Funny thing though, she was still willing to meet me, even after she was married, but only for lunch, not dinner."

"Can you remember when you last saw her?"

"Not exactly. It must have been a year or two after she got married."

"Did she talk about her new husband?"

"Hardly at all. She just said he was away a lot of the time, and that it was up to her to decide about going out with friends, which was what we were - nothing more."

"Where did she live? Did you ever go to her home?"

Clifford was taken aback. Vic laughed. "Hardly a discreet question, Adrian!" he said.

Adrian smiled. "Sorry," he said. "I don't mean to pry. I'm just after facts."

Clifford face's relaxed as he barked a throaty laugh. "Apology accepted. Anyway, I can assure you that I never did go to her home. I knew her address because I used to drop her a line before I set off on a tour, so that she would know when to expect me. And before she was married, I used to take her home in a taxi after dinner. I may be able to find the address somewhere at home in England, but I haven't got it on me."

"I was just thinking that if by any chance you had seen the baby, you might have noticed if he looked English or Levantine."

"I never saw him or even a picture of him; I've no idea what he looked like."

"Can you think of anyone you know, still here in Beirut, who might have known her too?"

"The people I saw regularly have moved on. The Embassy staff has changed. And since I'm no longer a QM, I'm not in the loop. Getting older, don't want to go out so much. Vic here is my contact and a very good friend. Knows everyone and everything there is to know here and almost everything about the Middle East. The old crowd I used to drink with aren't around. Sad. But I had many very good times. Can't complain."

Vic meanwhile had gone into the kitchen.

"He's a marvellous man," added Clifford quietly. "He doesn't like to hear me say it though."

Adrian nodded.

"Adrian, you're neglecting your food again," said Vic from the doorway. "Josette will be very disappointed if you can't do better than that."

"Multi-tasking," replied Adrian, smiling. "A male Achilles' heel. I speak so I can't eat. Such a pity, as I'm terribly hungry. I didn't have breakfast."

"While you finish eating what's in front of you, I'm going to tell Clifford about the party where you and I first met," said Vic. "It was at Glyn's regular New Year's Eve bash. All the usual suspects were there, plus Adrian – not yet qualifying as a suspect – and he was sporting a lion's head. Glyn was his usual bounteous self. And Trisha kept it all going. The Arnott's son, Mark, was there too. He's on a gap year, and he's been helping Adrian by going through old British Council records."

"That was a memorable party" interjected Adrian. "My introduction to the ex-pat world in Beirut on only my second evening. And meeting Mark and Jean."

"Eat up, Adrian."

Adrian ignored the order. "By the way," he said, "how did you know who I was at the party?"

"I put two and two together and made four. I knew when you were arriving in Beirut, and I recognised Jean and Mark immediately they came through the door, (you must admit that even masked they are unmissable), so I assumed that it was you with them."

"I see" said Adrian, "it's obvious when you know." He thought for a moment. "By the way, what can you tell me about the gross Hameed El Saad? Why did he come to talk to me?"

Vic and Clifford laughed.

"True to form, he didn't waste any time in homing in on you. He's got a rare nose for a new body," answered Vic. "He holds an important post, and doesn't he just know it. His greatest pleasure is to manoeuvre people into compromising positions, and then make the most of the situation. He's closely related to the Emir of Sharjah, of course, as are most of the people in positions of influence there. Hameed seems to be a general agent or go-between for the Emir in every respect. Dodgy stuff. But some members of the ruling family are more or less honourable and decent, on their own terms."

"I remember Hameed," said Clifford, "an unrepentant paedophile. Bad news. Do you know what happened to that poor kid (where did he come from?), who got adopted by Hameed?"

"I do" replied Vic. "Hameed found him through some disreputable orphanage agency. Luckily the boy was soon abducted back by a French missionary and he's now in a special school in France." Looking gloomy, Vic shook his head. "I suppose that's a better fate."

"Indeed" said Clifford.

Adrian finally finished eating. Vic stacked the plates from the table and took them into the kitchen. Josette emerged with him and placed a bowl of fruit with plates and knives on the table and then went into the kitchen to collect her jacket and walked towards the flat door, calling "au revoir."

"Merci Josette," Vic called after her.

"Is there anything else you can remember about my mother, Clifford? Anything she said which might have hinted at her past, or what she was doing in Beirut?"

"Come to think of it, there is. She mentioned that she wanted to found an English language nursery school for tots. She was going to call it 'The Little English School'."

Adrian jumped up. "Let's try the phone books, shall we?"

"Good thinking," said Vic.

Adrian followed him into a small tidy office with box files on shelves all over the walls, stretching right up to the ceiling. Vic picked up four Beirut reference books from a shelf beside the printer and carried them to the lunch table. Eating fruit, they searched under relevant headings in all of them, but found nothing.

"I'll ask Jean if she knows anything," said Adrian. "She's quite clued up about education here."

Vic picked up the reference books to return to his study. "Choose armchairs and sit comfortably. I assume you drink Turkish coffee, Adrian?"

"Yes. Khalil calls it Lebanese coffee."

"Same thing. It's just a question of national pride."

Vic disappeared into the kitchen.

"Well I think I've told you everything," said Clifford, yawning and crossing his legs. "If being here brings back any other memories of your mother, I'll be certain to tell you."

Adrian understood that Clifford thought the conversation was over, but he still had a few more questions.

"I'm tiring you out, aren't I?"

"No. It's just that I'm used to having a snooze about now. But if you've got more questions, now's the time to ask. I don't know what plans we've got for the next few days, but I can't promise to have time to see you again."

"Just a few quick things. I haven't asked you yet if she was good company – fun to go out with. Did she have a sense of humour? And did she say anything about hobbies?"

"She wasn't exactly fun. She knew how attractive she was and she got full marks for playing the part. She knew how to listen, and she asked me lots of questions about my job, what the bag was like, and whether I knew what it contained and whether I'd ever had to accompany a really big object, or even a container. She was genuinely interested. She was also very obstinate, set in her ideas, and, I imagine, rather selfish. But that didn't matter. I enjoyed taking out a lovely woman and she was pleased to be with somebody who wasn't part of the local scene. You know, somebody who, er, how can I say this, people wouldn't think was her lover."

"So what did you say when she told you she'd got married?"

"I congratulated her, told her I was pleased for her. Didn't ask any questions. She thanked me but didn't smile radiantly or anything, or offer any information. I got the impression it was something she had to do, perhaps a forced marriage."

"Have you any idea what she did apart from working? If she had any spare time, that is."

"She played bridge. But being a mother naturally took up a lot of her time, although there was the nanny."

"Have you any idea who the nanny was? Perhaps I could find her?"

"I never saw her, of course. I think her name was Therese and I think she was French, but that's not much of a clue."

Vic brought in two cups of coffee, and put them on the table between Clifford and Adrian.

"I'm going to have mine in the study. I've just got a couple of emails to deal with."

Clifford and Adrian sipped in silence.

"Thank you for all that, Clifford," said Adrian, when he could see the grounds at the bottom of his cup. "I'm going to leave you in peace now. I'll just go and have a word with Vic."

He stood in the doorway of Vic's study, watching him concentrate. Vic looked up.

"Have you finished?"

"Yes, Clifford's tired and is going to snooze. So I'd better be getting off. I can't thank you enough. And sorry I got a bit overwhelmed."

"I'd have thought you very cold and unfeeling if you hadn't been unnerved. Now, when you get back to the Residence, write it all down, what Clifford said, and the AUB stuff. I'll need a copy of that."

"Yes, while it's fresh in my mind."

"Good lad. I'll be in touch. Bye."

"Bye."

Clifford was already asleep as Adrian tip-toed through to the door. He shut it quietly.

Twenty-one

"Hi, Tazie!"

"Hi, Max"!

"All well?"

"Yes, and you?"

"Fine. Tazie, I assume you've heard from Adrian?"

"I had an email on New Year's Day, but nothing since then. Why?"

"He sent me a brief message a couple of days ago, saying that he wasn't returning on 9th because he had two leads on his mother. Hasn't he let you know?"

"No, he hasn't."

"Well, perhaps he hasn't had time."

Tazie was shocked, both by Adrian's decision, and the more so by his failure to tell her the news himself. Reminding herself that Max wasn't good at sympathy, she quickly dismissed the idea of telling him about the last evening she had spent with Adrian, and replied in as neutral a voice as she could manage.

"Perhaps not. Tell me about it."

"Apparently he's found Patti Sandling's name in a list of people teaching at the American University in the '80s. And also, some chap who may have known her will be passing through Beirut for a few days next week, so Adrian's hanging on to meet him. Bad idea, I think. He could be in the shit-house for going to Arabic lectures instead of Chinese, except that nobody of importance knows."

"That's been plain stupid, and loitering around in Beirut doesn't seem very sensible to me either. It could all get quite mucky."

"Mm. Anyway, let me know when you hear from him."

"OK, Max."

"Bye."

"Bye."

Tazie pondered. What could Adrian's silence mean? It was understandable that several days would pass between emails to people at home, but that Max should be graced with a message of some importance whilst she was not, was hurtful, and didn't seem to make sense. Had Adrian started to write emails and then been interrupted? Was she perhaps first on the list for the next day, or the next week, or whenever it occurred to him to open up his computer again? Was he being simply negligent, or was he deliberately shunning her?

Loyalty to him was an issue just now. Over a casual early evening drink, Toby had invited her to go to a concert with him. The programme included a piece of music which was close to his heart; it was scored for four horn soloists with orchestra – the Konzertstück by Schumann. He had, he said, played horn no. 4 in a performance with his university orchestra, a physical and mental challenge which he had only just been good enough to meet. Since then, he revealed, he had never heard a live performance.

Listening to classical music was a pleasure for Tazie. However she had not accepted Toby's invitation immediately; to gain time she had asked him what else was on the programme. Although he had never made overtures, she knew that he was drawn to her and that there was more than ordinary friendliness in his invitation. Under the circumstances, would it be reprehensible, she asked herself, to go out with him a third time since she and Adrian were lovers? On the other hand, was it possible that Adrian's silence signified that he had met someone in Beirut? That seemed unlikely, for Adrian was not an importunate suitor. In the exotic ambiance of the Middle East however, he could have got carried away. Anyway, whether he had or hadn't, she decided, it would have no bearing on her decision.

Were she not attracted to Toby, it would not be a dilemma. She could accompany him to the concert without parting with a single 'atom' of herself. For her, the love or affection which she might exchange, offer or sacrifice, were represented by atoms of herself – tiny particles which departed, leaving an opening ready to be filled reciprocally. By now, however, she felt she had moved too far forward for her connection with Toby to be casual. She recognised that she had already let loose a small batch on each of the occasions when they had been out alone together, although she hadn't realised it at the time. And the rate at which atoms detached themselves seemed to be cumulative. Toby had doubtless received those atoms and absorbed them; likewise, she had absorbed some of his. The 'atoms' analysis was a juvenile notion which she and her closest friend at school had dreamed up to explain the way in which people fell in love. At the time, they had assumed that divorced people's atoms were returned.

A couple of days after issuing his invitation, a flyer showing the full concert programme appeared on Tazie's desk with 'For your consideration. No hurry' penned on it.

What the hell, she said to herself. I want to go, and Adrian's in the dog-house. Then, perceiving that she had correlated potential acceptance of the invitation with her dismay at Adrian's silence, as though the act of going out with Toby would punish Adrian, she thought again. Such a stance on her part wasn't right, nor would it be fair on Toby, not that he would ever find out. Her choice should be made purely and simply on whether she would enjoy herself; it was a matter of principle. On those terms her answer had to be 'yes'. So she phoned him to thank him and accept the invitation.

The concert was in the Festival Hall. They had a pre-concert dinner at a nearby restaurant, during which Toby filled Tazie in on Schumann and the piece they were going to hear. When the main course arrived, his explanations moved on to the other pieces on the programme: Mozart's piano concerto no.17, and Tchaikovsky's symphony no.6, the 'Pathétique'. Toby was knowledgeable about all three composers but modest, volunteering that there was plenty he didn't know.

They walked over to the hall in the pouring rain. As Tazie had no umbrella with her, Toby gallantly tilted his to shelter her rather than himself, causing the drips from its edge to dribble down his neck. They had just a few minutes in which to dry themselves off and find their seats before the hall lights dimmed. The sight of the four horn players walking to the front of the platform between the orchestral players, instruments gleaming, to line up at the front of the stage with the conductor, drew a great swell of applause from the audience, many of whom stood up.

"There are loads of horn players here tonight," said Toby in a loud whisper into Tazie's ear. She nodded as the audience settled down. She watched the horn players as their parts interwove in glorious harmony. Afterwards she remarked to Toby how marvellous it sounded, and that it must have been a thrill for him to play it. Toby agreed that the horn players had got it just right. Next was the piano concerto, a sparkling piece, typical, said Toby, of Mozart's drive and finesse. Then during the interval, he outlined to Tazie Tchaikovsky's tormented life, situating the symphony within it. His expose did not however prepare her for the depth of feeling the symphony evoked in her. After it was over, Toby, sensing her mood, took her arm as they strolled towards the exit.

"Perhaps it's because I'm Russian that this music moves me so much?" she said. "Maybe I have a genetic affinity with it."

"It's possible," replied Toby, "you never know what influences may be in your genes. I always feel different when I hear Jewish music."

He stopped walking to turn her towards him.

"Are you in a hurry to get home?" he asked. "Or are you up for a nightcap?"

"Since home is Battersea, I don't have to hurry."

"Fine. Let's go to the bar under the railway arches."

He propelled her across the street and into the bar which was on several levels. They found a table on the top floor. Tazie ordered the nightcaps – cocoa for both of them.

"It's a sombre piece, isn't it?" she said, referring back to the symphony.

"Yes, but beautiful. He finished it in August 1893, conducted the premiere on 28th October that year and died nine days later. Perhaps he had a premonition."

They drank silently.

"Next time we go out," said Tazie, "I'll get the tickets, and it'll be a happening or a jazz session, something jolly, nothing to arouse our feelings."

"Mm," said Toby, suddenly serious.

"You don't sound keen," remarked Tazie.

"Tazie, it's *if* we go out again," he said, "not when."

Tazie was stunned.

"Sorry, I didn't mean to be presumptuous. Are you already tied up with someone?"

Toby stretched across the table to take her hand, and held it tightly in his.

"Your presumption feels good," he said, "and I'm not tied up with anybody." He seemed to be searching for words. "Tazie" he continued after a moment, "there's something I ought to tell you. I didn't intend it for tonight, but we seem suddenly to have reached that stage."

Tazie didn't reply.

"You see," said Toby with difficulty, looking at the table, "I've always found you attractive and liked you, and now I'm sliding precipitously towards something else."

He looked up at her to see her reaction. Her eyes expressed surprise; she said nothing.

"My imagination is galloping forwards, seeing myself as your partner and perhaps more."

Tazie instinctively pulled her hand away.

"We all have dreams," she said, turning her head to avoid his gaze. "Your words are rather unexpected. Don't think I don't like you; I like being with you, but I hadn't got as far as you."

"But it's anyway of no consequence. A future with you has to be out of the question because I can never live with somebody or get married."

This time he saw consternation in her expression.

"Go on," she said.

"I'm unhealthy, Tazie. I wouldn't want ever to foist my illness on anybody else. It wouldn't be right. My reason for telling you now is that I can't envisage going out with you if our friendship isn't going anywhere, but it can never go anywhere."

Tazie's mind leaped into the worst case scenario – AIDS. But, *Toby, AIDS?* How could such a seemingly proper man have contracted it? Caution was best.

"Well," she said, her heart in her mouth, "without knowing what you're talking about, I can't comment." She thought for a moment and then said, "you can tell me, you know? I won't be shocked, I promise. We can talk about it."

Toby was at a loss, pulled in one direction to tell her, held back in the other by his shyness and compunction. His silence led Tazie to prepare herself for the worst.

"Go on," she said.

"Nobody knows about this except my parents, and of course the Directors at work. It's difficult to talk about it."

"Discretion is my second name, I can assure you. Give me the short version."

"I've got hepatitis B. I caught it from a dodgy blood transfusion in Turkey. I had a bad fall at an archaeological site."

A gasp of relief escaped from Tazie's throat. She felt suddenly dizzy.

"Explain it to me. I don't know what that means."

"Most people clear the infection spontaneously. But I have chronic hep B, which has to be treated to reduce the risk of cirrhosis and liver cancer. One in twenty hep B patients has chronic hep B. Of those, some go on to develop scarring of the liver, and cancer."

"But what were you doing on an archaeological site?"

"I went to Istanbul on a Thursday for a business meeting which we couldn't finish by the end of Friday. I had to stay over the weekend, so my Turkish hosts, ever kind and hospitable, decided to show me the sights. That's when I fell."

"Where was the damage?"

"A big hole in my left shin – and my trousers too, of course."

"What happened then?"

"Hospital, lost a lot of blood, and a transfusion. I stayed another couple of days and then limped on to a plane home. After about a month, when the wound didn't heal properly and I began to look yellow, the doctors tested me for hep B and that was it."

"But that doesn't stop you from being with someone, does it?"

"I wouldn't want to inflict it on anyone. You see," he swallowed, "it's transmitted through body fluids."

"Ah," said Tazie. "But there's a vaccine, isn't there? I'm sure I've seen it on travel inoculation forms."

"Yes, there are various ways of preventing infection. But none is 100% certain. So you see, I can't risk passing it on."

There was a long silence. Tazie was lost for words. She was far from imagining Toby and she together as a couple; the best option was to return to their former position. Finally, she said:

"There are lots of ifs and buts about all this. As I said, I do like being with you, but I don't know you very well. I wouldn't like you to feel that our going out together meant a commitment. If we got to know each other better, you might decide that I'm not right for you, or vice versa. And as we work together, the whole thing could become a mess. Doing things together is nice. Couldn't we just be natural about it, continue to see each other every so often, and stay friends anyway?"

"You're the epitome of rationality. In this instance I'm not. I don't know what to say."

"Let's try it Toby, just being friends. Mm?"

"I'll think about it." He looked at his watch. "Time to go home now."

Tazie, much relieved, went to pay at the cash desk. They walked out together to Tazie's bus stop. There, Toby put his hands on Tazie's shoulders.

"Thank you for being kind and sensible. I'll think about the possibilities, assuming of course that your position doesn't change."

He turned and walked away. Tazie's stomach gave a lurch. Atoms going in both directions, she thought wryly, plenty of them. It was only when she got home that she realised Adrian had completely slipped her mind. What sort of a sign was that, she wondered?

Twenty-two

On Saturday morning, 15th January, Adrian didn't wake in time to have breakfast before Khalil arrived. The previous evening he and Jean had been invited to dinner with the Arnotts at home, during which Dr. Arnott had briefed him on the British Government's perspective on Lebanon and its position in the Middle East, as well as how the situation there at any given time informed the Government's position and influenced the Embassy's actions. Dr. Arnott and Mark had answered Adrian's questions tirelessly; the discussion had continued until well after midnight. On the way back to the Residence in Jean's car, she had taken the subject further by explaining the British Council's remit and how it fitted in with the Embassy's position.

At 7.00 a.m., watching for Mukhtar's car through the Residence window, Adrian was still turning over in his mind the information he had heard. He would have liked to make copious notes on what had been said, instead of heading off with Khalil on a jaunt, which felt like an unwanted interruption. When the car arrived, Adrian was surprised to see an unfamiliar face at the wheel. Khalil jumped out and gestured to Adrian to get in the back, where Khalil joined him. The car pulled out into the traffic.

"So what marvels are you taking me to see?" asked Adrian lightly, with a note of sarcasm, fortunately unrecognised by Khalil. "And where's Mukhtar?"

"He cannot make today till later, so Sabir comes instead."

"Oh. Hi Sabir!"

Sabir turned his head round briefly to nod unsmilingly at Adrian. Adrian began to feel uncomfortable.

"Where are you taking me?" persisted Adrian.

"We're going first to Khiam. Do you know the place?"

Adrian's insides gave a lurch.

"No, I've never heard of it."

"We're going to the Khiam Detention Center Museum to meet a friend from external relations of Hezbollah."

Adrian was horrified. "What are we going there for, and why didn't you ask me in advance if I wanted to go?" he barked.

"I didn't ask because I thought you refuse to come."

"Too right," he replied, bristling, "I would indeed have refused. Sabir!" he said, poking him on the shoulder, "stop the car and let me get out! Stop Sabir, stop!"

Sabir slowed down, but didn't stop. Ah, thought Adrian, he understands English. "You sly bastard!" he said to Khalil.

"Adrian, let me explain," said Khalil, with a sigh. "Hezbollah is an integral party of Lebanon. Since the 1990s, it has a powerful and respected political position in our country. It participates in Government, and its army is very strong. Hezbollah fought the Israelis until they leave our country last year."

Sabir interrupted Khalil with a stream of sentences.

"What's he saying, Khalil?" asked Adrian, when Sabir had finished.

"He is saying I must tell you that it is a big privilege for you to be invited as a guest to speak to one of the leaders at the Museum. Most English people do not get this invitation."

"Privilege, my foot," muttered Adrian, simmering. He didn't understand whether 'most' signified that Britain was one of the most undesirable sources of potential visitors, or whether Khalil meant that most requests from potential British visitors were turned down. It didn't matter anyway. There followed a swift conversation between Khalil and Sabir, then Sabir pulled off the road and stopped in front of a row of simple shops.

"Come, Adrian," said Khalil. "We eat breakfast here."

In a small quiet cafe, Sabir led the way to a table in a corner while Khalil ordered coffee at the bar, returning with three sesame rolls.

"I explain," said Khalil softly, after the coffee arrived.

"No, I explain," interrupted Adrian firmly. "I am NOT coming with you to visit some terrorist people whom my Government doesn't approve of. I want to stay safe here in Lebanon. I don't want to take any risks. I won't go with you to meet these people. End of story." Adrian subsided.

"Adrian, listen," said Khalil. "When I was studying at university, I worked in spare time as a guide for foreign visitors from the world. I saw many Americans and Europeans, as well as from other parts. Many visitors are not interested in the Middle East, in Lebanon, in our history, in our problems. They want to go to Baalbek, and skiing, and shopping." He stopped to glance at Sabir. "Hassan says you are a good person, so I meet you at the airport. I try to be your friend. I like you. And I want to show you Lebanon because I think, I hope, you are different from those tourists. You don't like terrorists, I understand. But perhaps you just come to listen to what the

Hezbollah people say. You don't agree with them, but you listen. I think you open-minded person. You get a view of Lebanese politics."

"I can read about Lebanese politics on the internet and in the press," retorted Adrian heatedly.

"Not the same, to read and to see, and what you read on the internet about Hezbollah is often biased."

Adrian looked from Khalil to Sabir. Both were watching him intently.

"No," he said grudgingly after a few moments, "it isn't the same, I know. But the whole idea seems preposterous. I've only been here just over two weeks, and you're already trying to drag me into something dodgy. It sounds terribly unsafe to me. I don't want to end up like Terry Waite. He wasn't safe."

"The Terry Waite affair was over ten years ago," replied Sabir. "Things have changed. Hezbollah has changed. The responsible people see some foreign visitors – journalists, politicians – who don't sympathise, but the visitors are safe. You must trust us. We trust you."

Adrian was momentarily embarrassed. "I do trust you, both of you" he reciprocated hurriedly, instantly regretting his words, not knowing what 'trust' might signify for a Lebanese, nor what demands this trust between them might make on him, apart from involving him in what seemed to be a foolhardy expedition.

"Good to trust. Today Sabir and me we take you to meet someone who will welcome you and explain about Hezbollah. He will answer all questions. You are lucky that we have a way to a personal contact there. This is a private, personal visit, nothing official. No notes, no photos taken.

We hope you will have a good impression of Hezbollah. You come, yes?"

So Sabir was a link in the chain to Hezbollah and, Adrian reflected, not drafted in today because a driver was needed. Adrian looked at him more closely, noticing his smart jacket and striped shirt. Sabir caught his eye then looked away. Adrian hesitated.

Khalil continued. "The Museum was built in the 1930s by the French for army barracks. After it was a base for the Lebanese army before was taken over by the South Lebanon Army – Christian collaborators of the Israeli occupiers – traitors of Lebanon. Under the Israelis the base was a prison camp where many Lebanese were tortured and died, until Hezbollah forced Israeli troops to withdraw in May last year. The South Lebanon Army disappeared, many to Israel and to live away. So Hezbollah took over the prison and turned it into a museum. In our country we feel more relaxed and positive now, thanks to Hezbollah. So you come, yes?" he repeated.

Adrian didn't reply. Khalil continued.

"As we trust each other, I ask you now not to tell about the visits today to Western friends in Beirut. It might not be an advantage."

"I see," said Adrian slowly. "But it would be ok to talk about it in England?"

Khalil glanced at Sabir. Again, a hurried conversation.

"We think you be careful who you talk to. Family, ok. Jewish and Israeli friends, not ok. Journalists and public people, not ok."

"Well, I think I've got that straight," said Adrian, thinking the opposite. It was time to take control of the conversation. "Sabir," he continued, "I want to be convinced that this visit today would not lead me into any dangerous circumstances at all. Where is this place?"

"It's about 130 kilometres from Beirut, in an area controlled by Hezbollah," answered Sabir in fluent textbook English. "I am here because I know the people we will be introducing you to. Our connections, those of Khalil and myself, are enough to ensure that you will not be in any danger anywhere. We have made a case for taking you to meet them by saying that you are a student at the famous School of Oriental and African Studies of London University"

"Thank you," replied Adrian. "Now who is the main person I would be meeting, another of your cousins?" The irony in the question was lost on them. Sabir leaned forward to exchange a few words with Khalil.

"He is a cousin of Sabir. You will call him Nawaf," replied Khalil.

There followed a short silence as Adrian digested the reply, wondering how many aliases the man had, and for whom he might use them.

"Then will you come?" persisted Khalil.

"Against my better judgement, I will come," replied Adrian finally, scowling.

"And you promise not to talk in Beirut?"

"I promise," replied Adrian unconvincingly. "In return, Khalil, "he continued seriously, "I think you should tell me now where we're going for the second visit today, so that I know exactly what my promise covers."

"This will be to Baalbek to see the archaeology, and to a Palestinian refugee camp close by."

Adrian wasn't shocked; in fact, if he had thought about it, he would have guessed. Khalil explained that, like the

271

prison, the Al-Jalil Camp (also known as 'Wavell Camp', after an English General) had also originally been a French Army barracks, built after the First World War. Lebanon had gained independence from France in November 1943, and the last troops had withdrawn in 1946. Just two years later, the first Palestinians fled from the new country – Israel – arriving in Lebanon, where the empty barracks provided shelter for the refugees. Mukhtar had a personal connection with the place: a great-uncle had lived there on arrival in Lebanon from Palestine, and his family was still there. Baalbek was close by – hence the choice of Al-Jalil for a visit, rather than any other refugee camp.

At least I haven't brought my camera in vain, thought Adrian wryly, as he considered his position and contemplated his resistance to Khalil's planned activities. His outbursts were, he felt, appropriate; Khalil had anticipated his reaction and was evidently not surprised or upset. Sabir, on the other hand, was an unknown quantity. Adrian suspected him of being, in some hierarchical body, Khalil's superior; he was a 'cool customer', unfazed by Adrian's words and exuding self-confidence.

The rest of the journey was accomplished in near silence, interrupted only by Khalil's descriptions of various sites on the way.

By the time they arrived, Adrian's anger and anxiety had abated. Having relented and decided to go along on the visit, he told himself he should now take the consequences with dignity. He would take everything in his stride, remaining poised and calm, listening carefully to what his host said, and asking only innocent-sounding questions. Even though he couldn't possibly condone the violent actions of Hezbollah, it would be interesting to hear some spiel from the horse's mouth and indeed, it probably was a privilege to have been singled out for such an encounter.

A series of bright yellow and green flags strung up between poles fluttered alongside the stony road leading to the museum, where a yellow notice over the entrance bore the name 'Al Khiam Detention Camp' in green, with the Arabic script in red. Uniformed guards flanked the entrance. A small swarthy man appeared, embraced Sabir, and then shook hands with Khalil and Adrian. A brief conversation in Arabic ensued, during which the small man looked penetratingly at Adrian.

"Nawaf says we go first to look round the museum, then he will meet us for coffee and explain about Hezbollah, and you can ask him about what you see," said Khalil. "He doesn't speak English but I translate."

Sabir led the way. The torturers had left, but the horror remained. Openings in outdoor corridors gave access to small cells with light filtering through ventilation holes in the ceiling. Yellow Hezbollah notices bore red (Arabic) and green (English) indications of the use made of different spaces by the captors. Grisly interrogation rooms contained unidentifiable equipment dangling from hooks; small cupboards, large enough only for a single crouching person, were labelled 'Solitary confinement.' Sabir said prisoners remained in there sometimes for as long as ten days. There were window grilles to which prisoners were tied naked for days, with freezing water thrown over them at night. A single pole across a narrow cell was where prisoners were hung by their wrists with their toes just touching the floor. Then there were electric leads for a small dynamo – the machine having been carted away to Israel by the retreating interrogators – which had the inmates shrieking with pain when the electrodes were attached to their nipples, fingers, tongues, or penises. Thick wire bound in blue plastic was used to beat prisoners, including women.

Inmates used their walls as canvases for expressing themselves. In the women's section Adrian saw a drawing of a fish with a heart attached to it. Prisoners used garbage for art materials, made *misbaha* (prayer beads) from olive stones, and combs from drift wood. The squalor was everywhere, even in the rooms occupied by the South Lebanon Army and the Israelis, whose presence was ratified by the numerous notices in Hebrew. Pornographic magazines, comics and puzzle books were strewn around their sordid quarters. By the time the three of them emerged, Adrian was gripped by nausea from his first encounter with real evidence of recent gross human cruelty.

Hundreds of people were by now surging into the museum. Nawaf was waiting to lead them through a heaving cafe area into a simple room, containing a few plastic chairs and a table. A wide window afforded a splendid view of meadows and mountains. Nawaf left the door open; a small boy brought in four cups of coffee on a tray which he put carefully on the table with a toothy grin. He hovered for a moment until dismissed by Sabir with a smile.

Adrian looked curiously at Nawaf. He wasn't wearing a uniform nor did he look threatening in any other way. His hair was cropped very short, showing a bald pate on the top, contrasted by a thick black beard. Under a shiny dark suit, he was wearing a maroon shirt buttoned up to the neck. While they drank coffee, (Adrian struggling), Sabir talked to Nawaf; Adrian knew from their gestures that Sabir was explaining about his visitor's reasons for coming to Lebanon, and his background.

"Now Nawaf is ready to talk to you," said Sabir to Adrian when the conversation ceased. "Khalil will translate."

Nawaf first questioned Adrian carefully about his search for his mother, showing a particular interest in her husband's identity and nationality. Adrian reassured him that the man was, as far as his family knew, a Saudi Arabian, who had met his mother whilst working in Britain. What kind of work did he do, was the next question. Here, Adrian guessed. Probably an oil executive, he said. Nawaf spoke quickly to Khalil; Adrian could tell that in his answer Khalil was vouching for him in some way – his honesty, perhaps. Khalil turned to Adrian.

"Nawaf wants to know, you are not Jewish, not Jewish family or groups in England."

"I am not Jewish," replied Adrian. "Nobody in my family has ever mentioned my having any Jewish relations."

Nawaf rattled off another sentence.

"Nawaf says how are you sure, you living with not birth parents?"

"I can't be sure that there is absolutely no Jewish blood in me. But I can assure you that I have no aunts or uncles or grandparents, in fact no blood relations at all to refer to, and no affiliations with anybody who is Jewish. So I hope Mr Nawaf will find that a satisfactory answer. I can prove nothing, but I can assure him of my goodwill towards the Lebanese people."

Nawaf seemed almost satisfied with his answer. He then asked for information about SOAS, and took copious notes of Adrian's answers. He was particularly interested in relationships between students of different nationalities, the total number of full-time students, and the percentage of Jewish Americans among those. Naturally Adrian was totally at sea. He explained that those sorts of statistics were unlikely to exist in SOAS, where students from all over the world were welcome, and that he certainly had no idea. Nawaf's next questions referred to Adrian's impressions of Lebanon; it was easy to answer those positively. Adrian enthused genuinely about the beauty of the seashore, the grandeur of the mountains, and the friendliness of the people.

Did Adrian want to ask any questions? No, not at this stage. Nawaf would now explain about Hezbollah.

The essence was distilled by Adrian from Nawaf's account, which Khalil translated into English, sentence by sentence, with numerous pauses whilst he searched for words. Hezbollah first began to take shape in the 1980s, funded by Iran, with the main objective of protecting Lebanon against foreign invasion and occupation and later, in particular to counter by whatever means necessary the 1992 Israeli occupation of Lebanon. Essentially Hezbollah's position was one of opposition to the very existence of Israel. Initially a resistance movement which grew into a revolutionary group, after 1990 Hezbollah became a political organisation, with ambitions to participate in government. Tolerance of the other religious groups embedded in Lebanon was an essential factor in this transformation, except that it did not encompass groups connected with Israel. In 1992, Hezbollah's first year of participation in parliament, it won 12 seats out of 128, and had continued since then to hold seats. This, Nawaf stressed, demonstrated the importance Hezbollah had achieved in national and international affairs.

A key moment was in May 2000, when the persistence of Hezbollah's military arm, the Islamic Resistance, finally disbanded the disloyal and evil South Lebanon Army and chased its members and Israeli sponsors from South Lebanon, after eighteen years' occupation. This was of enormous importance for the security of the country; the people of Lebanon were rightly grateful, and there was renewed enthusiasm in the country for restoration and rebuilding. Hezbollah was establishing schools, hospitals, and was instrumental in distributing help to the poor.

Adrian responded by sympathising with Nawaf over the Israeli occupation, particularly having seen the horrific evidence of the Khiam museum, where prisoners were kept and tortured without trial. For several moments, while Khalil translated, Adrian toyed with an idea: to ask about Terry Waite, held without accusation or trial. Should he do it? Eventually, when Nawaf paused in his narrative, Adrian took the plunge.

"Mr Nawaf," said Adrian politely, "I want to ask about the truth concerning Mr Terry Waite. Please can you explain to me Hezbollah's point of view?"

If Nawaf was surprised by Adrian's question, he didn't show it, being ready to respond immediately.

"Always British people talk about Waite, Nawaf knows," said Khalil. "But you have read what your British say, haven't you?"

"I have, but there seem to be some doubts about certain aspects of it."

Nawaf launched into an explanation. Threatening behaviour and violence towards non-Israeli individuals was not a policy of Hezbollah. And indeed it had never been proved that Hezbollah had had anything to do with Mr Waite's abduction. However, there were occasions when an individual's position could be suspect or compromised by his or her contacts or activities. As Mr. Adrian would know, Mr Waite had had frequent meetings with the American, Lieutenant Colonel Oliver North, who was instrumental in bringing about the clandestine sale of weapons to Iran, intended to encourage the release of U.S. hostages then held in Lebanon. Colonel North's subsequent action was to divert proceeds from the arms sales to support the Contra rebel groups in Nicaragua who were fighting the Communist Sandinista Government. Such action, said Nawaf, was discouraged, perhaps even forbidden by the Americans' own legislation. Colonel North had been seriously discredited and found guilty in American Courts of three charges, a sentence which the corrupt Americans had eventually overturned. Under such circumstances, it was understandable that Mr Waite's frequent comings and goings to the Middle East had been brought to a close.

Adrian nodded, determined to remember the details of this expose. Nawaf moved quickly on to hopes for the future. Ideally, Hezbollah would like to see world peace. But less ambitiously, the aim was to secure all Arab country borders with Israel against invasion from those Zionist warmongering colonialists, to recover the homeland of the Palestinian people and resettle them there, and to support Syria's bid to retake the Golan Heights occupied by Israel during the 1967 June war. Furthermore, Lebanese prisoners of Israel would all be released.

Adrian agreed that these were good objectives, without asking whether the obliteration of Israel was also on the list. That question, he felt, would be a bridge too far, as would a question about the whereabouts of the three Israeli soldiers being held since October 2000, or an outburst about Hezbollah atrocities.

Nawaf looked at his watch, placed his hands palms down on the table, and nodding to all three of them, said what Adrian assumed was the equivalent of 'time's up'. As they shook hands, Nawaf said to Adrian, in stumbling English: "Now Arabic, no Chinese!"

"I am starting, and thank you for welcoming me," replied Adrian. Nawaf had to get that translated.

As Sabir drove off, he asked Adrian, now sitting beside him in the front of the car, for his impressions. Adrian wasn't sure what kind of truth Sabir wanted to hear. After a moment's thought, he replied diplomatically that the Lebanese people owed a huge debt of gratitude to Hezbollah for ridding South Lebanon of the Israeli occupiers. He hoped that this triumph would allow everybody in Lebanon to settle back into a peaceful existence, and that border tit-for-tat skirmishes between Lebanon and Israel would cease. Sabir glanced at Adrian and nodded – a nod that seemed to Adrian to say, 'I know that you're sitting on the fence, and I understand why.' Adrian felt uncomfortable with Sabir's apparent knowledge of his position, but wanted to avoid a discussion, heated or otherwise, on the rights and wrongs of Hezbollah's terrorist forays.

"There are many checkpoints on the way to the Beqaa Valley," said Khalil, "so you need your passport ready."

"But don't speak," enjoined Sabir. "I do the talking, ok? For those guards, we are going just to Baalbek."

"OK," replied Adrian, a little startled. "Who runs the checkpoints?"

"Some are the occupying Syrians, under the control of Ghazi Kanaan, the man who is in charge of security in Lebanon," said Sabir. "But they do things as they like. Others are Hezbollah, who control much of the Beqaa Valley."

The first checkpoint was surprisingly close to Beirut. Adrian sat staring ahead as Sabir had a rapid conversation with an armed soldier; he was uninterested in Sabir's passengers and waved them through on a nod.

As the car started up into the hills, Adrian, feeling the change of temperature, pulled a scarf out of his backpack and tied it round his neck. It did not help that Sabir drove with the window open. Further on, at the next Syrian checkpoint, they were ordered to get out of the car while their documents were scrutinised by a thin fair-skinned man collected from a decrepit hut by a young soldier. The man was not wearing uniform; Adrian could tell by Sabir's attitude that showing respect was essential in fending off any inconvenient questions. After a few minutes, a nod indicated that they could go.

The traffic was dense, and the car wound precariously along poorly maintained roads, the sides of which were strewn with litter. The sun was now obscured by a layer of mist, further cooling down the inside of the car. Eventually, emerging suddenly above the mist, they were catapulted into sunshine and bright blue sky, before reaching the snowline and continuing on over the top of the mountain. On the other side, they stopped briefly for a snack at Chtaura, a small town boasting magnificent views of the valley and the Anti-Lebanon mountain range beyond. By that time Adrian had lost count of the number of checkpoints they had passed through. Beyond Chtaura, they were stopped again at a road block.

"Hezbollah," said Khalil. Sabir got out immediately and walked over to shake hands with two of the soldiers. They talked for a while, much to the annoyance of drivers in cars backed up behind them, who started hooting aggressively. The taller of the soldiers walked over to look at Adrian, whose neck began to tingle as he stared. The other soldier started a shouting match with the driver of the car immediately behind them.

"OK, Baalbek? You go?" said the taller one to Adrian.

Adrian glanced at Sabir, who nodded imperceptibly, then answered. "Yes please, we go!"

The soldier waved them on, whereupon Sabir got back into the car and they resumed their journey in silence.

The road was now flanked with hoardings demonstrating the domination of Hezbollah in the area, backed by Iran. Triumphant Hezbollah soldiers brandished guns at the backs of fleeing soldiers bearing the Israeli flag; Iranian mullahs conferred solemnly, heads together; Ayatollah Khomeini, his white beard too long for the size of the poster, glared down at them ominously. Yellow, green and red Hezbollah flags fluttered on poles alongside the road in the light breeze. They entered Baalbek. Sabir brought the car to a stop on some rough ground where Mukhtar was waiting, along with a tall skinny girl dressed in jeans, a jacket and a hijab.

Adrian got out of the car and went to greet them. Khalil and Sabir got out too, but only to explain that they were going somewhere else to see some friends, but would be back to collect Adrian and Mukhtar. They arranged the time between them quickly in Arabic; Khalil reassured Adrian that Mukhtar's relation spoke English and would do the translating.

The young woman whose name was Latifah introduced herself by explaining that her grandfather had come from Palestine to the camp soon after it opened in 1949. His older brother was Mukhtar's grandfather – he had been killed in 1948. Latifah was born in the camp and had always lived there.

She led Adrian and Mukhtar along a maze of narrow alleyways between dilapidated buildings and up a crumbling concrete staircase to a battered door, which opened on to a tiny entrance space. Beyond was a small room full of people – the family. Adrian was introduced to them: grandmother, parents and Latifah's brother and sister, Alim and Hiyam. Alim, the boy, was rather small and not at all shy; Hiyam was a little taller, wearing a hijab, as were the two older women.

Bedding was piled high all around the room. They were lucky, said Latifah, that there was running water and a toilet on the floor below. A gas ring on a table in the entrance, fuelled by a cylinder, enabled them to cook. Mukhtar went to make coffee. Latifah's grandmother pushed Alim off the chair beside her, beckoned to Adrian to occupy it, and then plied him with talk in Arabic. Latifah tried to interrupt the flow and translate the questions, but the idea of a foreign language was anathema to Grandma. All Adrian could do was nod and smile. Mukhtar handed round coffee then produced a camera, whereupon Latifah spoke in English, translating each sentence into Arabic as she went along.

"We are all very honoured to welcome our friend, Adrian, from London, to our home. We hope he will see that happiness is possible in our camp, and that we have many good things: medical centre, schools, mosque, and a social place where families can meet and talk. We hope that you will take back to London a good memory of your visit here, and that we will always be friends."

Adrian answered appropriately, both moved by the obviously genuine welcome and appalled by their living conditions. Mukhtar was busy with the camera. Alim, who had been prancing around as best he could in the restricted space, stopped to tap Adrian on the shoulder and point at his cup of coffee.

"No, no, Alim!" admonished Latifah. "He's not allowed coffee, it makes him too excited." He hung his shoulders forward and pouted. Then he had a new idea.

"Football?" he said in English. Everybody laughed. Latifah explained that Alim would be playing football in a while. Would Adrian join in? It was the last thing that Adrian wanted. He looked around at their hopeful faces, and gave in.

"But first," said Latifah, "I'm showing him our camp."

On the way round, with Mukhtar and Hiyam in tow, Adrian learned that Al-Jalil was one of the smallest of the Palestinian refugee camps in Lebanon, having about 3000 inhabitants, although many more refugees lived just outside the official area of the camp. In 1952, the United Nations Relief and Works Agency for Palestinian refugees in the Middle East had taken over responsibility for the camp in respect of services and administration of installations; at that time, the camp was officially named 'Wavell Camp'. Latifah showed Adrian the original barracks which were now home to many refugees. During the Lebanese civil war, because of its remote location, Al-Jalil had been spared the worst structural damage, but living conditions were nevertheless now very poor. Another problem for the refugees was that of identity: in Lebanon they had no legal status other than that of 'Palestinian refugees' and only very menial jobs were open to them. Many families were short of food because of unemployment, despite UNRWA's best efforts.

"We have a good education system," said Latifah, showing Adrian the bare classrooms and antiquated furniture in an empty secondary school. "Today there is nobody here because it is Sunday, and the teachers have the free day. I have two more years here, and then I want to go to university."

"Good for you," said Adrian.

"I am sixteen. Hiyam has five more years – she's only thirteen."

"What do you want to study at university?"

Latifah stood still and her bright eyes looked straight into Adrian's. "My parents said I must ask you something, but I …" Her voice went quiet. She swallowed.

"Come on," said Adrian gently, "there's no harm in asking." He had guessed the gist of what was coming.

"Well, I want to be a doctor, and I want to study in Europe. Can you help me get there, to England, perhaps?"

"Latifah," said Adrian quietly, "I promise I will see if there are any possible openings for someone in your position. But I must tell you frankly now that I think it's unlikely."

"I see. That is what I think."

They were both silent for a moment, unhappy. The schools, the medical facilities, the meeting rooms, all poorly equipped but obviously cared for, were a timely reminder for Adrian of his own easy circumstances. He was a university student – no problem.

Round the earthy football pitch, families were gathered, cheering on two teams, both of which seemed to have many more players than eleven. Adrian was conscious of being stared at, as he had been throughout his walk within the camp. Nobody had made him feel unwelcome, or shown any animosity towards him; he evidently wasn't regarded as an intruder of any sort. Indeed, on the contrary, people had stopped to say "Welcome" and "Where are you from?" in English, or had questioned Mukhtar and Latifah about him in Arabic.

A burly boy scored a goal. Alim immediately spoke to the referee, then came running towards Adrian to pull him on to the pitch. A discussion ensued, the outcome of which was that Adrian was to join Alim's team, and to compensate for the extra strength, two more players were added to the opposing side. Adrian was quite sure that his prowess didn't warrant such an enhancement; his trainers were unsuitable for football – he felt clumsy wearing them, and awkward because he was seriously out of condition among the vigorous little chaps darting all round him. However, he joined in and even enjoyed himself. In the end his side won, to the delight of Alim, who insisted on holding on to his sleeve proprietorially, while all the players clapped him before lining up to shake his hand.

It was time to leave. Latifah and her family said an emotional goodbye to him; she would stay in touch and hoped he would respond, even if he couldn't help her get to

England. He promised not to forget them; Mukhtar would keep him abreast of their activities.

***

In the ruins at Baalbek, Adrian climbed slowly up to stand between the two central columns of the Temple of Jupiter. He was too exhausted to make sense of where he was, to relate what he was seeing to Roman sites in England. Bath, he thought, but could find no thread of connection. I'm completely out of my depth, he said to himself. His mind was trying to process the scenes and conversations of the previous hours of the day. Sabir, Khalil and Mukhtar were sitting a short distance away on the remains of a wall, deep in conversation. Adrian sat down where he was and rested his forehead on his folded arms. He was roused from a muddled waking dream by a tap on his shoulder. Sabir was there.

"You were asleep?"

"I don't know, I think so."

"You sat there like that for ten minutes."

"Then I probably was asleep."

"I think you're tired. We go back to Beirut now," said Sabir firmly, helping Adrian to his feet. "Some other time you can come again to Baalbek."

On the way back, Adrian realised he had forgotten to take any photos.

Twenty-three

Adrian woke at midday. The previous day's activities, for which he had been completely unprepared, had shaken him to the core. Knowing that he had followed paths few other Britons had trod, and had met people considered to be terrorists in Britain, was deeply disturbing. The stares and smiles had been unnerving. Not for the first time, Adrian had wished he could understand what was being said, particularly at the Hezbollah headquarters. Straining unsuccessfully to recognise even one word was extremely frustrating. Khalil had translated to the best of his ability, but Adrian knew, not only from the brevity of his explanations but also from his and Sabir's body language, that more was being said than reached him. Some of it was evidently not intended for his ears anyway.

In his waking slumber, images flitted before his eyes: women wearing the abaya swayed past him, men gesticulated and shouted, small children trotted behind him then darted off when he turned to look at them, chickens pecked in the dust, and checkpoint guards pointed heavy rifles at him, smiling or scowling. Gradually these fleeting visions dissolved, to be replaced by real memories: the dignity and pride of the Hezbollah leader and the sense of community in the refugee camp where everybody was recognised. Adrian had to remind himself that some of the people he had met were fiercely defending their positions with aggressive and murderous actions, armed with modern weaponry. For a moment he wished that Gemma were standing beside his bed with a cup of tea and that he could describe his impressions to her. She would, he was sure, have understood his rage when Khalil had sprung the destinations on him, as well as his sombre reflections afterwards on what he had heard and seen.

He pushed the covers off, pulled on his underwear, and put the saucepan filled with hot water on to the hotplate to make a cup of coffee. That would clear his head. Funny, he thought, this was the first time he had, in his imagination, cast Gemma as an accomplice, someone to share his experiences, rather than a little sister, someone to be needled and protected. As he drank, he thought back to Khalil's insistence that he promise to tell nobody in Beirut where he had been. Khalil had hinted that talking could be dangerous, but had said nothing further. Adrian remembered Glyn Morgan's assertion that people were reluctant to pass on information, but that there could be money in both keeping quiet and selling secrets. He hoped he wouldn't be approached by anybody offering money for either service; wryly, it occurred to him that Khalil might have organised the visits as a means of filling his pockets. Unlikely, he reassured himself. If he himself spoke of his tour and his impressions, he could, he reasoned, be sought out and perhaps caught between different factions, offering him bribes or targeting him for multifarious purposes.

As for emailing home, any hint of the itinerary they had followed, other than sightseeing at Baalbek, was out of the question. Fen and John would be horrified to hear where he had been and whom he had met. A sketch of the atmosphere and the subjects of discussion would be completely beyond their imagination. But perhaps one day he would tell Gemma. Not yet, but in a few years' time. Meanwhile, Adrian typed several pages of his impressions, then filled a separate file with the information he had learned at dinner with the Arnotts.

It was afternoon by the time he had finished, so he went out to the grocer. On his return, munching falafels, he started drafting an email to Tazie, who had written twice since his New Year message, without his having answered. She had said she was disappointed that Adrian had not told her himself of his decision to stay on in Beirut, instead of sending a message via Max, and that she wondered why Adrian hadn't replied to her emails. Adrian drafted the most soothing answer he could, telling her that he was extremely busy, and describing in detail his discovery of the links to his mother, as well as the possibility that she might have started an infants' school. The best excuse he could find for first telling Max about his delayed departure from Beirut was that the information had to be relayed urgently to the Head of Department at SOAS.

Not often given to introspection, Adrian pondered. Was he in love with Tazie? Had he ever been in love? His answer to the second query was easy: his gap year adventures had been enjoyable but dismissible, nor had his teenage infatuation with a young science teacher left any dent in him. His feeling for Tazie was strong, which made it all the more regrettable that he had run out on her. Could he relate his feeling to, for instance, the love between his parents? There didn't seem to be many similarities: his parents' love was an everyday permanence, characterised by respect, friendship and understanding. Could he envisage reaching such a stage of comfortable familiarity with Tazie? He certainly liked her enough, and she, in wanting to solidify her connection with him, seemed ready for living together, perhaps even engagement. But was he to be the person? Were he and she really suited, well-matched? Would he feel like settling down in the foreseeable future? He felt love for her, not only in tender sexual moments, but in the morning too, cuddling warmly; and he always felt a special surge of happiness when they met.

Adrian could find no satisfactory answers to these questions; time would tell. He knew only that he had been comfortable with how things had stood before their final evening. He was certain, too, that he wasn't ready for parenthood. Perhaps everything would fall into place once he had found his mother and returned to England.

So what should he write of all this in his email to Tazie? His musings were not helpful. He wanted to find the right form of words to convey his regrets at his behaviour, without offering an apology, which could give her a false impression. He continued drafting. Eventually he found a satisfactory paragraph, explaining that he was hoping to see her very soon after his return, and to spend a Saturday and Sunday with her to make up for their last evening together, when he was so fidgety and preoccupied with his journey the next day as to be thoroughly ill-mannered. He finished by saying that he would be booking his flight home within a few days. He also emailed his family to say that he was following up a few last leads and would be home soon.

Adrian phoned Vic.

"My notes on the discussions with Clifford are ready. Shall I bring them round, or would you like to see my abode and taste students' coffee?"

"I remember visiting the Residence last year; I think, regretfully, that I can forego the pleasure of savouring its charms again. But come here tomorrow morning – any time you like. I'm not going out until later."

"Fine. I'll print it out now."

"Did Jean take you on an outing yesterday?" Vic's tone was avuncular.

Adrian was taken aback. How odd. Was that an innocent question?

He replied hastily, "No, she had a visitor," (this was true), "and Mark was with his family, so I did some wandering around on my own, sort of poking about."

"Good for you. See you tomorrow. Bye."

Vic didn't revert to the matter the next morning, for which Adrian was grateful. While Vic made coffee, Adrian looked out of the window and thought again of the many places where his mother might be living. Vic joined him at the window.

"Any progress with the infants' school?"

"Not yet. This is one of the loose ends I want to tie up before returning to England, as well as any address that the AUB might provide."

"Time to go home, Adrian," said Vic. "You're just clutching at straws. Your degree course awaits you. Stop procrastinating."

"It's not really procrastinating, Vic," protested Adrian. "These are real leads."

"All right then. One morning collecting an address at the AUB and going to check it out. And the afternoon for infants' schools in any reference books or files that Jean may have. Then that's it. Book your flight, Adrian. Bye bye

Beirut. After all, you can come back during the Easter break."

"It's the momentum," said Adrian thoughtfully. "I feel she's within my grasp. And I really like Beirut, the vibrancy, the energy, the colourful people, even the conflict's interesting…" he tailed off, realising he was on the edge of giving something away. As though to separate himself from what he might have said, he moved away from the window.

Vic was firm. "I appreciate that you're enjoying it, and finding your way around on your own. Laudable, when you think how many of our compatriots coming here for the first time find it bewildering and alienating. It *is* a fascinating place. I'm the proof. I wouldn't be here otherwise. Still, there's no final cut-off in your going home now. I'll be watching and probing. Keep Beirut alive in your thoughts and look forward to next time. Meanwhile Chinese awaits you impatiently."

"I know you're right," said Adrian grudgingly, taking his empty cup into the kitchen.

"And I'll still be here," added Vic. Putting his arm round Adrian's shoulders, he propelled him towards the door. "Off you go, Adrian. I hope it all goes well at home and at SOAS. Email me from time to time to tell me how things are."

"Yes, I will. Bye, Vic. I can't thank you enough for your help and support. I'll be back, no doubt." He went towards the lift. The door shut behind him.

Almost in defiance of Vic's advice, that afternoon he got out his Arabic text book which he was dipping into in his spare hours. Restlessly, he persuaded Jean to provide space for him in her office, and to set out all the reference books she could find with entries on infants' schools. He found a school named the 'English Junior School', but disappointingly Jean had never heard of it. Adrian returned to the Residence disgruntled.

His spirits rose the next morning with a call from Maddy, Personal Assistant to the HoA at the AUB, who informed him that an address for Mrs Al-Zaini had been found in the Accounts Department payment records. Adrian raced straight there, where Maddy handed him a piece of paper showing the address in Arabic and French. He found it on his Beirut map and called Khalil, who knew the district and agreed to take Adrian there on Thursday, when he had finished an urgent piece of work. If Adrian wanted to go straight away, Khalil could send Mukhtar with the car. Adrian vacillated; on the one hand he was impatient to go immediately, but on the other, interpretation was essential. So he decided to wait.

On Wednesday morning, Mark called to say that he had found a leaflet on the 'English Junior School' in a pile of old brochures at the British Council, and that he was free to meet Adrian straight away. The leaflet turned out to be a single glossy sheet folded in three, showing coloured photographs of infants and toddlers sitting on floor mats, playing with toys. There was no mention of the fees on the brochure, but it specified that children of all nationalities were welcome, on the understanding that English was the main language spoken. The address – near the Residence – and phone number of the school were in large letters at the bottom of the back page, along with the name of the headmistress – Samantha Bauer.

They stopped at a swanky bar on Hamra where Adrian immediately tried to call the school number expecting a recorded message, but the number didn't ring. This did not, he felt, augur well. Mark agreed. They set off together on foot to investigate the place. On the way, Mark talked about his plans for the rest of his gap year; Adrian observed admiringly how focussed Mark seemed and how carefully he had planned the time, compared with his own wanderings.

The anticipated school premises turned out to be a large second-hand English bookshop. The owner, an American called Briggs, explained that the school was now being run at the headmistress' home. They could, if they liked, return at the weekend in case he were able to find the new address. Adrian thanked Briggs. Mark went home by bus whilst Adrian walked back to the Residence, reflecting despondently on the lack of progress, and contemplating the reality of flying home. Mark called later to say that he had searched the Beirut phone books but found no number for Samantha Bauer – a further blow.

The following morning's visit with Khalil to the address provided by the AUB was similarly unfruitful. The caretaker had only recently taken over the job from his father and had no memory of Mrs Al-Zaini. He would speak to his father that evening, and Khalil could call him the following day at midday to find out if his father had any memory of her.

Adrian felt stuck, squeezed between that day in the very near future when he would have to go home, and the blank wall with a couple of chinks in it that was pushing up against him on the other side. A call to the airline disclosed that there was space on all flights in the next seven days. He needed at least a day, he self-indulgently told himself, in which to take leave of his new friends and acquaintances, and to thank them for their help. To allow himself flexibility, he decided not to book the flight in advance, but simply to turn up at the airport on the chosen day. He would call his parents from the airport when he had checked in. Meanwhile, despite holding out little hope, before going to the airport on Saturday he would return to the bookshop to see if Briggs had found the English Junior School's new address.

Khalil was at the Residence to be with Adrian for the Friday call to the caretaker. This produced a crumb of encouragement; the caretaker's father did remember Mrs Al-Zaini, but had forgotten when she had moved out, and had no forwarding address for her. Trying to be positive, Adrian reminded Khalil that the caretaker's father was the second person to verify her existence in Beirut, which was an important factor. But there were no further clues to follow up at the moment and Adrian had to go home to continue his previous life as a student in London. It felt worlds away. While they ate sandwiches together, Khalil launched into a speech, obviously carefully prepared, to say how much he appreciated Adrian's friendship. Adrian reciprocated sincerely, thanking Khalil for the time he had spent looking after him, and promising that he would have learned a lot more Arabic before his next visit to Beirut. Adrian refused Khalil's offer of a ride with Mukhtar to the airport, since he didn't know what time it would be. He told Khalil (truthfully) that he didn't like farewells at stations and airports, and that he had to do it on his own. Khalil made Adrian promise to call him from the airport to confirm that he was safely on his way.

That evening, over the final burgers, Jean and Mark tried to be encouraging, but Adrian was anything but chipper.

"Look," said Jean, "you've achieved heaps. You've found out that your mother was really here, and you've made lots of useful contacts. And you'll be coming again, won't you?"

"'Course I will. I can't stay away from you two. You're great chums. I just wish I had a real, current address for her."

"Hang on in there," said Mark. "I think she's here, and I think you'll find her."

Parting from them was painful, as had been his earlier farewells.

In the morning, Adrian left everything in his room when he set off to the bookshop, hoping that Briggs might produce a reason for an additional day in Beirut. Briggs was welcoming, but had not found the address. Adrian explained his circumstances to Briggs, who called to an assistant in the nether regions of the shop to make coffee for them. Adrian felt forlorn; he had, seemingly, reached the end of the path. Reluctantly, he trudged off in the direction of the Residence.

"Hi," said a voice behind him, as someone tapped him on his shoulder. "How's your friend Briggs?"

Adrian turned his head. Instantly, two men drew level with him, one on each side, taking hold of his upper arms with iron hands. A scream got stuck in Adrian's throat as he felt the nozzle of a gun in his back. They marched him down a side street which Adrian did not recognise, and pushed him into the back of a waiting car, where they sat on either side of him. Passers-by had taken no notice. The man who had spoken blindfolded him.

"We are taking you to a place to answer some questions," he said quietly.

Twenty-four

The car sounded as though it had hit rock bottom; the engine roared deafeningly when the driver accelerated, while every turn and gear change was accompanied by an ominous sound of metal clanging and scraping below the floor. The smell was terrible – evidently the exhaust disgorged its gases inside rather than outside the car. Adrian recalled these details later when he was left alone in his cell.

Nobody spoke to him in the car, nor did his two captors converse together. Occasionally, the driver blurted something out, to receive a fast blurted reply. Adrian had little idea of how long the journey lasted, but later guessed that it was less than an hour. When the car stopped, he was hauled out, dragged a few paces and up two steps. One of the men opened a door or a grille and pushed Adrian through. Loud noises outside suggested a market: stall-holders touting their wares and people bargaining. The access door was slammed shut but it made no difference to the level of sound. It was a grille, then.

"Now we take you to the room," said the man Adrian identified as 'Alpha', the one who spoke. Beta opened another door and they dragged him down a steep spiral staircase into a basement room which reeked of stale smoke. There, Beta removed the blindfold then flicked a switch by the door which turned on a dim bulb hanging from the ceiling. Alpha arranged the only two rickety chairs to face each other. A barked order to Beta sent him from the room.

"Sit," said Alpha, pointing at one of the chairs. Adrian sat, Alpha standing beside him. "Give me your watch," he continued, his portly stomach pressing against Adrian's arm. Adrian slid his watch off and deposited it in the podgy hand up against his chest. "And show your pockets."

Adrian pulled out his mobile, his Residence keys, a scrap of paper with Briggs' shop address on it, a packet of tissues, and a wad of Lebanese pounds, as well as a US$20 note, all of which he handed to Alpha, who stashed away the booty, including the watch, in the numerous pockets of his vast safari vest. What a repulsive creature, thought Adrian; even his voice was slimy.

"Good, you are obedient boy. Tell me your name." So saying, Alpha sat down opposite him. No advantage in giving a false name, thought Adrian swiftly.

"Adrian Goodfield."

"Now, Goodfield, tell me about your friend Briggs. Think carefully before you speak. I want the truth."

"Briggs isn't my friend," replied Adrian coolly.

"But you go there and you come out with no books. Twice we see you go there, once you go with a friend, once alone. And the friend, he buys no books."

Adrian didn't know if he was supposed to fill the ensuing silence with explanations, but thought it expedient to stay quiet, observing his interrogator attentively.

Alpha walked over to stand behind Adrian and then brought down a crashing blow with the side of his hand on his left shoulder, nearly knocking Adrian off his chair.

"You don't buy books, so what you do there, American boy?"

"I'm not American, I'm British."

"Of course you American. Briggs is American. People who go there are American."

A further blow on Adrian's right shoulder.

"What you do at Briggs shop?"

"I went there to collect the address of an English infant school."

"Why?"

"Because my mother may be there."

"Shit, you talk," said the man contemptuously, returning to his seat. "Mother too old for infant school."

"My mother is perhaps a teacher there."

"She's your mother, so you don't know where she is? You talk shit!"

"I'm looking for my real mother."

"So you have a not-real mother, in America?"

"As I said before, I'm not American, I'm British. And yes, I have adoptive parents in England."

"The Americans who go to Briggs all say they are English, or Canadian, or Australian, or New Zealand, but we know they are not. We know your friend Briggs has Israeli friends. You must tell us about Briggs, and what information you gave him on your visits. So, start! Speak!"

"I know nothing. I've only seen Briggs twice."

"OK. You stay here until you remember. Think about it."

With that, Alpha waddled out of the room and locked the door behind him with a key.

When Adrian stood up, he felt his whole body trembling. Steadying himself, he walked round the large dank empty space. In the ceiling on the opposite side of the room from the door, dappled light filtered down through a wide skylight made of thick patterned glass blocks let into the pavement above. Feet tramped to and fro on it. Apart from the two chairs, the room contained a plastic table, and a platform made of wooden slats screwed down on to metal feet a few inches tall. A rough grey blanket lay rumpled on it – presumably this was a bed.

So this is it, thought Adrian, this is where I am at the moment. Temporarily. He reminded himself of the exact way in which he had been seized, as well as the number of doors he had passed through, and the direction of the spiral staircase. Gradually the skylight dulled over; Adrian longed for his watch. He began counting seconds to try to keep pace with time. In a pile of rubble in a corner, he picked out the smallest stones he could find and put one aside to mark each hour that he counted. After over two of these, the key crunched in the lock and Alpha reappeared.

"So Goodfield, what have you remembered?" he said.

Better prevaricate, thought Adrian.

"I need the toilet," he said, hoping he would be led out of the room, which would give him an idea of the premises.

Alpha went to the door and shouted something. Beta soon appeared with an ancient metal bucket which he put in front of Adrian.

"This is toilet," said Alpha.

Having asked for it, Adrian knew he should use it. He took the bucket to a corner of the room and then glanced round in the hope that Alpha and Beta might leave him to it, but no, Adrian was destined to relieve himself in their presence. This is no different from peeing in any ordinary urinal, and no more exposed, Adrian told himself firmly, feeling nevertheless that it was, although the men were talking together without heeding him. When Adrian had finished, Beta disappeared carrying the bucket.

"Tell me about Briggs," said Alpha, pointing to the same chair as earlier and sitting down opposite him again.

"He's an American, as you say. And he was kind about me looking for my mother."

"Your mother excuse again! Where does Briggs live? Does he have family?"

"I know nothing of Briggs, truly nothing," said Adrian, who thought it best not to invent a life for Briggs, in case his captors did know the man and would punish him for lying. Alpha snarled at him, showing teeth stained brown.

"I can make you very uncomfortable," he said, "if you choose not to tell me what you know. I give you an example now." He stood up abruptly, went over to Adrian, and slapped him hard on both cheeks. "You see," he said. "And it can get worse." He walked out and locked the door, switching off the light.

Shaking, Adrian rubbed his stinging cheeks. He remained seated for a few moments in the darkened room, waiting for his eyes to become accustomed to the gloom. Eventually, a slight glow from reflected street lights through the ceiling glass blocks created shapes in the dark – the chairs, the table, the bed. Adrian went over to the light switch and flicked it on, but the room remained dark. The light must be connected to a master-switch outside the room he thought.

He spread the blanket on the planks and lay down to brood. Why was he here? Why had he been abducted? And what was all this about Briggs, who seemed to be an ordinary affable character? Was there a connection to the excursions the previous Saturday? Was it all Khalil's fault for taking him to meet the Hezbollah man and to visit the Jalil camp? It seemed unlikely since both he and Sabir had stressed that the visits would not put Adrian in any danger. And the emphasis both of them had placed on trust should eliminate any suspicion that they had a hand in his capture. Nevertheless, Adrian was uncomfortably aware of the short time lag between the day out and his abduction. Of the two visits, the morning with Hezbollah seemed the more likely to have been a catalyst. But did his captors have any affiliation with Hezbollah? He needed to find out who they were and what was the aim of their group. Suddenly exhausted from anxiety, Adrian stopped shaking and dozed off.

He was awakened by the key in the lock. Beta pushed open the door and tried the light switch in vain. Adrian heard him mutter to himself and retreat, leaving the door ajar. Adrian sprang up but by the time he reached the door the man was back, pushing Adrian in again. This time the light switch worked. Beta picked up a plastic bottle of spring water from the floor outside the door and proffered it to Adrian, who took it and put it on the table. The metal bucket was next; Adrian put it in the same corner as before. The man shut the door and sat down on one of the chairs. They observed each other.

"What is your name?" asked Adrian, walking round Beta's chair in an attempt to be intimidating.

Beta shrugged his shoulders.

"My name, Adrian," he continued, turning his hand to tap his chest with his forefinger.

Beta was tall and lanky, with a sallow complexion and enormous doleful black eyes. His short hair was greying at the temples, but he seemed young to Adrian, perhaps in his early thirties, certainly younger than Alpha, who looked to be over fifty. Adrian pointed at Beta.

"Your name?" he said.

"Zawar."

"Zawar," repeated Adrian. He took the bottle of water from the table, noticing to his relief as he opened it, that the screw top was intact. He hadn't realised how dry his throat was until now and drank thirstily.

"And his name?" he asked, pointing energetically at the door.

Zawar turned to look at the door uncomprehendingly.

Adrian jabbed his chest again. "Me, Adrian," he said separating out the words carefully. Next he pointed again at Zawar. "You Zawar. His name?" This time Zawar understood.

"Ahmed," came the answer.

"Ahmed" repeated Adrian. "And thank you for the water," he said, pointing to the bottle. Then he tried to say it in Arabic.

A small smile lifted the corners of Zawar's mouth, and he nodded.

"I'm hungry," said Adrian, pointing to his mouth. "Eat."

"No," said Zawar, shaking his head. "No eat."

"Tomorrow," said Adrian, searching in his mind for the Arabic word.

Zawar nodded, stood up, and strode out, leaving the light on but locking the door. Adrian waited for the light to go off, but it didn't. Zawar soon returned with a flat bread sprinkled with sesame seeds, which he put on the table, and a cushion, which he put carefully at the head of the bed.

This time he switched the light off as he went out. Adrian ate the bread and drank more of the water before lying down. He could tell by the way the cushion crackled that it was filled with husks. Enormously uncomfortable, he nevertheless fell asleep, restlessly plotting a fantasy escape with the help of Zawar.

Twenty-five

It was Sunday. Watching the rain through the kitchen window while working absent-mindedly on an easy maths homework, Gemma was trying to forget that it was nine days since Adrian's last email. When she had reminded her parents on Friday that a week had elapsed, Fen had told her not to worry, and that Adrian obviously had things to wind up and people to see before leaving Beirut. But Gemma could tell, from the look that passed between Fen and John, that they were concerned. Seb, too, had asked when Adrian would be back, and whether he would be stopping in London or coming home.

John and Fen lasted out until Wednesday, Gemma's half-day. She returned from school at lunchtime to find them sitting at the kitchen table with the big planning diary in front of them, Fen wiping her eyes. Gemma burst into tears, dropped her school bag on the floor, and went to put her arms round Fen.

"It's Adrian, isn't it," she sobbed.

"Yes, darling," said Fen. They clung to each other. John let them be until their weeping subsided, then cleared his throat.

"I think we should start making enquiries," he said.

"How and where?" asked Fen despairingly.

"Through people who are in touch with him."

"*We* are in touch with him," she replied. "If he's not contacted us, then why would he have contacted anybody else?"

"What I mean," said John "is that people in Beirut might know more. Or even somebody at SOAS – Max for example."

"I've got Max's number," said Gemma, brightening. "Shall I call him now?" She delved into her school bag for her mobile.

"Just a moment, Gems," said John. "We must think about what we're going to say."

"Yes, we must," agreed Fen. "We don't want to put the cat among the pigeons."

"I don't see that there are any pigeons for the cat," retorted Gemma heatedly. "I'll just say that Adrian hasn't turned up here, and is he in London. If the answer's 'no', then I can ask Max if he'll get in touch with what's his name at the Foreign Office."

John and Fen looked at each other. John nodded slowly.

"I don't see anything wrong in that," he said. "In fact, it's a smart idea, Gemma. I'd forgotten about the Foreign Office person. Do you see any objections, Fen?"

"Weellll," she replied, unable to voice her doubts about admitting that Adrian's family knew they weren't always the first to be informed about his movements. "If you're sure, John… But does Max know where to contact the man?"

"He'll find out," asserted Gemma. "Max is clever."

Gemma tapped in the number immediately, but Max wasn't answering, so she left a message asking him to phone, without giving a reason. When Seb returned from

307

school in the afternoon, Fen explained to him, as he demolished a jam sandwich and a mug of chocolate milk, that they were all hoping for news of Adrian via Max.

The call came after 6.00, while Gemma was working in her room. She soon bounced down the stairs.

"Max says he was wondering a bit, like, where Adrian was. But he doesn't think there's any reason to be unduly worried. After all, the Middle East is a different world, he said, and Adrian might have had a new solid lead and gone off somewhere else. I told him we were thinking about trying to contact Francis at the Foreign Office, and he says he'll try to find him, although he doesn't know Francis' surname. I told him we didn't either. So that's that, for the time being. He'll be in touch again as soon as he has any news."

The evening meal was soon on the table; Seb kept their minds off Adrian by chattering about sport.

Thursday started glumly, and dragged on with no call from Max, and most of Friday too until early evening, when there was good news. Max had got through to the Foreign Office and spoken to Francis Hacker, who had volunteered to phone Vic Appleton in Beirut. It was through Vic's introduction that Adrian had met the retired Queen's Messenger who used to know Adrian's mother in Beirut. Vic had, according to Francis, helped Adrian through this difficult period with useful information and moral support. If anyone knew where to find Adrian, Vic would.

***

The conversation with Francis set Vic thinking. Adrian should have been home in England by now. It was January 28th, nine days since Adrian had taken Vic the notes of his conversations with Clifford. Even allowing for his dragging his feet about leaving Beirut, this time lapse seemed excessive. Adrian was usually reliable – someone who kept appointments and remembered commitments.

Vic called Jean, who told him that she and Mark had said their goodbyes over a meal at Burger Hall on 21st. At that time, she said, Adrian's intention for the next day was first to get his belongings packed and then walk over to Briggs' bookshop in case he had found the new address of the English Junior School. Assuming, as seemed most likely, Briggs hadn't found the address, Adrian would then collect his bag, pay for his room and head straight off to the airport for the plane home. He intended to call his parents from there to say he was on his way. A quick chat with Glyn established that Adrian had said goodbye, Glyn thought, on Friday 21st, and had said he was planning to return to Beirut during the spring break.

Vic grew distinctly uneasy. In a further phone conversation, he briefed Francis, and they agreed that although the circumstances gave cause for alarm, discretion was essential; there would be no point in fuelling the anxiety of Adrian's family. Later that day, Vic went over to the Residence. A conversation with the caretaker was enlightening: Adrian had not checked out, nor paid a final bill. The caretaker was willing, (for a small consideration), to let Vic glance inside Adrian's room where he saw that two bags were packed and ready – one obviously containing a computer. A printer was still on the table. This was ominous.

Vic knew there remained one other person who might know where Adrian was, and that was Khalil. Phone calls to Mark and Jean revealed Khalil's surname to be Haddad – alas the most common surname in Lebanon. There would be several thousand Khalil Haddads in Beirut. Neither Mark nor Jean had met him; Mark thought Khalil lived somewhere in South Beirut but wasn't sure. Vic paced around in his flat, racking his brains for any other source of information.

Francis meanwhile obtained the Goodfield family's home number from Max. During a long conversation with John, Francis endeavoured to calm his fears by suggesting that Adrian might be exploring a new lead and would reappear soon. What he did not tell John was that he had alerted the Beirut embassy to Adrian's possible disappearance. Rum deal, he thought; a missing person searching for a missing person.

***

Not having received Adrian's promised call from the airport, Khalil tried to phone him on Sunday, two days after their parting. There was no reply. He tried again on the two following days with the same result. On Wednesday, he went with Mukhtar to the Residence. The caretaker, recognising Khalil from previous visits, volunteered the information that Mr Adrian had not paid his weekly rent nor had he checked out, but that his luggage was packed and ready. Did Mr Khalil want to pay and take the luggage? Mr Khalil did not, but noted down the caretaker's number and called him the next day. There was no news. He alerted Sabir, who had no advice to give, but offered to call his cousin at Hezbollah in case he had heard something; he drew a blank. And, Khalil and Sabir agreed, Adrian was obviously not at the Jalil refugee camp.

On Friday, he returned to the Residence to see if there was some misunderstanding, but the caretaker was adamant that Adrian had not appeared. Khalil anxiously scouted round the streets for a couple of hours, looking for his friend, but there was no sign of him. "Wait and see for a few more days," was Sabir's advice, which Khalil resolved to follow since he could think of nothing better to do.

Twenty-six

It's torture, it's torture, somebody was whispering. Adrian's head turned this way and that on the pillow. It's torture, it's torture, he heard it again, distinctly. Coming to, alone in the cell under the rough blanket, he recognised his own voice saying those words, and he knew why. He was lying on his front: his back, from his shoulders down to his buttocks, felt as though a sharp rake had been drawn across it, leaving furrows in his skin. How many times in the past had he flippantly said 'it was torture'? It wasn't, he reasoned, an expression to be used lightly in conversation – surely victims never did, nor would he ever again. How disrespectfully we use it, he thought, as he remembered bending forwards over the chair seat to receive Ahmed's punishment.

Now awake, Adrian wondered what time it was. Only dim electric lights filtered through the glass ceiling blocks so it must still be night. His stomach ached with hunger. He managed to stand up and walk over to the table to pick up his water bottle. Good, it wasn't empty. Unsure as to how much water Zawar would bring him, he didn't drink it all, just in case.

Adrian was surviving, somewhat. Twice the previous day, Zawar had brought him bottled water and flatbreads, some with sesame seeds on them, tastier than the plain ones. Zawar had also collected the stinking bucket to empty it – and brought it back. Ahmed, for his part, had persisted with the same questions about Briggs, to which Adrian had replied each time that he knew nothing of Briggs except that he had a bookshop and was American. His lack of useful information had prompted Ahmed's attack. Adrian had to assume that this activity would continue, but for how long? And for how long could he stand it? As he lay down again on his front, he decided that when there was enough light coming through the glass blocks, he should arrange stones in the corner to mark each day: bigger stones for one day, laid horizontally, and smaller ones in a vertical line downwards for the number of times he was tortured that day. This morning (assuming it was past midnight) was Monday, [24th] so it should be the third big stone, since he had been seized on Saturday. He dozed.

Zawar opened the door and turned on the light. Adrian gestured to him to show him his watch. It was 7.30. People were out and about on the pavement above. Zawar left water and a flatbread on the table and went out. About ten minutes later, he returned with an enamel basin of warm water and an old towel. From his gesture Adrian gathered that he should wash. He levered himself off the hard planks, removed his crumpled smelly clothes, even his shirt which was stuck to his back with dried blood, and did his best to de-grime his chilled, unhappy body. Then he dried himself, dressed, ate and drank. He longed to be properly clean, wearing clean clothes.

That day, the line of accusation was that Adrian was an Israeli spy. Ahmed gabbled on about Mossad, Aman and Shin Bet, stopping to question Adrian about his 'friends' who worked for them. The faster he spoke, the more difficult it was for Adrian to follow what he was saying, nor had he any energy to do so. Adrian's quiet denial of any knowledge of the organisations and their employees enraged Ahmed. The outcome was predictable – this time directed at Adrian's genitals. Afterwards Adrian's head was fuzzy as he lay aching on his front. In the evening, Zawar turned him over and propped him up with the pillow against the wall to pour water into his mouth. Adrian managed to swallow some. Then Zawar tore small pieces off the bread to push into his mouth. Again Adrian swallowed. "Good, good," said Zawar, continuing patiently until Adrian had eaten all the bread. Oh, said Adrian to himself, he knows a little English.

Adrian wondered what his captors' relative positions were in their organisation. Zawar-Beta was clearly the underling – indeed Adrian wondered what his instructions from Ahmed-Alpha were, presumably to keep him, Adrian, alive. He guessed that providing the basin of warm water was Zawar's own initiative. It seemed likely that Zawar lived in a room somewhere in the building. Perhaps Ahmed did too, but as he turned up only for the question and punishment sessions, Adrian surmised that he probably lived elsewhere. As far as Adrian could tell, Ahmed and Zawar didn't cross paths; he never heard them speaking together. Although Adrian saw them only one at a time, escape was impossible. There was no way he could crack the glass ceiling blocks nor break down the door; attacking Ahmed or Zawar was also out of the question in his weakened state, and would certainly incur more severe reprisals.

The line of big stones lengthened, each day thus marked bringing fresh physical insults and weakening Adrian's morale and bodily defences. It was all Adrian could manage, to remember the stone diary every day, and to shuffle or crawl over to the pile of rubble to mark the days, which were merging bewilderingly with the nights. On day five, the torture line stretched to three stones. Meanwhile Zawar continued his ministrations, even taking it upon himself to wash Adrian. The bucket was now placed permanently beside the bed and the basin on the table ready to be refilled. Adrian speculated on the kind of punishment that could be meted out to Zawar should Ahmed discover his kindness. Or was it kindness? Adrian scrutinised Zawar's expression each time he came in; he believed he detected pity in the man's eyes, but since he hadn't known Zawar in any other circumstances, it was only conjecture.

The next day, Zawar brought in a dirty thin mattress which he put on the bed, and a second blanket. Adrian lay down shivering. For that afternoon, Ahmed had prepared something special. Relishing his power, he explained slowly to Adrian that if he persisted in denying all knowledge of Briggs and the Israeli spy ring, he would be obliged to damage Adrian's feet. Adrian was too weak to protest with any vigour, but repeated the same answers to Ahmed's questions as previously. The result was broken toes – the middle one on each foot. It was agony, an agony that merged with all the other agonies of the preceding days. That evening, Zawar brought cold water to bathe Adrian's feet. The diet changed too: there was milk and Lebanese beans. Adrian knew that whatever else happened, he had to eat and drink. Zawar fed him slowly; by Adrian's reckoning, it must have taken a couple of hours. Then there were pills with the water. He slept fitfully and wretchedly, dreaming of being at home with his family, and of the light of day, and of opportunities, and of friends.

Was anybody looking for him? It seemed likely. He would have been expected at home by now. Vic too would probably have heard that he hadn't arrived back in England. Adrian's illusions of his self-sufficiency had been shot down. He needed them, Fen, John, Gemma, Seb, and his friends in England, Max, Benny, and Tazie. He tried to dream himself into her arms, but each time a spasm of pain shot through his right foot, causing him to grunt. Poor me, he thought, how feeble I am – I haven't even the strength to shout with pain and all this because I wanted to find my mother. Why should I be punished for that? It was normal, and despite everything, he still wanted to find her.

When Zawar woke him in the morning, he felt worse than he had at any other time in his life. His whole body was racked with pain, and he was by now afraid that months would pass before anybody found him. He also worried that he might not be able to walk. I have no future, I have well and truly cocked up, he thought. Zawar levered him into a sitting position on the side of the bed and held him while he pissed into the bucket. I must try to stand up, Adrian said to himself resolutely. Zawar moved the bucket and caught his arm when he saw what Adrian wanted to do; after two tries, Adrian was standing unsteadily on his badly misshapen feet. He gestured to the rubble pile; Zawar nodded. Each step was excruciating; Adrian rocked dangerously, prevented from falling only by Zawar's support. When they reached the rubble pile, Adrian sat down on the floor, still supported by Zawar, who crouched down beside him. Adrian pointed at the day stones one by one, and counted them aloud on his fingers, whereupon Zawar nodded and counted them in Arabic. At that moment, a sort of complicity was born between them;

Adrian was sure Zawar understood what the stones represented.

Breakfast was again milk and beans. Adrian recovered a little energy. Damaged feet seemed somehow to be a milder type of injury, further removed from the essence of himself than were the parts which had been so horribly violated by Ahmed's cruelty. Then he slept again, more serenely this time, the effect of the pills not having worn off. When Zawar returned at the end of the afternoon as usual, he found Adrian sitting up in the bed. Ahmed had not come. As the glass blocks in the ceiling ceased to glow with daylight, Adrian kept touching his head: was he dreaming or was it really evening, and had he really escaped punishment today? Zawar was bearing a tray: rice and vegetables, milk and water. Adrian couldn't find real hunger, but the change of food was a sign... of what? Adrian couldn't think.

Zawar helped him to eat, as usual. When Adrian had taken all he could, Zawar removed the tray to return a few minutes later with a piece of paper and a pen. Sitting on the bed, he wrote down a few words in Arabic then pronounced them for Adrian, who repeated them. They counted the stones and then went through the days of the week, and the months. Adrian's head buzzed from the effort. Suddenly he fell asleep. Zawar left.

A rude awakening. Ahmed waddled into the cell at daybreak, followed by Zawar.

"Up Goodfield, get up. We are taking you somewhere else, for a change. We go." Adrian, shaking uncontrollably, moved his legs slowly sideways until his feet touched the floor, stood up tentatively, and fell back on to the bed. Zawar came to help him.

"I need the bucket," he said. Peeing in front of these people was no longer embarrassing. "Where are you taking me?" he asked when he had finished.

"You will see later," replied Ahmed. Zawar dressed Adrian, picked up his trainers to hand to him, then blindfolded him. The men trundled him upstairs and out into the back of a waiting car. As before, they sat on either side of him. The car sped off erratically. Convulsive acceleration and braking jolted Adrian's damaged body, sending spasms of pain from his sore head down to his broken toes. After about forty minutes, Adrian guessed, the car slowed down and stopped. Ahmed opened the car door, pulled Adrian out with him, and pushed him to sit down on the kerb. His trainers, which were on the floor of the car, were chucked out at him. He heard the car door slam shut and the engine rev up. He sat for a moment, wondering, then pulled off the blindfold; his eyes, unaccustomed to daylight, shut tight. He shielded them with his right hand before opening them again cautiously a few moments later. The line of traffic was a glinting swirling snake. His captors' car had gone.

Was he free? Adrian wondered. Or would Ahmed reappear to scoop him up and ferry him off for some new form of torture? A pain flashed across Adrian's head from ear to ear. Gradually his eyes adjusted to the level of light. He noticed that his left hand was clenched tightly, holding something: a wad of small denomination Lebanese pounds. How did they get there?

Somebody was crouching beside him; Adrian recoiled. A hand went to hold his; he tried instinctively to disentangle it.

"N'ayez pas peur," said a soothing female voice, "Je suis là pour vous aider."

Adrian turned his head gingerly to look at the person: she was a nun. Behind her stood a second nun; both were wearing black habits and black headscarves with a white border all round. They both had kind wrinkled faces, and one wore glasses.

Adrian swallowed hard before launching into a garbled explanation in French and English. He had been wounded in a fight, could hardly walk, and needed to return to the Residence. One nun stayed beside him while the other ventured into the road to hail a taxi. Adrian vomited into the road; the nun beside him produced a huge white handkerchief with which she gently wiped his mouth and his face. Soon he found himself sitting between the nuns on the back seat of a taxi. At the Residence, they pulled him out and helped him to the door. He tried to hand the wad of notes to them to pay for the taxi, but they refused. As Adrian no longer had any keys, one of the nuns rang the bell. Soon the caretaker appeared. That was all Adrian remembered until he woke up lying on his bed aching from head to toe. Khalil was sitting in a chair, and moved over to the bed with a bottle of water. Adrian drank gratefully.

Twenty-seven

During the next twenty-four hours, Adrian drifted in and out of sleep, his body working at banishing the searing pain which penetrated every part of him and, in his waking moments, his mind dwelling on the terrible days he had experienced. True, he was apparently free, since Ahmed had probably conceded that Adrian had nothing of interest to say, but Ahmed could change his mind, or a different group could take Adrian hostage. Meanwhile, Khalil looked after Adrian gently and quietly, administering strong painkillers and tending his feet, first bathing them in cold water and then smothering his toes in arnica cream, as well as giving him a bed-bath. He sat Adrian up to feed him bean soup and then lay him down again. Adrian appreciated being clean and felt that his muttered thanks to Khalil were inadequate.

On Sunday afternoon, Khalil woke Adrian to say that two nuns were with the caretaker, asking to see him. At first Adrian didn't remember who they were, but smiled wanly when Khalil reminded him of his return to the Residence the previous day. His eyes released tears when he recalled the comfort of the hand that had held his. The nuns had, Khalil told him, stayed with him until he himself had arrived, summoned by the caretaker.

Having manoeuvred Adrian into a sitting position, Khalil went to fetch them up from the entrance lobby. First they kissed Adrian and then they introduced themselves. Sophia, who had held Adrian's hand and spoken to him on the street, sat down on the bed to take hold of his hand again, while Marie-Therese busied herself with a wide basket from which she carefully produced two small ramekin dishes, a couple of oranges and a bunch of bananas. Khalil took them from her and put them on the table, gesturing to her to sit on the chair. Khalil's offer of a soft drink from the array of bottles he had brought in to cater for Adrian's every wish, was accepted. Sipping cola from a plastic mug, Sophia explained that the ramekins contained creme caramel, composed of milk, egg and sugar, especially nourishing and recommended for sick people. Khalil produced a spoon whereupon Adrian, suddenly hungry at the prospect of different food, immediately tucked into one; it tasted delicious. Having taken the empty ramekin from Adrian, Khalil sat down on the floor.

It turned out that the two nuns had been on their way to buy vegetables when they had noticed Adrian slumped on the kerb and had come to his rescue. They regularly helped distressed people, regardless of race or creed, they said. Sophia, puzzled as to why Adrian's middle toes were broken, as though symmetrically, tried to prise more information out of him, but Adrian simply shook his head vaguely.

In due course, Marie-Therese came to the point: she and Sophia believed that Adrian needed medical attention. They lived in a Catholic convent with a nursing home, where it might be possible to find a bed for him. A doctor would examine him and recommend appropriate treatment. Nurses would look after him, and of course he would be fed and watered. What did Adrian think, they asked.

In his confused state, Adrian found it difficult to make a decision, and said so. His security was, in his mind, linked to being back in his familiar room, and he feared any change; although he didn't voice this, Sophia understood. To persuade him, she mentioned the burden that Khalil was bearing in looking after him; besides, Khalil had his work to take into account. Adrian would be safe in the nursing home, she stressed: the doorman at reception was well equipped to prevent any intruders from making their way into the premises. She had guessed, he realised, that his wounds were not the result of casual mugging. With Khalil's encouragement, Adrian accepted the offer. Marie-Therese took a mobile phone out of her bag and called the nursing home. The result was positive: a bed would be prepared for him for arrival the following morning. Suddenly the possible financial implications occurred to Adrian; he needn't worry, Marie-Therese reassured him. The nursing home belonged to a well established religious foundation which covered the costs of accommodation, food, and initial medical examination. Any specialist treatment would be chargeable, at a minimal rate. All being agreed, Khalil accompanied the nuns downstairs to show them out.

Late in the afternoon, leaving Adrian asleep, Khalil returned home for a few hours, but was back in time to administer chicken soup, followed by fruit. Once again, he slept on the floor, fitfully, for Adrian was now prey to terrifying nightmares, from which he awoke howling. In the morning, Khalil prepared Adrian's backpack with his passport, and a wallet with a little money. He dressed Adrian before enlisting the caretaker's help to get him down to the entrance. They took a taxi to the nursing home, which Adrian paid for out of the money he had found in his hand when his captors had thrown him out of the car. He now realised it was a final kindly gesture on the part of Zawar. Marie-Therese was waiting for them in the doorway of the nursing home with two burly male nurses who bore him into a fresh-smelling bed with smooth sheets. He fell asleep immediately, despite the raging pain in his toes.

***

"Francis, it's Vic again. I had an idea over the weekend. Adrian has a Jordanian friend in London called Hassan. Did he ever mention him to you?"

"Yes, in fact he did. He told me that Hassan's cousin would be meeting him at the airport when he arrived in Beirut and would look after him. Why?"

"Well, the cousin is called Khalil Haddad. He's the most likely person to know where Adrian is. I've never met him and I don't know where he lives, or his phone number. And Khalil Haddad is a very common name in Lebanon. I need to find the right one."

"Well so you do."

"Hassan in London will have all the details. Can you find him?"

"I, personally, no. But I'll ask Adrian's friend Max if he can help. Hassan's at SOAS too, isn't he?"

"I think so. Let me know asap will you?"

"Yes, I will."

"Thanks."

Vic had done all he could.

***

Adrian's health took a turn for the worse. He developed a fever; the pains from his torture increased, and his headache, severe in captivity, intensified. He could hardly move. The house doctor diagnosed pneumonia and prescribed antibiotics.

Adrian remembered little of the next few days. He knew he was in a room 'for foreigners' with one other patient – also suffering from pneumonia, he was told. He swallowed the pills handed to him, and ate a little when a nun came to feed him. He couldn't manage to wash himself so the nuns obliged, nor could he walk alone to the loo because his aching legs and damaged toes gave way underneath him. He was propped up on three pillows during the day and lay down on two at night. He would sweat profusely some of the time, then shiver uncontrollably immediately afterwards. His sheets were changed each time. In those chillingly bleak moments, he could feel and smell again the dank cell around him, although the hospital lights and noises were comforting. Marie-Therese seemed often to be there then, ready to comfort him.

"Reposes-toi, Adrian," she would say. "Tu n'as plus rien à craindre."

Sometimes he stayed awake at night on purpose, to avoid his agonising nightmares, with the lights a reminder that he was free. At such times, he wondered whether he would ever shake off the pneumonia. Was it only old people who died of it? Could he be, quite simply, lying on his deathbed? Or would he be permanently disabled by sickness? Was he clinically depressed?

Khalil visited him regularly, anxious and puzzled by the persistence of his friend's illness. The clinic doctor told Khalil that pneumonia did sometimes linger, but that someone of Adrian's age would normally get over it easily. When his fever abated, he would improve quickly. Khalil talked to Adrian, trying to rouse him and interest him by recounting the day's happenings in Beirut. However, Adrian's eyelids would soon droop, whereupon Khalil would leave.

Adrian dreamed longingly of home, of Fen or Gemma holding his hand, of Sebastian bouncing around on his mattress, and of John, smiling from the doorway. Sometimes the images were so real that he would wake up with a jerk expecting to see them there, but it was a nurse or doctor or Khalil who stood beside his bed. In one of his dreams, he was standing in the middle of a circle of his university friends who were holding hands around him. Suddenly they all shouted "Get better! Get better!" and danced around. He woke to find his sick roommate beside his bed, looking down at him.

"OK mate?" asked the man.

"Yeah, getting better by the minute," said Adrian. "Was I saying something peculiar? I keep getting these dreams…"

"You were grunting and mumbling – it sounded like 'dance, dance."

Adrian managed a small smile. "They were all circling round me," he said.

"You thirsty?"

"Yes, I must drink. They've told me."

His mate reached for the plastic beaker and helped Adrian to gulp down a mouthful of water.

Adrian had lost all sense of time. He had known, from his rubble stones in the cell, that he had been released on Saturday 29th January, but had lost count of the days since then. Besides, days and nights no longer followed each other logically but were all jumbled up. Khalil tried to tell him on each visit which day and what time it was, but Adrian never remembered. He kept thinking that Fen and John would be worried, not having heard from him for some time. They had probably tried calling him on his mobile which was in Ahmed's hands. Horrors. Would Ahmed answer incoming calls, or try the numbers in the directory for fun? Anyway, Adrian reasoned, he couldn't face calling his parents; he wouldn't be able to reassure them or explain anything. Recounting his agony was out of the question. So it didn't matter that his mobile was gone. He tossed and turned in semi-sleep, muttering to himself.

***

One morning, when the nuns had finished washing him and he was slumbering on his pillow heap, somebody touched his arm. He opened his eyes to find Vic looking down at him.

"Hullo Adrian. I've come to find out what you're doing."

"Oh, Vic."

"Yes, that's me."

"They say I've got, erm, what's it called…"

"Hm, well, we'll see about that."

"How did you know I was here?"

"I asked Khalil."

"Oh, of course. Khalil comes often. It was he and the nuns who brought me to this clinic."

"So you're being well looked after."

"Yes, everybody's very kind. Sophia and Marie-Therese come often. But I don't feel any better."

"You look pretty poorly, to tell the truth."

Adrian's mind rumbled up a gear. "You said Khalil told you?"

"Yes."

"You know him?"

"Mm."

"How?"

"Most people are findable – perhaps even your mother."

"Oh." Adrian thought, not for the first time, that 'omniscient' seemed the right word to describe Vic. "Then you probably know I've got pneu... pneu... pneumonia"

"Yes, that's what they're saying. But why are you just lying here like a heap of bedding?"

"I feel rather feeble, and a bit depressed."

Vic bent over Adrian, pulled his pillows up brusquely with one hand while he supported Adrian's back with the other. Adrian winced and twitched as he was moved. The pillows repositioned, Vic hauled Adrian up into sitting position. Adrian groaned.

"That's better," said Vic. "Now I want you to think. Look around yourself. The world's still here, isn't it?"

Adrian nodded.

"And you're still alive, aren't you?"

Adrian nodded again.

"But you need to get well again, otherwise you won't be able to carry on with your degree or find your mother."

"Er… yes. But I can't budge, really; I feel a bit too weak for any of that at the moment."

"I bet you do. I think we should move you. We'll get you to the AUB Medical Center for a full check-up and accurate diagnosis, and then when they think you're well enough to move, you can come and stay with me until your father comes to collect you."

Adrian started weeping. "How do you know he'll come?"

"Well I'm sure he will when I tell him how ill you've been."

Adrian turned his face away from Vic. "But I've got things to do here. I haven't found *her*. I can't go home now!"

"Finding her can wait. The most important thing is for you to get better. And I can't and don't want to be your nurse for months on end. Now give me your home phone number."

"I can't. I've lost my mobile."

"Can't you remember the number?"

"Not now, no, I can't."

"You are in a bad way if you can't remember your home number. Where are your things?"

Adrian pointed at the locker beside his bed. Vic opened it, pulled out some crumpled clothes, under which were Adrian's passport and wallet. He put them back.

"There's not much in here – stinky clothes and your passport."

"Everything else is at the Residence."

Adrian closed his eyes.

"I'm just going to make a couple of phone calls and I'll be back very soon," said Vic, walking briskly out of the room.

Adrian slept fitfully, wondering whether Vic's appearance had been a dream. Eventually he woke to see Vic standing beside his bed again.

"So you are real," he said.

"Was that ever in doubt?" asked Vic. "Now it's all arranged. You must get up and get dressed. Can you do that yourself? I've got a car and a driver waiting below."

"I don't think so. I can't even walk to the loo."

"Would you like the nuns to dress you?"

"Yes please."

"I don't suppose they can do away with that grisly growth on your face."

Vic left the room. In a few minutes two nuns appeared. They took Adrian's clothes out of the locker and wrestled them on to him as he lay on the bed. Vic returned, found Adrian's socks on the floor and pushed them on to his bruised misshapen feet. He picked up Adrian's passport and wallet and then checked that there was nothing else of his anywhere. He got Adrian to stand up, held him round the waist with his right hand, using his left hand to steady him.

"Gosh, you're strong," said Adrian.

"I need to be with a lump like you to haul along."

"Sorry, my feet aren't much good, nor my legs."

"You can say that again. Adrian, didn't you have a watch?"

"Yes, but I lost it."

"As well as your mobile?"

"Yep."

Both Sophia and Marie-Therese were in the entrance waiting to kiss Adrian goodbye. Tears ran down his face as he thanked them for rescuing him.

On arrival at the AUB Medical Center, Adrian was wheeled into a luxurious single room, part of a ward for infectious diseases. A needle was inserted into the back of his hand and a drip attached to it. Vic produced a bottle of water and filled a beaker.

"Where's the gin?" asked Adrian, with a sudden spark of wit, noticing the bubbles. Vic smiled.

"That's not even tonic, it's mineral water. So no gin for the time being. But it's there, waiting for you at home. Gin or no gin, you must keep drinking this water."

There was a silence.

"Why are you being so kind to me?"

"Because at the moment, there's nobody else to do kindness for you."

"Oh." Adrian looked puzzled. "But Khalil…"

"He's a good friend, and he did the best he could."

A doctor and nurse wearing starched clothes appeared and introduced themselves. "They are going to do lots of tests to find out what's laying you so low now. It's unlikely to be pneumonia. I'll come back later to find out what they've discovered, and to see how you're getting along."

"Thanks for everything," said Adrian to Vic's receding back.

He was in no fit state to take in or recall later the numerous tests that he underwent that afternoon, nor the many people who trundled him around in his wheelchair with his drip. Doctors came and went and discussed quietly. His feet were examined carefully. Eventually Adrian was bathed, returned to his room wearing a pair of white cotton hospital pyjamas, and was lifted into the most comfortable bed he had slept in since he had left home. A nurse came to bind each broken toe to the larger toe beside it. For the first time, the pressure of the bed cover on the injured toes was relieved. At about 6.00pm a meal was brought in.

"You must eat," said the nurse. "This is a special high nutrition meal for people who are losing a lot of weight. You're anaemic and rather thin for your height. See what you can manage and I'll be back to check up."

On the plate there were four dollops of differently coloured mashed food. To Adrian's sickened palate they all tasted bland, but he ate as much as he could. Afterwards the nurse brought a chocolate pudding, also high nutrition. She fed him three big mouthfuls of that too.

While eating, Adrian thought about his mother, the original reason for his voyage and the reason, by extension, for his captivity. 'Now or never' – it still seemed to him. He had to extricate himself from the mess he was in and stay on in Lebanon, never mind England. He needed to become brave, to face possible danger again, to slog it out until he found her, whatever the consequences. But what would his family say? Adrian vacillated. Would John and Fen disown him? Did he really want to repay their kindness in that way? The answer was 'no', of course.

When the tray had been collected, Vic appeared again. He sat down in one of the comfortable armchairs beside the bed.

"There's good news for you. As we suspected, you haven't got pneumonia. The doctor's given me permission to tell you what you have got, and he will explain it to you in detail tomorrow morning. It's called brucellosis and it's not life-threatening. But the symptoms are very similar to those of pneumonia, hence the confusion."

Adrian began to cry again. Vic put his hand on Adrian's arm and squeezed it.

"It's relief that's upsetting you now, isn't it," he said.

Adrian nodded. "I feel such a wreck. Blubbing all the time. I've fucked up SOAS and I haven't found my mother. I'm a loser, aren't I?" he asked pathetically.

"No, you're not. You've been very brave in coming to Lebanon on your own knowing hardly any Arabic, you've been persistent in following up all the leads, and you've adapted very quickly to the way things are here."

"When things were going quite well and I was feeling strong, I felt I was making progress. Now I feel … ugh."

They were quiet for a moment.

"You've just been in the wars a bit, by all accounts," said Vic.

Adrian wasn't sure he had heard right. "What do you mean?"

"I mean that nasty place where you had a forced holiday for some days during which you acquired quite a lot of bruises and some broken toes."

"You know about that?" asked Adrian incredulously.

"Yes. I assume you got brucellosis from infected milk they gave you. And if I were you I wouldn't tell anybody about the whole episode. Just say you drank some milk in a dodgy place."

"Right. But how did you know about that? Nobody knows."

"I have extra ears all over my body. And did you really think that the doctors and nurses wouldn't notice those weals and bruises, not to mention your broken toes? They have a lot to do with your feeling so low."

"You astonish me, how much you know. It's still all so awfully painful. And, Vic, I'm frankly terrified that they'll be back for me - if not them, someone else."

There was mounting panic in Adrian's voice and he began to tremble. "I thought I'd never get out. I thought they'd murder me. It was so unjust, sooo…" Adrian's voice crackled.

"Take it easy, you're safe now," said Vic gently, stroking Adrian's shoulder. Gradually, the shaking subsided.

"You know, Adrian," continued Vic after a moment, "they discovered you were no help to them, so they let you go. They have no further interest in you. It's highly unlikely you'll be taken again. Word will get around that you're not joining in the games they play here. Rest assured. You're ok."

Adrian was a little cheered by Vic's words; if anybody knew what was what in Beirut, it was he.

"So what is brucellosis anyway?"

"It's a bug which is endemic the world over, mainly in animals, but much less in humans, most of whom catch it from infected milk."

"Did those people give it to me on purpose to make me ill?"

"That's unlikely. Incidentally, it was irresponsible of Khalil to take you on those two visits."

"You know about that too? He swore me to secrecy about them. Sabir is the only other person who knows. He drove us." Adrian paused. "Is there anything you don't know?"

"Plenty. I don't know exactly where you were captured or how many captors there were. I'd like to hear how it all happened some time, when you're stronger and feel up to talking about it."

Vic withdrew his hand and stood up. "Now it's time for you to go to sleep. I'm going home to have dinner. Tomorrow Khalil and I will collect your things from the Residence and pay off your room there. And then you can give me your home phone number so that I can tell your parents that you're ill but recovering. I've called Francis so I hope they know by now that you're in safe hands, but I'll be able to tell them more when I speak to them. The nurses will keep checking up on you during the night. You may still have to have the drip for a while. They're pumping the antibiotics in through it. The nurse will be in soon to settle you down for the night; she may even ask you if you'd like a sleeping tablet. Either with or without, get plenty of sleep. Goodnight."

Adrian looked up at the strong man and felt a surge of gratitude; it took a lot of self-control to prevent a further flood of tears.

"Vic, what day is it?"

"It's Friday 4th February."

"Oh. Thanks. Good night, saviour."

"Good night."

Twenty-eight

'come straight home after school news of adrian love mum' said the text message on Gemma's mobile at the lunch break. Gemma ran into the cloakroom, grabbed her anorak and charged out of the building, struggling with the sleeves. She must, absolutely must, know immediately. Changing arms, she dropped her school bag into a puddle. Ugh, she said to herself, remembering, as she retrieved it, that it was Friday and she hadn't taken the books she needed for weekend homework. She got as far as the school gateway and then stopped in her tracks. If the news were bad, Mum would have come to fetch her from school, she reasoned. And her parents would be angry if she missed the afternoon's classes. And she would be cross with herself for not having what she needed for the classical civilisations work. Reluctantly and reasonably, she turned back into the school building, replaced her anorak on its hook, and hung up her bag. She ate lunch deep in thought, trying to imagine what the news could be, unaware of her friends' chatter. Back in the classroom, she congratulated herself for hanging on; Mum and Dad will be pleased about that, she said to herself.

As soon French was over, she hurried off, forgetting even to wish her friends a nice weekend.

Fen and John were in the kitchen, drinking tea.

"Tell me, tell me!" said Gemma, plumping herself down, panting.

"The short version," said Fen, "is that Adrian's in hospital in Beirut with brucellosis."

Gemma took a breath to speak.

"Don't interrupt, Gemma," continued Fen. "John's going to tell you the long version and then you can ask questions."

Gemma sighed.

"Late this morning we got a phone call from Francis Hacker at the Foreign Office," said John. "You probably remember – he's the person Adrian met several times before going out to Beirut. Vic Appleton in Beirut had rung Francis this morning to say that Adrian was in the American University Hospital in Beirut, being very well cared for after a diagnosis of brucellosis. It seems that Adrian had been taken ill about ten days earlier. His friend Khalil – the cousin of Hassan at SOAS – had arranged with some nuns for Adrian to go into a Catholic nursing home where the doctor misdiagnosed pneumonia. The symptoms are very similar. Vic went to see Adrian there and moved him to the University Hospital. That's all we know so far, but Vic will be calling us to tell us how Adrian's doing."

"When? When will he call?"

"Tomorrow probably."

"What's brucellosis?"

"It's an illness caused by bacteria that humans get from infected milk."

"I'll look it up on the internet," said Gemma agitatedly, taking her bag and going up the stairs two at a time.

She spent a couple of hours in the study, sifting through the various sources of information, before synthesising the facts and printing off a synopsis. Fen and John read it attentively.

"I want to speak to him when he phones, this Vic," said Gemma emphatically.

"We don't know when it will be, darling," said Fen. "And you've got lots of things planned for tomorrow, haven't you?"

"It's only swimming and play-reading. I can miss them."

"Didn't you say you were going to work with Nell on some history project?" asked Fen.

"Oh, that. It can wait," replied Gemma defiantly. "Nell will understand."

John and Fen glanced at each other.

"Well, we'll see," said Fen calmly. "I don't think you should reorganise your day for the phone call. Suppose Vic doesn't ring until Sunday, then you'll have wasted Saturday."

Gemma didn't deign to reply, deciding to stay in and wait for the call.

However, the decision was taken out of her hands the following morning. Nell's mother arrived with both Nell and Susie to take them swimming, to be followed by a family lunch for Nell's birthday which couldn't happen on the actual day that week. Gemma couldn't refuse.

***

It was raining heavily when Khalil arrived at the Residence. Vic was already deep in conversation with the caretaker, negotiating price and terms for his silence about everything to do with Adrian. Khalil stood by until, within minutes, Vic and the caretaker shook hands, and Vic opened up his briefcase from which he removed a brown envelope. He counted out the amount: rent owing plus hush money. Khalil took the key and they went upstairs to Adrian's room. It didn't take long to sort it out. Some clothes were on the chair and only a few papers were still lying on the table. Adrian hadn't unpacked his computer from before he was abducted and Khalil found the original carrier bag for his printer under the table. Vic went down to the caretaker to ask for an additional bag in which to put the unopened bottles of drinks that Khalil had bought when Adrian returned from captivity. Vic picked up Adrian's diary from the table and put it in his briefcase.

They set off in the chauffeur-driven car which was waiting on the kerb outside. Khalil was impressed; it was the first time he had been in such a grand vehicle. He tried to strike up a conversation with the driver, but he responded with disdain, evidently accustomed to more distant and distinguished passengers. On arrival at his flat, Vic dropped Adrian's clothes into a basket in the utility room for washing by Josette on Monday, while Khalil set up Adrian's computer and printer (to be connected later) on a table in a large airy bedroom. The bottles went into the fridge.

The car then took them to the hospital. On the way, Vic questioned Khalil carefully about himself and his family. Almost certain that he was innocent of any involvement in Adrian's abduction, he hoped that Khalil would say nothing to make him change his mind. He needed to be sure about him. Khalil's answers were transparent.

Adrian was asleep on his back, his head and shoulders propped up on a considerable pile of pillows, while his legs were underneath what was obviously a frame, with covers draped over it reaching up to his armpits. Although the drip was gone, the line was still in the back of his left hand. He woke when Vic said his name, and apologised with a grimace for not being ready for his visitors. He had indeed been given a sleeping tablet – the first ever – and although he had eaten his breakfast, sleep just seemed to keep taking over. Encouragingly, he was feeling a bit better although still feverish. His toes felt secure and protected, and the weals on his back weren't so sore. Thank goodness for painkillers, they all agreed.

Vic explained that Adrian's possessions, except for his diary, were now in a guest room at his flat and that he had paid the outstanding rent on the room at the Residence. He removed the diary from his briefcase and handed it to Adrian.

"Before you give me your parents' phone number, there are a few things to discuss and settle between the three of us." He looked at them. Khalil nodded. Adrian looked puzzled.

"What things?" he asked.

"Well, first and foremost, what are we going to say about your activities in the past few weeks? We need a uniform story, the same one for Beirut as for England, a no-loopholes story."

"I don't conceal much from my parents," said Adrian pensively. "But I suppose…" he tailed off.

"There is Sabir to think of too," said Khalil. "He drove us to Al-Jalil and Khiam, and Mukhtar."

Vic nodded. Adrian consulted his diary.

"I was supposed to be going home on 9th January, originally. Then there was Clifford Turner and the notes on that, and the discovery of my mother's name in the AUB records and the things that evolved from that, including Briggs…" he lapsed into silence, his lips quivering.

Vic was immediately on his feet beside Adrian, his hand on his shoulder.

"Keep calm, you're ok now. You're safe here."

Adrian looked up at him and gradually smiled.

"I sincerely believe it," he said simply.

"So," said Vic, returning to his chair, "we've got about four weeks to fill in. I suggest that on Saturday 15th, instead of going to Jalil and Khiam, Sabir and Khalil took you just to Baalbek, and then for a meal with relations." Vic turned to Khalil. "Somebody's relations are up there, aren't they?"

"Yes. Mukhtar's uncle and family, they came to meet us there."

"Good. So that takes care of that. OK Adrian?"

"Yes, but I've got to remember all this."

"We can jot it down later. Then you had to follow up the leads from the AUB – your mother's address and the Little School, etc., which you stretched out into a week."

"I can't deny it," said Adrian with the ghost of a grin.

"So," continued Vic, "it's actually straightforward until the day you were abducted, which was Saturday 22nd, wasn't it?"

"Yes, it was. The day and date I shall never forget." He swallowed before turning to Vic. "Do you know anything about Briggs?"

"A little, his allegiances are somewhat suspect and ambiguous, he's probably dipping his toes in several incompatible ponds."

"What the hell does that mean?" asked Adrian heatedly.

340

"Just what I said. Hush. We'll talk about it some other time. There are more important things to decide now."

Adrian subsided.

"The point is, Francis told your family that I would call them today to tell them how you are. Naturally, they are very anxious indeed about you, Adrian. They will no doubt want to know what you've been doing and where you've been, and of course, how you caught the bug - at least a broad outline. This is the difficult bit. You said earlier that you usually tell your parents everything. Do you think that would be appropriate now?"

They were all quiet for a moment. Adrian drew a breath.

"I don't feel up to talking to them myself, not for a few days anyway," he said quietly and sadly, "and I certainly couldn't unmuddle everything in my mind. It would all go wrong on the phone, and everybody would cry, including me..." His head sank on to his chest as he swallowed back a sob, then he looked up again. "The truth would be terribly upsetting for them. They need to hear a story today which contains no bad news apart from me being in hospital, a story they can accept and believe without pain, and which will persuade them that they needn't have worried."

"I agree with Adrian," said Khalil. "Families always think they want the truth but don't like when they get it."

"So shall we carry on trying to sort out this calendar business?" asked Vic.

"Yeess," said Adrian slowly. "I can try to persuade myself that I am lying for their sake, not my own, although it *is* for my own sake too. I don't want them to prevent me from looking for my mother here. They would certainly try, if they knew what had happened."

Between them, they hatched out the cover story. They extended the nursing home period backwards in time, to give a total of ten days there, which Vic did not think excessive, given that brucellosis developed at different speeds in different people. They dreamed up a collision between Adrian and a cyclist, in which Adrian's right toe was broken by a pedal; for the left toe, Adrian stubbed it on a door frame going to the bathroom while ill in the Residence. Adrian doubted anyway that anyone, except his inquisitive monkey of a sister, would want to see his toes. Vic had to demonstrate the verb 'to stub' for Khalil.

Vic then took a lined sheet of A4 paper from his briefcase and drew up a quick schedule of the dates and happenings.

"I'll use this for my phone call, and make copies for both of you. Khalil, what do you want to tell Sabir and Mukhtar?"

"I trust them both," said Khalil. "But perhaps best not to tell them much. I'll say Adrian had an accident with bicycle and not well now in AUB hospital – brucellosis. If Sabir hears more somewhere, perhaps he tells me, but he understands about silence too. And Mukhtar also."

"So, now, the phone call," said Vic. "I'm going home to do it from my landline because the connection is better. I'll be back after lunch. Give me the number Adrian."

This time, Adrian remembered it. Khalil stayed with him until his lunch came after which Adrian, exhausted by the morning's decisions, fell asleep.

The phone call was as difficult as Vic had anticipated. It started badly when a tongue-tied Sebastian answered, making Vic edgy. Fen was next. She greeted Mr Appleton briefly before putting the handset on the table and

342

summoning John in from the garden, telling him that he was the right person to do the talking, and that he should wash his hands before holding the handset. Vic heard it all and waited patiently. When Vic and John did start talking, Fen kept interrupting, wanting John to relay Vic's every word to her verbatim. Vic, frustrated, did his best to keep his cool. When he had finished the shortest account possible of Adrian's illness, Fen's agonised questions were raised by John and the answers fed back straight away.

It was obvious that both she and John were exceedingly distressed, partly because Adrian hadn't told them himself that he was ill, but mostly because he wasn't at home. They regretted deeply their inability to do anything for him and, having read up about brucellosis, were afraid that Adrian might suffer some seriously debilitating, long-term damage. They went through the symptoms one by one, asking which Adrian was suffering from, and finally whether the specialists thought he would recover completely. Vic was able to answer truthfully that the consultant had said the development of any complications was extremely unlikely in Adrian's case, but the symptoms could persist for several weeks. Adrian was comfortable in hospital, where he should stay until the fever and headaches abated and he began to gain weight again. Vic also reassured them that the AUB hospital was the best in the Middle East, with a long track record of high-quality research, and staffed by expert consultants. Brucellosis was rather common in that part of the world, so Adrian was being treated by very experienced doctors.

Should they fly out to see Adrian? John asked. Vic replied that of course they would be welcome, and indeed if they came, he would expect them to stay in his flat, but now was perhaps not the best time. Being extremely fatigued – one of the symptoms of brucellosis – Adrian spent much of the time asleep. Perhaps Mr and Mrs Goodfield would prefer to come a little later, when Adrian's good progress would be more apparent. He was expecting anyway that Adrian would stay in his flat when he was well enough to leave hospital; Vic and Khalil had cancelled Adrian's room at the Residence and his belongings were already in the flat. Vic was planning to take his computer to Adrian soon, so he would be emailing home. And of course, Adrian would phone as soon as he felt strong enough. At the moment he was also recovering from a broken toe, the result of a collision with a bike. John's final question was one which Vic couldn't answer: where had Adrian drunk the infected milk? Probably in a dodgy milk bar, came the answer. John thanked Vic warmly for everything he had done.

When the conversation was over, Fen urged John to go to Beirut as soon as possible, a proposal echoed vehemently by Gemma when she returned home late in the afternoon. Sebastian had an opinion too he announced, when Gemma had spoken. He thought John should wait, as suggested by Mr Appleton who, after all, knew all about it and was on the spot, looking after Adrian. It would waste an awful lot of money to fly to Beirut just to watch Adrian sleeping, and it didn't seem to be an emergency anyway.

Gemma, John and Fen stared at him, astonished that he should express a view. Over supper, the argument developed, but Sebastian resisted all attempts to coax him from his position. Eventually John suggested a compromise: they should wait until Adrian could say what he felt, preferably over the phone. Fen agreed reluctantly (although she didn't show it), for the sake of peace, and also to show Sebastian that his word counted. Gemma burst into tears and stomped upstairs, calling out that none of them loved Adrian in the way she did. Fen and John knew that to be true.

Late in the afternoon, Vic returned to the hospital to find Adrian just waking up after several hours' sleep. He recounted the essence of the conversation, including John's suggestion that he and Fen should make the trip to Beirut to see him, whereupon Adrian shook his head decisively. Indeed, he needed to feel stronger before he would be ready to face them and confirm the version of the truth that they had heard. However, as soon as he felt a bit livelier, he would like to have his laptop, and could then email them. That would be the first step.

Twenty-nine

Adrian improved, although taking into consideration his youth and presumed general good health, the consultant would have expected faster progress. One of the problems was his weight: having temporarily no appetite or pleasure in food, he was some ten kilos lighter than the lowest appropriate level for his height. The consultant prescribed an appetite stimulant which was also recognised as useful for staving off any signs of depression, although Adrian, when questioned, replied that he wasn't depressed, only aching and tired. Hearing this, the consultant also decided that he needed iron and vitamins. Until he had made convincing advances, there was no question of discharging him, especially since his temperature was still high, and his headaches persistent. Adrian was still plagued by regular nightmares, in which he was held captive and tortured, not by strangers, but by Briggs. The consultant sent a psychologist to see him.

As brucellosis was not contagious in day-to-day contact between humans, Adrian was moved into a ward containing four beds, where he began to take notice of the people around him. There were two elderly men who, Adrian assumed, were in hospital for heart problems. They spoke Arabic together. The third, younger man, German, was recovering from an operation for testicular cancer. All three welcomed Adrian with a wave of the hand.

The next day a nurse unbound Adrian's toes and flexed them gently, causing a jab of pain in his right foot; the left, however, reacted less violently. Adrian looked at them, wishing that they weren't his, before the nurse bound them up again. The frame over his legs was removed. Later, the ward doctor appeared, accompanied by a physiotherapist called Thierry, who would, the doctor said, help Adrian to stand and walk a little; his muscles, by now weakened from many days in bed, needed to be re-animated. Initially, Adrian was frightened, but with encouragement from his fellow patients, and with Thierry holding him up, he succeeded in shuffling over to each bed to shake hands.

Vic and Khalil came regularly; soon other visitors appeared, alerted by them to Adrian's illness. Jean was the first. As she hugged him, he started to weep. She stroked his forehead, soothing him with comforting words. An ex-boyfriend of hers had had brucellosis – a horrible illness – but he was now completely cured. Adrian would soon be feeling stronger. She stayed about half an hour, left him some magazines, and promised to return soon.

Trisha Morgan was next, full of sympathy, and bearing homemade fruit cake to tempt his palate. Then Mark and his mother came, bringing clippings from the Beirut *Daily Star* and a recent copy of *The Economist*. Mukhtar, curiously, brought a teddy bear which Adrian relegated dismissively to his bedside locker as soon as Mukhtar had left; but on reflection, a few hours' later he extracted it for Mukhtar to see, if or when he returned to the hospital. It sat on one of the bedside chairs, where, over the days, it became an indispensable part of the furniture, saluted by hospital staff, wardmates and visitors alike. Looking at it, Adrian was reminded of his first teddy (which was probably still in a cupboard at home), and of the poem he had loved in his childhood:

Our Teddy Bear is short and fat
Which is not to be wondered at;
He gets what exercise he can
By falling off the ottoman…

At around nine one evening, Sabir slipped in quietly. In hushed tones, he expressed his 'most sincere regrets' that Adrian was suffering so much, and reassured him that he was in the best possible place to make a speedy recovery. Of course it was the first time they had met since the excursion with Khalil; Adrian was surprised at how easy it was to talk to him, how fluently he spoke English, and how worldly he seemed. In response to Adrian's probing, Sabir revealed that he had spent two years at Yale University, writing a Ph.D on the Palestine situation. After some twenty minutes, Sabir slipped out as quietly as he had arrived.

A few days later, Khalil touchingly brought Adrian a new mobile – one with a sim card that would work for Europe. Vic brought in Adrian's laptop, with new batteries and a new internet connector, but warned him against spending the day staring at the screen, which would doubtless aggravate his headache. In truth, Adrian confessed, despite what he had said earlier, he didn't feel like booting it up or sending any emails as he wouldn't know what to write. Vic took it away again. Adrian was however glad to have the mobile in case he wanted to contact Khalil, Vic, or anyone else in Beirut, but he wouldn't be calling home for the time being.

A week after Adrian had arrived in hospital, Vic had a private informal chat with the consultant, who recommended that Adrian should stay at least another week under his care, perhaps as long as ten days. He needed supervision at meal times to ensure he ate everything on his plate, since the amounts were carefully measured to suit his needs; also his blood, heart, temperature, and many other bodily functions had to be checked daily. Furthermore, it was preferable for Thierry to treat patients 'in-house' rather than to waste precious time travelling to their homes. Adrian was still experiencing nightmares too. Vic, for his part, assured the consultant that when Adrian was well enough to leave hospital, he would arrange for him to be looked after at his flat until he was strong enough for the journey home.

***

"I've brought your laptop back. It's time to write home," said Vic, a few days later. "I had a phone call from John yesterday evening. They've all got the wind up that there's something more wrong with you than just brucellosis, so unless you want them to winkle out of you what's happened, you'd better bite the bullet and send an email. It needn't be long."

Adrian grimaced.

"As long as it's you telling them what's happened, it seems a little bit like your lie, but as soon I as have to write it…," he said.

"You don't have to mention what's happened. Come on, just a few words to soothe them."

Vic pulled Adrian up into a suitable position, opened the laptop and settled it on the blanket in front him.

"I'll be back later, got a few things to do today."

It wasn't so difficult after all. Adrian wrote that he was feeling better and that thanks to Thierry, his leg muscles were beginning to work again after all those days in bed. His toes weren't so sore, and his temperature was going down. He wrote character sketches of the consultant and Thierry, as well as of his wardmates, one of whom had been discharged and his bed taken by a Saudi Arabian. He devoted several sentences to Khalil, and a paragraph to Vic, who had rescued him from the kindly nuns and set him on the road to recovery. Vic would take him to his flat once he no longer needed daily nursing care and was well enough to be moved. Finally, he asked for news of what they were all doing, and sent as much love as he was able to express.

When Vic returned at the end of the afternoon, he found Adrian reading the Beirut *Daily Star* online. Adrian admitted that his neglect of his family had been getting to him and that sending the first email had somehow liberated him from a stifling self-imposed cocoon. Now, he said, he had only to break free from the hospital, which wouldn't be such a wrench. Vic replied that he would need, according to the consultant, at least another week before he was well enough to be discharged. There were three criteria to be met: he should be free of headaches and fever, be able to walk to the bathroom and look after himself in there, and his weight should reach 70 kilos at least.

As an incentive, Vic told him that Josette had washed and ironed all his smelly clothes, and he and she together had prepared his room for him. His papers, books and printer were on the table, along with Vic's backgammon board – Khalil was planning to teach Adrian how to play this extremely popular game.

"Are you sure about having me to stay?" asked Adrian. "It's awfully kind of you."

"I don't mind guests, as long as they don't talk all the time and expect me to listen. I've got a low boredom threshold. Domestically it's no problem because Josette comes whenever I need her, and sometimes brings in relations to do a deep clean. I'm out a lot too, and the flat's quite big – you've not yet seen it all – so there's plenty of space in which to be separate."

"I'll try not to get under your feet. I'll be sleeping a lot anyway. And I've got my experiences to write up. I started today."

"That's excellent news. We need to get that done and dusted. By the way, I didn't tell you this morning, Adrian, but naturally John once again raised the possibility of coming to visit you here. I assume you didn't mention it in your email?"

"No, I steered well clear of the subject."

"If you're soon well enough to fly home, there won't be any point. But it depends on one's interpretation of 'soon' and 'well enough'. I imagine the consultant will have some advice to give about that. Anyway, what do you feel about it?"

"I'm missing them awfully, and I'm longing to see them, but I'm not sure…" he tailed off.

"Not sure of what, Adrian?"

"Several things really. They'd probably be very anxious about the whole scenario, and about the journey, and if they saw what things were like here, they might worry even more about me." He paused, before adding "and then there's something else."

Vic waited.

"It's to do with this being part of *my* world, my possible meeting with my mother, the things I've seen and done, Khalil, you, and the other people I've met, my independent life. And not part of *their* world. I'm not sure I'm willing to let them in – a little bit of me wants to keep all this private, for myself. Does that sound odd?"

"No, it doesn't. It's your prerogative to keep it for yourself. Nobody can ever know or understand all the truths about another person."

Just then, Adrian's meal was brought in by his 'feeding nurse' as he called her, so Vic left. When the tray was gone, Adrian began to examine what he knew of Vic, trying to match Francis' description of him with the person he had come to know. A mathematician with a phenomenal memory, an expert on the Middle East, the son of a spice dealer, Francis had said, and somebody who played his cards close to his chest. Adrian had seen only Vic's Middle East expertise, but he didn't doubt the rest was true too. What of his family? Had he ever been married? Vic had never mentioned relations but nor had he, when Adrian thought about it, ever said anything about himself. He was private, self-contained and self-sufficient. A closed book, but also generous, kind, and strong. And manipulative. He had coaxed out of Adrian everything he had wanted to know. Adrian was in awe of him, but felt strikingly at ease with him. How could that be so? That was another of Vic's strengths: the ability to make people feel comfortable. Clifford Turner was an obvious example – someone who always stayed with Vic when in Beirut. Vic was relaxed enough to allow people to be with him, but so essentially private that the presence of visitors was no threat to his shell. Adrian wondered if staying with Vic would allow any insight at all into the man himself. Wait and see, was the answer.

Adrian grew more alert in the next few days. The further he walked, the stronger he felt and the more he was able to eat. Thierry congratulated him on his progress. His body, reawakened, had set about ridding itself of his illness. The consultant told him one morning that he would be discharged soon. Adrian realised he had been at the AUB for over three weeks; it was hard to imagine being anywhere else.

He said as much to his family in his next email. Gemma had written a full account of happenings at home, including the fact that Sebastian seemed to be growing up, (Adrian wondered what was behind that declaration), and that Cadby had a boyfriend but would be spayed in due course – 'before anything can happen'. Mum and Dad were ready to visit Adrian if appropriate, and they hoped he would phone soon to which Adrian replied that he didn't want to call from the hospital but would do so as soon as he was out.

The next afternoon, Vic confirmed that Adrian was to undergo a full series of tests and that as long as the results were satisfactory, he would be discharged.

"By the way," Vic said casually, "I've got some news for you. Some Hezbollah fighters launched an attack against an Israeli military outpost in the disputed Shebaa Farms area at the foot of the Golan Heights on Friday, killing one Israeli soldier. Two other soldiers were injured in the attack. Also there's been a spate of shootings in central Beirut. Briggs was one of the victims."

Adrian's heart gave a thud.

"We never got round to talking about him. Tell me now."

"I will if we can walk together down the passage?"

Vic stood to hand while Adrian slid sideways out of bed, steadied himself and stood up looking triumphantly at Vic, who took hold of his upper arm.

As they ambled along, Vic spoke quietly so as not to be overheard.

"He's a chameleon. He states that he's not interested in Lebanese politics but in earning money from the English-speaking residents and tourists in Beirut. That's only part of the truth. His wife is Jewish, an Israeli citizen living most of the time in Jerusalem where she markets cloth woven by Palestinians. He and she don't get on, so they meet only occasionally. A whisper has it that through her he works for Mossad." Vic sounded doubtful.

"But…?" asked Adrian.

"But that seems rather unlikely, since his mistress, whom he keeps in a luxury flat here in Beirut, is a Kuwaiti princess from the Sabah family. She's a niece of the current Sheikh."

"Is it common knowledge that that's who she is?"

"No, it's not. Most people think she's Iraqi. She was sent to school in Switzerland, and then she refused to return to Kuwait. Exceptionally, the family allowed her to stay away, knowing that she would be more trouble in Kuwait than in Europe. I'm only telling you this because of your Briggs connection – not to be repeated – it's serious stuff."

"Oh. She's quite a girl then, is she?"

"I suppose you could say that. Anyway, he tries to sell what he knows from one side to the other. Somebody decided yesterday that enough was enough."

Adrian swallowed hard, his throat dry for his next question.

"Is he dead?"

"No, he's not, but badly wounded. He's here in the AUB."

Vic felt Adrian's body shake.

"Here? I thought I was safe here…"

"You are. As I told you before, there's no longer any interest in you. Briggs has a policeman outside his room 24 hrs a day."

"Nevertheless," said Adrian, "I'd like to be out of here as soon as possible. Who else got hit?"

"A couple of other dodgy people – I don't know yet who they were."

"But you will soon, I suppose?" asked Adrian sarcastically.

"Indeed." He held Adrian still while he turned to stand facing him, "Sarcasm! You must be feeling better. But no need to rile me."

"Sorry. I'm a bit shaken. How soon can I leave?"

"Consultant-God will decide on the morrow, and the day after is target day."

***

Adrian was duly signed off after the tests. The consultant wished him well, expressing jokingly the hope never to see him again. Vic was brought up-to-date on Adrian's nightmares, which were now less frequent. Adrian was given a bag of medicine with an instruction sheet, and was reminded to eat plenty. Vic brought him clothes and shoes and packed up his few hospital belongings, including, at the insistence of the feeding nurse, the teddy who was now named Karam, after a national hero who had led resistance against the Ottomans.

Adrian realised, during the bizarre transitional journey between his life as a patient and that as a guest, that he hadn't felt free since the day of his capture; the price of his new liberty would include making decisions again. Could he cope he wondered, as he looked at Beirut through the car window. Vic said nothing on the way, leaving him to muse.

It was luxury, at the flat. Adrian occupied a double room at the end of a passage from the entrance hall. It was spacious enough for a work table and chair, as well as an armchair, a stand with a television set and the latest electronic players. There were full bookshelves along one of the smaller walls. His clothes were in a cupboard and on his bed was a pair of new blue pyjamas and a bath robe. With Adrian hobbling behind, Vic breezed round, opening doors into two further bedrooms, a large study, and a room off the kitchen, intended for a resident maid but used as a utility room and for storage.

After a late lunch and when Adrian had rested, Vic insisted that he must call home. Adrian tried to procrastinate, but Vic pointed out that he had phoned John and Fen the previous evening to tell them the good news of Adrian's imminent discharge from hospital, and that they would be very cut up if he didn't get in touch straight away. He propelled Adrian into the office, shut the door on him, and retreated to the kitchen. After twenty minutes he went to open the study door cautiously and looked in. Adrian was sobbing quietly, his elbows on the desk supporting his hands which were covering his face. Vic went to comfort him with an arm round his shoulders. Neither of them spoke. When Adrian grew calmer, Vic led him into the sitting room and helped him into one of two armchairs facing the window. He poured two gin and tonics and they sat silently there, sipping, until Adrian felt able to talk. It wasn't, he said, that John and Fen had reprimanded him or even questioned him; it was rather that he could hear them both crying as they spoke. Their immeasurable love and sympathy were almost more than he could bear. His love for them was equally strong, but when he tried to speak of it, to reciprocate, his gulped words were clumsy and muddled. Vic tried to reassure him, but he knew that Adrian would need to forgive himself for his perceived inadequacy.

The sun sank below the horizon, leaving a gold and blue luminescence in the sky, which darkened to ultramarine. Beirut glittered whilst ships' lights pricked the blackness of the sea. Adrian got up and hobbled to his room, falling asleep on his bed immediately. Vic looked in on him later, shut the blinds and tiptoed out. At eight, he woke him. It was time to eat again, he announced. Adrian rubbed his eyes and sat up, feeling oddly refreshed, and wondering for a moment, where he was.

Over a large bowl of lentil and lemon soup, prepared that morning by Josette, Vic tentatively broached the delicate subject of his parents' possible visit. Adrian, now on an even keel, said that the question was still wide open since they had not discussed it during the telephone call. Vic relayed to Adrian the consultant's view: that Adrian should be well enough to fly to England in a couple of weeks, assuming that he continued to regain his strength at the current pace. Adrian replied firmly that he had to adjust psychologically to going home, and was reluctant to be precipitated into meeting his parents until he was ready. Soon they agreed on a compromise: Adrian would suggest to John that he could come to collect him and accompany him home, probably in about a fortnight. Vic would offer a couple of nights' hospitality, and together they would show John some of the splendours of Beirut. Adrian and Vic agreed that Fen should be encouraged stay at home rather than brave the flight and the maelstrom of Beirut. After all, Gemma and Seb needed her.

That night Adrian's screams woke Vic, who went to comfort him. He sat on the bed holding Adrian until he calmed down. The dream, Adrian explained, had propelled him from torture in captivity to torture at home at the hands of his family. Vic talked to him quietly, explaining away each phase of the nightmare until Adrian settled and fell asleep. Vic moved to a chair in the room, watching over him for another hour before returning to his own room.

The next morning Adrian, white-faced, phoned home to propose the arrangement he and Vic had concocted, to which John, with Fen's blessing, readily agreed. Once the hospital had given the go-ahead, Adrian said, they could make the plane bookings.

He began to feel at ease. Calls home became less traumatic each time. In the flat, he and Vic quickly established a tacit understanding as to how the days would pass: Adrian worked at his notes on the visits to Hezbollah and Al-Jalil refugee camp, as well as on everything he could remember of his captivity, shudderingly painful though it was. In particular, writing details of the forms of torture to which he had been subjected reawakened pains in the scars on his back, as well as producing a throbbing headache. One night, after recording the torture to his genitals, he dreamed that he was incapable of making love to Tazie. It wasn't a nightmare, but he woke crying. Vic was immediately there to comfort him. Later, when Vic read the account of that occasion, he commented on Adrian's bravery in recalling and including the information. A few days later, Adrian found the courage to voice a question which had been gnawing at him: who had taken him hostage? Vic answered that it was most likely a small specialist cell attached to the Syrian occupiers, whose aim was to check up on all possible sources of anti-Syrian activities, particularly those involving Israelis. Adrian knew better than to raise the matter with Khalil.

Vic came and went; Adrian never asked where he was going, or why, nor did Vic ever volunteer any information. Occasionally, they strolled together along the Corniche, when Vic would recount events in Lebanon's recent history, explaining the different factions and their positions, and pointing out significant buildings. For instance, the Hard Rock Cafe, opened in 1996, was considered, Vic said, to be a symbol of the spirit of reconstruction after the end of the civil war. Vic led Adrian round the Western point of Beirut to Raouché to watch the water swell and ebb under the Pigeon Rock, and to look from a distance at the Ferris Wheel in Luna Park. From the breadth of Vic's knowledge, Adrian assumed that he was privy to official documents and that his, Adrian's experiences, would be fed in some form or another, into the reservoir of knowledge. Adrian sent emails to Max and Benny and, without much hope of a warm response, to Tazie. In the evenings, he read or sometimes studied Arabic with Vic's help. Jean, Mark, and Khalil came often to keep him company and to play backgammon. Josette pandered to Adrian's appetite by preparing large quantities of delicious food, and even taught him some simple recipes.

***

"Are you thinking of your girl-friend?" Vic asked one evening when Adrian was staring silently into space. Adrian had mentioned her existence during his initial long discussion with Vic, but had neither named nor described her.

"No, I was contrasting my life here with my student days in London," he answered pensively, "but I do think of her often. I emailed the other day, but she's not answered. I'm in the dog house, understandably, since I've not been in touch regularly."

"I assume she's beautiful, charming, intelligent, accomplished, passionate, and all the rest?"

Adrian smiled.

"All of those, yes. But we've only known each other a few months, and I've been too preoccupied to connect properly with her. It's something that I'll have to sort out when I get back. But it'll be hard enough knowing what to say to my fellow students and family, without having to decide what's appropriate to tell her."

"Understandably."

"And then she's older than me, already established in a career and hoping to settle down. I can't be part of that, at least not now."

There was a silence. Adrian took the plunge.

360

"What about you, Vic? You never mention your family or anybody else. Who is there and where are they? Parents, siblings, spouses, children?"

"My parents are dead. I have a brother in Canada with a wife and five children, and a lively spinster sister in Brighton."

Vic got up and went to look out of the window. After a few moments, he returned to his chair.

"I also have a daughter who's a Professor of Neurosurgery in Oxford," he continued. "She's married with no children. That's all, except that I'm divorced."

"Oh?" said Adrian.

After a quick decision, Vic continued.

"My wife left me because I'm bisexual," he said, then fell silent, watching Adrian's reaction.

Adrian was surprised at first; then in the silence that followed, he began to fit Vic's avowal in with what he had seen of the way Vic lived.

"I might have guessed," he said slowly.

"Perhaps, if you had been less damaged."

"Did your wife know right from the start?"

"She did. Before we were married, she thought it would be all right, but after a couple of years, she couldn't accept it any longer. Besides, by then I wanted to return to live in Beirut, where she could never be happy. I left her and my daughter in London. My wife remarried – an engineer. I see them occasionally, when I go back to England, and my daughter regularly."

"That's good."

A bizarre thought occurred to Adrian, prompting him to chuckle.

"And you've been telling me that I'm safe now, here with you! Am I?" he asked archly.

"Perfectly, as you will have noticed" replied Vic, smiling.

They fell silent, thinking, from different angles, about the significance of Vic's words.

In the succeeding days, the essence of that conversation kept intruding into Adrian's mind, forcing him to mull over its possible implications. He wondered whether some of Vic's hours out of the house were spent with a lover, male or female. Or did Vic indulge in group frolics? Adrian imagined, with distaste, a room full of men undressing, men of all shapes and sizes, with Vic amongst them, or even a room full of people of both sexes. On reflection, it was unlikely; Vic seemed circumspect, and would doubtless avoid any kind of risk which that type of habitual activity could incur.

Why did the scenario disturb him, Adrian pondered? Had Vic become a surrogate father, to be respected, obeyed and loved, and fathers didn't indulge in group sex? Or had Adrian become possessive of his rescuer; was there a tinge of jealousy in his feelings? To test himself, he tried to imagine Vic helping another man in circumstances similar to his own; after all, anything was possible in Beirut. He resolved to ask Vic whether he had ever before looked after someone in Adrian's exhausted condition; he could then examine his own thoughts and sentiments in context.

Adrian remembered the power of Vic's arms and hands, as he had helped him to sit up or to walk, or comforted him with an arm around his shoulders. It had felt as though Vic were transmitting to Adrian some of his resources through these gestures, invigorating Adrian physically, and stimulating him mentally to overcome the terrifying memories of his torture. But although these actions had been strong, Vic's touch had been only reassuring and gentle. Adrian felt comfortable in physical contact with him, and he was certain that his knowledge of Vic's bisexual nature would not change that. Was there a seed of attraction in his feelings towards Vic? Adrian was sure, anyway, of his affection; if it encompassed desire, then Vic was certainly holding back, mainly it seemed, because of Adrian's temporary physical and psychological weakness; Vic would never take advantage of him. Adrian did indeed feel completely safe.

Vic's own preoccupations were with how Adrian would fit back into his family, after so many weeks of startlingly new experiences, some terrifying and some rewarding, which had pushed him into situations requiring tenacity and understanding. He had been toughened by adversity, but would not realise how far he had leaped into adulthood until he found himself back in the environment of his past. Vic hoped that home comforts would see him through the next phases of his healing, both physical and mental. He needed to be strong enough to keep his counsel about his captivity, so as to retain control for future visits to Lebanon. Conquering his nightmares before he returned to England was important.

Meanwhile, Vic was sure that Adrian had taken the knowledge of his bisexuality in his stride. Telling him had been a calculated risk, but Vic had been proved right: there was no awkwardness between them in the days that followed.

***

On the eve of John's arrival, Vic mentioned to Adrian the possibility of a job as an assistant to a Qatari lawyer who was involved in development projects and needed an intelligent person of English mother tongue to shadow him. Adrian was astonished. It sounded attractive: the salary and benefits were more than generous, added to which Vic was able to vouch for the lawyer as being a man of complete integrity, with a truly international outlook gained partly while studying in London and at Harvard.

The post was a new one, but should be filled before the end of the year. The incumbent would first be trained in the Middle East. Vic stressed that he did not believe it would be in Adrian's interest to abandon his degree course, but that he felt obliged to tell Adrian about the job since it could open many professional doors later. Adrian could think about it in the forthcoming months; if he were interested Vic would arrange an exploratory discussion with the lawyer next time Adrian was in Beirut.

John's plane was due to land in the early evening. Vic was reading in the sitting room, waiting for Adrian to be ready to go to the airport. When he appeared, freshly shaved, wearing a gilet and a pair of new shoes bought to accommodate uncomfortable feet, Vic stood up.

"The plane's going to be about half an hour late. But we're ready to go and the car's here, so we might as well have a G and T at the airport."

"Fine by me." Adrian was shivering.

"Are you all right, Adrian?"

"Yes, I think so – just a little nervous."

"Of what?"

"Getting too emotional."

364

"Don't worry. John will be emotional too. Just be natural about it. People do get emotional at airports."

He turned Adrian to face him.

"You look rather well. Well enough, in fact, for John not to worry."

"Mm. Do you realise the significance of today?"

"Apart from meeting John, you mean?"

"Apart from that. It's 4th March – exactly a month since you rescued me from galloping Roman Catholicism and virulent brucellosis."

"And which is the greater evil?"

"The second, I know."

"It's done me good having you here," said Vic, "seeing things from a different perspective."

"I don't need to tell you how much good it's done me!" said Adrian. "I can't thank you enough."

"Thanks are due to Josette too; you know, she even said you were no trouble at all."

"The ultimate plaudit from my cookery teacher; I must thank her properly before I leave."

"Time to go" said Vic, releasing Adrian. He turned away abruptly to hide his emotion. Quickly he regained sufficient control to open the door and usher Adrian through.

Thirty

Vic stood back, while Adrian leaned over the barrier facing the arrivals exit. Soon, a tall gangly man wearing a raincoat and carrying a small holdall walked slowly through. Adrian rushed round the barrier to hug him.

"Hullo old thing," said John.

"Dad, dad."

They both wept. When they separated, Adrian led John to Vic to introduce them.

Adrian was subdued in the car back to the flat, trying to adjust to the strange circumstances in which he found himself. His old self, from whom his new self had hatched out, was suddenly there too, reawakened by the presence of his father. Adrian had bounded away from the atmosphere of England into that of Beirut, discovering now an inner conflict when confronted by the collision of the two. Lovingly grateful as he was that his father had come to be with him for the journey home, he knew it would somehow be easier to relate to him once they were back in England. Here in Beirut, withholding from his father the information about his capture and torture, such recent horrors, seemed almost like treachery on his part, making him feel sad.

John, in the front seat beside the driver, calmly described the flight and some of the passengers. Between snoozes, he had conversed sporadically with the young Arab in a smart tailored suit with a tie, who was sitting beside him. Some fifteen minutes before the plane landed, the man had opened an overhead locker, removed a squashy bag and gone to the toilet. He soon emerged wearing the traditional Arab garb: a full length white tunic and a white flowing headscarf held in place by a cord. He had explained to John that he felt obliged by family custom to follow the traditional dress code when in the Middle East, but preferred western clothes – they were better for meeting western girls. John had replied laughingly that there was no suitable response to that.

After dinner, Vic went to his study leaving father and son alone. Adrian immediately plied John with questions about the family. When John had related all the news, it was Adrian's turn. He explained all the leads in the search for his mother, and described the people he had met along the way, as well as the areas of Beirut in which he had circulated before getting brucellosis. Fortunately for Adrian, John decided that home, with Fen, was a more appropriate place for hearing the details of Adrian's illness. Adrian was relieved when John told him so: he was thus spared trying to avoid any reference to its horrific origin.

There was a moment's embarrassment later when Vic appeared, to make the gentle suggestion to a flagging Adrian that it was his bedtime. Thereupon John apologised for keeping him up. After Adrian had retired, John asked Vic for his opinion on Adrian's recovery, as well as the progress he had made in looking for Patti Sandling. Vic stressed how brave Adrian had been in undertaking the search and how well he had adapted to being in Beirut. It was unfortunate that he had fallen ill and now had to give up his quest, for the time being anyway. John thanked Vic on behalf of all the family for looking after Adrian, and offered to defray the expenses Vic had incurred. Vic refused all, except the final payment on Adrian's room at the Residence. It had been a great pleasure he said, to meet and get to know Adrian, who was blessed with an even temperament and great intelligence.

The next day, the driver took them in the car round Beirut sightseeing, along the coast road in both directions, as well as up into the hills. John was shocked by the number of security posts they had to cross. They also spent an enjoyable hour in the souks, buying presents for the family as well as a silk scarf for Josette. Adrian was glad to see that John and Vic were soon easy in each other's company, although John was not embarrassed to say that he had never before met anybody like Vic, and was a little dazzled by him and his lifestyle. This amused Vic who was happy to ham up the part for their entertainment.

Farewells at the airport the next day were cordial. Vic, unexpectedly a little flustered Adrian noticed, patted him on the back and shook John's hand, wishing them a peaceful journey home. Adrian promised to email as soon as they arrived. After they had gone through the barrier towards Security, Adrian turned to look back but Vic had disappeared. Returning to his flat, Vic looked briefly into Adrian's room where his Lebanese computer, printer and mobile were still on the table, and the forlorn teddy bear on the shelf. He poured himself a G and T and sat down in a lonely armchair with his eyes shut, to reflect.

***

For the first few days after he arrived home, Adrian spent much of the time moving from bed to armchair, recovering from the journey which had taken more out of him than he had expected. A flight, a few hours, it's nothing he had said to himself beforehand, but the formalities, the luggage, and the waiting around were much more taxing than Adrian had remembered. John and he spoke little on the journey, both dozing in comfortable familiarity after the enjoyable days in Beirut. John had wisely ordered a taxi to take them home from Heathrow. Adrian was once again acutely conscious of his parents' extraordinary generosity in helping him on his way to and from Beirut, and of the emotional toll of his activities.

Everybody cried as he and John walked through the front door. Fen put her arms round Adrian and drew him in, caressing his head and saying "my poor darling." Gemma hugged him then slipped her hand in his and wouldn't let go. Sebastian, pretending he wasn't crying, held Cadby by the collar while she barked loudly and sniffed at Adrian's trousers. John detailed Sebastian off to carry Adrian's luggage up to his room while Fen and Gemma led him into the kitchen. Adrian looked around himself; it was all blissfully familiar, comfortable and secure.

The evening meal was soon on the table. Fen called Sebastian down from Adrian's room where, he said, he had been introducing Cadby to Adrian's things. When everybody was served, a stream of questions tumbled out. Adrian was happy for John to answer everything he could, to give his impressions of Beirut and Vic, and to describe how they had spent the days together. Adrian spoke of the kind nuns and of his rescue by Vic, as well as the excellent medical care in the AUB hospital. He talked too about the pleasant times he had spent when his friends came to Vic's flat to keep him company. Gemma grasped the idea of backgammon and begged Adrian to bring back a set next time he went to Beirut, whereupon John and Fen exchanged glances, noticed by Adrian but nobody else. He assured his family that he was almost a hundred percent well, just needing a little more time to gather his strength before returning to London. Gemma asked about his toes; Adrian had to remind himself to which toe he, Vic and Khalil had attributed which accident. Keep your cool he said to himself, as he wriggled them in his comfortable shoes, thinking absent-mindedly for a moment of other shoes.

Fen watched over him, feeding him a second helping of beef stew with dumplings and smiling continuously at him. By the time apple pie was on the table, Adrian was wilting visibly. Fen suggested he should go to bed straight away, but John announced that there were presents first. They were a success: Sebastian loved his knitted scarf in the cedar tree design of the Lebanese flag; Gemma opened up her book on Byzantine relics in Lebanon squeaking with delight, while Fen was rendered speechless by a plain platinum watch. John had had Vic's help in choosing it and in negotiating the best price. Excusing himself, Adrian went upstairs, promising to tell them about his search for his mother when Gemma and Sebastian returned from school the next day. In the morning, Gemma crept in to see if he wanted a cup of tea before she left, but he was sound asleep so she didn't wake him. He slept until midday.

He knew that his first duty was to email Vic. It seemed odd, telling him about the journey and about his family's welcome. Adrian had to admit to himself that he missed Vic – or, at least, Vic's knowledge of his experiences. It had become natural to speak together about every aspect of Adrian's time in Beirut, whereas at home he had constantly to guard his tongue, a habit he quickly adopted. Vic's almost instant reply was brief: he was glad they had arrived safely and he hoped that Adrian would settle in easily. Adrian also emailed Max, Benny and Francis. The former invited himself for lunch the following Sunday, while Francis congratulated Adrian on his recovery and wrote that he hoped they could meet as soon as Adrian returned to London. Benny wrote back an affectionate, touching email.

Max's presence created a party atmosphere. Fen excelled herself in the kitchen, John was his usual affable self, while Gemma and Seb vied for Max's attention. Adrian opened a bottle of Chateau Musar which he had brought with him from Beirut; Gemma and Seb were allowed to drink a little wine, sweetened and diluted with water, in 'proper' wine glasses. They all drank Adrian's health. Adrian told Max the bare bones of his quest for his mother.

"Well that's all fine," said Max, when Adrian had finished, "and it sounds as though you're going to find her in due course. However, it would be remiss of me not to tell you that Chinese at SOAS is pining for you. Vernon wants to fill you in on the work you've missed."

"Yes, that's right," said Fen, "you should go back to London as soon as possible, but not until you feel strong enough."

"I hope I'll be able to go this week," said Adrian. "Meanwhile I've got to learn the difference between recovery and sloth... Sloth will be taking over quite soon unless I watch out."

"The common enemy, sloth," said Max. "Vernon's sympathetic but he wants to see you clued up for the few remaining weeks of term and to outline what you've missed

371

so that you can spend the forthcoming holiday going at it. I'll help, of course – it will be a kind of revision for me."

"Thanks Max."

"Meanwhile, I've got some good news to tell you, I'm getting married in the autumn."

There was a chorus of congratulations.

"What, with mother's milk still behind your ears?" said Adrian.

"*Thanks!* With friends like you... Anyway, it's like this. Arabella and I are physically separated by our university courses, hers being in St Andrews and mine in London. Naturally, we'd like to spend time together in a steady way, at weekends, but it's always a question of where – in her digs in Scotland, in my room in London or at our parents' houses, none ideal. When I was talking to my parents about it, they mentioned that there's a legacy awaiting me – generous enough for a deposit on a London flat – and the condition for collecting it is that I must be married."

"What's a legacy?" asked Seb.

"It's any kind of property that a person leaves in his or her Will to somebody – money, furniture, cars, anything," answered John.

"Oh," said Seb. "Are you sad that the person died?"

Everybody laughed, except Seb who looked hurt.

"I was sad, Seb – it was an uncle, several years ago now. But it's serendipity," he said cheerfully. "We can buy a flat in London and I can live there all the time and Arabella can fly down Friday night from Scotland and return Monday morning."

"Another toast!" called Adrian. "To Max's matrimony!"

"Can I come to the wedding?" asked Gemma, emptying her glass.

"Of course you can, darling," replied Max. "I couldn't possibly get married without you being there."

In the afternoon, Adrian and Max talked in the study. Max said that he had eventually, after talking to Benny, told everybody where Adrian was and that he'd been ill. Adrian was instantly sorely tempted to open up to Max about everything that had happened to him, but he managed to resist, telling himself that doing so would be a sign of psychological weakness. If he found himself too isolated by the burden of his experiences, he could reveal it all to him at a later date, once he was settled back in London where it would be easier to talk, and more private.

Adrian returned to London on Wednesday. In the interim, he made contact with Francis and had a long conversation with Benny, who offered to meet him off the train at Liverpool Street. Adrian still didn't know what to do about Tazie; Max hadn't mentioned her on Sunday, which Adrian thought was ominous. He had, however, plenty on his plate for the time being; the meeting with Vernon loomed large. It was enough to crank himself up for that, without facing Tazie.

Benny was touchingly happy to meet Adrian at Liverpool Street and to accompany him back to Fletcher's. They spent a couple of hours drinking coffee and eating biscuits together in Benny's room, where the books had multiplied since Adrian had been there last. Benny was agog to hear Adrian's descriptions of Beirut, as well as to learn how he had manoeuvred himself through the spider's web of evidence which had, at least, proved that his mother had been there. He was sure Adrian would find her in due course. Adrian, for his part, noticed that in his absence, Benny had gained self-assurance and was now speaking with some authority on academic matters. He was also evidently perfectly at home in London.

***

"Ah, Adrian, good to see you back," said Vernon, looking up briefly. "Sit down. I won't be a minute, just got to sign off on this." He gestured to a chair across the desk.

Vernon's room still smelled strongly of smoke. There were books everywhere, crushed in together on the shelves, falling off each other in piles on the floor, and in mad disarray, along with papers, on his desk. While Adrian found a passage to the chair between the books, Vernon scribbled with a flourish, pushed aside one sheet of paper and then picked up another which he placed ostentatiously in front of him. Adrian sat down.

"You're feeling better, I hope?" asked Vernon, tapping his pipe in an ashtray before refilling the bowl and lighting it. "What was it?"

"Brucellosis. And yes, thank you, I'm feeling better."

"Max told me you've been looking for a close relation in Beirut. Your …er…"

"My biological mother."

"Ah yes. Any luck?"

Vernon stroked his beard. He had a long face and the droopy eyes of a bloodhound. In his imagination, Adrian could see bloodhound ears too. Pulling himself together, he tried to adopt a cool and collected mien, although he found Vernon's casual reference to his mother extremely offensive.

"No, but I've not given up."

"As I hope you've not given up on Chinese. You've missed some essential parts of this term's syllabus, you know. So what's your strategy?"

"Strategy?"

"Yes, your plans for catching up. You must have a strategy."

"Well, I…" Adrian floundered.

"No strategy?"

Adrian found his tongue.

"Max has been filling me in, and of course I'll be seeing Dr. Sun about the language syllabus."

"You'll need to set yourself a realistic timetable for all the elements of the course. You've got four clear weeks of holiday coming up soon in which to home in on it all. I hope you haven't got any elaborate plans for sunning yourself in the Med, or hiking in the Highlands?"

"No, nothing like that, no plans at all, just Chinese."

"Right. So here I've drawn up a list of the history topics we've covered in your absence." He proffered a sheet of paper to Adrian, who took it, glanced down it and then stood up. He couldn't wait to get out.

"Max is waiting for me, so we can start immediately. I'll be off then."

"No febrile malingering now. Come back and see me before the end of term."

"I'll do that. Thanks."

No thanks, he said to himself, as he banged the door behind him.

Max was reading in the cafeteria. Adrian thumped his backpack down on the table and pushed Vernon's sheet so energetically across the table at Max that it fluttered on to the floor. Max retrieved it.

"Fucking bastard, with his bloodhound eyes and mean little beard," said Adrian.

"What?" said Max, "mild Adrian, calling the HoD names! I've never heard you speak like that before."

"He asked if I'd had 'any luck' in finding whoever it was I was looking for in Beirut. It's not fucking luck. It's a hard grind, and I've been through a lot to get as far as I have. I'd like to see fucking Vernon handle the things I've fucking well handled."

Max, eyebrows raised, looked questioningly at Adrian.

"Such as?"

"Tell you some other time, perhaps," answered Adrian hastily. "He kept asking if I'd got a fucking strategy for catching up."

Max fetched him a coffee.

"Calm down, Adrian," he said. "Come to my place for a snack lunch, then we can start going over everything. My language notes are relatively clear, and I can advise you on which books are best for quick facts."

Adrian, who had been staring moodily at the table, brightened at the suggestion.

"OK then. Lunch chez Max. You're on."

Unlike Vernon Buckley, Dr. Sun was kindly. Family matters and health were most important, he told Adrian, and he would be happy to help Adrian through this crisis. He provided him with copies of all the Chinese exercises and texts he had used during Adrian's absence, complimented him on his facility for learning and writing characters, and told him not to worry. He also gave Adrian ten minutes' practice in spoken Chinese. With this encouragement, as well as Max's prodding, Adrian threw himself into work and began to make some headway. Despite this, he was still not convinced that a Chinese degree was what he wanted, especially since Vic had dangled before him the carrot of a well-paid job. If he were to seize this opportunity, he reasoned, he would be in an excellent position to learn Arabic, doubtless to SOAS degree standard, within a couple of years. He said so to Max who snorted, pointing out that in the current employment market, it was essential to have a degree, that magic bit of paper that opened doors. Adrian should look ahead. Suppose, Max said, he concluded after a year or so that he couldn't stand the boss or the office or the environment, and decided to throw in the towel, then he would have wasted all that time. Adrian tried to explain the tremendous pull of Lebanon and of the Middle East. Max retorted that these places would still be there in four years' time, unless someone meanwhile blew them to smithereens.

Alone, later, Adrian pondered. Since being home, rather than regarding his suffering in captivity as something to be forgotten, he had begun to embrace the experience as a time when he had discovered new aspects of himself. His Beirut life had enriched him – the proof being that he had come to accept his terrible damage as part of it. He knew, also, that he had made good progress since returning home, for the nightmares no longer reflected torture, but were replaced by a frightening dream in which he tried to push his way out of a body bag sticking to him. He would wake sweating, with aching toes, fighting the bed covers tangled around him. Fen had appeared at his bedside on one occasion, rearranged his duvet, and stroked his forehead.

"Don't worry, Adrian, you're well now," she said. That dream would, he was sure, gradually fade and cease.

Adrian was comfortable knowing that Benny was just along the passage in the unlikely event that he should need somebody in the night. The perfect neighbour, there was plenty of proof that Benny was unquestionably helpful. He had even, in kindness to Sadie, relayed to Adrian with a mischievous twinkle the message that Sadie wanted to talk to him alone. Adrian slipped quickly out of classes, skulked in the library and slinked around the corridors, but Sadie was not to be deterred. She finally caught him in the cafeteria, where he was munching a sandwich, alas, alone.

"It's wonderful to see you back, Adrian," she said. "Mind if I join you? I've got loads to tell you!"

She sat down firmly beside him. What could he reply?

"I'm not stopping long, just going to eat this before going back to Fletcher's. What do you want to tell me?"

"I want to say that I'm sorry you've been ill, and been in the shit and all that. I know what it's like. I've been there. Do you want to tell me about it?"

She's oozing kindness, but hasn't a clue, Adrian said to himself. Her circumstances bear zero resemblance to mine.

"That's kind of you, but no. I've not exactly been in the shit, but anyway, it's good to be back. How've you been?"

"Good, really good. I've joined a new group, to boost my self-confidence and keep me busy and out of trouble. I'm reelly, reelly happy. The group's called The International Federation for Revelation, Interaction and Peace – it's known as 'INFRIP'. We're looking for more members and I was wondering if you'd like to join too? I'm sure you'd love it!"

Crikey, what a great name for a whacky cult!

"I've got a lot on my plate at the moment, Sadie. I wouldn't have enough time to do justice to it."

(Might as well hear a little more while I'm still chewing).

"What do you do?"

"We all get together and sing and have meaningful discussions about love and peace. Of course, it's teetotal, so we drink green tea or cocoa, and eat muffins. The Revelation is when the men take off their tops, and then we hold hands."

(Good thing they don't try to hold hands while they're taking off the tops.)

"We're thinking, or rather planning, for the women to take off their tops too, you know, just to show equality in Interaction. And what's really good is that the organisers have lots of confidence in me and are suggesting that I could open up a branch in Canada when I go back there."

(Just up her street.)

"Well, that sounds like a great opportunity for you."

"Yeah. It feels so right. It's a really international movement. It was started in San Francisco, and there are already branches in Florida, Australia and Brazil. And there's one due to open in Belgium."

(Crumbs. Not to be missed.)

"And there's always China in the picture too, I don't doubt, Sadie."

"Well we have talked about it, but the Chinese wouldn't understand what we're about, and we wouldn't want to get into trouble."

(Groups of people stripping – they might like it.)

"Quite right. Keep your nose clean."

"What?"

"Keep your nose clean. It's an expression meaning to stay out of trouble."

"Oh."

Adrian stood up and scooped his belongings off the table.

"Got to dash now, Sadie. Nice to talk to you!"

She stood up too and leaned towards him, arms extended.

Oh no, her mouth looks kissy. He scampered off through the swing doors without looking back.

Thirty-one

In the weeks following their concert outing, Toby and Tazie had continued to go out together occasionally, when their workloads allowed it. Although the approaching financial year end put paid to any plans for extravagant entertainment, they had nevertheless found a little time in which to have a drink or a snack together at the end of the day. Max had joined them on one occasion; he told Tazie privately later that he approved of her new suitor. The friendship between Tazie and Toby was developing, based on mutual respect of each other's tastes, as well as similar views on almost every subject they discussed. They however avoided any reference to Toby's hepatitis, and to the burgeoning affection between them which, separately, each recognised. To avoid potential heartache, Toby was trying to ward off the hope that Tazie would be part of his future, whilst she sat uncomfortably on the fence, one suitor on each side.

One morning, Tazie arrived at the office to discover that Toby had phoned in sick. She called his mobile immediately to discover that he was in the Accident and Emergency Department at Barts Hospital, suffering from nausea and vomiting. He told her not to worry, but of course she did, thinking the worst: that hepatitis might be the cause. Later in the day, he sent her a text message to say he had been allowed to go home, since tests had revealed no cause for concern. After another day off, during which Tazie called him twice to check that he was resting comfortably, he returned to work, quite hale, but certainly not hearty, which he would never be.

Tazie understood then how vulnerable the shadow of hepatitis must make him feel, discovering to her surprise that she minded about it and wanted to reach out to him, to comfort him and to help allay his fears of future illness. These were strange new impulses for her, suggesting a type of attachment which included elements of possession, and which she hadn't experienced before. She tried, unsuccessfully, to gauge the level of her involvement. All she knew was that the idea of being at his side seemed appropriate.

But then there was Adrian. Tazie had learned from Max that he had returned from Lebanon and later, that he was back in London. How long would it be, she wondered, before he contacted her? The paucity of his emails from Beirut, excusable during his illness, but perplexing before then, had left her feeling in limbo. It wasn't in her nature to two-time men and she didn't like her position, although she had no formal ties with either Toby or Adrian, nor did she have to choose between them in the immediate future.

The contrast between Tazie's feelings for Toby and those for Adrian was running through her mind one evening while she was chopping carrots. She needed to see Adrian again, and to know where she stood in his scheme of things – if anywhere. There was no reason why she should wait for him to take the initiative; he had always been lackadaisical, and might now be feeling a little reserved if he had not completely recovered from his illness. Nervously, she called him. He sounded gratified to hear from her, accepting with alacrity her invitation to meet for a drink. Term was not quite over, he said, but going out would make a welcome change from the strict study schedule imposed by Max – a hard taskmaster.

Adrian took the trouble to look critically in the mirror before leaving Fletcher's to meet her. He was surprised: the person he saw was smarter, more upright, more manly than the one who had left for Beirut at the end of December. Fresh clothes and a crisp haircut had improved him. Stepping closer to his image, he could make out new lines on his forehead, and his facial expression in repose looked different, less juvenile.

They met at a bar in the City at 6.30. Adrian chose to drink ginger ale rather than wine, thinking that he needed to remain completely sober for the occasion. Tazie fetched it and a glass of wine for herself, joining him at a quiet table. As they began to converse, Tazie immediately noticed changes in him. For one thing, he was thinner, perhaps more muscular than before; for another, there was a consciousness of himself in the way he moved and spoke, and seemingly, a more considered awareness of her. The sunny lad had gone, replaced by an attractive man. He apologised for not being a good correspondent; she said she understood that he had been preoccupied, and probably still was. He replied that indeed this was so, and that his objectives now were to make up for the missing weeks of study and to return to Beirut as soon as possible. Tazie rightly grasped, without voicing it, that this placed their relationship on the back burner. She regretted her timing, she said, in trying to pin Adrian down in December when he wasn't ready for it. Gently, Adrian took her hand and squeezed it as he told her that he hadn't stopped thinking of her while he was away, but that the atmosphere between them before he left had deterred him from writing at length. They moved on to exchange news, about her job, about Max's engagement, and about Adrian's new friends, as well as the atmosphere in Beirut. At around 8.00 they parted: Adrian had promised himself to finish a written piece that day. They agreed to meet again in the near future. On the way home, Tazie reflected that despite his seductive appearance and affectionate gestures, Adrian had become more remote.

***

Knowing that Adrian was planning to see Francis, Vic decided it was time to call. He had held back until he knew Adrian was in London, thinking not to disturb his rehabilitation at home. The conversation was brief: Vic was encouraged to learn from Adrian that he was concentrating seriously on catching up, with Max's help, and that everything else was on hold until he had. For his part, Vic had nothing to report concerning Patti Al-Zaini. What he wanted to tell Adrian was that he had briefed Francis about his illness and sojourn in the AUB while Adrian was still in Beirut, but that it was up to Adrian now to decide whether or not to tell Francis of his captivity and torture; Francis had no need to know. If Adrian did decide to take Francis into his confidence, he could rely on Francis' complete discretion. Vic had also mentioned to Francis the job with the Qatari lawyer.

Adrian hesitated. On the one hand, some extra sympathy for his suffering would be welcome, but he felt confident that he was now over the worst of his trauma.

Besides, he had promised to himself that if he told anybody, it would be Max. But the next time they met, instead he told Max about the possible job.

Max was incensed.

"Remember what I said when you started skipping Chinese for Arabic?"

"Mmm."

"Well here you are again, the same old story, except this time it's more serious. Who knows about this?"

"Only you, and Francis, and of course Vic."

"… who must have been out of his mind to suggest it."

"Vic's the most sensible person I know," retorted Adrian hotly. "He's not suggesting it; he's laying it on the table for my consideration. That's different. He respects me enough to put it before me for my decision. He knows my strengths and weaknesses. He wants me to make up my own mind, and will doubtless have an opinion about whatever I choose to do. And by the way, he said he didn't think I should abandon Chinese to take the job."

"Oh well, whatever, rant on! But I'm bound to say that I wouldn't have offered to help you now had I known that my information might get flushed down the loo like the contents of a chamber pot."

"A disgusting description of the destiny of your words of wisdom Max, and hardly accurate."

"You've got to concentrate on the job in hand," said Max, choosing to ignore what Adrian had said. "Would you like me to ask Lily to instruct you in being completely single-minded?"

'What's Lily got to do with it?"

Max laughed. "Guess!" he said.

Lily couldn't have been further from Adrian's mind at that moment, but it came to him.

"Is this to do with her and Hardy?"

"Well spotted! She cast her line and has succeeded in hooking her favourite fish. Hardy and she are now engaged. But there's no wedding in view yet. The next step is trips to America and China this summer, to meet the respective parents. They've agreed that it's best to graduate before marriage. Rumour has it that this engagement and relationship are Very Proper and that they've not had nooky yet."

"Shush, Max, don't be vulgar. Don't forget, you're getting married soon and we, your chums, could find some neat epithets to describe your doings."

"I bet Benny knows lots of apposite words beyond our ken," said Max thoughtfully.

"Yes, I expect he does. All that north-east stuff. Clever Benny. And he's single-minded too."

"Do you know, he's already been asked to give a twenty-minute introductory talk on linguistics to some sixth formers in Hampstead. He's an intellectual star, in a way neither you nor I will ever be."

"I'm sure of that."

They were silent for a moment.

"Right, nose to the grindstone, back to Chinese trade figures."

"If we must."

This discussion left Adrian feeling disappointed. He had hoped that Max might have been sympathetic about the attractions of the job, and would have permitted him some latitude for wayward ideas. Adrian resolved to search out Hassan for a bit of Arabic conversation, to cock an imaginary snook at Max. However, in Adrian's absence, Hassan's grasp of English seemed to have regressed. After a frustrating hour of incomprehensible babblings, Adrian gave up and retreated to the safety of Fletcher's where a boring Chinese translation passage awaited him.

After a distracted half hour, he went to knock on Benny's door for some light relief. Sujit was there too; they were playing chess. Benny invited Adrian to come back for tea in ten minutes, by which time the game would be over. Benny, who had started playing chess only in January under Sujit's tuition, was already beating him sometimes, as well as other revered members of the SOAS chess club. Adrian was pleased to see Sujit; they hadn't bumped into each other since Adrian's return to London, so hard had Adrian been focussing on work. There was plenty to talk about, including the unfortunate end to Sujit's relationship with Mike, the man Adrian and Benny had vetted for him.

"He turned out to be hugely possessive," said Sujit. "One evening he turned up here unexpectedly, and I happened to be in Benny's room. I heard this banging along the corridor, so I went out to see what it was. Mike was giving vent to his frustrations on my door. When he saw me, he threw a mad wobbly. What was I doing in someone else's room? etc. etc."

"He threatened Sujit, then buggered off. The same day he emailed a list of rules for the relationship," said Benny, "which were, naturally, unacceptable. We were worried he would be back to beat us up."

"I didn't reply to the email," said Sujit. "A couple of days later, he dismissed me in an appallingly misspelt letter. End of story. Thank goodness."

"Crikey," said Adrian. "So what now?"

"I'm looking round," said Sujit.

***

Francis held, of course, the same view as Max about the Qatari lawyer's job. The nub of the conversation he had with Adrian over a drink was about Adrian's options. Francis stated firmly that Adrian should not consider switching from Chinese to Arabic at SOAS as being even a remote possibility. It was unlikely that SOAS would be willing to countenance it, and such a move would be a severe waste of the time he had already spent on the course, not to mention the money kindly put up by Adrian's bankers, John & Fen Co. Ltd. As for the proposed job, Francis pointed out that obtaining a degree was essential for a secure future. Chinese was well regarded by potential employers because of its intrinsic difficulty which needed special talents; Adrian was fortunate enough to possess these. In vain did Adrian eagerly wax lyrical about the fascination of Middle Eastern politics as compared with the Chinese equivalent. Francis agreed with him, but did not allow him to escape the reality of his situation. Adrian knew Max and Francis were right; he was clutching at straws.

***

At the end of term, Adrian was summoned by Vernon for a review of his progress. The smell in his room had not improved, nor had the book stacks diminished. Despite Adrian's real dislike of Vernon, he curbed his tongue and the conversation went satisfactorily; Vernon was persuaded that by the end of the holidays, Adrian would be ready for the challenges of the summer term, and first year exams.

Adrian called Max who was with his family in Sussex, to tell him the good news and to thank him for the part he had played in this modest success. They stayed in regular contact during the vacation; Max, knowing that Adrian could be forgetful, kept a log of themes that needed to be covered before the beginning of term.

In due course, Adrian told his parents of the job opening in the Middle East. He presented it to them as an interesting subject, rather than something he might consider seriously. Fen was predictably horrified at the idea, and said so in no uncertain terms. John made all the salient points about the desirability of gaining a degree, and the effort Adrian had put into Chinese so far. The matter was then dropped.

The tight vacation weeks passed. When Adrian felt easy about the headway he had made, he contacted Tazie. They met for a meal in an Indian restaurant they knew, close to where Tazie lived. Adrian admitted to Tazie that concentrating steadily on Chinese during the holiday period had been difficult, since his mother was constantly in his mind. He was planning his next trip to Beirut, although he had no idea of timing. When they had eaten, Tazie invited Adrian back to her flat for a nightcap where their mutual attraction took over. A contented Adrian left for home after midnight. Tazie, lying on the rumpled bed, wondered why she had let it happen, pleasurable though it had been. The next morning she acknowledged coolly to herself that the evening spent with Adrian had actually served a purpose: to show her that he didn't love her in the way that she would wish.

Thirty-two

On May 6th, Adrian received a momentous email from Vic.

Adrian

I write with caution to give you some news.

An acquaintance has told me about an English woman calling herself Patti Smith who has appeared in the ex-pat community here. It is thought she turned up at the American Drama Club for a play-reading one evening, and moved from there into a bridge group. Not a bad player, apparently. I have seen her although not spoken to her.

I realise there's no point in describing her to you, but I can say that she looks attractive and probably about the right age to be your mother, although appearances can be deceptive.

She claims that she's been resident in Beirut for over 15 years, that her husband died last year, and that it's only now she feels up to social activities again. Since she wasn't known in UK or European social groups here previously, presumably she moved in Lebanese,

Arab, and other such circles only. She understands Arabic but speaks it haltingly, well enough however to make herself understood in essential everyday circumstances. Incidentally, there are no traces of a British Mr and Mrs Smith registered here, but we know our records aren't comprehensive.

Meanwhile, there seems to be an underlying reason for her emergence from the shadows: she talks about 'a Lebanese boy' who needs to go to school in Britain, but she doesn't say who the boy is or if he's related to her. She has asked one or two people for information and help, but has not seen fit (yet) to approach The British Council. When it was suggested to her to do so, she shrugged her shoulders dismissively.

I realise that any advice about not rushing into another Beirut trip will most likely fall on deaf ears. So be it. Anyway, if and when you decide to come, I expect to be able to supply her address, and we can discuss the best way to approach her. I may have more concrete information by then.

By the way, when you return to Beirut, I can arrange a meeting with the Qatari lawyer, if you're interested.

You know, I am sure, that it will be a pleasure to see you again, and that if appropriate, you will be welcome to stay at my home again. Meanwhile, I hope all goes well and that you've managed to steer clear of any further maladies!

Best,
Yours ever,
Vic

***

The post wasn't usually delivered before lunchtime and that Wednesday was no exception. Fen, who was sorting out food, heard the mail plop on to the floor and the letter flap snap shut. She went into the hall to pick up the envelopes, journals and publicity leaflets that were lying in disarray. Back in the kitchen, she stacked them on the corner of the sideboard to sort later.

Sebastian charged in.

"Hurry up Mum, I'm hungry," he said, running two circuits round the table, brushing past her. She caught his arm and grasped it firmly.

"Seb darling, I've told you lots of times not to race around pushing into people. It's become a bad habit of yours. One day you'll knock somebody over and then there'll be trouble."

"Sorry," he said, looking genuinely contrite, and pulled his arm away so as to be able to drum his fingers on the table instead. Just then he caught sight of the pile of post and bounced round to rifle through it in search of sports equipment leaflets but there were none. Something else caught his eye though.

"Hey, Mum, isn't this Adrian's writing?" he asked, waving a handwritten white envelope at her. "It's got a London postmark, so it could be from him."

Gemma appeared from nowhere to snatch it out of his hand.

"Oi" he screeched, trying to grab it back, but she was too quick for him and held it high above her head. Turning her back on Sebastian, she lowered her arm a little so that she could read the address.

"It *is* Adrian's writing, he's right" she said turning back to face them. "How funny! Why does he need to do a letter? What's wrong with email or phone? Can I open it?"

"If it's addressed to you, then of course you can. Better look first," said Fen.

"It's addressed to you and Dad, but it must be for all of us, mustn't it?" said Gemma eagerly.

"Not necessarily, young lady, so put it back on the pile and Dad and I will open it later."

"What will we open later?" asked John, ambling in.

"Just a letter from Adrian," said Fen.

Sebastian soon forgot about the letter. He swallowed his lunch down noisily before being allowed to escape outside. Gemma ate slowly and silently, one eye on the letter. When she had finished, she said plaintively:

"Aren't you going to open that letter?"

"Gemma," said John with exaggerated patience, "we'll let you read it in due course, if appropriate, but Mum and I want to finish our lunch first, so buzz off and leave us in peace, please."

Gemma pouted and stomped out, tossing her head.

Over coffee, Fen slit open the envelope and pulled out a typed sheet of paper which she and John huddled over to read together, his head at an awfully uncomfortable angle.

Dear Mum and Dad,

Sorry -- sorry -- and again... By the time you get this, I'll be on my way to Lebanon, hopefully to see my mother. It's bad of me I know, to have gone off (on purpose) in term time, and not to have discussed it with you beforehand. My actions will incur the HoD's wrath and disapproval, Max's irritation and contempt (he has tried to keep me on the straight and narrow Chinese path), and will doubtless be an enormous disappointment for you. But I just feel a pull I can't ignore towards finding the person who bore me, someone with whom I have undeniable genetic connections and who decided to abandon me and my unworthy father. It isn't objective curiosity that drives me forward, its gut ropes heaving me along and twisting inside me. I've never before felt so disturbed or so full of anticipation, apprehension and anxiety.

Please don't think that you did the wrong thing in telling me about my biological mother. On the contrary, I know you were right to do it; first because everybody in your position (or similar) has, I believe, a moral obligation to reveal what they know. And second, because the information awakened in me the natural instinct to know

394

something more about myself and my antecedents, which must be the 'right' reaction.

I have to go to Beirut now because Vic has emailed me that he has a possible lead: he's heard about someone called Patti Smith who seems to correspond to everything we know about my mother. Please don't think that Vic has persuaded me to come back to Beirut now. On the contrary, he has always stressed to me the importance of my Chinese studies and my degree. But he felt he had to let me know straight away about the woman.

I've got this awful feeling that unless I follow it up immediately, the trail may evaporate and she, the object of my quest, may disappear as she did before, or simply move on before I get there. There are of course all sorts of potential difficulties, both practical and emotional. Will my elementary Arabic be any good for seeing me along? How will I feel if I find her? What is she like, and will she be glad to see me? And when I return to England, will I be disorientated or will I feel good? Will what I learn change the way I feel about myself and how I envisage my future, whether I've found her or not? I don't know and won't know until afterwards, so in one sense there's no point in thinking about it. But of course I do.

I've got a confession to make – something you may already have guessed. I have been attending Arabic lectures at SOAS from time to time, learning some rudiments of this extraordinarily difficult language, and reading up about politics and social conditions. It's all enormously complicated. The part of the confession which is directly relevant is that in the autumn I had been skipping a few Chinese lectures when they clashed with Arabic things. Max knew about it and tried to steer me in the right direction. Of course, I've not missed any Chinese lectures since I got back from Beirut.

Whatever happens about my mother, you must believe that I regard you as the best parents I could ever have and the only real parents I have and ever will have. Nothing can change the family ties and the sense of belonging I have with you, as well as of course with Gemma and Sebastian. I believe I am able to take this step and leave for the Lebanon now because I feel 100% secure with you behind me, and that whatever the outcome, you will be there waiting for me when I return. Meanwhile, please forgive my waywardness.

With all my love as always, and to Gemma and Sebastian,

your son and brother,
Adrian

Choking back her tears, Fen put the letter on the table. John rubbed his neck as he sat back in his chair, a big clod in his throat preventing him from speaking.

"We did have to do it, to tell him," croaked John eventually, "no question."

"No, no question."

"And it's a letter with a second class stamp, so that it wouldn't reach us until after he'd gone."

"Yes – deceitful so-and-so," replied Fen vehemently. "He'll get a piece of my mind when he comes back, or rather *if* he comes back."

"Don't forget, these are emotional times for him – special circumstances," said John.

"Finding his mother, yes, that's special. But it was cowardly of him not to tell us he was going."

"Mm."

They were both quiet again. John broke the silence.

"At least there's still money out there for him. And Vic on hand to help."

"Yes, at least there's that. I assume he's staying with Vic."

"Yes, I suppose so. It's probably uncharitable of me, but I wonder a bit about the influence that man's having on him."

"You liked him, didn't you?"

"Yes, but… There's something unfathomable about him. Ah well. Adrian's a steady person. I just hope this woman, Patti thingamajig, does turn out to be his mother, and that he comes back and settles down again to finish his degree. He'll need it."

For a moment Fen was silent and then said:

"It's out of our hands, John, for the time being. All we can do is to wait and see what happens, if he comes back, and try to nudge him in the right direction."

"We'll let Gemma and Sebastian read the letter, won't we?"

"Yes, it'll upset Gemma and be good for Sebastian," said Fen with a sudden smile. John pushed his chair back and stood up.

"I'm off." Then he bent to kiss Fen on the forehead. "You're wonderful," he said as he went out.

Fen was right. Gemma took the letter upstairs to read alone in her room with the door shut. When she emerged with it, her face was blotched red and white. He's toppled off the pedestal where she'd put him, thought Fen. She feels betrayed and probably jealous of this potential mother. Fen put her arms round Gemma who allowed herself to be hugged for a few seconds then pulled away, reasserting herself. She'll be fine, thought Fen.

When Sebastian came in from the garden, Fen told him to sit down and gave him the letter to read. He took ten minutes over it, a puzzled frown lining his forehead as he kicked his legs back and forth. On finishing, he asked a stream of questions, about Adrian's mother and father, about families, about Adrian's life in London – what he did at university and where he lived. And, perceptively, what Max (Sebastian's hero) thought about all this. Fen was pleased that he was taking it seriously.

Thirty-three

A freak wind was buffeting the Eastern Mediterranean. The pilot warned passengers that it would be a bumpy landing. Adrian, not afraid of flying, was disturbed by the young woman sitting beside him, who groaned into her handkerchief every time the plane lurched. Suddenly she grabbed his arm with both hands and the handkerchief, clinging on with an iron grip.

"I don't want ... to die ... I mean, ... to fly ever again," she croaked to him. Adrian was in the window seat; the plane was low enough for him to see white ruffs of foam frothing on the wave crests chasing towards the shore.

"It's all right," he said, "planes are built to fly safely in the wind. We'll be landing in just a few minutes."

He remembered what it was like to feel scared. Captivity-scared. This woman's fear was irrational, but no less real to her than his had been to him. With his spare hand, he covered her fist which he stroked gently. Best to keep talking and make her talk, he thought.

"Is someone collecting you at the airport?"

"My husband," she managed to say.

"He's probably watching the plane on the horizon. As soon as it lands and you're in the arrivals hall, you'll feel quite different."

"Mm."

"Do you live in Beirut?"

"No, we live in London."

Adrian kept it up until the plane landed, veering slightly in a sudden gust. In the baggage hall, the woman sought out Adrian to thank him for his kindness.

The sun was just dipping below the horizon as Adrian walked out of the airport into the warm fume-filled air, rejoicing to be there. At last, an essential person in his life might become real to him. During the flight, he had tried to curb his elation at the prospect, reminding himself that the woman mentioned in Vic's email might not be his mother, but he couldn't quell his optimism. I shall remember this moment, here at this airport, for the rest of my life, he said to himself.

He took a taxi to Vic's flat where the caretaker welcomed him back. Vic put his arm round Adrian's shoulders and squeezed him. To sit comfortably facing the sea, G and T in hand, was to reawaken, for both of them, memories of the hours of recovery Adrian had spent there. They looked at each other.

"Corny though it is, I'm nevertheless going to say it," said Adrian, "just like old times, except thank goodness, not quite."

Vic nodded. They sat quietly for a few minutes.

Soon they exchanged news. Vic told Adrian that Briggs had died; his wife had asked for his life support machine to be disconnected.

"Afterwards, the American Ambassador called on the Lebanese Foreign Minister to demand that an official inquiry be conducted into the unlawful killing of a well-respected American citizen. Those were the exact words. The Foreign Minister replied that a thorough internal inquiry had been under way since the shooting incident had occurred, and the information gleaned would be transmitted to the Ambassador when the inquiry was concluded – again the exact words. Meanwhile, Mrs Briggs has offered a reward for information leading to the arrest of the murderers."

"Oh dear. I ought to feel sorry for him, but his double-dealings were indirectly responsible for my abduction."

"You would have interesting information to offer," said Vic, "but don't even think of it."

"Quite. The idea of reliving what happened to me to help render limpid – or muddy up – the waters of a dodgy death is a no-no. The whole truth will never be uncovered anyway."

"Nicely said! Your perception of Middle East politics is pessimistic, but alas, accurate."

"By the way, I didn't tell Francis about my captivity – we talked mainly about the Qatari lawyer and his job. One day soon, though, I think I'll tell Max. But it won't be to help me get over it. It'll be because I think he'd like to know, and I'd like to share with him this important thing that happened to me."

"You've been admirably strong Adrian, in keeping quiet about it."

"You know, for a long time all I wanted was to lap up sympathy, and I got it from you."

"I was glad to give it."

"But at home it was different. I got sympathy for my illness, but of course none for my torture. So there was a hurdle to clear: I have to finish healing myself on my own, which entails accepting what had happened as part of my life, rather than rejecting it as something that didn't belong. Difficult to explain… I'm not there yet."

"I understand, and about why you want to tell Max. So what did he say about you coming back here?"

"Nothing, he doesn't know yet. Only my family knows. I sent them a letter from Heathrow with a second class stamp on it, so that they wouldn't try to prevent me from coming or get upset on the phone. Cowardly, I know, but the best way, I think. I'll email Max and Benny tomorrow. Everybody will be furious, Mum, Dad, Max, my HoD."

"You know that I agree with them that you shouldn't have come now?"

"Vic, this opportunity may be my only one. I can't wait," said Adrian urgently.

Vic didn't reply immediately and then said:

"All I can say is that at your age, in your shoes, I would have done the same thing."

"Thanks for saying that, Vic."

"You'll have to face the music back home; fortunately it's nothing to do with me."

They moved to the small dinner table where Vic set out the food. It was then that he raised the subject of arrangements for the forthcoming days.

"How long are you staying, Adrian?"

"I've got an open return," he answered, smiling. "But if you need me to move out, then do say so. I daresay the Residence will have me back."

"Good idea! Perhaps you'd like to pop along there anyway to say hullo, and see if it's nicer than here? It can be arranged. I'm sure the caretaker would be happy to accommodate you."

They both laughed.

"I don't want to get in your way, that's all."

"You're welcome to stay here as long as you like, or as long as it takes to get everything done. I may have to disappear for a couple of days, but I know you can manage on your own. I'll give you a key."

"So when can I call on Patti whatever her real name is?"

"Not yet. I still have to find out exactly what she's said about the boy she wants to send to school in England. Then we'll know what kind of information you need to take with you when you go to see her."

"Oh."

"You sound disappointed – don't be. I'm not procrastinating. It will happen. Your speedy arrival caught me on the hop."

"Vic, do you think there's a Mr Smith, whom I might meet?"

"That's something else. Did he really exist, and if he did, was she really married to him? How would the timing of that marriage fit in with her marriage to Al-Zaini, her current husband – who is probably the man she met and taught in England? I think she just landed on Smith as being the most anonymous surname in England. The convenience of inventing somebody is that it's ok to kill the person off when you want to. For obvious reasons, she wouldn't have wanted to revert to Sandling."

"Perish the thought," said Adrian with a wry smile, "and Smith wasn't her maiden name; she was Patricia Newbold." He paused. "People who want anonymity have something to hide."

"Quite. I came to the conclusion it must be something to do with Al-Zaini. A minor diplomat with that name at the Saudi Embassy in London in the early to mid 1980s left back to Saudi under a cloud – something to do with shoplifting – the details aren't important. Patti may not have known about the incident when she met him, but found out eventually after they were married. If this is indeed the same man, she wouldn't want the British community to know, in case somebody were aware of the shoplifting. This could account for her steering clear of the Brits up to now; wanting help for the boy has put her in an awkward position."

"Gosh. So if I turn up there, very typically English, saying I've come to meet Mrs Al-Zaini, she probably won't be very welcoming."

"Right. You'll have to call her Mrs Smith."

Adrian sighed. "It all sounds so difficult and complicated. She ran away from my violent father into the arms of a thieving Saudi Arabian. She must have a rather dim view of men. How on earth do I go about talking to her?"

"I think it would be best for you too, to hide behind anonymity, just to get in to see her. We can arrange that without her knowing your name. When we know more about the boy, we can decide on your opening gambit."

"It sounds so deceitful."

"This is a delicate matter, Adrian. You have to face up to the possibility that she might not want to see you. She abandoned you all those years ago, never got in touch with you. We can't assume that she would welcome you."

"I realised that at the beginning, but it's a hard truth to face now that I'm nearly there," said Adrian, after a moment.

"But you've come, and you're going ahead with it."

"Yes."

"Well, let's get on to something more cheerful. I'll get the coffee first."

Adrian carried the plates into the kitchen and then went to sit looking out towards the dark blue sky and the black sea. Vic returned with two small cups of coffee.

"The good news is that I can now fix an appointment for you, if you're interested, with the Qatari lawyer, Rashid Al-Kuwari. He comes to Beirut roughly once a fortnight. His office people say he's due towards the end of this week. I haven't got any paperwork about the job – it hasn't been advertised yet."

"I didn't realise it would be."

"Oh yes, Rashid's trawling around for people. You're not the only person he'll be interviewing. He's got several projects simmering. How he's going to structure the various developments he has in mind, I don't know. As time goes on, he's going to need more staff with different qualifications. He'll tell you about it himself." Vic paused. "So what do you think?"

"My view is that I've got nothing to lose by seeing him. After all, an interview is a two way process, and I need to look at what sort of a person he is. I'm not making a commitment by meeting him. I'm sussing out the man, the job and the environment."

"Good, then I'll fix it up for you."

On Friday 13th May at 5.00 pm, Adrian presented himself at Rashid Al-Kuwari's luxurious suite of offices in Beirut Central District. Almost an hour later, the company driver took Adrian back to Vic's flat. Adrian's mind was whirring. Al-Kuwari was younger than he had expected – probably only in his mid-thirties – and spoke very fluent American English. He wore a suit and tie that made Adrian

405

feel shabby (despite his best clothes and a tie borrowed from Vic), and was completely clear about what he wanted to say, and know. A toughie. Adrian suspected that he had allowed himself fifty-five minutes in which to conduct the interview, and then needed five minutes before a six o'clock appointment.

Vic was at home, waiting to hear how it had gone. Adrian explained, pacing up and down.

"Well, essentially, he's hiring a series of young men – not women of course – one at a time. Each will spend about three months shadowing him so as to learn the business. They may overlap. He doesn't know yet how many people in total, maybe as many as a dozen. He wants as many different nationalities as possible, so as to cover Europe, the Far East etc. He mentioned probably two Europeans, one of whom must be British, a Chinese, a Brazilian, an American, and so forth. He's open-minded about the level of education of applicants; he doesn't want to exclude anyone very promising without a university degree. His businesses will encompass several areas – I think you know about that? Top end luxury goods, real estate, finance, and other things too."

"For goodness sake, stop prowling around like a hungry lion!" said Vic. "Sit down while I fetch some drinks!"

Adrian obeyed and then continued talking.

"Next, he got round to talking about me. By the way, thank you for the overly generous recommendation you gave. I could never live up to how you described me."

"I'm sure you could, otherwise I wouldn't have done it."

"Anyway, he asked me if I'd brought a cv which I hadn't, but that's ok: – he wants me to fax it to him. He was interested in where I imagined I might be in five years' time and what I might be doing. I had to dream up something quickly. Francis had mentioned the Foreign Office at one point, so I latched on to that. I couldn't tell him I was just a meanderer, doing what happened to come along."

"You aren't, not any more. Perhaps you still were last summer, but that's a long time ago now, or rather, many experiences ago."

Adrian looked thoughtfully at Vic.

"Maybe."

"Carry on."

"We got on to the question of my degree. He understands that the Brits regard it as essential for good future employment, and he said how much he appreciated the opportunities he had had: AUB, Harvard and LSE. So then we talked, inevitably, about my position, Chinese versus Arabic, and I tried to explain how I felt about it. And do you know what he said? He said it might be possible for me to study for a degree in Arabic at the AUB at the same time as shadowing him."

"The Adrian charm has obviously worked. Congratulations!"

"Stop it, Vic," said Adrian heatedly. "It was an objective suggestion in an objective conversation."

"Yes, but step back from it. Al-Kuwari's nobody's fool. He's looking for adaptable people who he thinks will fit in. And part of that is the way you present yourself, how you are with people, and how receptive you are to facts.

407

You score on all three. So he's trying to make the position attractive to you."

"I suppose it's possible," said Adrian pensively. "Well, I think I've told you everything."

"Except how you left it with him."

"Oh yes. I told him I must finish this year at SOAS. He agrees that it's the right thing to do. He'd like to meet me again afterwards – perhaps in London."

"That gives you plenty of time for contemplation."

"Yep. You know, what he told me puts a completely different complexion on the job. I thought it would be a simple question of deciding before the end of the year whether I wanted it or not. But it's not like that at all. It was a very rounded session."

Adrian turned the matter over in his mind in the following days, between daydreaming of conversations with his mother and trips with his half-brother. Joyful reunions with his friends also helped fill in this period of anxious anticipation. Jean invited him to dinner alone (Mark was travelling in South America); their conversation reached a level of intimacy which would have been unlikely in cerebral Mark's presence touching, as it did, on relationships. Dinner at the Morgans with Jean and Vic was as animated as ever, Glyn booming with bonhomie and Trisha intent upon feeding everybody up. Khalil brought Sabir to lunch with Adrian in a cafe in the suburbs, known for its Iraqi specialities. All made Adrian promise to let them know the outcome of the next step in his search.

***

In due course, Vic found out what he wanted to know. Although Patti Smith had still not imparted to anybody the identity of the boy whom she needed to send to school in England, she had revealed that he was sixteen years old, of Arabic mother tongue, but with quite good English. He had to improve his English reading and writing so as to be able to qualify for entry to a British university. After consulting Jean, Adrian typed a list of possible schools and sixth form colleges in London where the boy would be able to study for GCSE and/or A level exams.

Vic arranged, along a circuitous path, that a go-between, Gloria Bjorklund, Chairperson of the American Bridge Club, would speak to Patti Smith about a young man (unnamed) who could advise her on education for the boy. The information would reach Mrs Bjorklund, apparently casually, through a string of acquaintances, thereby ensuring that its source, and Adrian's identity, remained unknown. Fortunately she was somebody who collected friends airily and introduced them around, without remembering their names.

Vic and Adrian chose a possible date: Sunday 22nd May, at 4.00 pm. The date was fed via the chain to Patti Smith who agreed. There was no indication as to whether the boy would be there at that time. Once the date had been fixed, Adrian's anxiety swelled by the hour. His fear of rejection was acute. He wanted to love his mother and brother. Vic, who by that time had heard negative whispers about Mrs Smith's personality, was extremely anxious for Adrian, but kept his knowledge to himself and could offer neither advice nor comforting words. He arranged for the car to take Adrian and wait for him; Adrian decided that Vic shouldn't accompany him.

Mrs Smith lived in a tower block in Ras Beirut. It didn't look particularly new, but the outside was well maintained. Inside, it was spotless. Adrian, his mind in turmoil, spoke to the caretaker and was directed to take the lift up to the sixth floor. There were three doors. On the middle one there were two plaques, one above the other. The top one said 'Al-Zaini', the one below said 'Mrs P Smith'. Adrian pressed the only bell.

A woman opened the door. She was quite tall, with shoulder length blonde hair curling inwards; she was wearing a smart ivory-coloured dress which revealed the generous curves of her body. A heavy gold necklace with large purple stones emphasised her long neck; her bracelet matched the necklace. Adrian stared at her well-proportioned bronzed face, hoping for a hint of recognition, she of him, or he of her, but none came.

"Hi," she said in the husky voice of a smoker. "Come in and sit down. Would you like tea or coffee?"

"Yes, please, coffee," said Adrian.

"Arabic or instant?"

"Arabic, please, sweet," he replied. It was as though his voice were speaking without his brain triggering it.

The woman disappeared. Adrian didn't sit down, but walked softly round the spacious living room, hoping to recognise something, anything. There were oriental rugs on the floor, some looking very old. At the far end, there was a glass dining-table with eight black leather chairs. On one side of the sitting area, a collection of copper and brass objects was exhibited on a long sideboard beneath two portraits of men dressed in Arabian clothes. Proudly displayed in front were three photographs in silver frames, of a smiling, dark-skinned boy, at different ages.

The woman returned carrying a tray with two cups and a plate of small biscuits, which she put down on a coffee table.

"Sit here," she said, gesturing to a generous settee alongside. They sat next to each other. She handed Adrian a cup and pushed the biscuit plate towards him.

"Is that the boy?" he asked, pointing at the photos.

"Yes, that's Fouad," she replied, looking curiously at Adrian. He returned her gaze. "Mrs Bjorklund didn't mention your name," she said, after a moment. "You look a little familiar."

Adrian took a deep breath and a sip of coffee, before turning towards her and replying.

"That's not surprising. I'm Adrian Goodfield, formerly Sandling, and I think you're my mother."

"No, no, no, not Adrian," she whispered, sliding instinctively along the settee, away from him. "No, not you."

"I'm sorry if it's a bit of a surprise," said Adrian calmly, hoping to reassure her.

"A bit of a surprise? It's an awful shock," she said sharply, her eyes scanning his face. "When did you get here? What are you in Beirut for?" she demanded, a spiky tone in her voice.

"I arrived a couple of weeks ago. I came to look for you, to find you. I was here before, in December and January. I've been…"

She interrupted: "So you thought that bringing information on schools was a neat way of spying on me."

"I've not come to spy on you, I'm…" Words failed him, as he saw the anger in her face.

"Mrs Bjorklund should have told me who you were."

411

Adrian noticed she was retreating further along the settee.

"She may not have known."

"Then you should have said who you were when I opened the door."

"But you might have refused to see me. I was afraid you'd shut the door on me."

"I would have done. It was deceitful of you not to say who you were." Her voice grated unpleasantly. "You must go now, I can't have you here," she said restlessly.

"But I made a list of the schools for you. Here's it is." Adrian took it out of the inside pocket of his jacket with a shaking hand and proffered it, but she didn't take it.

"I don't want anything from you, and I won't let you anywhere near Fouad. Please go, now."

When Adrian, bewildered, made no move, she suddenly jumped up, stumbling against the table which wobbled dangerously. Adrian, on his feet immediately, put out a hand to steady her, but she pushed him away and backed off.

"Don't touch me," she shouted, "leave me alone."

"OK, I won't touch you. But are you all right?"

She shook her head slowly and then stepped towards him to stand right in front of him, her face inches from his.

"I was until you appeared," she said, spitting the words emphatically in his face. "Why did you want to find me?"

"Because I wanted to see you, to get to know you. It's normal to want to know one's mother," Adrian replied urgently.

"I left you behind in England. I didn't want to take you with me."

Adrian shivered. "I know that. But why?"

"It's obvious, isn't it? Because I didn't care about you."

"I'm your son, why didn't you care? Didn't you love me when I was a baby?" There was a crack in Adrian's voice.

"Adrian, you were conceived in a moment of violence – how could I ever love you?"

"Oh no!" said Adrian, putting his head in his hands. She gave him a little push. He stepped back and she forward, menacingly.

"Do you want to know what happened that evening? I'll tell you, even if you don't. I was doing the ironing. Your father came back from the pub, drunk, and took off his trouser belt …" Her voice was bitter.

"No, no, no, please don't tell me," cried Adrian covering his ears with his hands.

"I was terrified. I ran upstairs and locked myself in the bathroom. He raged around the house shouting insults at me – I learned lots of those from him – until quite late. Eventually, when he had gone quiet, I crept out, but he was waiting for me."

"Stop, stop, stop it, I don't want to know. I believe you. Please don't tell me," begged Adrian.

"He forced me to have sex with him on the floor. It was rape, even though we were married. Then he beat me with the belt," she said.

Adrian's legs were rocking him back and forth.

"Can you imagine how I felt afterwards, when I knew I was pregnant?" she continued. "I wondered what I was carrying in my womb – a clone of Leslie, or some other kind of monster?"

"Not a monster. That was me, and I'm ok," answered Adrian in a low tone.

413

"Shut up and listen. I wanted to have an abortion. Leslie knew, so he did everything he could to prevent me, not because he wanted a baby, but because he was a control freak and was determined to contradict me." Her voice was rasping. "When I couldn't stand up to his threats any longer, I escaped to my mother's in London where I felt safe. Leslie wanted me out of the way anyway, so that he could drink and cavort endlessly without coming home to a silent, reproachful wife. Silent because I knew if I said anything he didn't like, he would go for me – it was better not to speak at all. Abortion was out of the question as my mother, a proper practising Catholic, was firmly against it. After you were born, my mother persuaded me to try to live with Leslie again. But I couldn't look after you properly; I was in a terrible state, really frightened. Leslie took you to his mother where you stayed a lot of the time, except when you came with me to my mother's."

Adrian felt a terrible constriction in his throat which prevented him from gulping. It was the result of trying not to cry.

"What was I like, as a baby?" he croaked.

"Dunno. You were just a baby. You wanted attention all the time, which I couldn't give."

"Didn't Leslie's mother like me?" asked Adrian desperately.

"Probably. She didn't mind keeping you."

"Oh." Adrian swallowed, with difficulty.

Patti turned to sit down again on the settee.

"I started giving private English lessons. I lived with my mother during the week, and only went to see Leslie occasionally, at weekends, usually when we were passing you from grandmother to grandmother. He'd lost interest in me by then. He had a coven of girls down at the boozer. I think they shared him around between them." She was nodding, almost talking to herself. "Then I had an opportunity to leave. I had met a kind man – he worked at the Saudi Embassy. I was teaching him English. He said, come to Beirut with me. I'll marry you and give you a nice life, but you can't bring the baby. I'll make a new baby with you. In due course, I took some of my things and went to live with him in London for some weeks. Leslie looked for me after I left my mother's house but never found me. He didn't dare threaten my mother. In due course we got divorced. He knew I was abroad, through the solicitor. And I ended up here."

"But aren't you frightened by the fighting in the Middle East?"

"No, my husband looks after me. He doesn't live here all the time. He has to spend a lot of time with his other family in Saudi. He comes here when he can, and when things get bad here, he sends me to Switzerland. Fouad goes to stay with him regularly in Jeddah."

They were silent for a moment, she, hands clasped in her lap, lost in thought, Adrian still standing. He took a step towards where she was sitting and looked down at her.

"Did you never think about me? Wonder what was happening to me?"

"I had to think of you after Leslie died, when your adoption was going through. It was an enormous relief when it was done. After that I knew I didn't have to think about you again."

"Don't you want to know anything about me, about my life, about who I've become and what I'm doing?" He was beseeching her.

415

"No, I don't," she replied bluntly, raising her voice again. "Don't you understand? I came here to forget all about a horrible period in my life; you were part of that life, and I don't want to have anything to do with anybody connected with it. As to who you've become, you're doubtless just like your father." She looked at him contemptuously.

"I'm not like him. I'm me. I have no memory of him."

"Well, perhaps not like him *yet*. He was so attractive and charming when we first met, but then…"

She started to cry. A big blob of a youth, the face in the three photographs, appeared from a passage, looking puzzled. He stopped to take in the scene and then went over to perch beside his mother, putting his arm round her. They spoke a few increasingly loud sentences in Arabic, she pointing a shaky hand at Adrian.

"Don't you get it, Adrian? Watch my lips," she said tremulously. "I'm OK here, can't you see? I've got a nice life, money, friends, a nice flat, a husband who doesn't bother me. I got away from your nasty violent father. I got a job, worked hard, and I don't want to have anything to do with his son."

"But I can help you find a school for the boy. Is this him? Is this my brother?" Adrian, his stomach churning, gestured towards the boy. "If he is, I'd like to get to know him."

"I'll tell you," she said, more calmly, but bitterly. "Yes, Fouad is your brother, your half-brother. And he's sweet and gentle and kind to his mother. His father says he's a mummy's boy, and that he should go to England to university. But I don't want you to have anything to do with him. You'd be a bad influence."

"I'm a good law abiding citizen," countered Adrian desperately.

"I don't care what you are. You must go now, and that's that." There was rising panic in her voice. "I can't cope with this situation, you standing there, looking at me like this. Get out of my life."

"But we've not talked…"

"I don't want to know what we've not talked about," she interrupted harshly. "When I left England I didn't want anything more to do with your father or you. Leslie was a vile man. He did disgusting things. He wanted me to do disgusting things too." She was becoming hysterical. "He beat me black and blue when I refused. And you're his son, so you'll turn out just like him. You'll be a woman beater too." By now she was screaming.

Something was banging hard inside Adrian's head.

"Fouad, push him out!"

Fouad went to grab Adrian, who had no difficulty in escaping from his flabby grasp. With a sudden spurt of vicious energy, he kicked Fouad who fell heavily to the floor.

Patti bawled at both of them in Arabic; Fouad picked himself up and limped off down the passage, rubbing his arm.

"Can't we just…" Adrian's voice was plaintive.

"Go away, clear out. You've hurt him." Adrian hesitated. "Bugger off!" Her shrieking voice reached its highest decibels. "Leave me in peace, you fucking interloper."

Adrian tottered out of the door which slammed shut behind him. He leaned up sideways against the wall, his head swimming. A moment later he bent over and vomited on to the shiny marble floor. He stepped back from the mess, fumbled in his trouser pocket and found a handkerchief with which he wiped his mouth and his spattered shoes. Trembling, he called the lift and got in. Down on the ground floor, he shuffled to the caretaker's desk where he explained hesitatingly that he was ill and there was a mess on the sixth floor. He was able to dispose of the handkerchief in the caretaker's bin behind the desk. The driver, smoking in the parking bay outside, saw Adrian's unsteady progress, threw down his cigarette and ran in to collect Adrian and help him into the car. Adrian heard himself groaning, but couldn't stop.

The driver supported Adrian up the steps into Vic's block of flats. The caretaker called Vic, who ran down the stairs, and guided Adrian into the lift and the flat. There, he sat him down on a sofa and fetched him a large glass of water and a plastic bucket. Adrian was crying, desperately. Gradually Vic was able to get him to drink down the glassful. Either it would go down or it wouldn't, Vic said to himself. Adrian vomited again. Vic arranged two pillows and a couple of cotton blankets on the sofa for the perspiring and shivering Adrian. He fetched his pyjamas, got him into them, and tucked the blankets round him.

"Adrian," he said gently, "you've had a severe shock, and you need to take in some sugar. Do you think you could manage to drink some sweet tea now?"

"I'll try," said Adrian. These were his first words.

Gradually he swallowed some tea, and his head stopped swimming. Vic disappeared and reappeared with a couple of tablets which Adrian took with the remainder of the tea. Vic sat down. After a few minutes, Adrian broke the silence.

"I've been wasting my time, thinking and hoping. She'll have nothing to do with me. She hates me and everything to do with me. My dream's shattered."

Little by little, between sobs, Adrian related to Vic what had happened in the short time he was with his mother. Vic was furious on Adrian's behalf. To reject Adrian was one thing, but to insult him as she had, was excessively cruel. Adrian, wracked with guilt at having kicked his brother over, agonised about the possibility that he had indeed inherited his father's vicious genes, especially as he had been conceived in a moment of violence. Vic tried to reassure him but Adrian was, for the time being, inconsolable.

Later, Vic warmed up some soup; still propped up on the settee, Adrian managed a few mouthfuls, as well as some fruit. Eventually, they talked again. Adrian, by now much calmer, got up to fetch his airline ticket, so that Vic could book him on the early plane home the next day. Vic upgraded him to business class so that he would be as comfortable as possible.

Before midnight, when Adrian began to doze, Vic suggested he should go to bed and offered him a sleeping tablet which Adrian refused. It was a long distressing night for both of them; Vic, immensely sad, stayed in the room, watching over his troubled friend, who tossed and turned and muttered. He soothed him a little by caressing his forehead. Between Adrian's fitful slumbers, they talked, sometimes only for a few moments, sometimes for longer.

When morning came, Adrian, now steadier, prepared his luggage. Vic went with him to the airport. At the security barrier, they hugged tightly. Adrian wept.

"I'll miss you," said Vic.

Adrian nodded. "Thank you, and I you."

Thirty-four

Adrian called home as soon as he was out of the arrivals hall at Heathrow. Fen and John were immensely relieved to hear he had arrived safely; they clung to each other when the phone conversation was over. An earlier call from Lebanon had been extremely distressing, with a very poor connection making it impossible for them to understand more than that Adrian was about to get on a plane back to England, and that a meeting with his mother – the first indication for them that he had found her – had made him extremely unhappy.

He called again from Liverpool Street station to tell them his train arrival time. Like a wounded animal, he was fleeing home, (avoiding the real and potential complications of stopping in London), in the knowledge that only there could he be healed of his unhappiness, in peace, with the physical and psychological support of the people he loved – the members of his real family. John collected a sad, silent man at the station. After news of Vic and remarks on the journey, neither spoke on the way home; John understood that Adrian would speak freely about his ordeal when he was ready. When they reached home, John carried Adrian's luggage upstairs while Adrian kissed Fen, who then led him zombie-like up to his room. Once under the covers, he fell asleep immediately. In the afternoon, he woke with a throbbing head and stumbled down to the kitchen in search of painkillers. Fen told him to sit down, made him tea and gave him a couple of tablets. As he sat with his head in his hands, she asked him when he had last eaten; he mumbled that he didn't know, so she made him a nourishing sandwich of cheese, ham and tomato, which she put in front of him with a yoghurt. He swallowed it all down obediently, staring into space, remembering from his childhood Fen's voice saying 'Eat it all up, Adrian.'

As he swallowed the last mouthful, Fen put her arm round his shoulders, leaning over him to pick up the empty plate. The safety and familiarity of her gesture released a spring in him and his contained emotions spilled out. He put his head on the table, alternately sobbing uncontrollably and howling like an injured fox. He wept for his mother, and for his futile efforts to link up with his background. John, alerted by the noise, came in to find Fen sitting beside Adrian holding him and stroking his head. Gradually his howling and crying abated until he found a creaky voice to begin telling them everything. It was all etched chronologically in his memory: the arrangements made in advance for getting access to his mother, his feelings during the ride to the apartment block, the words he and his mother had spoken to each other, the presence and appearance of his half-brother whom he had kicked, his hasty departure in severe shock, and Vic's compassionate care. He was able to speak of the deep chasm that had formed inside him when Patti told him she wanted nothing to do with him because her life was tidy, settled, and because Adrian had doubtless inherited his father's violent genes. Since that moment, Adrian had been tormented by that thought. Fen reassured him that even as a toddler, he had never shown any signs of violent behaviour, had never raised his hand against Gemma or Sebastian, and had sometimes come home from school black and blue, having been roughed up by schoolmates without giving as good as he got. Adrian took in what she said, but knew he would be seeking proof within himself of his non-violent nature for months, perhaps even years to come. The whole encounter had left him feeling bereft; he had lost something, but it was something he had never possessed, something that had taken shape and identity in his mind but not in fact: the affection and love of his biological mother.

John and Fen comforted him; they were relieved that Adrian had found her, which in one sense would mean he could move forward, but they generously shared his unhappiness that nothing positive had come of the connection. By the end of the day, Adrian was exhausted, having repeated his story for Gemma and Sebastian after school. Gemma sat on his knees and hugged him, which was also tiring. Immediately after supper, Adrian went to bed. He slept on through the next morning, his thinking, speaking and listening capacity exhausted.

Sleep and affection were of the essence for a few days. Adrian appeared for meals, said little and went back upstairs afterwards. When Fen asked him if he was depressed he answered "no" with a slight smile, but said that he felt very sad and terribly tired. John was surprised that Adrian didn't seem tormented or agitated, but Fen pointed out that Adrian's was a calm disposition and that he had never been clinically depressed, so was unlikely to show symptoms of it now. They were, however, enormously anxious for him, thinking that his expressing the intention to return to London would be a step in the right direction, although they anticipated that being accepted back at SOAS would take some arranging. In due course, when Adrian told them with a tinge of enthusiasm, about his interview with Rashid Al-Kuwari, they became greatly alarmed that this option, with immediate financial rewards and avoiding the awkwardness at SOAS, would tempt Adrian away from completing his degree course.

Adrian's apathy lasted until the weekend.

On Saturday, Max rang Gemma to find out what was happening.

"Adrian sent me a short email to say he was back," said Max, "and about his mother but that's all. Benny looked for him in vain at Fletcher's."

"He's hardly got up yet," said Gemma, "only for meals and the call of nature. He told us about Beirut and that woman, but hasn't said anything otherwise."

"It's time he came back to life, to face the music. I've been talking to Vernon Buckley, the HoD, but don't tell him that."

"Ooh, that sounds serious. Is it going to be ok?"

"Well, let's just say it's not a closed door. But Adrian's got to want to come back."

"I'll take him a cuppa – yet again – and prod him a bit."

"OK, call me back if you want me to come and help get him going. I'm free today. You've got my mobile number?"

"Yes, you gave it to me last time you called."

"OK then. You're a good sister. Bye."

"Bye."

Gemma carried the mug of tea upstairs to Adrian's room, banged on the closed door and went in. She put the mug on the bedside table and tickled the lumps under the cover which must have been his feet. Adrian wriggled and grunted. She did it again. He opened his eyes and said, "Leave me alone."

"I've brought tea," replied Gemma brightly, sitting down on his bed. "Why don't you get up? You must be bored with looking at the four walls."

"I've been asleep."

"What, all the time, twenty-four seven?"

"Well, not quite. I got up this morning to get a glass of water and some toast and I've been reading."

Gemma picked up a sticky plate just visible under the bed and put it on the floor inside the door to remind her to take it down.

Adrian levered himself into a sitting position, picked up the mug and drank.

"Nice tea, Gems," he said.

She looked at him seriously for a moment.

"It smells in here; it smells of unwashed man. Time you had a shower. And you could get rid of that stubble, or make it look a bit more trendy. It's definitely not cool now. Unless of course you intend to look like a tramp."

Adrian raised his eyebrows.

"Besides, Max is coming later," she continued, making a swift decision.

"Max? Who told him he could come?"

"I did. He called to say he would be passing this way and wanted to see us."

"Us? Passing this way?"

Adrian looked questioningly at Gemma for a moment; she held her head high, chin slightly raised, defiant.

"Yes, us."

"You don't usually lie Gemma."

She didn't reply.

"Well, since he's coming, you can see him if you want. I don't. Max is a successful person. Why would he want to talk to somebody like me who's fucked everything up?"

Gemma sighed.

"Adrian, you can't loll around for the rest of your life. And you haven't fucked everything up. You're just not thinking in a straight line at the moment. Max is a good friend and wants to help."

"Help with what? I don't need his help."

"Yes you do. Come on," she said cajolingly. "The rest of your life's waiting for you. Mum and Dad are worried. Yesterday I heard them yelling at each other; they were arguing about you. Mum said they ought to stop your allowance, but Dad disagreed; he says you still need time. Mum then said we should stop pussyfooting round you and that she'd stop putting a plate out for you at mealtimes if you didn't get up during the day. And I can tell you that I, for one, won't be bringing you any food up here."

She stared at him as he turned his head away, avoiding her gaze.

"Gems," he said quietly, "you're a pushy little blighter. I'll get up when I feel like it. Maybe in a couple of hours."

"What's wrong with now?"

"I need time to crank my spirits up. Leave me alone and don't pester me." Having finished his tea he slid back lower down into the bed.

Gemma took the mug and the plate down to the kitchen and then called Max to tell him to come.

By the time he arrived, just after lunch, Adrian was dressed and shaved, sitting reading the paper. Gemma answered the door. Hearing welcoming kisses, Adrian wandered into the hall.

"Hi Max," he said, running his hand through his hair.

"Hi Adrian. I'm glad you're back. I've come to hear what happened in Beirut."

They occupied the sitting room. By now able to talk about it without tears, Adrian related the whole episode with his mother. Max was as angry on Adrian's behalf as Vic had been, and expressed enormous sympathy. Soon they talked about the future. Adrian said he wasn't sure about returning to SOAS. Understanding his anxiety, Max toned down what Vernon Buckley had said, in anger, about Adrian's sudden absence. He stressed however, the urgent need for Adrian to put in an appearance, in order to show willing, and to pick up the threads of the course. Defiantly, Adrian told Max that while he was in Beirut, before the bitter meeting with his mother, he had had a preliminary interview for the job in the Middle East; his prospective employer was business like, shrewd and somehow likeable. Max, appalled, knew that an outburst on his part would be both unkind and unproductive. Instead, he told Adrian calmly that now was not the right time to be thinking of that job. After all, he argued, if the Qatari lawyer were really keen on employing Adrian, he should still be interested in three years' time. Adrian didn't reply immediately. After a few moments, he said quietly that he simply felt he didn't deserve any more financial support and trust from John and Fen; Max retorted decisively that he certainly didn't if he continued moping in his bedroom, and that it was time to broach the whole matter with them. Adrian protested that he wasn't ready to talk to them yet, but stood up resolutely when Max accused him of being a coward.

John and Fen were sitting in the kitchen, hoping and speculating on whether Max would influence Adrian into returning to London. Adrian joined them. He mumbled how sorry he was for all the anxiety he had caused them, before and during both his visits to Beirut. It was wrong of him, he said, to have departed the second time without telling them in advance, and he felt guilty at having wasted so much time and money, rushing into things head first without considering the consequences. In short, he believed he had well and truly cocked up.

Kindly as ever, Fen and John accepted his apology and agreed to draw a line under his waywardness, on condition that he returned forthwith to continue his course in London.

"You must carry on with your life, Adrian. Time to pick up where you left off," said John. Adrian nodded.

"We'll have afternoon tea now, as Max is here," said Fen briskly, and called Gemma down from her room to join them. Sebastian was out at cricket.

"So what's happening?" she asked bluntly, as she came in.

"I'll be going back to London," said Adrian. "Facing up to things, getting going."

"'Course you must, I told you that this morning."

"Hush, Gemma," said John. "It's not easy for Adrian – he's missed an awful lot."

"I know, but…"

"Stop it Gemma," said Fen firmly.

Gemma obeyed.

Later, as Max was about to leave, Adrian told him quietly that there was more he wanted to explain, but that it would wait until he was back in London. Max looked at him quizzically, but Adrian shook his head.

"Definitely not now, Max. Other things that happened in Beirut."

"OK then. It's just occurred to me, do you want to come up to London by car with me now?"

"No, I've got to get ready. I'll come early next week to see Vernon, and everybody, I suppose," replied Adrian with a sigh.

"Procrastination…." started Max.

"Shut up Max."

After a moment, Max said:

"If you want, I can accompany you to see Vernon, or is that an insult?"

"It's an insult. I'll do this on my own."

"Right you are. Well I'll be off now. I'll just go and say goodbye to your family. By the way, call Tazie!"

With Fen's pushing and John's gentle encouragement, on Monday morning Adrian got busy. He sent Vernon an email to announce that he was returning to London the next day and wanted to see him as soon as possible. Then he called Francis, who had already heard the essential news from Vic; they arranged to meet towards the end of the week. Adrian also sent a long overdue email to Vic. It was a relief to write it, Adrian felt, because he could be completely open with him, the person who had seen him through his worst moments. There was nothing to hide. Vic replied by return, that he had been alarmed by Adrian's silence but was pleased to know that he was returning to London. Benny had sent a text message to say that he hoped everything was tickety-boo and that he was hungry for tea and biscuits together again, so Adrian emailed him.

To Tazie, he wrote that he was looking forward to catching up with her soon; her reply seemed less than completely enthusiastic.

Benny was at Liverpool Street to meet Adrian. On the way to Fletcher's, he filled Adrian in on the latest news of the chums. Sujit had come out, and was single at the moment. Hardy and Lily were still going strong; he had presented her with a beautiful promise ring to seal their attachment. Sadie had disappeared off to Canada to work full time for her wacky cult. They had had an uproarious farewell party for her in the SOAS cafeteria, attended also by Sadie's flatmate Holly, who had tried in vain to prevent Sadie from overindulging in vodka. Lily and Hardy had dropped in on the party to wish Sadie well and then made a hasty escape. Wallowing in tears over the sad occasion of leaving her friends in London, Sadie had said that the party wasn't complete without Adrian, which all agreed to be true. Eventually Max had put Sadie and Holly into a taxi. A couple of days later, Benny and Holly had gone to Heathrow with Sadie to see her off. They were all happy, Sadie going off for what she believed to be a worthwhile challenge, whilst Benny and Holly were simply glad to be rid of the responsibility she had been for them. Sadie had left a note for Adrian, which Benny handed over. In it, she promised everlasting friendship and offered hospitality in Canada whenever Adrian wanted to turn up.

"She's sweet," said Adrian, "unfortunate, misguided, but sweet."

"Yeah," said Benny. "I hope that cult doesn't turn out to be something rather awful. I went along to an open evening – against my better judgement – and I got some nasty vibes from the 'Master', as they call him. He was standing close up to the women, pelvis forward, metaphorically licking his chops."

"Poor Sadie. I'll write to her."

On Tuesday late afternoon, Max turned up at Fletcher's. At the end of a lecture the previous day, Vernon had collared him with a message for Adrian, to say that he would like to see him on Wednesday at 12.00 pm. Essentially, he had told Max that in circumstances such as Adrian's, SOAS liked to try to be understanding; it helped that Adrian was a very able student. These encouraging noises were, however, tempered by Vernon's assertion that there would always be stiff conditions attached to such an approach.

"It's aye aye Sir, isn't it?"

"Definitely. You've got to be there. Try not to lose your rag."

They went out to eat together in an Indian restaurant nearby that Max had discovered. He was curious to know what the other Beirut events were that Adrian was planning to tell him about. Adrian first swore Max to secrecy, which Max thought overdramatic, until he had heard what Adrian had to say. During the course of a long meal, Adrian revealed everything: about Hezbollah and the Al-jalil refugee camp, about Khalil and Sabir, and finally about his captivity and Briggs. Max listened, astounded. He asked many questions about Beirut itself, about the political situation and about how, after his extremely negative experiences, Adrian could still find the place so seductive that he had wanted to return there. Adrian replied that his captivity had usefully taught him much about himself, especially since it was followed by a debilitating illness, misdiagnosed until Vic stepped in. During his weeks in hospital, and afterwards at Vic's flat, Adrian had had a great deal of time in which to reflect on where he was, how, and why. He had eventually succeeded, with Vic's advice and support, in rationalising his internment as a learning experience. Without Vic's intervention at the Catholic hospice, Adrian said, he might not have emerged in one piece from all that had happened. Vic was a rock, a crutch, and a mentor; he had propped him up at the worst times, chided and shaken him when necessary, and celebrated his recovery with him. As for the disaster with Patti Al-Zaini, it had little to do with the Middle East and could have happened anywhere; but once again, Vic had helped him through the first hours of severe shock. Vic's knowledge and understanding of Lebanon and of the Middle East were second to none; Adrian's fascination with Lebanon was of course coloured by what he had learned from Vic – the circumstances behind conflicts, the unofficial causes of certain events, and the reality behind politicians' posturing. Adrian vowed that he would, in the future, visit as many other Middle Eastern countries as possible, so as to place them in the context of the economic, social and political maps that Vic had drawn for him.

"You know, Max, countries smell different, and Lebanon to me smells more different than China."

"I understand. This Arabic versus Chinese thing is a very real dilemma for you, isn't it?"

"Yep."

"You'll be weighing it all up carefully. Getting a degree is paramount. Going for the job with an Arabic degree thrown in sounds attractive, but there are lots of unknown quantities. Presumably the Qatari lawyer hasn't mentioned fees and accommodation?'

"Accommodation, yes. A flat would be provided – it might be sharing with another shadower. I, or we, would only be paying for services."

Max walked with Adrian back to Fletcher's. They stood for a moment on the pavement outside.

"By the way," said Max, "I gather your parents know nothing about Hezbollah, the refugee camp or your captivity?"

"No. I'll never tell them – it would just be too much. But perhaps one day I'll tell Gemma."

Max grasped Adrian's arm.

"I'm awfully glad that you emerged of sound mind from your ordeals. I must say I respect you enormously for how you've coped with it all."

"Thanks, Max."

***

Adrian's discussion with Vernon Buckley was cordial and restrained. Vernon refrained from dwelling on Adrian's second absence, mentioning it only in passing. Rather than discussing Adrian's future, Vernon simply told him the conditions for his continuing on the Chinese degree course. Adrian was to spend the whole holiday period, from the end of term until the beginning of the new academic year in China, in a university town of his choice, subject to Vernon's approval. During that time he should write an essay in Chinese on an historical subject relevant to the town of his choice (5,000 characters), as well as an analysis in English of the socio-economic development of the town since 1980 (at least 10,000 words). On his return to London, he would need to pass an exam set at the same level as that taken by his fellow students at the end of the past academic year. It would help too if there were a summer course for foreigners that Adrian could attend. Adrian wasn't taken aback; the conditions seemed reasonable and apposite to him, although he baulked at the financial implications for his parents. Vernon gave him a week in which to decide on the town where he would go, and the subject of his Chinese essay.

***

Francis invited Adrian out for a meal in a French restaurant, as he said, to celebrate his survival and return to Britain.

"You're well kitted out now after your experiences, for all eventualities, I imagine. Good material for a job at the Foreign Office," said Francis, after they had ordered.

"I haven't been thinking about that. After my mother and her hysterics, I fell into the doldrums and lay around in bed for several days. My busybody of a little sister summoned Max, who came over to give me a jolt or three. I felt awful vis-a-vis my parents for having wasted time and money, but they pushed me to come back to London. So here I am, still wondering a bit about everything."

"Such as...?"

"Well, as you can imagine, some of me is still thinking about my non-mother, and the things she said. Those thoughts will take ages to settle. But more important, I've got to decide about my future."

"Just as I said, the Foreign Office, in due course."

"You keep saying that. But no, it's about my immediate future. Did Vic tell you about my job interview with Rashid Al-Kuwari?"

"I knew he was putting you in touch, but he didn't tell me you'd met."

Adrian related the details.

"I'm now at a crossroads," he continued. "My interest is in the Middle East whilst my loyalty is, or should be, vested in my Chinese degree. My parents have invested in full fees and accommodation for me in London, while I have irresponsibly escaped to follow a dream – an understandable dream, but one that would have waited. Patti Al-Zaini is firmly established in Beirut with her son, and will almost certainly still be there in three years' time. So I've wasted about five months of this academic year. I saw my HoD this week who stipulated the conditions for my continuing on the degree course. I must spend the whole holiday period attached to a Chinese University, (preferably attending a foreigners' summer course), I'm to present some specified written work in Chinese and English, and take an exam in September – an equivalent of this year's end-of-year exam. This implies more financial input from my parents: flights to and from China, probably an attachment fee to the university there, accommodation, course fees. Plenty bucks. I imagine I may be able to earn something by teaching English but if so, it will only nibble around the edges of the costs. Whereas…"

"Yes, Adrian," interrupted Francis, "whereas taking a job would release your parents from an additional financial commitment, almost certainly enable you to repay them some of what they've spent and, most importantly, allow you to take control of your position, bolstering your self-respect. And it would place you physically in the place where you believe, at the moment, you want to be."

"Precisely so."

Francis looked at Adrian with a smile.

"Not exactly a no-brainer, is it?"

"No."

"So when are you going to decide?"

"Within a week, I've got to tell my HoD, (who knows nothing about my Middle East interests), where I intend to go in China. It doesn't mean a final decision though. I'll be meeting Al-Kuwari again before the beginning of the next academic year."

"Ah, the decision dates don't coincide."

"No. Francis, I really want to know your opinion about all of this."

"Well, you've been out of the Chinese orbit, so to speak, for several months so re-plunging yourself into it would be good for you – put you back on to the planet you originally chose. You may find a renewed interest in things Chinese, living there in an academic environment. So my opinion is that you should meet the challenge set by your HoD, go to China and come back refreshed. You can mull over all the pros and cons of your alternative paths while you're there, and then decide what to do when you get back."

"And accept more financial input from my parents, whatever?"

"Your father isn't exactly short of a bob or two, is he?'

"No, but…"

"I know," interrupted Francis, "it's the moral dilemma of accepting their support and possibly afterwards rejecting what it gave you. So be it. I don't mean this cynically, but parents often face this kind of situation. They survive. Besides, completing first year Chinese can be its own reward, regardless of what you do afterwards."

"And Rashid Al-Kuwari?"

"I've researched him. He's a man with an excellent reputation in diplomatic circles. Straightforward, well educated, sophisticated. If he's interested in employing you now, he may find you even more interesting in three years' time with a Chinese degree, and a continued strong interest in all Middle Eastern matters."

"Thanks for the advice. I've got to be wise about this. You've certainly laid it all out for me."

"Talk to Vic again. Can you call him?"

"I can Skype, I suppose."

"Good."

Vic agreed with Francis' analysis, and had nothing to add to it, except to say that Francis would not have mentioned the Foreign Office as a potential career without thinking that it would be the right niche for Adrian.

Thirty-five

The idea of three months in China began to sound attractive to Adrian and the choice of an appropriate place and affiliation was easy: he would go to Yangzhou, a prosperous and attractive town in Jiangsu Province which he had visited with great pleasure during his gap year. Although there would be no specific taught course at intermediate level for the whole period of Adrian's stay there, he thought suitable arrangements could be made. On his previous visit, he had met a Professor of Chinese language, who had spoken about the University's wish to encourage foreign students to come to Yangzhou during the summer holidays for Chinese language studies. An email to Professor Huang produced an enthusiastic reply which Adrian submitted to Vernon. Professor Huang would arrange for tutoring, and personally supervise Adrian's progress; in addition, he would be able to find plenty of Chinese students interested in improving their English. Professor Huang also wrote that he hoped this connection with Adrian might lead to collaboration and academic exchange arrangements between Yangzhou and London Universities. Vernon was satisfied with the arrangements suggested, as well as with the subject of Adrian's proposed Chinese essay: 'An historical account of the Grand Canal in Yangzhou.' He concurred that the lack of a suitable course for Adrian could be an advantage since Adrian would not be tempted to spend time speaking English with fellow foreigners. Adrian promised to be on his way before 7th June and to stay until mid-September.

Fen and John agreed to fund Adrian's visit there, at a cost which seemed exorbitant to Adrian. He hoped he would earn enough giving private lessons to pay at least for the fares, as he wanted to stop off in Beirut. He emailed Vic about his decision to comply with Vernon's catch-up proposal, without mentioning a possible visit to Beirut. As he had expected, Vic read between the lines and replied that Adrian would be welcome to stay with him if he passed through Beirut on the way to or from China. June wasn't possible as Vic would be visiting his sister in Canada, but September would be good.

***

With his plans well under way, Adrian felt ready to call Tazie. During the flight home from Beirut, he had thought of her wistfully. The last time he had connected with her fully had been before his first journey to Beirut. Their only meeting between his two trips now seemed rather inconclusive to him – neither a continuation of the past nor a move into the future.

Tazie's phone was on voicemail so Adrian left a message: "Hullo Tazie. I'm back at Fletcher's. Hope to see you soon. Please will you call me?" He sent an identical text message. Three days later, after he had left another message, she called first thing while Adrian was eating cereal in his room.

"Hi Adrian!"

"Oh, hi Tazie. Great to hear your voice. How are you?" replied Adrian eagerly.

"I'm fine, really fine."

"I thought perhaps you were away on a trip as I hadn't been able to reach you."

"I have been away, but only for a couple of days. I had to go to Scotland and got back yesterday. There was a conference in Glasgow and then I went to visit the people in the Edinburgh office as I'm going to have quite a lot to do with them in the coming months."

"Is this a promotion then?"

"Not exactly, it's more of a move to different responsibilities for the time being. I've been taken off the Home Counties. Good thing too!"

"I'm glad it's working out well for you." There was an embarrassing silence then they spoke simultaneously.

"Adrian, there's …"

"Tazie, I'm…"

"Go on," said Tazie.

"I was going to say that I'm really looking forward to seeing you again. I feel as though I've lost touch with life here. There's so much to tell you and lots of other things I want to say, including plenty of apologies."

"I'm glad you're back safe and sound. We were all worried about you."

"Who, we all?"

"Max and I. And Benny's been fretting; nobody's as nice to him as you are. And Sadie missed you at her leaving party."

"I heard about that. Max and Benny have filled me in on the news. Anyway, I'm not planning any more trips.

Tazie, something important… I found my mother, for what it's worth."

"Yes, I know. Max told me. I want to hear about it when I see you. I gather it was rather awful."

"Yes, it was. Anyway, when can we meet?"

"Today early evening if you like. I mustn't be late getting home though. I've got an early breakfast meeting tomorrow." She swallowed, anticipating Adrian's disappointment.

"Can't we have an early dinner together?"

"Not tonight. My flatmate's cooking for me."

"Never mind, it'll be for another time." Was he consoling himself or her?

"OK then?"

"Yup, I've got nothing planned."

"I'll see how things go at work and call you this afternoon."

"Fine."

They hung up. She sounded different, cool, distant. He was worried. He had wanted to convey his regrets at the distance between them straight away, but somehow the conversation hadn't gone in that direction. Anyway, he told himself, it'll be easier to say when we meet.

Tazie heaved a sigh of relief. The first hurdle cleared. Adrian was his usual passive-sounding self. She now had a few hours in which to prepare her next words.

Adrian spent some of the morning walking aimlessly round the streets in all directions from Fletcher's Hall, feeling simultaneously keyed up and exhausted. Finally the appointment with Tazie was set for 5.30 outside her office. Adrian was there early, having spruced himself up and tried not to hurry. Tazie looked cool and neat as usual.

"Adrian, I need to talk to you in private. Can we go over to your place?"

Adrian was taken aback.

"It's a bit of a shambles – I haven't tidied up."

"I don't mind, I've seen your shambles before," she replied with a smile.

On the way, Tazie asked about Adrian's mother. He explained the line of contact leading him to her, describing only briefly the people involved. He told her of his shock at meeting his half-brother, Fouad, and of his poisonous conversation with his mother. He didn't go at length into his feelings, but simply said with conviction that he would never see her again. Tazie's impulse was to put her arm through his, but she didn't do so in case it implied an unsustainable level of intimacy.

In his room, she sat down immediately on his chair while Adrian made tea; he put one mug on the table and went to perch on his bed holding the other. Tazie lost no time in saying that she had something important to tell him. With no preamble, (for after all nothing could soften the blow), she divulged that she was going out with a colleague and that they were planning to get engaged within a few months. Adrian choked on his coffee; Tazie took his mug from him and tried to stroke his back but Adrian pushed her away.

"Who is he?" he asked eventually, his voice deep. "How long have you known him? Were you going out with him before? "

"He's someone in the office. I've known him ever since I went to work there, but a few months ago I was transferred to his group. And no, I wasn't going out with him at the same time as with you. I don't do that."

"But we weren't apart for very long."

"Adrian, we spent an unhappy evening together at the end of December, and then saw each other just once when you were back between your two visits to Beirut. That's two sightings in five months. Not much of a record. And I sent you several emails to which you didn't reply."

It was true; Adrian hadn't known what to tell her, or how.

"I was ill, Tazie. Don't forget, I've been really ill."

"I know. Max told me. It would have been nice to hear it from the horse's mouth," she replied bitterly.

"I was completely absorbed in the search for my mother. Also, some people and situations I saw in Lebanon were very upsetting. Sometimes I didn't know what was going on or what might happen next. I was in physical danger part of the time, and all sorts of weird people flitted in and out of my life. Seriously, Tazie, I was in quite a state – I lost track of time completely when I was in hospital."

"If you'd called me or contacted me, I would have been sympathetic and tried to help. I was very concerned."

"I'm sorry Tazie, I really am. But I lost my Lebanese mobile just when I got ill, and I didn't have access to my computer some of the time. It wasn't until Vic collected me and moved me to the American University Hospital that I got a new mobile. Now that I'm back, I was hoping we'd get together again, but you've moved on to Mr X." He swallowed painfully. "How far has it gone with him?"

"We've been discussing the timing of everything, but we've not made any firm plans yet. He's Jewish and although not practising, his parents are and he's an only child, so there are lots of issues there. His folks are rather

443

doubtful about me. They wanted him to marry an Israeli girl he saw at a family wedding in Tel-Aviv."

"I suppose you've been sleeping with him?"

"It's none of your business but no, we've not made love. He's a bit of a mummy's boy, old-fashioned. We're going to wait until we marry."

"How odd."

"We respect each other."

"But how will you know if you're sexually compatible?"

"I'm sure we'll manage."

"I don't get it, Tazie," he said, "why are you in such a hurry to get married?"

"Time's moving on. My biological clock. I'm ready for it, and I realised in December that you weren't. End of story, brutally speaking, and the beginning of another."

She was sitting white-faced, quite still, on his clothes-strewn chair. His body was hunched up on the bed. The warm untidy room smelled close.

"You're right there. I'm not ready for marriage."

"There's something else. It's partly to do with my sister."

"Your sister? What sister?"

"The only one. The one who died. There wasn't ever another. Don't you remember, the first time we met, you asked if Max and I had any other siblings with long names, and Max replied that we had a sister who had died?"

Adrian thought for a moment then said slowly, "I do, now. But at the time, it didn't seem right to ask any questions as neither of you volunteered any information, so I forgot. When did she die?'

444

"Almost exactly seven years ago. Max didn't tell you any more about her either, I gather."

"No, he didn't."

She sighed. "And nor did I. I should have done so, and would have if we had, so to speak, got tied up."

"Tell me now."

She took a deep breath.

"She was called Natalya Galina – Tasha to everybody. We were identical twins and she committed suicide. Aged 19. I felt as though half of me had gone." Tears flowed down her cheeks unchecked.

Adrian got off the bed and bent over to put his arms around her, while she wiped her eyes. It was, he realised suddenly, their first physical contact that day; their separate distress had made an emotional connection between them. In a few moments she pulled away and squeezed his hand as she detached him from her. Adrian returned reluctantly to sit on the bed.

Tazie was recovering her composure.

"She was artistic, in all sorts of ways. She wrote plays which she directed at school, she was a great cellist, and she made wonderful clay models of people's heads, real likenesses. But when she started art school, she got to know some freaky people in an occult sect, where suicide was considered an ultimate heroic act. It was really sick. She went away a lot and didn't say much about what she was doing or where she was going, although she told me a bit about it. She knew Ma and Pa would disapprove, as I did. She was away at a weekend retreat with the sect when she and another young woman did it. There was an awful rumpus: the media and photographers, the well-wishers, the sensation-seekers, the nosy neighbours, the inquiry into the activities of the sect, and we were right in the middle of it all. Anyway, when I lost her, I felt as though half of me had gone. The bond between twins is stronger if you're identical, you know. All the usual stuff: friends couldn't tell us apart, we had identical reactions to people and situations, all that. So since then, deep down, there's always been a feeling that I need to guard against wanting to do the same, to follow her, although luckily for me, we appear to have been very different in that department." She swallowed.

Adrian looked up. "Tazie, I'm so sorry. But you're not in a sect and I don't think you're easily led. So you weren't like her after all, and you have no suicidal tendencies, do you?"

"No I don't." They were both silent for a moment. Then Tazie drew a breath to continue.

"For me, marriage seems a bit like finding another half again. I'll feel safe and complemented when I'm married." Adrian was looking at his hands, flexing his finger joints.

"And I suppose you've chosen this man, whatever his name is…"

"He's called Toby Sterne."

"… Toby Sterne, because you're older than me and he's presumably older than you and he's ready for it and I'm not," Adrian said softly.

"Some of that. Toby wants us to have a family. You're different, you've no career path, you have more years of study ahead and a new preoccupation with your family. And you disappeared the second time without telling me you were going. It was frustrating trying to contact you, and never hearing back. You didn't give me your new Lebanese mobile number or call me." Her voice had gained strength, and her words emphasis. "That's a real put-down, you know."

"I forgot to tell people about the new number. Nobody here had it. Not even my family."

"That's it, you see," said Tazie vehemently. "You don't think ahead, you don't plan. You don't see what effect your actions are going to have on people."

"I must admit I didn't put myself in your position. I had too much stuff to deal with. I couldn't think about another world. I was miles away, physically and psychologically. I was searching and finding. And now I've found my mother and she's not up to much, I've got to step back, readjust, and find my direction, as my dad says."

He paused, hoping Tazie might respond, but she just continued to look at him thoughtfully. He continued.

"I suppose you think of me as a loser while Toby's a winner."

"You're not a loser, certainly not, you mustn't think that. But until you've sorted yourself out, you won't be on the way to anywhere and ..." she tailed off.

"And what?"

"You don't seem to have a devouring zeal for your Chinese degree, and you've not told me you've got any other plans. You're certainly not in the right frame of mind for a relationship or anything like that, are you?" It was a statement, not a question.

Adrian acquiesced. "No. You're right, I'm not. And at the moment I'm hesitating between Arabic and Chinese. There's the possibility of a job in the Middle East, in the autumn – shadowing a Qatari lawyer with considerable business interests, a fine opportunity to carry on with Arabic. Big salary, useful connections."

"You see!" cried Tazie. "That's typical – you're vacillating. It just goes to show that what you're doing at the moment doesn't fit in with what I'm doing, my plans. I want stability, a good lifestyle, to have children soon so that afterwards I'll still have enough energy to pursue a career within family life. Toby's steady and kind, he's ready to be a father now and he needs me." Tazie had decided Toby's illness was no concern of Adrian's.

"Great, great." Adrian looked away, not wishing to meet Tazie's gaze and thus reveal his sarcastic expression.

"And I'm planning to move jobs before we announce our engagement. Neither of us thinks that working together and being a couple is a good idea."

"If you were with me, that wouldn't be an issue."

In the silence that followed, each was stretching out towards the other. There was mutual tenderness, even though their lives had moved apart.

"Adrian… I was in love with you."

He didn't react.

"And I still have love for you, you're a lovely bloke. But the timing's wrong for us as a couple. You'll see that I'm right when you meet someone else. It will happen."

"Yeah. I suppose so."

She stood up. "Perhaps I'd better be going now?"

"Yes. Do that. Before I say something I'll regret." He stood up too. Both hesitated delicately.

"Well, let's keep in touch via Max," said Tazie, stepping forward and then back again. Adrian went to her, put his arms round her and held her firmly against him. They kissed passionately and then she left. He took his clothes off, threw them on the floor, and slumped on to the bed, pulling the duvet over his head. In the space of a few weeks, he reflected, he had lost the love of two women. The love of the first, his mother, had been an illusion. The second, Tazie's, had been real.

Thirty-six

It was a Saturday at the beginning of June. Adrian interrupted his sorting and packing to get himself some breakfast. In the kitchen, Gemma was sitting reading, a block of sticky notelets and a pen to hand. Shredded wheat today, Adrian decided, then made two mugs of tea and put one in front of Gemma who looked up quickly to smile.

"Here's yours!" she said, pushing an envelope across the table to him.

"My what?" he replied, looking at it.

"Invitation to Max's wedding. Mine's come too."

Adrian slit the envelope open with his finger.

"Confirmation of the fun," he said slowly and quietly. "Good for Max, - perhaps more of a merger than a marriage. It's happening now because he wants to buy a flat and can do so with a legacy that'll be available to him when he gets married."

"So what! Don't be so cynical! Just because it didn't work out for you with Tazie, that's no reason to get funny about Max's wedding. He really loves her."

"How can you judge? Did he tell you himself?"

"As a matter of fact, he did." There was a defiant note in her voice.

"Was that when you were discussing me? For you did discuss me, didn't you?" Adrian stared straight at Gemma.

"Yes, we did." After a moment, she added, "Adrian, I'm glad you're going to China. It's the right thing to do. This Lebanon thing sounds really dodgy – not viable."

"Funny, that's a word Max used," answered Adrian sarcastically. "'Viable' indeed."

"He only said it because it's right."

She returned to her book. Several notelets were already marking pages.

"You look busy, Gems," said Adrian in a conciliatory tone as he sat down with his bowl of cereal. "What are you reading?"

"It's a book I got from the library at school. Nobody's borrowed it except me in the past six years. It's about archaeology in Turkey. I'm marking each page where there's a reference to Byzantium. I'm hoping I may be able to do archaeology at A level."

"Good for you. You'll always get there, covered in chocolate."

She nodded and continued reading.

"Gemma," he said hesitantly. She looked up again.

"Yes?"

"Max wants me to be an usher at the wedding."

"Great, I hope you've said yes."

"Not yet."

"Why not?"

"Because…" he paused.

"Oh I get it, like you're worried Toby may be an usher too."

"Not worried exactly, but it could be embarrassing."

"Why? Toby will be there with Tazie and I'm sure they'll be glad to see you."

"I don't know about that."

Gemma, wise from her own experience, said self-righteously: "Sometimes you just have to move on. It's more important to do the right thing by Max now, than to worry about your own sensitivities."

"You're right of course."

"So you'll tell Max you will? Promise me?"

"I'm not promising you anything, except to tell you my decision in due course. Now get on with your beautiful Byzantium."

Adrian had noticed how much she had changed in the past few months: her skinny body had filled out, altering the way she carried herself. Her voice had changed too: it would never be deep, but it was a decibel or two lower, and her speech less chatty, less impulsive.

***

Adrian accepted Max's invitation to be an usher before leaving for China. Once there, he put his time to good use. It took him a few days to settle into a routine and to start planning his written papers, with the help of relevant material provided for him by his enthusiastic young tutor. His ear quickly became attuned to speaking Chinese again, especially from contact with local students who sought him out of an evening for reciprocal language practice. He managed to earn good money from giving regular, remedial English lessons to a group of rather slow teenage boys. Occasionally, he was invited to meals with the Huang family and, unknown to Adrian, the Professor emailed progress reports to Vernon Buckley. Adrian's concentration improved as the painful memories of his meeting with his mother receded. He discovered a new pleasure in working in Chinese, getting ahead quickly with the Chinese essay. The piece in English proved more difficult since he had to find a focus for it and organise interviews, in halting Chinese, with key people.

Meanwhile, he was punctilious in calling home regularly, knowing that he had to prove to his parents that he was serious about his studies, and that he genuinely regretted his past behaviour. Nevertheless, he still hankered after a spell in Beirut. When, in August, the time came to plan his journey home, he scheduled a week there for early September. He had anyway completed his assignments for SOAS, so felt no compunction in taking a holiday.

Staying with Vic, he was able to make his decision about his future. His fascination with the Middle East had not abated, but his renewed interest in Chinese language, as well as his perception of his responsibilities, were sufficient to prompt him to decide to complete his degree, renouncing the job with Rashid Al-Kuwari for the present. Over an extended lunch with him, Adrian learned, to his astonishment, that this was the outcome Al-Kuwari had hoped for: that Adrian would show the right persistence, setting out to finish what he had started. He urged Adrian to keep in touch, and to let him know when he visited Beirut again.

Vic was unsurprised by this, and glad that Adrian had made the right decision. Their common feeling for Beirut remained, stimulated for Adrian by seeing all his friends again. The days flew past; Vic and he decided to try to travel together to Algeria and Tunisia after Christmas, conflicts permitting.

John and Fen were predictably relieved that Adrian's thinking was back on the right track, especially when he was able to tell them later that Vernon was satisfied with the content and style of his written assignments, as well as with his year-end exam results.

***

Adrian saw his London friends again at Max's wedding, the day after his return from Beirut. For Gemma, this was an occasion for dressing up. She felt pretty nice in her cotton frock; on a white background, groups of vertical blue stripes alternated with garlands of pink and blue flowers cascading down from her shoulders - unambiguously retro, but fetching. She liked her new next-size-up bra too. A blue cardigan and white pumps, as well as a large white canvas shoulder bag containing an umbrella, purse, make-up and a tiny Sudoku book, completed the outfit. It was her first wedding without her parents. Max, in his grey tail coat and all that went with it, looked immensely handsome, and Gemma told him so as she kissed him. He was suitably gratified and put his arm around her shoulders, telling her he hoped she'd have a really nice day and that she herself looked marvellous. Sometimes stiff, critical, disdainful and uncompromising, he was at his best, radiantly happy.

Adrian joined the crowd of ushers. He had imagined Toby to be pleasant-looking but not handsome; he was surprised by Toby's serious, almost severe expression. Toby was indeed feeling uncomfortable, alien in this social group.

Tazie, looking superb in a dark blue silk bridesmaid's dress, detached herself from the group of bridesmaids and went to greet Adrian. He took her firmly by the shoulders and kissed her on both cheeks.

"You're well?" she asked.

"Yes, glad to be back from China. And you?"

"Fine, and happy." There was a moment's silence.

Then Tazie asked: "You've met Toby?"

"'Met' is pushing it a bit – more like spied him in the crowd of ushers."

"Yeah, well, trust Max to want fifteen of you. I suppose he told you each exactly what he wanted you to do, and when?"

"Precisely. His wedding day's got to be perfect."

They both laughed.

"Max couldn't be Max without perfection," said Tazie. "Where's Gemma?"

"Around somewhere, probably talking to Benny."

With mixed feelings, Adrian watched Tazie walk away. Affection, certainly, and regret, but his summer musings in China had planted him emotionally back on his feet. He felt released, seeing her again in their changed circumstances. He smiled to himself.

Gemma was indeed talking to Benny. He was wearing a shiny black top hat, which, he said, he had borrowed from his father's circus costumes, with a dark blue velvet jacket with bald patches on the cuffs and at the elbows, and a bright red bow tie with dark blue spots on it.

"Can we sit together in the church?" said Gemma. "I think Usher Adrian's got a special seat."

"'Course he has and 'course we can."

Adrian went to hug Benny.

"Great to see you. Where've you been?"

"Here and there. A conference – one of those 'everybody welcome' things which produce rather little in the way of research. And my family. My sisters want to meet Gemma."

While they were waiting to go into church, Max brought a young woman over to introduce to them. She was Tiziana Morelli – Arabella's Italian flatmate in St. Andrew's, studying English literature. Hullos all round. Adrian had never, he thought, met anybody as immediately attractive as her. Gemma watched him laying it on, and tried to see what it was about Tiziana. She was petite and slightly rounded, with a straight nose, neat teeth and tiny ears. She wore her thick light brown hair in a plait to the side of her head, with a cascading ribbon at the top. Beneath a dark pink silk jacket was a medium grey slinky gossamer dress. As she and Adrian walked off to talk to Lily and Hardy, Gemma said to Benny:

"Perhaps that's what I need, a pink jacket?"

"You look great just as you are," he replied.

After the service, Adrian, Gemma and Benny, joined by Sujit and his new boyfriend – a tall Iranian actor – lined up to meet the proud bride, Arabella Winton, a big-boned honey-blonde woman with large hands and feet, a wide smile and a booming voice. As they moved on, Gemma whispered to Adrian that she had a horsey face; he shushed her.

Gemma watched Adrian's charm working on Tiziana. She was glad for him and sad for herself, not because Adrian would never be hers, for she had simply outgrown that phase. No, rather because she grieved for the child she had been and for her puppy love, which she would never experience again.

Saturday morning. Gemma was propped up in bed; Adrian was perched on the end of it.

"Thanks for the tea, Adrian," she said.

"The least I could do," he murmured. Gemma was recovering from flu.

"Nice to have you back," she continued. "Everything peaceful at Uni?"

"Mm," he replied. "No traumas like last year. I'm a model student now – or for the time being anyway."

Gemma smiled.

"Things aren't the same, are they," she said, "but we're out of a rut, at least I am. You've moved on too, haven't you?"

"Well I wasn't in a rut, but I created a whacking great hole for myself and jumped in, with both feet. I had to do it, all of it, and it was good for me, laid some ghosts. Now I've got a new beginning and a direction for the next three years."

"Adrian…" she started to say.

"Sshh, Gems," he interrupted, "don't say anything more. Subject closed." He took her empty mug from her and went downstairs, whistling.

Epilogue

Adrian married Fabiana, sister of Tiziana, whom he had met at Max's wedding. She was the perfect wife for the diplomat Adrian was to become. Tactful, adaptable and imaginative, she never baulked at Adrian's outlandish or dangerous postings, and was ready to shore him up in his rare moments of doubt about the route their life had taken.

To Adrian's surprise, he had achieved a first in his final year Chinese exams, a well-deserved success according to Vernon Buckley. During the final year, while his friends made plans for the future, Adrian (to Max's great frustration) continued to navel gaze, trying to place himself, in his imagination, in a 'socially meaningful' job. His only firm decisions were to continue learning Arabic and to volunteer in the British Library. Immediately after the end of term, he enrolled in an Arabic immersion course which he supplemented with extra hours of conversation with Hassan, whose patience was not inexhaustible. The perfect career niche seemed to elude him. Banking and business were not to his taste, nor was he attracted by the prospect of academic life despite encouragement from his former professors and tutors. And there was no pressure to take over his father's boat-building business, which John and Fen had tentatively earmarked for Sebastian.

Francis stood by, meeting Adrian every few weeks, observing him, but making no suggestions. Nine months on from Adrian's graduation, over a drink on a bright chill April day, he reminded Adrian of the Foreign Office graduates' fast track recruitment scheme. He had chosen the right moment; Adrian had exhausted his own list of possibilities and had not given any further thought to the FCO since Francis' remarks when they had met previously. Francis pointed out Adrian's strengths to him: practical intelligence and an enquiring mind; a knowledge of Chinese and Arabic, as well as French, German, and a smattering of Italian thanks to Tiziana and Fabiana; a strong interest in international relations; an unflappable personality; an outward friendliness to all and sundry, etc. Adrian didn't recognise himself, but with Francis' encouragement, he sat the highly competitive screening, was accepted, and soon embarked on his career, surprised and relieved to discover how well it suited him.

An initial disappointment was his and Fabiana's inability to have children. Adrian pointed out drily that this would at least ensure none of his mother's and father's ghastly genes would be inherited. After much heart-searching, they decided on adoption. A long-drawn-out process ended in the arrival in London of twins, a boy and a girl aged two, from Colombia. Later, during postings abroad, the physical dissimilarity between parents and children caused some local bewilderment.

Adrian and Max saw each other regularly, the families even spending holidays together in exotic places. Max always congratulated himself on having goaded Adrian into action at difficult times.

Once, in his mid-thirties, Adrian saw Patti again. He wanted confirmation, rationally this time, that she was reprehensible and that nothing was to be gained from any sort of connection with her. To be able to see her, he dangled the carrot of his diplomatic career before her, which naturally had the desired effect: Madam would be delighted to welcome her important first-born son in Beirut as would her second son, Fouad. During the visit, she fawned, whined and wheedled, trying to butter him up, which repulsed him. He treated them coolly, satisfying himself that this would indeed be the last time he would see them. He later felt little regret on refusing to help Fouad emigrate to Britain to find work.

Gemma advanced admirably in Byzantine studies, holding a joint British Museum and London University post, funded by a rich Turk living in London. In her early thirties she married a gentle sculptor called Archie, who resembled Adrian in character. The pressures of Gemma's work – juggling teaching and research – as well as her desire for perfection in everything she did, caused her some stress. Her husband's relaxed nature and the latest natural treatment therapies kept her on an even keel. They had a gifted son who, from vacillating between a career as a painter and a dancer, eventually moved into arts management.

Sebastian went to a sports academy. On his second attempt he managed to pass GCSE maths and English; at the age of sixteen he started to work part-time at a leisure centre where he became very popular. Fortunately, he continued to enjoy the boatyard and gradually, in an unstructured way, learned how to build boats. In partnership with his wife Abigail, a plump local girl with masses of blonde curly hair and common sense, they took over running the boatyard when John retired. Along with their four bonny, naughty children, they kept Fen and John happy to the last.

Vic remained important in Adrian's life. Although he never had to rescue Adrian again, he continued to be Adrian's port of call for advice. Luckily Fabiana and Vic hit it off from their first introduction in London; she immediately understood the whys and wherefores of Vic's and Adrian's mutual affection. Adrian went to Beirut several times to be with Vic during the weeks leading up to Vic's death from cancer.

Max and Arabella lived principally in London, although he spent several weeks each year in Hong Kong and Beijing, where she joined him sometimes. He gradually took over and developed his family business, his wealth eventually surpassing that of his father. Arabella did not seek a paid job, preferring to be active in local as well as national affairs. They lived a lavish life, albeit with discretion so as to avoid being named in lists of wealthiest people. Theirs was a good marriage, despite fidelity lapses on the part of Max, guessed at by Arabella but stoutly ignored. Their three children were all clever.

Tazie and Toby married early in the year following Max's wedding. His parents, at first dismayed by Toby's intention to marry a Gentile, were soon won over by Tazie's warm personality. She and Toby were ideally suited to each other, grateful for the other's qualities and smoothly compatible on a daily basis. Toby's hepatitis B was regularly monitored until, in his fifties, he was declared free from the infection. They lived contentedly in Berkshire where Tazie gave birth to two perfectly healthy children. When the children reached their teens, Tazie swapped freelance tax work for a part-time job in a private hospital.

They met Adrian and Fabiana from time to time, although Toby never really unfroze in Adrian's presence.

After graduating, Hardy returned to South Carolina, where Lily soon joined him. They were married there with all due pomp, and then flew to Shanghai for a Buddhist ceremony (to please her parents) and a wedding party (to allow her to show off her catch). Hardy trained as an insurance broker. In due course they moved to Hong Kong where he became the linchpin for Asia of a global company. Lily worked as an analyst for a security services conglomerate. They owned an enormous Mid-Levels flat with a staff of three, as well as a large house in South Carolina. Max saw them regularly, Adrian and Fabiana, occasionally. Their only child died at birth, but young relations, particularly on her side, took full advantage of their hospitality and amenities.

Sadie had returned to Canada without finishing the year at SOAS. She was immediately funded by a shady sponsor to open the Canadian branch of the International Federation for Revelation, Interaction and Peace (INFRIP). An aid worker called Jock, who soon joined INFRIP, enticed her away from her parents' house, much to their dismay, to live with him in two sordid mobile homes well stocked with beer and vodka. They were married without her parents' knowledge; Mr and Mrs Klein discovered it only when they were called to see her in hospital after a serious binge. On looking into INFRIP, they learned that sexual rites were among the activities of the group. Along with similarly concerned relations, they were able, after many months, to get INFRIP banned; Jock was indicted for rape and gross indecency. At that point, Sadie moved back to live with her parents, along with her four children. They tried to keep her sober, sometimes successfully. It was Benny who remained in sporadic contact with her.

Sujit had several tries at finding a permanent partner, and was once arrested for attempted seduction of a minor. The case was dismissed when it was discovered that the 'minor' in question had misrepresented his age and already had a conviction for blackmail. Eventually Sujit settled down with a Bulgarian cellist; after a few years together, they married. Sujit became a Chartered Secretary, soon headhunted by a consortium of Indian businesses. He also founded a school for teaching their ethnic language to first and second generation Asians in Britain, dabbling in Indian languages himself. Although his siblings knew he was gay, he never told his parents, believing that for them, their inklings were easier to live with than the enormity of confirmed knowledge.

Benny fulfilled his and everybody else's ambitions for him. He accepted a Professorship in semiotics at Oxford at the age of 38, and was described by some as a natural successor to Noam Chomsky. Honest with himself and others, he was considered to be one of the most advanced thinkers of his time, earning plaudits and honours worldwide, whilst trying hard to live a private life and to avoid becoming everybody's favourite visiting professor.

His partner was Sidonie, an Oxford mathematician; theirs was not a sexual relationship – more a meeting of minds. He maintained close links with his family (his siblings visited him regularly), as well as with Gemma, Adrian and their families. In his forties, Benny fathered a daughter with a young woman in her twenties called Lottie. They never lived together; nevertheless, he, Sidonie, Lotti and the child formed an unconventional but comfortable clan. Benny adored his three women, as well as Gemma of course.

***